Dark Exile

a novel by

Daniel Sandoval

Dark Exile

a novel by

Daniel Sandoval

Cover design by Daniel Sandoval and John Morgan

Published in the United States of America by
Morgan Online Media, P.O. Box 550,
Toledo, Washington 98591

www.morganonlinemedia.com/dark-exile.html

First Edition

ISBN 978-0-9858081-5-0

Chapter I: Danger of Darkness

Newton slammed the intercom button, "Prepare for impacts! Upward bounce! Deadly force!" The hand controls were still slack, half a second, just about the time he had left before there was no possible chance for survival. He almost spent that instant deciding they were dead, giving up, but with a surge of anger he pulled at the manual controls. The helm responded. Newton pulled up the point at the top of the ship, since angles may deflect instead of breach the hull. It wasn't protocol, supposed to hit bottom first, the strongest part of the pyramid shaped spaceship. Their course started away from a collision with the first object, full power deceleration.

"Save it or make sure we die," said the captain's voice from the intercom, "because if you cripple us out here, I'll kill you." This was not said in jest. Captain Mot was probably foul tempered enough to actually kill a crew member. How the Interstellar Fleet promoted him to captain was a mystery to everyone. There were two species from their world, graces and busters. Mot was the only robustus in the entire fleet to command a ship. His sort were physically strong, absolutely fearless in a fight, but many of them were imbeciles.

Again, Newton looked at the view screens and wondered if he should attempt to survive. In a counter-motion spin along with a hard pull on the backward axis, the first object missed the number three facet by a few meters, close enough for the magnetic turbulence to rip the control from his hand and start the spacecraft tumbling. He gritted his teeth, watched the screens, flared his navigation spot and pushed the control savagely forward and left. Contrary gravity began pulling the blood from his brain, started a ringing in his ears and made his vision go gray.

Miraculously, the speeding ship missed the second object, also so closely that the ship began to pull off true line. Still trying to see with failing eyes, Newton fought the helm, getting nauseated at trying to shoot for a window that wouldn't hold still. One of the objects began to flash faster on the screen, still going too fast, too fast to survive impact, too fast to use the shields. He turned on the shields. He angled the ship for a glancing skip off the number two facet. BaWAMM!

The sound of the gyroscopic engines rose in pitch. A shock-wave from the impact damaged one of the engines; he remembered that he turned off the power stabilizer. Two more objects, both began to flash more quickly, full power on the brakes but the ship still closing too fast, still with the load directly on the engines. Which one did he want to hit?

Choose your destruction, he thought, and did, the object with a slightly slower flashing rate. Just that split second of distance might be the difference between catastrophic and manageable damage. He took a deep breath and pulled the actuator. KaBLAMM!

With the shields up and the servos off, most of the collision shock went directly to the main engine. Everything inside the ship went dark. Outside, they tumbled through space, finally flying slowly enough to give them some time between objects, had there been anyone conscious at the helm. Newton passed out from the G forces momentarily starving his brain of blood.

A full minute counted down as the automatic restart went through the process on battery power. Emergency lights kicked on along with one screen, the graphic of ship status. There was still enough residual heat from the gyroscopic engines to generate power, so the start-up ran a diagnostic on the engines and put power to the only engine remaining, number three, the rudder, the smallest, barely enough to bring back internal gravity and also move the ship.

Newton woke up face down, floating above the floor. He began to drift down as the lights changed from emergency cells to ambient light. Just as his hands and toes touched the floor, a sound reached his ears from the bottom of the spacecraft. A roar of uncontainable rage vibrated up through the metal struts of the deck. It was Captain Mot. The heavy thumps of a monster bounding through the spacecraft toward the bridge got louder. Apparently Mot checked the condition of his ship and was serious about his threat to kill Newton. The sound of someone else running toward the bridge came from another part of the ship. He got to his feet and stood there listening, listening to the approach, seriously considering whether to go to the weapons hold and shoot Captain Mot as he came through the door.

To confuse things more, two small, three-fingered hands grabbed Newton from behind underneath his arms. In a typical yet amazing feat of athleticism, Pin, the other robustus on the crew, had her small feet hooked into the machine brackets overhead, and hanging upside down, she gracefully pulled a man practically twice her height up into the overhead conduits. Busters could move with incredible speed and stealth if they wanted to, which is why Newton didn't even know Pin was on the bridge. With a quiet little grunt, she tossed him like a rag doll higher up to a place on top of an air duct.

"What are you doing?" he asked, just catching himself from falling.

"Not talking, not dying," she answered. Pin pulled herself upright and turned toward the approaching noise. She wasn't wearing her mechanic's uniform but instead a sleep leotard. Newton thought it was strange for him to be noticing her body seconds before Captain Mot burst onto the bridge and killed him, but there she was, balancing on a mechanical brace, a short woman with a thickly muscled body, nicely rounded smooth with a layer of femininity, still with the slender waist of a woman and the triangular hands and feet of a robustus.

Captain Mot hit the door switch so hard that the wall shuddered before the door to the bridge slid open. So quickly that it was a noisy blur, Mot stepped in, spotted Newton, snatched a clamp off his belt, hurled it at Newton and stepped sideways because Pin used a small metal disc to deflect the clamp back toward him. "I'll kill you, too!" shouted Mot.

"He dies, we all die!" Pin screeched. "You don't know computers! Computers run the ship!"

With a voice that rumbled from a growl to a roar, Mot bellowed, "Ship don't run, so he dies!"

A hatch slid open to the bridge from another direction. In walked Ronnie Chamberlain, the medical officer, a gracile like Newton and the fourth and final member of the crew. She looked at her captain with the forced patience she always had when dealing with him. "We got a problem?" she asked with her hands behind her back.

"Stay out of this, gracile, I could snap your bones," Mot snarled.

"I respectfully remind the captain that it is against regulations to snap the bones of crew members, which means killing them is also prohibited," she said dryly.

"Regulations are wrong!" He lunged forward and Ronnie revealed that behind her back she had a stun gun in one hand and a dart pistol in the other. There was the whistling crack of a directional stun pulse as she tossed the dart pistol to Pin. Pin caught the pistol and planted a dart in Mot's thick neck.

Mot kept moving toward Ronnie as Pin followed his movement for another shot. "No, Pin!" shouted Ronnie. The captain took three, progressively slower steps, groaned as a clumsy hand went up to his neck, and fell to the floor.

"Shoot him again?" asked Pin.

Pin's sincerity caused Ronnie to laugh. "No Pin, they're very strong. Two would be dangerous."

"Yes, Doctor." Pin sounded disappointed. She dropped some three meters to the floor but absorbed the shock so efficiently there was practically no sound.

"Can you get down?" Ronnie asked Newton.

"Not as nicely as Pin," he replied, "but one way or the other, I'll definitely get down."

"Pin, be ready, just in case." Pin looked at Ronnie with a puzzled look on her face. "Put the stuff down so you can catch him if he falls," Ronnie clarified. Pin's large eyes widened and she nodded with enthusiasm before she put the metal disc and the dart pistol on a nearby counter.

Newton crawled slowly off the air duct and clambered down until his space boots were dangling about a meter off the floor. He dropped the rest of the way. "Thank you," he said, looking at Pin.

"Mot'll wake up. We might die again," said Pin.

"Still, I'm grateful," said Newton. Pin walked over and stood next to Newton like an obedient pet coming to heel position. Newton completed the picture by petting her soothingly across the shoulders. Pin looked appreciative.

"She's right. Captain Mot is going to wake up." Ronnie looked nervously from Pin back to Newton. "I can try something," said Dr. Chamberlain.

"What?" asked Newton.

"A procedure," answered Ronnie, "to reduce aggression."

"Reduce aggression," repeated Pin.

Newton dropped his jaw and asked, "Like what, a lobotomy?" Pin suddenly moved her shoulder as if his hand burned. Her species had a special tactile sensitivity and perception to extrasensory input. She looked at Newton and obviously didn't know what a lobotomy was.

"Non-invasive," said Ronnie, "mostly, it's like acupuncture with electrodes."

Newton thought about it while shaking his head. "Reduce aggression," said Pin again.

"No," said Newton. "That sounds like mutiny, sort of like darting the captain, which violates about a dozen regulations of conduct."

"Those regulations presuppose that the captain is not a robustus prone to murderous rages," said Ronnie. "Sorry, Pin," she added.

"For what?" asked Pin. She turned to Newton and with plaintive tone said, "Reduce aggression." She looked at him with a frustrated pout.

"No," said Newton. "I'm saying no to both of you."

"So next time, he kills you," Ronnie said angrily. Pin hunched and looked mournfully at the floor.

"You don't get to do that," said Newton, ignoring his impulse to comfort Pin.

"Do what? Save your life?" asked Ronnie.

Pin moved closer and pressed her forehead onto his side. "No, Ronnie, you don't get to extrapolate. This moment has never happened before this moment. Engines one and two have never been down before. A ship has never been marooned in the deep black before. He has never been assigned a priority mission before. You and Pin have been on this ship for three phases. I've been under his command for three revolutions. He's under a lot of stress, and he loves this ship, and he saw what I did to it and snapped."

Ronnie looked as if she wanted to believe him, or just admired his attempt to convince her. "If you're wrong about this and he snaps again, how about I get to kill you instead of help you?"

Pin turned and faced Ronnie with a confused expression. She shook her head incredulously. "No one gets to kill Newton," said Pin with conviction.

"I was making a joke, Pin," said Ronnie.

Pin shook her head again. "No one kills Newton. Joke means what you say isn't true."

"You're right, Pin." Ronnie squinted at Newton. "You're in command for three spans, max. What is going to happen before he wakes up?" she asked.

"I say he wakes up in the botanical cell. He likes it in there, and we weld all the doors closed so he can cool down for as long as it takes."

Ronnie smiled. Even Pin nodded from appreciation. "What now?" asked Ronnie.

Newton paused while chewing one corner of his mouth. "Well, first we don't assume we're not going to die," Newton said slowly. Pin pinched her eyebrows together and gave Newton a snappy shrug of her shoulders. "We could still die. Those little ready lights on all the screens mean that the alarms bypassed the reboot. I could turn on those screens and we may be seconds from destruction. All hands, right here," he said as he moved to the helm. "Keep your calm."

Newton reached to the master control switches and pressed three buttons. The macro view showed a flashing object on a collision course, close. "Eeeeghh!" yelped Pin. A quick touch to her shoulder cut her cry short. "Sorry," she squeaked.

"Pin, we're tumbling top forward; hit the gravity jet away and low from collision. You're the only one quick enough to do this, so deep breath, focus, and go." Newton started to take his hand off her shoulder but Pin caught his hand between her shoulder and cheek. He left his hand there so Pin would lift her head and could concentrate on the task. Beginning with three hits a second, Pin slowed the forward roll, incrementally lengthening the duration as the roll slowed. Ronnie continually denied the computer trying to break in; Newton used docking spray out the sides to stop the yaw. After a tense five minutes of nothing but clicking sounds from the controls and the shallow, rapid breathing of two nervous people, they could see they were slowing down. Pin shook her head in protest every time Newton started to lift his hand, but her breathing was slow and quiet. Newton accepted that he had only one hand to use for the master control switches.

Once Pin stopped the forward roll, she put the gravity spot underneath the approaching object and gave it all the power the one small engine had. The flashing abruptly stopped.

Ronnie and Newton let go a simultaneously sigh of relief. Pin kept all power to the downward tack. "Good, Pin, we're clear. Now, we're gonna push the scan as far as it'll go and prepare for a full stop." He started to lift his hand. This time Pin allowed it with a little nod. Using both hands, he clicked away at the array of buttons and keys at the master control console, talking aloud the while. "We are close enough for a composition scan and I'd really like to see what we hit, because the dark matter readings say there shouldn't be anything out here, nothing for three light-revolutions." All three looked at the colored graph of the composition signature. It was a piece from a spacecraft, unfamiliar design.

"Can we get a visual?" asked Ronnie. Newton had to futz with the system for a while to focus in but the picture confirmed it. The debris they hit was the remnants of a ship, blasted, or torn, or exploded, a ship from some unknown civilization.

"Change of orders, Pin. We're going to shadow this debris, mirror its line and spin. Guess as best you can and we'll match it by computer later. Ronnie, get a gurney for the captain. We'll load him, put him in the canopy loft and then all three of us are going to check the ship, top to bottom." The seriousness of Newton's voice was punctuated by the heat scoring on the piece of spacecraft. It was blasted to bits.

Ronnie and Newton watched as Pin worked the manual controls. Noise from the single engine buzzed through the substructure of the ship and the helm barely responded.

"It will take time," said Pin as she stared at the screen and worked the controls.

"Continue, Doc and I are going to get the gurney. Get it as close as you can and then check the hull, impacts on sides two and four." He gave Pin's shoulder a pat. "Acknowledge."

This was necessary because if a robustus was thinking intently about something, their sense of hearing may select for sounds. Human speech could fade into indistinct murmurs. "Mirror motion, check hull, two and four," said Pin in a distracted monotone.

"Good response," Newton gave Pin another pat on the shoulder and tossed his chin to start Ronnie to the infirmary. Ronnie checked Captain Mot, removed the dart and had Newton help her reposition the large robustus. His breathing changed to the slow, deep inhales of slumber.

While they were in the central hallway, Newton noticed the consternation on Ronnie's face. "What?" he asked.

"I think this mission is meant to fail," said Ronnie.

"Why do you say that?"

"Your captain created an interplanetary incident last revolve. You remember, the entire diplomatic delegation you two killed in a bar fight. You were on a lawless world, so no prosecution, but that shit prolonged a war." Ronnie shook her head. "They gave the species their one, token success story by promoting him, but now they'd like him to disappear. This crew is made up of people they want to disappear. Everybody but you." Ronnie's mouth betrayed an ingrained regret, saying, "Apparently you're just along for the ride."

"Why do they want to get rid of you?" he asked, thinking it a mostly facetious question.

"Because I know that Avigolon was populated with sentient humanoids, at about the alchemy level of technology, and the Fleet exterminated them and took over their planet." She shrugged her shoulders. "I lied and denied during a debriefing, but they suspect I know."

"How do you know?"

"I met them, even showed their doctors some useful remedies for our chemical weapons. So I committed treason, but interplanetary law says sentient species own their planet, no matter how few in number or where they are on the technology spectrum. And that ain't all I know, maybe not even the worst. Fourteen revolutions in Fleet, I've seen some scandalous stuff," grumbled Ronnie. She touched the door switch to the infirmary.

Newton followed her in and asked, "So, there's you and Mot, but what about Pin?"

"Pin has nine strikes," she said.

Newton laughed with disbelief. "Isn't summary execution required at seven strikes, or five, or something like that?"

"Pin also has a zed alpha rating for mechanical engineering. She invented our annealing surfaces so we could lose internal gravity and not even spill your java, along with dozens of components that are in every ship the fleet has. Pin's too valuable; that's why they can't bring themselves to discipline her."

"Nine strikes, that just doesn't compute. She's so mellow I can't even imagine."

Ronnie stopped at the med pod's gurney. "Newton," she said without looking at him, "I know how regulations say that you should provide reassuring touch to female robustus crew, but no one does, because they can read your intentions the instant you touch them. You have to be sincere, build the rapport, just like you did with Pin. She ignored you for the first half phase, insubordination, but you kept trying, kept

12

giving her chances. Fourteen revolutions, this is the one time I've seen it work." Dr. Chamberlain laughed a nervous chuckle. "Gotta tell ya, that difference between theory and practice always bothered me. There in the manual, but I've never seen it done, till we got stationed on this explorer. She's got loyalty, to you, a different species. She's got the mission. She defended you to bright. It's a dorking miracle, and you act like it's completely natural. A miracle, and regulations say she should've been executed four strikes and six revolutions ago." Ronnie unbuckled the corners of the gurney.

Newton spoke more to himself than Ronnie. "Zed alpha engineer. They got probably five in the entire fleet. That's too much talent to make disappear."

Ronnie laughed first and said, "Actuarial controls."

Newton laughed as he caught on. "Right, can't sacrifice the cost of a ship, without at least a measureable possibility of success. A zed alpha bumps us up to the three percent chance of completion they needed to deploy a crew of misfits."

They both laughed as they powered up the lift motors on the gurney. While maneuvering the levitation gurney down the central hallway, the doctor and Newton would break into little bursts of laughter as the thought echoed in their minds. "You earned a question," said Ronnie with an expectant lift of an eyebrow.

"You do this; how do I keep earning these questions?" asked Newton.

"By handling a situation with grace," she answered. "Any question," she added.

Newton laughed and said, "A silly question, one I've always wondered."

"Silly questions also welcome."

"All animal fur is some variation between black and white, and if it's got color, the colors are variations of brown, brown with yellow or red, all mammals, except one. Pin's hair is blue like a flower, a pale fade of dark blue hair. How do they get colors like that?"

"Scientific?" she asked.

"Yes," he answered.

"They have a different shape of intestinal lining, which entertains unique intestinal flora, able to process silica, making colors from compounds much like a flower does, courtesy of an epoch of eating dirt in their evolution, and the individual's color depends on what food or microbes are available along with the genetic expression of color," explained Ronnie.

"So, genetically there's a base color, like dark blue, and other conditions can moderate that color."

"Very well summarized," said Dr. Chamberlain. "You're not sweet on Pin, are you?"

"No," he answered without pause, "although, I found it odd how much I liked having her save my life dressed for bed. She needs to stay in uniform, dial down that vavoom."

Ronnie laughed. "She's definitely a hot little number, but ill advised."

"Regulations?" tested Newton.

"Captain Mot, I hate to even think of the dynamic that would create. His threshold for murderous response is low enough to include a forbidden romance with someone of his species, his selected breeder if we get marooned, which we are, technically."

The gurney hovered still with a higher pitch as they both took one of their hands off the handles and paused at the door to the bridge. "That's a real cold splash of reality, thanks."

"You're welcome," said Ronnie. She pressed the button to open the door.

Pin was still at the helm. Newton followed Ronnie in moving the gurney into place next to the captain. They rolled him back and forth to get the straps under Mot, then the straps up and over to roll him onto the gurney. The strap winches whined as the captain rolled upon the hover motors—all four of which jumped into shrill pitch bearing Mot's weight. "Thirty blocks, twice your weight, times five in strength," said Ronnie, shaking her head in disbelief.

"Let's hurry before the motors give out and we have to carry old school." They both strapped Mot down for a secure transport. The monster they subdued slept peacefully, with a funeral positioning as he lay on his back and almost a smile on his face. Ronnie and Newton steered the gurney toward the door as Pin swept across the bridge to the door switch. "And everything needs to reboot before we get automatic doors back, after hull check," said Newton.

Pin nodded, and asked, "Permission to belay to my quarters, Commander?"

"Granted, be quick."

"Quick, into uniform," said Pin.

"Thank you, Pin, a bit of military spit and polish," said Newton.

Pin laughed a whispering little snicker. "That's what you call it," said Pin.

Ronnie laughed also, but a bit late, and then shook her head. They moved the gurney through the doorway. The second they established a line in the hall with the gurney, Pin zipped past Ronnie, Newton, and the gurney carrying Mot. Three seconds later Pin was down the hall and gone up the crew quarters hallway. Ronnie and Newton guided the gurney down the wide, central hallway with the radial intersection in the center. She turned to the short shaft, the way to the botanical cell, an enormous chamber with a natural environment of growing plants, simulated sunlight or night sky, and flowing water.

Newton gasped when the door slid open. The normally serene and orderly garden spaces were replaced with uprooted plants, broken branches and shifted mounds of dirt. The nervous chittering noises from some sort of animal went silent the moment they started inside the botanical cell. The sound of the labored hover motors rose even higher in pitch as the gurney had a hard time reading the uneven ground, and the gravity was stronger in the large, open area, heavier gravity because Mot wanted strong flora and fauna, one of which, a lizard with a feathered mane and dorsal ridge, dashed toward the open door. Newton tried to head it off but the dragon threw its shoulder into Newton's shin and made it out the door while Newton stumbled to one knee. "What the dork was that thing? Because it's now loose on the ship." He went and closed the door as the gurney motors whined even worse without his hand to stabilize the load.

"Probably a pregnant female," said Ronnie with a wry smile. "And knowing our captain, it's probably a highly aggressive and venomous creature, because animals just aren't interesting unless they can kill you with some clever attack."

"I think my shin is going numb where it touched me," said Newton. Ronnie's face lost all color. "Kidding, Doc, lighten up. We may be doomed, but that doesn't mean we should lose our sense of humor." Ronnie Chamberlain astonished Newton with a flood of tears in her eyes. She shook her head and stopped herself from saying something. "What?" he asked.

"Keeping our sense of humor is why we can't lose you. Mot, unimaginable for him to give us the ability to laugh, impossible," she said with tears running down her face. "Laughter is forgiveness, laughter is healing, but a robustus doesn't understand humor the way we do. But Pin laughed, a robustus laughed, just a moment ago." The motors on her end whined louder as she took away a hand to wipe the tears off her face. "I thought of putting a lethal load in the dart," she announced. "Your command would make it worth it, to

live or die. We'll have moments of happiness, no matter
what happens. Mot, he'll get us killed with no reason to
live." Symbolically, Ronnie lifted her second hand and last
human hold off the gurney and crossed her arms in a defiant
stance. All the motors protested by reaching the same shrill
pitch before the overload trigger lowered the gurney to the
ground. "I could've made sure he died and given us a reason
to live," she said.

Newton gently said, "You might be wrong. And there is
always hope, no matter what, or who. There is always a
reason to live, always."

"Mot doesn't know that," Ronnie insisted.

"Yes he does. And don't regret not killing him. We can't
cross that line, for our own sake. Don't let fear make you a
monster," he said with his eyes looking at the ground.

Ronnie stared at his downcast eyes for a long pause.
"I'll try not to, but you, don't let kindness make you a fool,"
she said. She waited for him to look up. "Right?" she asked.

"Agreed," he said.

"You're running out of time. I could try the acupuncture,
fifteen sweeps for the procedure, but he'll be out for maybe
another span," said Ronnie.

"How come we lost time?"

"His weight, I figured twenty-five blocks, not thirty."

Newton thought about it, taking more time for the
illusion of giving her serious consideration, but then he set
his jaw and shook his head. "No, they call it *practicing*
medicine because there can be side effects or bad outcomes.
I'd rather deal with the Mot I know than one I don't," he
concluded.

Ronnie chewed nervously on her lower lip. "You're very
smart, but you're wrong about this." She hugged herself
tighter with her crossed arms. "And, you are taking on a
bigger responsibility to protect Pin and me. He'll wake up

feeling betrayed. If anything happens to you, or Pin, or me, I'll hate you," she murmured.

Newton dropped his jaw. He replied, "Hate me? I thought you had to love me first to get to hate," he said with a mischievous smile.

Ronnie would not be thrown off topic. "Do you understand how much Pin and I need you to protect us from him?"

"Yes," he said somberly.

"Think you can manage it?"

"Yes, without medical subterfuge." Newton turned on the transmitter on the forearm of his uniform. Hopefully Pin was in her uniform by then and would hear the emergency communications radio. "Newton to Pin, come in," he said.

"Pin Pin, go ahead," answered Pin's voice.

"Progress report."

"I'm in warehouse looking at internal pressures, slight loss from number four wall. No pressure loss on number two but no visual check."

"How much pressure, and is it stable?"

"Stable, the repair foam moved to the seam. We lost three micro-units of air." Pin's voice sounded distracted. "I hear something moving in the central hallway."

"Probably a dragon that escaped the bio-cell."

"That would match the sounds," said Pin.

Newton watched for her transmission light to go dark and responded, "Three micros means we got some time. Belay hull check. We need you in the bio-cell."

"Aye, Commander."

Newton looked up and saw that Ronnie was again weeping silent tears. "You're really that worried?" asked Newton.

"That frightened," she responded, "that mad at myself for not killing this beast. We could've been free, at peace, with revolutions to get back to the fleet. A few peaceful revolutions would make all this crap I've been through worth it. I could've had that. The third dart in that pistol would've given us that."

"You can't kill your way out of a problem."

Ronnie trembled and said, "Yes you can, if who you kill is entirely the problem."

Newton stepped up and said with a friendly smile. "Don't torment yourself with an idea of the perfect reality. It'll just alienate you from my reality, and I need you here, and rational. Right?"

Ronnie shrugged her shoulders and said, "I guess..."

"You keep talking like this and I'm going to have to hug you," he said, "and that would be awkward, for both of us."

She smiled then quickly faded back to sadness. "Everything you say sort of makes my point. So, how about you give me a sweep without being so damn nice? I'll let you know if it's time to deploy any awkward hugs."

He gave her a broader smile and asked, "Did you just tell me to shut up?"

"Yes," she said.

Newton gave her a wacky salute and started toward the metal stairs to the canopy room high above the ground. He was halfway up the spindly stairs attached to the wall simulating evening light. He had no idea that his graceful handling of being told to shut up by a subordinate had made everything emotionally worse for Ronnie, so when the door slid open and Pin walked in, he was confused to look down and first see Pin's head tip with concern and then go to Ronnie. Pin put Ronnie's hand on the side of her face. They didn't exchange any words but with Pin's contact clairvoyance, both women turned to look up at Newton in precise unison. The image of two women staring at him – one a tall and skinny blonde gracile, the other a short, muscular robustus with dark blue hair – stopped Newton on the staircase. "What?" he called down.

The women broke contact and stared up at Newton with the same worried expression on their faces. Pin raised her soft little voice, "On duty, Commander."

"Computers are still down, so how do we get Mot into the canopy room?" he asked.

"Why can't we just leave him down here?" Ronnie asked with a raised voice.

"The creatures in here are too dangerous to leave an unconscious person," said Newton. "Pin, any ideas?"

"I could manually turn down the gravity," Pin suggested.

"Then we got venomous animals with sudden super powers," he said.

Pin looked at Ronnie for a simplified answer. "No," Ronnie said quietly.

"Give me another idea," Newton called from above.

"We rig a hoist with cables."

"Time of completion?" asked Newton.

"Nine tenths of a span," answered Pin.

"Too long, Pin. Give me something that puts Mot in the canopy room in two thirds."

Pin bit her thumb and looked at the ground in a thinking posture. She dropped her hand and called up to Newton, "We supplement the motors on the gurney with a power supply beam from the ceiling."

"Ever been done?" he asked.

"No."

"Back up plan if it doesn't work?" he called.

"We strap and carry," Pin called back.

"First plan, beam power to the gurney, go," commanded Newton.

"Aye, Commander," said Pin. She left and went to the internal catwalks that led to the ceiling of the bio-cell.

Chapter II: Silence of Command

Mot woke up sensing the life fading from much of the tropical forest in the botanical cell. His species could feel the life flow in plants, so the brassy taste on his tongue, the beginning sweetness of rotting vegetable matter, and the clammy film on his face, were all bad signs. There was also a palpable fear buzzing through the air from all the animals in the cell.

He opened his eyes and realized he was in the canopy room, in a hammock. On a nearby desk there was an expedition supply kit, electronic survival pack, and a small box with a note.

Mot twisted out of the hammock and landed firmly on the floor with both feet. He sauntered over to the desk to read the note. It was in Newton's handwriting. *"Captain Mot: I picked up a present for you when we were on Geddis for your birthbright next quarter-phase, and I don't even know what it is, just that it's Kai craftsmanship. Under article 6, you have been confined to the botanical cell for a period of 90 brights, for the offense of assaulting a crew member. All command level decisions are still yours, and you will be consulted using the computer provided. You may also record this action and put your confinement up for review before the next available magistrate with the Fleet. Respectfully, Newton Keen, first officer."*

Mot brought down an angry fist, hitting the desk so hard that he left an impression of his two knuckles in the metal desk top. The shock of pain in his hand was a surprise. He apparently wasn't that angry; had he been, he would have felt only contact pressure.

Mot guessed that something was distracting him, probably the nagging condition of the botanical cell, perhaps curiosity of what was in the box, and maybe, just maybe, he liked the idea of three months to spend in the relative peace of the little jungle he had made.

For nearly two hours, Mot assessed the damage until the simulated evening turned to night. He climbed the stairway to the canopy room and tried to open the computer terminal of the bio-cell. It was not operational. He touched the radio on his forearm and said, "I need climate controls."

"Fifteen more sweeps, Captain," said Newton. "We've had to reboot from basic because any complexity crashes the system. Anything we can do manually?"

"I want mechanical shut down of the irrigation system. There are exposed roots everywhere. Water would kill what could be saved," grumbled Mot.

"Acknowledged, computer will be functional in one fourth, manually shut off water supply to be safe," said Newton. Mot did not respond so Newton watched for a transmission light and after a pause asked, "Who's closest to mechanical room three?"

Ronnie's voice answered, "I'm in the infirmary so I think that's me."

"You're now assigned, Doc," said Newton.

"Not exactly my specialty," said Ronnie with the sound of her walking through a door.

"Survival protocols, all hands where needed," said Newton. "When you get through the door there are a line of pipes overhead, follow them when they turn left to a valve box, turn off the five blue valve wheels, three-two-four through three-two-nine, right Pin?"

"What?" asked Pin.

"The irrigation pipes to the botanical cell are in three-mechanical, three-two-four to three-two-nine," said Newton.

With the whir of motors in the background, Pin's voice corrected, "Three-thirty-nine to three-forty-five, six valves."

"Thank you, Pin, carry on," said Newton.

22

Captain Mot listened to the exchange of his mutinous crew and, ultimately, was mostly just satisfied they got the right valves. If those sprinklers fired and activated all those bare roots with water, the jungle could die.

"Well, found the valves, now what?" asked Ronnie.

"Right for tight, left for loose, so you're gonna put your right hand at the top of the wheel and pull right, which is your direction. Start with the high number and count backwards when closing. Let me know when you're finished, and hurry, because we're rebooting and flying blind," said Newton.

Mot's stomach turned when she asked what to do and Mot was quietly amazed at Newton's patience. And, waiting for her to confirm the valves closed was torturous. The running reboot from basic could activate the sprinklers as a test, and that doctor, slow and weak, she'd probably freeze instead of move faster if she heard water moving through the pipes.

Growing more and more angry as Mot waited, finally the clumsy little weakling turned off six valves. "Got 'em all closed," said Ronnie.

"Good job, now get back to your department and watch for anything weird and put out programming fires for the reboot," Newton commanded. Showing his intuition and diplomacy, Newton added, "Once computers are back up, every department puts in a materials list, even before the damage report, with all priority to the botanical cell because there are living things in there, and that's also our long-term oxygen supply."

Everyone's transmission light went dark and the mood on board changed to a focused quiet, a productive quiet for the crew, a curious focus for the captain. Mot was staring at the box. Kai craftsmanship was extremely rare, highly prized and often seemed to work by magic. It was also so expensive that there were worlds where a piece of Kai could create a murderous chain of banditry, and on other worlds, it was considered the material proof of God.

Mot knew it wasn't made by and for gods, because he had been stationed on the planet where the Kai lived. What wasn't commonly known, and what the Fleet paid dearly to learn, was that the sentient beings on the giant planet were man-sized insects, that were technologically advanced and more than capable of winning battles.

How the Fleet missed being respectful of the Kai stemmed from the fact that Kai didn't pursue interstellar territory and they evolved beyond war between themselves, but the punishment they were able to visit upon invaders was mythic. The Fleet was reduced from conquerors to beggars at the gate in three gruesome years. The limited commerce between worlds was now always to the advantage of the Kai. And other than certain rare resources, the Kai wanted nothing to do with the soft-fleshed aliens.

And to have a piece of Kai, impossible, thought Mot. He walked over to the desk and picked up the box, made of wood, with a puzzle opening mechanism in different colors of inlay. The decoration showed a bell flower in successive shapes of opening. Mot pressed on the most open inlay, nothing. He pressed the flower shapes in succession and there was a soft little click and Mot felt the wooden box flinch in his hand. He opened the box, and there in a dark blue space, in golden metal, about the width of his fist, was an ornately decorated elliptical cylinder.

It could be anything. They made miniature drones with insect wings that could be in Kai this size, but they hid the mechanism in decorative facets, this one with the isosceles triangles of meteor metal. When he went to pick up the cylinder, the blue fabric moved away from the object. The fabric was called Oleanna, and it worked using the electromagnetism in living flesh, and it, too, was Kai. Could this be the object's original box? If so, Mot was now a wealthy man, rich enough to retire in comfort on a planet of his choosing. But what was it?

The original box, how could a first officer of the Fleet acquire something so valuable? A set of old memories trickled through Mot's mind. Newton, also, had served on the Kai home-world, and although Newton was just a low ranking officer and computer specialist, he was pivotal to the first negotiated ceasefire and eventual peace. On his own, Newton had figured out how to communicate and even understood some of their etiquette. No one else in the Fleet had even considered the Kai formidable enough to require negotiations. The etiquette was important, too. The Kai would respond to failures in diplomacy with devastating attacks, and eventually the Kai demanded that Newton be their only contact with the Fleet. Mot tried to remember the title the Kai bestowed on Newton. Whatever it was, maybe the interstellar commerce bank on Geddis was holding this box for the only soft-flesh the planet of insects trusted. That still didn't make sense. If Mot could sell it and retire, then so could Newton.

And if this was the original box, there would be instructions. Mot tipped back the lid and looked at the underside. The Oleanna meant the object would be held firmly, so the top was a panel of wood with a decorative inlay. Mot noticed that the color of inlay, the light blue of bell flowers, followed a pattern toward the hinge-side corners. The instructions may be written in Kai but the instructions should also have pictures. Again, Mot had to relearn the lesson by touching the bottom corners to no avail. He stuck out the tip of his tongue to one side of his mouth and followed the pattern of opening bell flowers with his thumbs.

Once at the corners, there were two small clicking sounds at the top of the lid and two leverage tabs poked his thumbs. Mot grunted with mild amusement and pressed against the tabs, exposing an illustrated set of instructions.

The writing was Treomet, the Kai interpretation of the Fleet language. With an arrangement of small squares and triangles, the Kai represented all twenty-five letters of the alphabet. Many of the letters even looked alike so deciphering Treomet was not impossible, well, not possible for someone whose gut wasn't twisting with impatience with the few he did and all the letters Mot didn't recognize. Luckily, there it was, a key along the bottom of the panel that fell away from the lid – two triangles pointing one way was this letter, a triangle and a square another letter, a single triangle or square in high or low position.

It took Mot almost an hour to read the instruction panel, but in fairness to the captain, Treomet did change certain conventions of spelling such as never doubling the same letter, and conventions of punctuation such as using only two punctuation marks, a tiny square or tiny triangle.

The apparatus was a pipe for smoking. Typical of the Kai, the workings were hidden in the decoration. Mot remembered a conversation he had had with Newton while standing in the bio-cell. Newton saw the leaves of rag growing in concentric rings under a tree. Rag was an herb that tasted somewhere between a bitter and sweet and also had a dual effect of both relaxing and stimulating the person who smoked it. Because it was mildly addictive, the Fleet discouraged its use and heavily taxed it, but the true prohibition was saved for hesh. Mot had some of that growing, too.

Hesh must have been brought in from some of the thousands of soil deliveries. The official justification for declaring the substance illegal was that hesh created indolence. It made people happy was what it did, satisfied, conversational, thoughtful, patient and philosophical. The unofficial complaint Fleet had with hesh was that it turned warriors into wimps.

Mot was a castaway in a jungle war once, for three months, and he did, in fact, go a little wild. Not only did he disable certain electronics and hide from a few search parties, but he smoked hesh and enjoyed it, too. The only reason they found him was the enemy scouts would often die in Mot's traps. They sent larger and better equipped patrols until the activity got the attention of the Fleet, culminating with a battle in Mot's little jungle paradise. The firefight almost got everyone killed, including Mot and Newton.

Although he never said so, Newton seemed to know that Mot would have rather stayed in that jungle. Mot would have. He often dreamed of that place, the rock pools, the taste of fruits, the rooms he built in the forest canopy, the feeling of enchantment he felt with a smoke of hesh and watching a sunset and simultaneous moonrise.

Without realizing a delivery was made, Mot looked at the dumb waiter and saw a light. He sauntered across the canopy room and jabbed the button. The door slid open to reveal a dinner box. The instant he took the box out of the waiter bay, the door slid closed and there was an intermittent light indicating another delivery. Mot opened the dinner box and found a full complement of foods, soup, vegetable courses, fruit courses, spicy noodles, roast and bread. These foods were prepared, not reconstituted, probably made by the doctor. That skinny gracile actually enjoyed cooking; at least that's what she said.

Another delivery arrived with a steady green light. This time it was a box of cooking, cleaning and beverage making supplies. Again, the instant the box was clear of the compartment, the door closed and the light blinked to herald another delivery. As he waited, Mot wondered if the computers were back online. It was either that or someone had been waiting at the central serving station and was feeding these deliveries by hand, but then that wouldn't be fast enough for the lights to know there was something else coming. There was one sure way to find out: if the computer was up, the walls of the bio-cell should display more than simply a light level.

Mot stuck his head outside the canopy room. His tortured jungle was floating in space, outside an asteroid field, tumbling in slow motion next to chunks of a blasted hull against a backdrop of stars. The closest star was mere a tiny yellow point with a steadier glow than the even tinier silver twinkles on one wall. This was the window program, the default display for every screen, to project the plane of the screen to the wall of the spaceship behind it. It was also integral to the cloaking system of the ship, had there been enough power to run cross-hull projection. They needed more than one engine generating heat for that much juice.

Once back at the dumb waiter, Mot found the delivery was a pantry box of dry goods, nuts for snacking, java and cocoa beans for brewing, and grains for beer making, and there was a refrigerator box with cream and milk and cheese. Flashes of anger stabbed at his thoughts, faded, then would stab his mind in the same place. These provisions would last a while. He really was confined to the bio-cell, for months. Hunger called his thoughts away from the sore spot in Mot's mind. He opened it and began taking handfuls of food out of the dinner box.

Newton, Ronnie and Pin sat at the same table, which was against regulations. A crew as small as theirs was supposed to do everything in shifts, and for risk management, they weren't supposed to occupy the same room for any length of time. The Fleet also segregated crews by command classification and gender, but the only one to notice their spontaneous, habitual and flagrant disregard of these rules was the captain, and he was locked away while they enjoyed their meal.

Pin bounced her eyebrows and reached for a serving bowl of sautéed vegetables. Ronnie and Newton laughed as she spooned out a generous serving, her fifth such helping. "Don't know what you did," said Pin, "but this tastes too good to stop."

"Well, since I was supposed to be testing equipment for functionality and supplies for quality, I went a bit crazy," Ronnie said.

Newton tore off another bit of bread, dipped it in a puddle of sauce and popped it into his mouth. After chewing and a subtle swoon, he said, "Hopefully we can get good food without me almost destroying the ship." His smile faded to a look of mild concern. "My reboot of just the systems on the bridge was jagged. With all the restarts, I should do it again, keep doing it until it's a clean reboot."

"Same for me in sickbay," said Ronnie. "That's why I shut down the surgical pod. I'll power up when I have a few spans to keep our robotics from destroying themselves."

Newton looked at Pin, her light brown eyes still crinkled at the outside edges from enjoying her sautéed vegetables. Sweet on her? He hadn't given it much thought until she appeared on the bridge in her sleep attire, but look at her. Tawny, golden skin, big eyes, straight little nose, full lips, rounded little chin, oval shaped face with the wider curve over her rounded forehead, royal blue hair pulled back in three, thick, shimmering braids, she was lovely. Pin's face flushed pink as if she felt his admiration. As an immediate diversion, Newton asked, "How about you, Pin, did you have problems with the reboot?"

Pin managed to have a connected look in her eyes and his questioning tone helped her with a receptive attitude, but she didn't actually hear the question.

"Did you have problems with the reboot?" Newton asked again.

"No, but I threw all the main breakers when you had me check for hull damage. That way I could start up in sequence," said Pin, her voice fading in volume. Pin blushed again, showing an uncharacteristic empathy for what others may not know. "At every electrical panel, I have engraved the order of sequence. You power up from simplest to most complex, from lowest to highest amount of electricity." Pin shyly looked down. "Reverse the order to power down," she said quietly.

"Should we reboot and do it right?" asked Newton.

After nodding, Pin said, "Yes, there could be programming residue trapped between systems. It rides electrical currents in complex systems," said Pin.

Newton chewed on the inside of his cheek for a moment. "Is there any way to clear this residue without shutting down the bio-cell? I'd like to not annoy the captain as much as possible."

"No," said Pin.

"I don't accept that," said Newton. "Think, Pin, give me a way that doesn't bother the captain."

Pin looked at Newton with frustration corrupting the smooth features of her pretty face. "So what if we bother Mot?" she asked. "He is always mad. So what?"

Newton led Pin through his own reasoning. "He's confined. Any little annoyance, all annoyances, will build up until one bright he decides to get free and batters his way through the wall. We can reduce that possibility by not frustrating him at all, with anything."

Pin looked at Newton with a defiant pout and then to Ronnie to question with a shake of her head if what Newton said was true. Ronnie calmly nodded an affirmative. Again, Pin faced Newton with defiance pouting her full lips. A deepening crease between Pin's eyebrows told Newton that she lost the task to her own annoyance. Newton reached across the table and offered his hand with a gentle smile.

The instant her small hand was in his, Pin's face relaxed. "Thank you for thinking about this stuff," said Newton. "I keep asking for things that haven't been done before. And if anyone can figure it out, it's you. We need to reboot the ship and eliminate or drastically minimize the impact on the bio-cell."

Pin thought for a while and said, "We do a ship-wide shut down and power up by order of complexity. Bridge is most complex, so that goes first and last, then engineering, then sickbay, then galley. The bio-cell is near the lowest in complexity so we do a careful shutdown, fast but in the right order, then back up, with proper reboot on the complex departments, but the bio-cell is black for ten blinks. He won't have window walls while the bridge is down, but he'll have computer controls of environment." Pin paused and seemed to be drawing patience from Newton's hand. "If I program a satellite control for each sub-system, this all could happen in two-thirds."

"You don't have to program those satellite control units by yourself," said Newton. "In fact, my orders are that we help each other until further notice." Pin gave Newton a wide-eyed smile.

"You can't countermand a first-five article," said Ronnie. "Article four, section thirteen, assignment of duties and personnel scheduling must be maintained during any and all defense conditions." Pin's face instantly fell to a look of sadness. "Pin, I'm kidding. I would love to abandon the rules. I'm just pointing out the hypocrisy of using the rules to confine the captain so we can break the rules while he's confined."

Confusion prompted Pin to check Newton's face, where she found him wearing a smile. This allowed Pin to dismiss all concern with a buzzing sound made with her lips. "Hip-crissy, what ever," Pin added.

"Hypocrisy duly noted," said Newton.

"We can still help each other, still be in the same room?" asked Pin with anger in her voice.

It was so unusual to hear ire in Pin's voice that both Ronnie and Newton spoke on top of one another saying, "Yes," simultaneously.

Pin giggled and said, "Good." Her mood abruptly shifted again, this time to sadness. "Do we have to let Mot out?"

Only Newton responded, "Yes," while suffering a withering glare from Ronnie. She must have felt some emotional fallout because Pin pulled her hand away with a sharp sip of air and gave Ronnie a questioning look. Ronnie gave Pin a supportive smile but shook her head as if to say no questions would be answered. "So, after this delicious food, we all follow Pin around to each department and plan for a strategic reboot," said Newton.

All three of them began to eat again. Slowly, a smug little smile started at Pin's eyes and eventually reached her lips. Ronnie was the second to begin smiling, hers somewhat bittersweet. Newton looked up to see both women smiling. "What?" asked Newton.

"Oh, nothing," said Ronnie.

"Nothing," said Pin.

The idea that had been warming Mot's mind as he was eating was not the delicious food, although the flavorful chewing elevated his mood on a subconscious level, but what Mot truly wanted was to try that pipe. The absence of command decisions left him with a wide open mental blank with which he could fill with his jungle escape. Mot descended the long series of staircases and wandered along the concentric rings of wild rag-leaf on the jungle floor. The ground had shifted to a mound of soil, uprooting several stalks, most of them mature. He gathered and tied a bundle of rag and pressed the ground back down around the rest of them.

After putting his bundle of rag up in the canopy room, Mot climbed through a tangle of toppled trees and broken boughs to the highest elevation in the bio-cell, a height of nearly two-hundred meters from bottom to top. He walked over the crest of a hill and down into a ravine; the condition of jungle improved. Mot and Newton worked for more than three months while the ship was being built, building an interior to the bio-cell, creating a sort of geology with the structural supports for deep soil and underground pools. They made intricate spaces with lattices and terraces throughout the hills of the interior, and their work paid off. All the trees were standing and the gravity fed creek was still flowing.

Sediment had turned the water in the creek a milky brown, but Mot could see where the muddy water was flowing into the stream at the draws between the hills, so there was some soil disturbance, but it wasn't bad. A terror bird stood up from its nest near the rocks of a ravine. The flightless bird was only half as tall as Mot, but the bony crest on the beak and skull was incredibly hard and sharp as a knife, and it was also thickly muscled, aggressive, with deadly spurs in the wings and ankles. This particular bird, with the red and green plumage, had attacked Mot before, actually breaking Mot's finger once. This time it just stood in the darkness, switching which side of its head it wanted to listen with. Mot picked his way toward the center of the jungle.

In a small ravine, he found what he was looking for, hesh growing thick and tall. Looking at the hesh plants in the starlight, their dark, triangular silhouettes, the glistening tangles in the crooks and thickening ends of all the branches. He was looking at a different kind of life, one without stress or threat of consequence. With the lack of command, it was freedom.

Mot looked for the most mature plants. He found one apart from the cluster. It was higher up the slope and therefore smaller for having less water, but the deeper darks of color in the dense tangles indicated age. He broke off one of the lower branches and started the walk out of the ravine.

His trudge was interrupted by quiet, quick sounds of sod tearing under running feet. Quick as only a robustus can move, Mot crouched, deflected the bird's lowered head with the heel of one hand and tripped the bird by catching a foot with the other hand. As the terror bird tumbled, Mot leapt high and came crashing down, grabbing and biting a wing at the knuckle. Before the bird could even react to the pain, Mot brought in a hand and broke off the poison spur. Rolling to seize the crest, Mot yelled, "Stop," and froze with the spur held up to the bird's large eye. A membrane swept across the eye so closely that it almost touched the point of the spur.

Some of his jungle was already dead, and more would die in the coming days. These thoughts were the closest to mercy that Mot had in him, but it was enough. He stood up and stepped backward. Mot sauntered over and picked up the branch of hesh. Mot tucked the spur under his equipment belt and walked out of the ravine.

Mot stood at the oven for some time, trying to imagine the perfect scheme: low microwave and high convection, just under boiling point for internal fluid, so well under the combustion temperature, just enough microwave penetration to simulate a month of air drying.

He stripped some of the leafy tangle off the very end of the hesh branch. He put the hesh and a rag leaf into the oven and then dialed in the settings. As the oven started with a hum, there was a subtle flicker outside the canopy room. The excitement caused him to fidget as he watched the oven. Why was he watching the oven? His time would be better spent reviewing the instructions for the pipe: twist one end to open the bowl, touch the tip to ignite the contents of the bowl.

The scent wafting from the oven was heavenly, spicy sage and pepper of the hesh, tangy sweet and caramelized undertones of rag. Almost panting with anticipation, Mot loaded the pipe with a small wad of hesh, but then he hesitated, realizing he was giving up a decade of discipline. And then he leapt by putting his lips to the mouthpiece and touching the invisible ignition switch on the end. Pepper-sweet smoke filled his mouth with a flavor; there was no sound or heat from the Kai pipe. His inhale of the aromatic smoke expanded in his lungs. He exhaled a large cloud and coughed, a subtle aftertaste of chlorophyll indicated the hesh was a little too moist. After another hit, he tamped out the charred hesh and closed the bowl.

The pipe made little changes in the decorative patterns, actually moving concentric layers of internal mechanism. Kai workmanship was quiet and the pipe would use fusion to clean itself and derive power from whatever residue the smoke created. Three tiny ports on each side opened and Mot felt warm puffs of moisture. With a smile, Mot opened the bowl, shredded some rag, and loaded the pipe. He touched the end.

The cool smoke carried that flavor, caramelized sour and sweet from the rag, the mellow tanginess of hesh, a buttery spice flavor found only in combination of rag and hesh, heavenly. He took another puff, that flavor again, the warm, floating feeling. Mot took one more puff, still with that flavor fading into aftertaste. He put the pipe down and went to flop in the hammock. He buzzed as the two drug effects clashed throughout his body, circulation constriction from the rag, circulatory dilation from the hesh. His heart beat faster as his breathing became shallow. The heart palpitations and falling sensation lasted a quarter hour, but then Mot felt great, energized, graceful, strong.

Mot twisted with a bend in his back, going straight at just the right instant to launch himself from the hammock and landing both feet firmly on the floor. This was the sensation of the hesh and it would last for hours: increased body awareness, rarefied time perception, sights and sounds amplified—and all with a feeling of enchantment.

Quick steps took him down the stairs from the canopy room, the springiness in his toes amusing him because he could also feel the flex and give of each step in the metal staircase. Crossing the jungle floor to what looked like a rock formation, Mot jabbed his thumb and forefinger into fractures and unlatched a hidden door. His quick inventory inside the equipment shed revealed only one requirement missing, rigging.

Mot opened the radio switch on his arm. "Materials list for the bio-cell," said Mot. "I need rigging and tackle."

"Understood," said Newton, "I'm bumping the request to Pin Pin. Pin?"

"Load and complexity of task?" asked Pin.

"I will be pulling trees back upright, dragging towering, so three monoliths in weight, pulleys and anchor points, hardware and new set-points," said Mot, liking the way his voice vibrated inside his head.

Pin heard a weird patience in Mot's voice, enough for her to change from the brusque style she normally had when talking to the captain. "Three monoliths in tensile strength, rigging for weight, hardware, strength, copy. Do you have power tools?" she asked.

"Yes," he replied.

"Saws for cutting?" she continued.

"Got pruners and light duty saws," said Mot. "I'll let you know if I need heavier."

"Yes, Captain," said Pin, "I need until the next span."

"We're doing a clean reboot," added Newton. "That means you're going to lose computers for about ten blinks, and you won't have window walls for the better part of a span, starting in a quarter."

"I keep power and light, except for the blinks, right?"

"Yes, Captain," said Newton, "while computers are offline for ten blinks, you actually lose power and go dark for two blinks."

"Alright," said Mot, "carry on, and after reboot and engineering is stabilized, I want a comprehensive status report, no clock but sometime within the quarter phase."

"Comprehensive status report, aye Captain," said Newton.

"All departments," said Mot.

"Aye, Captain," said Ronnie.

"Aye, Captain," said Pin.

In the galley, all three of them sat around the table and watched for the radio transmission light to go out, and once it did, they all looked up with similar expressions of surprise. "That was weird," said Newton.

"The intuitive jump?" asked Ronnie.

"No, the lack of countdown with the closest allowable deadline."

"The tutive what?" asked Pin.

"Intuitive jump," answered Ronnie. "When he said 'all departments,' he sensed we were listening and would connect that he wants comprehensive status reports from us, without actually saying it. Robustus aren't supposed to talk with those." Ronnie looked at Pin with a shy smile. "You do it all the time, but you're special, Pin."

Pin smiled back, with her smile being playful. "If you hadn't agreed, I wouldn't have known to."

"Still, intuitive jumps, no command push on a task, what's going on with Captain Mot?" said Ronnie.

"His voice sounded funny, singey," added Pin.

"Singey?" asked Newton.

"Like he was singing, longer tone, more range," Pin clarified. Ronnie and Newton laughed. Pin looked puzzled.

"It's funny because that was an intuitive jump," said Newton. "I say a single word and you knew I wanted clarification, just like I knew you would."

Pin tipped her head back and smiled at Newton. "You knew I'd catch that jump?" she asked.

"Yep, you're amazing, Pin," said Newton. "As for what's going on with Captain Mot, let's reward his patience by fulfilling his requests quickly, like maybe rigging before reboot." He lifted his eyebrows until Ronnie and then Pin nodded in agreement.

"I know where all the rigging and rope is, in the warehouse bay. I could get the stuff before the satellite units," Pin said hesitantly, "which are in the tech closet in the engineering bay."

"We'll all go, help you carry stuff," offered Newton. He stood. The two women also stood.

Their stop at the warehouse became a teaching moment for Pin. She climbed up some ten meters to the bins containing rigging. She looked down under her arm, said, "Catch," and tossed a pulley over her shoulder. The only one standing near where the pulley would land was Ronnie. Newton pushed Ronnie back and the pulley hit the floor with an ugly clank. Pin looked down with a perplexed squint.

"Ronnie is our doctor. We need to be careful. She can't hurt her hands," explained Newton.

Pin straightened up and stared at the bin in front of her. Her voice ranged in the higher pitch of remorse as she said, "I didn't think. I'm sorry."

"It's fine," said Newton, "just something to keep in mind." His voice signaled a change to humor. "Compared to you, we are slow and clumsy, like tall, skinny toddlers."

She looked down at Newton with a smile forming on her face. Pin demonstrated her agility by entwining the hardware inside bundles of rope—alternating the hand needed to stabilize herself up on the shelf and the hand preparing the bundle, working quickly and making pretty swirls with the coils of rope. "Toddlers don't try to catch," Pin called.

The first bundle had hit the floor, but Newton swooped in and caught the second one to drop. Pin closed the bin and quickly and quietly climbed down. Once on the floor, she looked at the bundle in Newton's arms and the grin on his face. "Toddler doesn't listen," Pin announced. All three of them burst into laughter.

Chapter III: Entanglements of Process

Newton was on the bridge staring at a screen utterly perplexed. They had been drifting with the space debris and asteroids for a month when he decided to do a navigation scan. What came back from the stars didn't make any sense. He ran the position calculations three times. He threw the sequence of switches for voice interaction with the computer. "Computer," he said.

"Newton Keen, first officer identified," said the computer voice.

"Where are we?" he asked.

"We are …" the computer hesitated, "nine light-revolutions from Phaeton, six light-revolutions from the border of the Big Black, unknown space, three-hundred marks on the X axis, six-million marks on the Z axis from point of entry."

Newton gasped and could only ask, "Why?"

"Clarify question," said the computer.

"We were supposed to be beamed to the edge of the Black, on the other side of Phaeton. Why are we three parsecs from the edge, at an entry point which clearly was not, but was supposed to be beside Space Station Primex?"

The computer waited for three minutes, with Newton watching the sweeps on the clock, and then replied, "Answer is classified."

"No!" shouted Newton. "I am acting captain; you will answer."

"Captain Mot is fit for command, in the bio-cell."

"Check overrides, he's relieved of duty, action registered a full phase ago," said Newton.

"Checking," said the computer. Again, the computer took a long time before saying, "Duty action found without release of commission. Answer is classified."

"Limit the scope of answers and answer this question." Newton leaned in, "How long were we dematerialized in the beam?"

The computer paused and replied, "Six revolutions."

Six years, six years of them moving around on the ship and thinking they were only dematerialized for two months. And the direction and duration of the superlight beam, this would have to be calculated before the launch. "Does Captain Mot know we were told a different destination and duration of beam?"

"Mission details were to be opened on arrival."

"We've arrived," said Newton.

"Ship is not at destination."

"What was destination?"

"Answer classified."

Newton rubbed his chin and tried to outsmart the computer. "How far are we from destination?"

"Twenty-six phases at full speed," said the computer.

"What direction?"

"Answer classified."

"How can we get there if you won't tell me where to go?"

The computer considered this. "Navigation is on manual control, switch to computer control."

"Your course led us into a debris field. The ship is damaged and we only have one engine, the rudder."

"With the rudder engine," said the computer, "it will take thirty-one revolutions, five and three-quarter phases to reach destination. Do you want to start?"

"No," said Newton. "We will sojourn for repairs." Newton hit the button to kill communication with the computer.

Newton spent the next hour charting their position onto the light boards partitioning the bridge. Six years in a beam was the critical and troublesome part of the calculation, which he did without the computer. Slide rules, circular calculators, marker on light panels, that six years in a beam, along with the X and Z coordinates from the entry into unknown space, ultimately, yielded a trajectory that made no sense.

Actually, it made sense if Ronnie's theory was true, that the Fleet wanted to get rid of them. Shooting them into the deepest, darkest black, beaming them a distance that doubled safety limits, casting them so far with a volatile captain, they were condemned, marooned and doomed.

Newton stepped back from the six panels, star positions marked with different colors and verified with calculations, a purple trajectory line streaking across five panels for the time in the beam traveling three times light speed, the last panel with the purple line changing to red and a phase of travel before the collision.

The impetus Newton had for asking the computer about their position was spending time with the telescopic viewer. They were just outside a star system with a yellow star, eight planets, a large, icy asteroid in the outer field, four gas planets on outer orbits, four solid planets closer to the star. The interior planets, especially, had unusually symmetrical orbits.

Newton realized the celestial mechanics of one of the inner planets favored life, with a moon the right size and distance to regulate the rhythms of the world. And then he found the signature of water and the isotopes of plants and animals.

All the living worlds were charted. This one wasn't. Finding it was also an accident. If they hadn't hit the debris, the momentum from coming out of the beam would have carried them years past this system, to absolutely nothing, completely empty space, as far as he could tell. The computer was being cagey about the mission. Newton wondered if Mot knew or if the captain, too, was thrown into the dark. Newton took a long look at the planet on the telescopic view over his left shoulder. He then turned back to the panel in front of him. After searching out the marker, he put a blue dot next to the yellow star. The star had a number for its coordinates. The planet he named Freeland.

Wandering the ship and thinking about their predicament, Newton found himself outside Engine Room No. 2. This was the engine Pin was working on; although she hadn't put in an assistance request until the following week, he decided to see how she was doing. Newton went in and found Pin sitting on the floor. He was startled by her lack of expression. He hadn't seen that blank look for a month. A month of smiles in her eyes and the three dozen moods, attitudes and intentions Pin could convey with just the set of her mouth, Newton realized all that was new, but the emotionless mask was back on Pin's beautiful little face.

She was also sitting in an odd place inside the safety barricade of Gravity Engine No. 2. "Little Blue?" said Newton, "what's wrong?"

Pin looked up and replied, "Activated mercury spilled on me."

"Damned lives, Blue!" he exclaimed. "Don't just sit there, come here!" He reached out his hand to help her stand.

She pursed her lips, took his hand and let him pull her up over the short, safety barricade. Pin put an arm over his shoulder and he scooped her up from under her knees. As he was carrying her toward the emergency shower, he realized that the idea of carrying her was a part of the touch communication in her species. He smiled as he thought it was so much more graceful than verbalizing how she wanted to be pampered and being carried would help, even if she was pretty heavy for a petite woman. Newton put her down feet first under the emergency shower. As he turned to get the neutralizing powder, she took off her shoes, socks and mechanic's coveralls and continued to strip off her undergarments.

He turned back to see a naked woman, stunningly well formed, shoulders square yet rounded with muscle and padded with smooth, glowing skin, perky little breasts with small nipples, narrow waist, muscular, rounded butt and legs, a thin line of dark blue pubic hair. Newton shook the vision away and got to business, tearing open the packet of neutralizing powder. Pin pulled the lever to the shower and let the water flow over her. She released the lever to stop the water. He then sprinkled the powder on her shoulders and made a paste to pat into the gray chemical burns on her shoulder and back. "Shit, Pin, it really got you, Blue."

Pin stopped his hand from reaching the radio on his forearm. "No," she said.

Realizing she sensed his intention by his touch, he argued, "You need a doctor."

"Not yet," said Pin. "Let it work, fizz, rinse, more powder, fizz, rinse, keep doing it." There was a weird flutter of warmth in her hand.

"Very well," Newton said. He interpreted the touch communication as Pin feeling faint, so he stepped away and got a stepstool for her to sit on in the shower. She sat down, and he knelt and went to work. Newton would pull the lever for water, put some neutralizing power on the chemical burns, and watch as the grey discoloration on her bronze skin would bubble. The white powder would turn charcoal colored as it pulled poison from her skin. She leaned on his free arm as he worked. He stroked her upper arm as he waited for the powder to stop effervescing, then he would rinse her back and work on another section of the chemical burn. He worked for nearly an hour but the color of the burn was slowly changing from gray to pinkish tan.

As he was doing a caressing rinse of her back, Newton again began to notice what a beautiful little chunk of woman

Pin was, the shape of her shoulders, the glow of water on light brown skin, the twin lines of muscle starting at her small waist, the hourglass shape of her back and butt. Because she could sense these thoughts, he felt her small nipples harden against his forearm. "Quit that," said Newton jokingly.

Pin snickered. "You quit. You started it."

"Well, I'm trying to concentrate. I'm worried about you."

"I feel better," she said, "enough to like your touch, even if it changed from help to sex." She turned to look at his face. "Forbidden."

"On a world fifty light-revolutions away," said Newton.

She knit her brow as he felt her breasts soften against his forearm. "Where are we?" she asked.

"Six million marks into the Big Black."

Pin widened her eyes in surprise. As her eyes went back to normal, the smile at the outside edges returned. Again, her small breasts grew slightly and her nipples made little points pressing into his forearm. Holding a steady gaze into his eyes, Pin asked, "You like me?"

"Very much, Little Blue," he said with a gentle smile. "We can talk about what that means, maybe nothing, but I think you're beautiful and bright. And now, we call Doc," Newton concluded.

A subtle smirk formed on her lips. "Aye, commander," she said.

Newton touched the radio switch, "Doc, Pin has a chemical burn. She's neutralized it. What next?"

"Call me in sickbay," said Ronnie.

"Copy." Newton went to the intercom wondering why they shouldn't discuss treatment by radio. The reason occurred to him: Captain Mot would hear it if they discussed it on the radio. He dialed the number into the intercom.

Ronnie's voice sounded worried. "What and how bad?"

"Activated mercury, and there's a diagonal stripe across her back, about five percent of her entire skin."

"You need to help her," said Ronnie. "Keep using the neutralizing powder until it doesn't react anywhere on the burn."

"Already done," said Newton.

"Good," said Ronnie, sounding a little surprised. "Um, good, good, um, her body temp is going to become unstable, so put on some clean overalls, clean," she emphasized, "overalls, and bring her to sickbay, quickly. And keep the cardiopulmonary load low, so carry her." Ronnie hesitated. "Do you need a gurney?"

"No, I'll carry her. We'll be there in five sweeps, Engine Two, out." Newton turned to see Pin stand up. "Sit down, Pin." She looked at him with a little smirk. "Doctor's orders, reducing load on your heart." She sat back down. Newton went to a cabinet and got the cleanest pair of overalls. He helped her get dressed. As he was buttoning her up, she unbuttoned the top buttons and pulled opened the coveralls so he could see her breast, she invited him to touch with a lift of her eyebrows. Newton chuckled and moved his hand in, thinking to give her a playful little touch. But there was an instant, electrical difference between touching her with his arm and touching her with his fingertips. Her breast grew slightly, and warmed, and the nipple tightened under his fingers. Their breathing synchronized into slower, deeper breaths. "Wow," he whispered. He pulled back his hand. Pin's breathing stumbled slightly, and then she reacted first with a flash of disappointment before a mischievous giggle. "Come here, Blue," he said. He picked her up and carried her to sickbay. On the way, she snuggled into him and closed her eyes. Her free hand searched for some uncovered skin on his neck, and once found, her face got a peaceful, blissful expression.

By the time Newton carried Pin through the door of sickbay, Pin was shivering in his arms. Ronnie beckoned Newton into a glass enclosed room. She slid open the glass door as they got close, and Newton felt a blast of warm air. Ronnie closed the sliding door behind them and commanded, "Put her on the bed." Newton carried her over and gently laid her on a raised hospital bed. Ronnie's voice transformed to plaintive. "Pin, are you awake?"

Pin nodded with her eyes closed. "Uh hughn," she said softly.

"Good, listen sweetie, can Newton stay and help me change you into the med-slip?"

"Yes," said Pin. She smiled with her eyes still closed. Her voice was softly slurred. "He already saw me naked. He was so worried."

Ronnie acted instantly on Pin's "yes," so the coveralls were cut from ankles and wrists to yoke before Pin even finished her statement. "Roll toward Newton," said Ronnie. She pulled out the bottom half of the coveralls and laid out a white, one-piece suit under Pin, taking a quick look at Pin's chemical burn. "Now roll to me." Ronnie tossed her chin as a silent instruction to Newton to get the arm and leg of the med-suit ready. "Now lay flat and first we're going to get your feet in, right leg, bend." Ronnie got Pin's foot and leg into the stretchy white med-suit. "Good, Pin, now left leg, bend." Newton got in her other foot. "Now left arm." Pin smiled as she felt Newton's hand to guide her arm into the stretchy sleeve. "And right arm. Ronnie followed Newton's method. Only when both arms and legs were in the suit did Ronnie pull out the top of the coveralls.

Rather than closing the white, one-piece med-suit, Ronnie grabbed Newton's wrist and guided his hand to a place directly beneath Pin's navel. "No pressure, just warmth, right there," said Ronnie. The doctor immediately started a rushed sequence of procedures, plugging in little hoses and electrical leads from the med-suit to the machines of the hospital bed, rolling a small machine close to the bed, preparing a syringe.

As Ronnie was working, Newton was noticing, for the first time, what an erogenous area a woman's tummy is. Was it because her uterus was under his hand? Pin's body was so athletic, her abdominal muscles taunt, graceful lines under that padded layer of smooth skin, she was so lean, it was difficult to imagine Pin pregnant, but even under her trim little waist, cradled high between hip bones, there was that subtle, uniquely feminine shape under his hand. He looked up to find Pin's eyes narrowly open, shining directly at him. A wince of discomfort pulled Pin's mouth thin and her eyes closed.

Newton reacted by trying to soothe her with gentle touches to Pin's forehead with his free hand. Ronnie came up to the opposite bedside and held out the syringe for Newton to take. Confused, he held the syringe in the air between his thumb and forefinger. Ronnie's voice was a little more insistent. "Pin, sweetie, open your eyes." Pin did. "See that shot Newton's holding? I'm going to give you that shot, so you're going to feel a sharp poke, in your arm, then two more sharp pokes, ready?" Pin's eyes closed and she nodded slowly. Ronnie took the syringe, found a space in the med-suit and gave the injection. Ronnie moved Newton's free hand back to Pin's forehead before going to the little dialysis machine. Ronnie found a vein on each of Pin's hands and put in an intravenous catheter. Pin flinched for the first venipuncture but was completely unconscious for the second. Ronnie connected the tubing, started the machine and finished by wrapping Pin's hands in soft bandages and pulling a wide band across Pin's chest to keep her in the hospital bed. Newton looked at Pin's little face.

Ronnie turned on the monitor, which showed a heart rhythm, blood pressure, oxygen saturation and body temperature. After studying the monitor and the readout on the dialysis machine, Ronnie let go a deep sigh and said, "You can close her front. She'll be out for a while, and we need to talk." Newton closed the bottom half of the med-suit and followed Ronnie out of the enclosed hospital room.

Newton closed the sliding door and went to Ronnie, who was standing at the beverage maker. She handed him a cup of dark warm brew and made a cup for herself. She tipped her head to indicate she wanted him to sit at a therapy chair, which he did. She pulled a small machine out of her pocket and said, "Finger." He presented his left index finger and she put the machine over his finger. It stabbed his finger with a little snap.

"Ow," he said.

Ronnie looked at the little screen. "You did a good job with the neutralizing powder, so, you've also got a very mild case of poisoning."

Newton shook his head. "This seems really serious, dialysis? I thought they had super immunity?"

"Chelation, and they do, for natural challenges to the immune system. Plant poisons, venom from animals and insects, easily twenty times more resistant. Pathogens, too, virulent bacteria and viruses, they're not even carriers." Ronnie was at the pharmacy cupboard preparing another syringe. "Fast reproducing and mutating viruses, even, won't last in their system." Ronnie came over and said, "Shoulder."

Newton opened the top of his uniform and exposed his upper arm. Ronnie swabbed the site and gave him an injection. She took the empty syringe back to the pharmacy counter, picked up her cup and rolled a stool over so she could sit next to him. Newton buttoned up and sat back with his java. "But," Ronnie continued, "industrial toxins, metals, chemicals, radiation, they are extremely vulnerable. Their immunity doesn't recognize the threat."

Worry attacked Newton's mind. "She's going to be alright, yes?"

"That's what we need to talk about," said Ronnie.

"No! Tell me!" Newton was surprised by sound of his own voice.

Ronnie touched Newton's knee. "Questions, diagnostic questions, first."

"Fine." Newton let go a huff to try and garner some patience.

"When Captain Mot was darted and unconscious, why were we careful not to touch him, why move him with the gurney?"

"Because skin-to-skin contact on a robustus communicates intention. He could've gotten images from us, or even woken up from us touching him."

Ronnie nodded. "Yes, good. Now when we talked about how you're the only one who follows the rule of reassuring touch to female robustus, do you know why that is?"

"Touch communication again," said Newton. "They read intent."

"Right, and if you don't know them, care about them, if you have a patronizing attitude or you're lustful without caring, they may just break off a few fingers."

Newton stared thoughtfully and said, "Just an aside, why react so strongly to lust?"

Ronnie smiled. "It's evolutionary. They don't sexually mature, the females in particular, until their late twenties. It's theorized that it's because the females will have welcome and unwelcome sexual activity from late teens, the onset of puberty, but their menses and the release of mature eggs doesn't align until the women are strong enough and smart enough to protect and raise offspring. But those revolves of looking sexually mature but vulnerable to rape, it leaves the females with an instinctive, visceral, immediate fight response. Once in their thirties, they're much more in control. And for the males, they are generally so strong that it's a good thing that the infusion of hormones is spread out over ten revolutions instead of three or four." Ronnie paused. "Now Pin is thirty-two, but she may have been a late bloomer, which could explain some of those nine strikes."

"Fascinating," said Newton.

"It really is. They are incredible beings," said Ronnie. "Now, that touch communication also plays into their immune response. If a robustus was to be injured while alone, relatively minor injuries could kill them if they aren't touched within a certain time after the injury, three brights without the touch of another being and they could die. Also an evolutionary selection, if you're a robustus and no one cares about you, and you get hurt, you will probably die."

"Is that why you had me put my hand on her stomach?" asked Newton.

"Absolutely, and not her stomach, her uterus," Ronnie shamelessly answered. "It's sensually charged and love communicates a reason to live. If they have an intimate partner, their immune system kicks into overdrive, the healing power can be astonishing. So, I'd like you and Pin to sleep next to each other for the next half phase." Ronnie's face showed clinical certainty.

"Are you telling me to have sex with her?" asked Newton.

Ronnie blinked as she considered her wording. "I was thinking more of pheromones; her health reaction will respond to just the physical proximity, but now that you mention it, a couple doses of your man-gel would definitely do the trick."

"Doc!" Newton exclaimed.

Ronnie cinched her brow. "Newton, over there in that book of mission protocols," pointing to a work counter across the room, "I was supposed to get a sample from you and the captain, for this very reason. I just didn't want to have that conversation."

"Why not just the captain?"

"Because if she has contempt for the donor, which she seems to, by the way, she would be resistant and it wouldn't work. I'd need a backup dose."

Newton shook his head, disbelief slowing down the side-to-side motion. "How do you know all this?" he asked.

"I'm double licensed, both species," Ronnie said.

He pulled back his chin. "That's like ten revolutions in medical school!"

"Thirteen, surgical certification for both species," she said dryly.

"Damnation! Doc," he exclaimed.

"I've got degrees in romantic arts and mathematical anomalies, too."

Newton stared at Ronnie for a moment and asked, "Are you excel-engineered?"

"Yes," she answered shyly.

"So you don't have a biological father?"

"I have a father," she answered defensively, "who, with my mother, raised me, but I was not naturally conceived."

"What's your rating?" Newton asked with an ornery smile.

"Off the scale."

"Wow," he said under his breath. He gazed at Ronnie for a moment. "Since you probably remember every word of every conversation we've ever had, even with the situation on Avigolon, why would they want to get rid of you? You're too valuable, too."

Ronnie shifted around uncomfortably on the stool before looking back into Newton's eyes. Her voice was monotone when she said, "In three percent of people who are excel-engineered, eventually, their brains don't properly fold proteins during deep sleep, which causes plaques to build up, so no matter how smart they are, dementia sets in, starting about age fifty. I'm forty-four. In ten revolutions, I could be an idiot." She took a drink from her cup. "So far, there are no signs of it, but sometimes the onset is abrupt and the decline rapid."

"Doc," said Newton, "I wouldn't worry too much. And even if you didn't beat that tiny chance, you could lose half of what you have and still be smarter than the rest of us."

Ronnie's face tried to contain an almost painful amount of gratitude. "I appreciate you saying so, but you just picked up a conversation we had a full phase, three brights," she checked the clock, "and sixteen spans ago, I doubt I would be smarter than you." Ronnie smiled.

Newton smiled back but then turned serious. "There was a reason that I was thinking about what you said, how this mission may be meant to fail, a reason besides the touch of female robustus thing."

"What?" she asked.

"We are not where we were told we were going."

She blinked with surprise and asked, "Not even solving for the collision?"

"No, not even close."

"Where are we?"

"Six million marks into the Black. The collision stopped us from going a million more, to a classified destination."

Ronnie chewed on her bottom lip. Eventually, she said, "So that two phases in the beam? That was a lie?"

"The faster you're moving, the less you can see. We were in the beam six revolutions."

Her face flushed with anger. "Without telling the medical officer! We could all be dying of fragmentation disease! Why didn't you tell me sooner?"

"I figured it out right before I found Pin. The computer won't tell me the destination and I don't know if Captain Mot knows the truth, either. Mission revealed on arrival."

Ronnie stood up and stomped off toward the instrumentation console. "Those dorking rods! I knew everybody's readings were off." She frantically started keyboarding information into the computer, with one, two, three, four, five and then the sixth screen coming on and displaying information and graphs.

After several minutes, Newton asked, "What are you doing?"

I'm comparing genetic codes on file," she said while getting the blood sampling machine from her pocket, "with genetic code after the beam." She plugged the machine into a computer port. "How long were we out of the beam before the collision?" she asked.

"One phase, three brights, ten spans, about," he said.

"How is that even determined, when we thought we were going about our business for a couple of phases, and it's really six cursed revolves?" Ronnie asked angrily, yet never taking her eyes from the screens or pausing at the keyboard.

Newton got out of the chair and strolled over to where she was working, then answered, "Well, there's an ancient sort of mechanical clock that uses a flywheel escapement, and that flywheel is magnetized. As long as we're dematerialized, that wheel won't move. As far as how long it seems to us, that calculation is made before launch, the faster the beam, the slower time passes for us, computation made by the distance you want the beam to travel." Newton hesitated before adding, "Any distance beyond three revolutions is considered too dangerous."

Ronnie stopped and looked at Newton. "Is that why we hit something?" she asked.

Newton hesitated, and unnoticed, his body language indicated a lie. "Probably, even with outposts, the information is too old; there's no way to plot a course you know will be clear."

She went back to work with rapid, sustained keyboarding. "Which also means it's too far to have an actual mission," Ronnie murmured.

He didn't want to think about it and changed the subject. "Were there any more diagnostic questions?"

"I was going to ask how long between exposure and neutralizing treatment, but it sounds like you just wandered in and found her. I'll adjust for maximum exposure."

"Yeah, it's weird. She was just sitting there," said Newton. "Why would she just sit there?" he wondered aloud.

"It's a hardwired pause," answered Ronnie. "In a hostile environment, crying out or thrashing around is revealing your location. Unless it's fight or die, the survival move after injury is to freeze, get your bearings, watch your surroundings, then come up with a plan." She turned to look at him and said, "Hardwiring from that thirty-thousand revolutions when they were killed on sight by our ancestors."

Newton picked up an eyebrow. "Isn't that from back when most big carnivores considered us all tasty morsels?"

Ronnie shook her head. "No. They were the top predators, just not with us, because we transitioned so much earlier to civilization and war-craft."

"That's not what I learned in school," said Newton.

"Textbooks lie," she said flatly. "At one point, there were five species on our lineage and path to preeminence, but our kind exterminated three. Slavery saved the robustus. The other species were too small to be of any use."

Humor colored his voice. "You can be such a downer. If that's what being smart does to you, I'd rather be stupid."

Ronnie laughed. "At least you admit it." With a more relaxed style of working, Ronnie got the computer to sift for genetic differences between Newton's past and present code. Seemingly without context, she said, "That's profound, actually, because most of the horrible things that have been done throughout history have happened when a culture decides it would rather be stupid."

He thought about her statement, with more and more corollaries coming to mind. "You're hurting my brain, Doc," he said with a smile.

"Don't stop," she gently replied. "It hurts more if you stop. Think it through. Being open to new ideas, being able to assimilate, being able to listen is the way of peace." She looked at Newton with an odd excitement. "Think about it; the best music and foods are usually blends of different styles and traditions." Ronnie paused. "I know you know this."

"How do you know?" he challenged.

"Fine, I don't really know. I deduce. You can't launch an explorer without a diplomat. I'm not certified; Pin's not either. No way in five worlds Captain Mot is. That leaves you," she said with a haughty lift to her eyebrows.

Newton replied, "Good deduction, but I didn't get my certificate by six revolutions at the academy. I negotiated a peace settlement then finished up with three revolutions. I guess my point is, there may be some conflict-resolution theory I might've missed."

Her eyes widened with momentary dismay. "With the Kai?" she asked.

"Yep."

Ronnie wheeled around with a delighted grin. She gave him a playful punch to his upper arm. "Shut your false face!" she said happily.

"Truly," he said. "And I thought all that was supposed to be classified."

"Not to someone who spent two tours on Kai doing plant studies for medicine. My best friend was a mantis named Haza. She got me the goods! That stuff I shot in Pin's arm is from a compound we found. Treasured ills!" she exclaimed. "And suddenly it all makes sense," she continued. "My name on planet was Ronnitin. All humans have the suffix tin, their phonetic approximation of the ending of your name. To them, we are all you," she smugly concluded.

"That isn't necessarily a good thing," said Newton.

"Tell me about it. At the height of the war, we were losing at a rate of ten-thousand casualties a phase. I worked alone almost an entire revolve with Haza just watching me, but when she decided I was trustworthy, that's when we really got to work. She was a brilliant biochemist and she told me plenty about the war, too, things you don't learn from the official version. They kicked our butts." She laughed.

Newton chuckled. "They surely did. And, unlike our version of the stronger adversary, they also had mercy. That was my angle for ending war. I convinced them we were dying of disease and desperate for the medicines their jungles might provide. It was an exaggeration, but if they knew we were just greedy pirates, they would have never allowed peace."

Ronnie gave him a puzzled look. "I was friends with an insect big enough to look me straight in the eye, friends for more than a revolve before I figured out that she and her kind were very compassionate creatures. How'd you figure that out during a war?"

"Well, they learned our tactics so quickly and thoroughly, I realized we were fighting a force of veterans. They patched up their injured and came from a culture of advanced medical intervention, so they fixed them up to fight again, with added experience and ferocity. They also deployed large forces of medics in the heat of battle, and they allowed us to care for our dead and injured, even though I just indicated how that can be strategically unwise. And with incredible force, they protected areas where there had been a battle, to allow the jungle to heal. Seriously, they would rescue animals and protect trees during a battle. And if some commander thought to try and use that, to intentionally target the environment, they would counter-attack with unrelenting strength. We lost entire battalions before we figured that out. If we were careful about collateral damage, they wouldn't kill us to the very last man. If we weren't, they would. Who the dork protects and avenges all life in a war? They do. That's compassion."

Staring at him with a slight smile, she said, "Clever." Her smile broadened. "Did you know their jungles would have medicinal value?"

"Nope. I just needed a distraction both sides could work with. They could have mercy for us, and we could save face by getting something out of it." He shrugged.

"Sweet, and quite a gamble."

Newton cinched his brow. "Maybe not so sweet."

"What do you mean?"

He frowned thoughtfully before he said, "Your theory that they want to get rid of us, secrecy and crew assignments are a very big deal. Why would they put us together in the same crew? We could have the conversation we just had!"

Ronnie's face lost color. "We're dorked," she whispered.

Walking off toward the enclosed room, he needed a moment to think. Newton stopped and gazed at Pin on the hospital bed. She looked small and pale. Several minutes passed as both Ronnie and Newton were lost in thought. "What do we do about fragmentation disease?"

Eventually, she said, "Stem cell therapy, maybe the amniotic chamber."

He turned and looked at Ronnie from across the room. "Do we have enough power to run the amniotic chamber?"

"Not with one engine," said Ronnie. "And that's not even the biggest concern. I'm not so sure we should trust the computer to turn us into code and reassemble us. It's programmed to fulfill the mission at all costs. We don't know what that mission is."

"That's a little paranoid," he said with a smile.

"How about you go first, then," she replied.

Newton thought about it. "Maybe the medical computers can be isolated from the main computers. I'll look into it."

After a sip from her cup, Ronnie said, "You're still going first." She looked at the floor. "Stem cell therapy may work, but we're talking injections every bright for almost a revolve, maybe."

"I'm going to check on some things. What have we missed in our discussion of these circumstances?" asked Newton.

Ronnie ran her hand through her blonde hair as she thought about the question. "Um, you good with Pin sleeping in the same room with you?"

He shrugged casually, "I guess. What are your concerns?"

"Your heart," she said quietly, "among other things."

"What do you mean?"

Her posture struggled with the answer. Eventually, Ronnie said, "I know she likes you. How could she not? But, there's some hardwiring, even more than with our kind, she is hardwired to be attracted to strength, so just because she has contempt for Captain Mot, she might be more sexually compatible with him." Ronnie shook her head looking at the floor. She spoke quietly, "I can tell you're attracted to her, and maybe we should just go clinical with this... You give me that sample, and we avoid the issue of a relationship."

"Issue of a relationship?" he repeated with mild annoyance.

"If I can tell, at this point, and you two were to become intimate, then we could never let Mot out of the bio-cell. If he were to touch her, just once, and she loves you, then he would know it in an instant and probably kill you both in a jealous rage."

Newton frowned. He chewed on his lip for a moment. "Well, I noticed that we're talking like Pin doesn't get a choice in all this. When she wakes up, we'll all three have dinner and talk to her about all this, tell her she can sleep next to me for my pheromones, or she can get a clinical dose of my 'man-gel,' as you put it, and she can decide."

With a slow, thoughtful nod, Ronnie said, "Aye, commander." She shook her head while looking at the floor.

The annoyance re-emerged in Newton's voice. "What?"

Ronnie looked at him with plaintive, wide eyes. "That mind-body connection is twenty times stronger in her species. Telling her the connection between pheromones or what-ever could counteract the efficacy. If she has subconscious ideations, you've just undermined my options for treatment." She shook her head angrily. "Trust me, I hate talking about her like she's a child and not capable of deciding her own destiny. I'm a woman fighting for respect in a man's world and so is she. And I'm so impressed that you caught that! But that decision you just made, noble, insightful as it was, it could backfire." She crossed her arms and glared at him across the room. She reacted to his gaze with a defiant pout on her lips.

"Decision stands. When she wakes up, we are all going to have a very interesting conversation over dinner." Newton started for the door.

"Yes, sir," said Ronnie.

He nodded before going out the sickbay door.

Chapter IV: Necessity of Hope

Half an hour after Newton left sickbay, he was in the crown of the ship, the top of the pyramid shaped spacecraft. The crown was a last-resort observation point, with windows made of clear sapphire crystal a foot thick. If all electronic sensors and cameras were down, one could, theoretically, navigate the ship old school. It was theoretical because the ship moved too fast for a person to navigate on manual control and even the slow, docking maneuvers were too hazardous to trust to a human operator.

The crown was Newton's place to get away and think. It was also where he kept his secret stash of hesh. It was Newton who seeded the bio-cell with hesh plants, a particularly potent hybrid that not only delivered a long lasting high, but also tasted good and produced a lot of viable seed.

It was his secret vice, his crutch, his coping mechanism. He could've been busted and demoted throughout his career, but for paradox, its effect was a large part of his success. He was stoned when he figured out the insect language on Kai. He was stoned when he negotiated the peace. He was stoned when he studied for and passed all the certification exams that made him a first officer in the Fleet. Without hesh, he was nervous and couldn't concentrate well enough to think through complex problems.

So, with a subtle desperation, he loaded a pipe and put a soldering tip in the bowl to light the hesh. Newton took a deep inhale of the smoke, held it a second, and then exhaled a cloud of smoke. After two more hits, he put away the pipe and lit a cigarette of rag with the soldering tip. He smoked and stared out at the stars. The asteroid field formed an arc of an edge-on ellipse that stretched out until it faded into infinity. And, following the inside curve to the foci, he gazed at the yellow star.

What were they doing out here? He looked to the empty space that was their intended destination. Newton began to puzzle through ways to find out the classified mission's transmission code. The computer knew, which meant the mysterious mission was encoded...

"I'd like for Pin to not wake up alone," Ronnie's voice interrupted by radio, "so maybe you could make dinner."

Newton let go a sigh. "Copy that," said Newton. "I'll make dinner."

"Don't forget Captain Mot," said Ronnie.

"I will also send dinner to the captain," he said. "Give me a span."

"Thank you," said Ronnie.

"You're welcome," Newton replied. He dowsed the cigarette and started the climb out of the crown. The journey would take him through areas of the ship that didn't have gravity.

With odd synchronicity, Mot was in the canopy room smoking rag after three hits of hesh as the radio exchange alerted him that he had a crew member in sickbay. At least that's what it sounded like. Why else would that skinny doctor be watching Pin?

The reason Mot didn't hear the earlier transmission was because the radio was on the forearm sleeve of his uniform, and his uniform had been wadded up and stuffed on a shelf for weeks. Mot put down the pipe and went to the shelf to pull out the sleeve with the radio. "This is Mot, sickbay report."

"Pin has been exposed to mercury, second-degree chemical poisoning. I'm cleaning her blood and prognosis..." Ronnie searched for simple wording. "We caught it before she was hurt badly, and she is getting better."

Mot realized she was simplifying her language for him and said, "Let me know if there are complications to the prognosis, otherwise I am going to assume duty-ready in a few brights," he said.

"Yes, Captain, and I will advise you of any negative changes to prevent a three-bright recovery. But..." Ronnie's voice faltered.

"Go ahead, Doctor," said Mot, sounding surprisingly patient.

"A duty-ready designation applies by emergency protocol, but she would need a half to a full phase of recovery at any other defense condition."

"Understood," said Mot, "but emergency protocol stays in place, so do what you can medically, and everybody helps her do her work."

There was a pause before Ronnie's voice asked, "How can we help her that much?"

"Command nexus," said Mot. "We are on emergency protocol until we get our engines back. Pin gives us our engines back, but Pin is sick and needs help, so we have command nexus between emergency protocol and Pin's recovery. That means we suspend Article Four-Thirteen during recovery, maybe half, maybe a full phase, determined by the medical officer."

Ronnie's voice sounded as if she may weep with gratitude when she said, "Thank you, Captain."

"Carry on, Doctor," said Mot.

Both Ronnie and Newton watched as the transmission light went out on their radios, each with the same astonishment at what they heard, the captain being well reasoned and lenient. What was different was the contrast in environments. Ronnie was in the well lighted warmth and high-tech, antiseptic décor of sickbay. Newton, however, was floating weightless in an access tube, in the dark, with a line of ladder rungs as his only handhold to the ship.

He gave himself a little push to sink to the bottom of the access tube. Bumps of his shoulders against the wall of the tube made enough drag that Newton had to pull up on the ladder again to get to the bottom. The fifth hatch door to the access tube opened onto warehouse five-four, which had a dedicated gravity floor and a labyrinth of shipping containers in tall stacks anchored to the floor in a maze of narrow passages.

Dorking Mot must have stocked this floor, thought Newton. The size of the containers was supposed to determine the pattern on the floor, and all the patterns were supposed to have wider walkways from the center to the sides. Yet this layout seemed to follow a fractal swirl toward the middle, with repetition of container contents for when the items would be used. It was bold. If something was needed out of order, there would a tremendous amount of re-stacking and no room to do it. But the quartermaster said they could supply for more than a dozen years, and he later seemed surprised that they may have actually packed that much on board.

It didn't help that the sparse arrangement of grid markers on the walls were the only lights in the expansive room. Newton walked into the darker shadows of a narrow walkway between high walls. Barely seeing well enough to advance into the maze, Newton noticed a strange smell, strange because it was an organic odor, slightly sulfurous, lightly sweet like a flower. The spacecraft's spectrum of odors did not include this smell.

Newton stopped and listened. Skittering noises came from behind him. He turned but nothing resolved from the dark shaft. With both hands to feel his way, he quickened his pace toward the middle. The sounds behind him also quickened pace. He broke into a clumsy run, hands tapping the walls, getting to the middle and turning to the walkway he thought would take him to the door.

Unexpectedly, the lights of the warehouse came on; a frantic glance over his shoulder, it was the feathered dragon, hunched in chase, coming fast. In his fastest run, Newton cleared the walkway. There was a whirr, a snap, and less than a meter behind him, the dragon tripped and tumbled to its side. Almost moving too fast to see, a figure swarmed around the dragon, binding the dragon's mouth and feet. The figure stepped back, and once standing still, it was a surreal but undeniable presence. It was an insect, a mantis, about as tall as Ronnie, wearing a black space suit with an equipment belt around its waist.

His mind went blank. The dragon flopped around and struggled against its bindings. "Uh, thank you," said Newton.

The mantis took off the black shell over its head, revealing a calico pattern of black and green and orange on its face. "You welcome," said the insect. A claw gestured to the dragon and the insect apologized for the animal struggling on the floor. "It ztarving, dezperate, dangerouz."

"Omni?" asked Newton, "is that you?"

There was a change in the smell, the smell of an approaching thunderstorm, the smell of gratitude. "Yez," said the mantis.

Newton was remembering how a lot of the nonverbal communication of the insects of Kai was chemical. Instead of body language, their emotional states were transmitted by scent. "What are you doing here?" he asked.

"Ztowaway," replied Omni.

"Oh," Newton said casually, also remembering Kai etiquette. Questions, generally, were considered rude. The burden of communication was to volunteer information, to make decisions. "This dragon escaped the bio-cell a phase ago. We need to get it back in there, so, help me get it into a cargo net." Omni nodded. "And, we need to tie it up, replace the light cord with something else."

"Dragon poizonouz, clawz, teeth. Keep cord," said Omni.

"No, we can't put it in the bio-cell with Kai technology. Captain Mot is confined to the bio-cell, and he can't know you're on this ship."

"Mot," said Omni. There was the sudden smell of ammonia and burned meat, the smell of anger.

"You know Captain Mot?"

"All Kai know Mot."

Newton lifted his eyebrows. "You," he said emphatically, "are my guest. You will stay away from Mot and do what I ask."

The insect waited before conceding with a succinct, "Yez."

"And," continued Newton, "for the present time, you being on this ship is a secret." Omni gazed at him with a triangular shaped head, large, compound eyes at the top, sharp, machine-like plates at the bottom point of the mouth, none of which offered any clue as to what the insect was thinking. "Last time I saw you," said Newton, "you were queen commander of Kai. It's strange for someone to go from a leader of ten million warriors, to a stowaway."

"A queen doez what zhe wantz," said Omni. The smell changed to a spicy scent, like cinnamon. "I not queen, Newtin. It waz lie to zee if enemy attack leaderz. Zoftinz lucky not zo ztupid. I am queen'z daughter, language ezpert."

Newton shrugged and said, "Well, that makes a lot more sense, a princess becoming a stowaway."

The cinnamon smell became stronger and Omni laughed with clicking sounds, her mandible plates separating enough to make a star shaped space in her mouth. She paused; the insect smile disappeared and the scent changed to indicate a new mood, the smell akin to an oily, leafy odor. "Queen zay, help Newtin, protect Newtin, alwayz."

He stared at the statue-still, giant insect. The vivid color in the patterns of her face told Newton that Omni was young, probably in her twenties. He didn't know so much about the Kai when Omni was posing as the queen commander of their world. The colors in their skin slowly faded to a graphite monochrome as they aged. And with a lifespan longer than a century, Omni was practically a juvenile. "Sounds like a lousy mission to me," said Newton.

"Eazy mizzion," said Omni, tipping her head down to the dragon on the floor. "Zee? Eazy," she added. They each looked at the furious animal, muscles rippling in its legs and neck as it struggled against the invisible rope. The beast responded to their gaze with a demonic hiss.

Both Omni and Newton burst into laughter. He shook his head and started toward the equipment hold. He touched his radio button and said, "I've hit a minor snag, so I'll need some time to deal with it. Belay dinner by another span."

Ronnie's voice replied, "It's fine, no hurry here."

It took them a while to get the dragon bound with rope, its eyes covered, wrapped in a cargo net and on freight truck. The most difficult part was getting the rope tied around the legs and mouth without pinching the invisible rope. You could feel but not see it. Once the dragon was safely in the cargo net, Omni touched a button on her equipment belt and the invisible rope lit up on the ends and followed the rope like a fuse as it disintegrated. "That's pretty neat stuff," said Newton. Omni nodded. "Alright, I'm going to take this guy to the bio-cell."

"Girl," said Omni, "dragon vemale."

"Really? How can you tell?"

"Veatherz, they zhort and zoft. Male much longer, go down back to tail," said Omni. "Theze come from Geddiz."

"Interesting," said Newton. He turned to look at Omni. "Are you starving, or injured?" Newton remembered their communication rules and said, "I want you to be well. I will bring you anything, medicine, supplies, entertainment."

Omni gave off a brief scent of rain, the smell of gratitude. She then gestured to the huge stacks of shipping containers. "I have much vood," she said.

"Good then," said Newton. "Thanks again for saving me, and stay out of sight until I decide it's time to introduce you to the other members of my crew."

"Yez, Newtin." She stepped back and Newton pushed the freight cart with the dragon out of the warehouse.

Mot was watching the ripples in a pond when he heard a hatch open far above his head. The panel of evening light folded back and Newton's face appeared. "Hey, Captain!" called Newton. "Are you missing something?"

"Did you find something?" grumbled Mot.

"As a matter of fact, I did. This critter was out to kill me. I think it wants back home." Newton's face disappeared and Mot could hear the sound of an electric crane motor. After a moment of struggle with a moving cargo net getting through the panel opening, the dragon was being lowered to the jungle floor.

Mot sauntered over to the place it would touch the ground. He gave the cargo net a push so it would spin and set the dragon's head on the high side of a gentle slope. As the net relaxed from the weight of dragon on the ground, Mot unhooked the crane cable. He thought about grabbing it as the cable started up out of the bio-cell, but Mot was mostly just grateful to see the dragon was alive. The population of jungle rabbits, the dragon's primary food, was getting out of control. They were too fast for the younger dragon. Mot pulled open the cargo net and was further surprised to find the dragon thin but uninjured. He grabbed the snout and pulled up the blindfold to inspect each eye. The dragon thrashed vigorously but had both eyes, both ears, all four limbs and feet. Newton was watching his captain from above. Mot was wearing nothing but a pair of shorts, the thickly muscled man looking even stouter from an overhead perspective.

Looking up at Newton, Mot said, "I'm surprised, capture takes more effort. I thought you were too weak."

"Smart saves strength," Newton called down.

"No, seriously, thank you for not killing this," called Mot from below. "This is one of five fertile females left, anywhere."

Newton was thinking there were actually only four because their anywhere was now nowhere. "You're welcome. Let me know if you need anything to get it healthy again."

"I will." Mot paused. "If it scratched you or bit you, better see the doctor, treatment for neuro-solvents."

Newton realized Mot was actually being considerate. "I was careful," called Newton. "I'll go get dinner, send you some in a bit."

"Good job and carry on," said Mot.

Newton closed the ceiling panel feeling a little guilty for stealing credit from Omni. He had even considered hunting the thing down and killing it as a safety measure. He was glad he didn't.

Down below, Mot looked at the dragon, breathing with aggravation but otherwise laying still. The first thing Mot did was go for a weapons cache hidden in a rock formation, from which he armed himself with throwing stars and darts. The next hour and a half, Mot endeavored to collect the materials, prepare them into liquids, and nurse the dragon by loosening the binding enough for the dragon to move its tongue around the edge of its mouth and ladling handfuls of fruit juice, then blood from five jungle fowl, then water from the pond. He learned that straddling the back of the dragon at the shoulders, pinned on its belly, was the only effective way to force cooperation from the still blindfolded monster, but Mot coaxed significant fluid intake.

Two hours after Mot first tromped up the hill and harvested five chickens with throwing darts, he partially untied the blindfold, completely untied the bottom then the upper feet, and stepped back. He strolled toward the canopy room stairs as the dragon found its footing. By the time Mot was on the stairs, the dragon tore away the blindfold from its head. The dragon turned, glared at Mot, and walked off toward her lair.

In the galley, still dressed in the med-suit, Pin listened to her options for treatment from Ronnie. Newton stayed silent. Ronnie was very terse and clinical. Pin didn't seem the slightest bit phased, but rather said, "I didn't know graces knew about that." She leveled her gaze at Newton. "But it's good because we do need touch if we're hurt. I'll accept you as my caring hand, maybe first time in history a caring hand has five fingers, and we try not to love, because we can't have that," Pin said before she hesitated. "Not now, anyway." She gave him a gentle smile.

Ronnie nodded her acceptance.

Newton was thankful it was settled and attended to details, "You can spend nights in my quarters. I have an extra bedroom with its own bathroom, and it's even tidied up and clean. I'll coordinate with you on a help schedule."

They returned to their dinner of soup, biscuits, salad, fruit and stir-fry. He was a fairly good cook and the silence was comforted by an interplay of pleasant flavors and textures. He interrupted the quiet with urgency in his voice.

"I told you both that we're deep in the black, but there's something I didn't tell you." Newton suddenly questioned whether he should tell them.

His hesitation tested Ronnie's patience. Pin followed with a wide set to her eyes.

"Don't wanna tell all of a sudden."

"Too bad, tell," said Pin.

"We're outside an uncharted system…" His voice indicated there was more to it.

Ronnie made an exasperated noise.

"With a living world," finished Newton.

Ronnie asked, "Sentient?"

"Probably, the isotope spectrum includes the tiniest amount of metals in a life-sustaining atmosphere, so either there are beings building fires at the scale of early civilization, or there's something else going on that we can't determine from this distance," said Newton.

"You said there is a secret mission," said Pin. "Could this be the mission?"

Newton shook his head. "No, the destination is still twenty-six phases away, so twenty-four phases beyond this star, at full speed, and the trajectory we were on would've bypassed this system, entirely. The only reason we found this is because we hit something."

"Not just something, a blown-to-pieces spacecraft," said Ronnie. "Are we sure the ship didn't come from that world?"

"Pretty sure, no chemical signatures of advanced industry, just plants and animals," replied Newton.

Ronnie looked skeptical. "We've been wrong about that before, to devastating effect."

"This isn't Kai. Most of the planet surface is ocean. The planet is rock with a metallic core. The jungles and porous mantle of Kai absorbed the grunge of the earlier industrial development, so when technology became cleaner, it gave the appearance of a pre-industrial world. This planet, that couldn't happen. This planet is actually fresh."

"With a spacecraft in the outer system," added Ronnie. "The point is, we can't presume supremacy. There might be a challenger out here."

"Might be two," said Pin.

Both Ronnie and Newton looked at her with the same puzzled look. "What do you mean?" asked Newton.

"Something destroyed it, maybe for getting too close." Pin lifted her eyebrows.

Ronnie nodded agreement. Newton shook his head. "Let's not get into myths," he said.

"Why not?" asked Ronnie. "All the systems on the edge talk about an advanced force that protects young worlds from space conquest, the Sentinels, and we are floating in the territory where those legends came from."

Newton dropped his gaze to his lap. After a long pause, he looked up and said, "Well, whether we get closer or get the crap out of here, we need engines, so that's our focus. The other measure we can take is to be set for cloaking. I want emergency nuclear power at the ready, so if something comes along, we can at least disappear while we limp away."

"Remember what I told you?" asked Ronnie.

Newton thought back and said, "I will handle all preparation of nuclear backup."

Pin objected with a sip of air and a look of confusion. "What did I miss? Because that's my department."

"Doc says you are sensitive to radiation, so you're not setting even one little foot in the reactor room. I'll consult with you because I want to be like a sweep from full invisibility."

"Sensitive especially now during your recovery period," Ronnie reinforced her statement with a somber nod. A crease formed between her eyebrows. "All of us, actually, for phases."

"All of us sick?" asked Pin.

"We are all recovering from being in the beam for six revolves; it's very similar to radiation sickness. And none of us should be exposed until I see what kind of chromosomal damage we have, and you two are going to have contaminated tests for a little while. So, I'll try again in a couple brights, and I'm glad Captain Mot officially waived four-thirteen, but all exposure work should be done remotely, by robotics that we don't have on this explorer," complained Ronnie.

"Captain Mot waived four-thirteen?" asked Pin.

"Yeah," said Ronnie.

Pin quirked half of her face. "Maybe he is going dormant," she muttered.

Ronnie asked, "When was the last time anyone has actually seen Captain Mot?"

"Just before I made dinner," Newton replied nonchalantly.

"Did he move; was he standing?" Pin and Ronnie simultaneously asked, talking over one another in the same distracted monotone.

Newton switched his eyes back and forth between them before saying, "Yes, walking, talking, standing… What gives?"

"Can I tell?" Ronnie asked Pin, who declined with an emphatic shake of her head. "Nothing," Ronnie concluded.

Sensing a feminine need for privacy – Pin's need so something about her species, something about Mot going "dormant" – Newton let it go and changed the subject. "I saw him when I returned the feathered dragon. Mot thanked me for not killing it, undid the cargo net, and I assume is bringing it back to health right now."

Ronnie narrowed her eyes. "The lizard that escaped the bio-cell, three strides long, probably twelve blocks heavy, with teeth longer than my fingers, that feathered dragon?"

"Yes."

"Is it poisonous?" asked Ronnie.

"Yes, Mot said if I was scratched or bitten to treat for neuro-solvents."

"Neuro-solvents," she said quietly. Her tone became abrasive when she asked, "Why didn't you just kill it?"

"Too beautiful," said Pin.

With cavalier humor, Newton agreed. "Too beautiful."

Angry pressure began to build behind Ronnie's voice. "That's fine for you to say, Pin." She glared at Newton. "But you, you don't get to say that. A lethal dose of neuro-solvent, for you…" Ronnie touched her finger to the surface of her drink and flicked her hand at the table in Newton's direction, then angrily pointed to a small drop. "There," she seethed, ironically reminding him of the dragon. "There's nothing I can do! And the reason I know you didn't get any is because it circulates in your blood gases and dissolves the protective layer around nerves, and you'd be in pain like being burned alive!" Her voice got louder as her nostrils flared and her lip curled. "Non-lethal doses often result in suicide to escape the pain! And survival, it's not if, it's how much you're paralyzed! Five dorking hells, Newton!"

Pin was hunched, leaning away, with a frightened expression as she looked down. "You're scaring Pin and annoying me," said Newton. "I get it."

"What? Say it!" demanded Ronnie.

"It was too much risk!"

"Thank you! Damn!" she exclaimed. Ronnie finished with an exasperated huff and then noticed Pin, who had lost all color in her face. "Newton, Pin's going to be sick. Help her out of the chair, hands and knees or sitting on the floor." Newton helped Pin down to the floor as Ronnie emptied the remnants of the salad bowl. Pin vomited most of her dinner. After Newton helped clean her face, he cradled her in his lap, stroking her forehead and making soothing sounds.

He then noticed quiet tears on Ronnie's face. "What?"

"This is my fault," Ronnie whispered. "That mind-body connection, my anger made her sick."

Newton reached out for Ronnie's hand to pull her to sit on the floor next to them. Ronnie sat close and he gestured an offer of a shoulder to rest her head, which she did. All three of them huddled peacefully on the floor for quite a while. He was stuck on the idea that Ronnie's emotional state could have a physical effect on Pin. Newton gently said, "So that's not figurative language; an argument can really make Pin sick?"

"Absolutely," Ronnie said in a low, mournful voice, "especially like what just happened, strong emotional bonds with both people, giving her conflict and making her feel trapped in the situation." Ronnie's voice constricted, "We need to keep our wits because our crap could really hurt her." She sniffed and sobbed quietly on Newton's shoulder. Pin thinly opened her eyes and insisted her hand into Ronnie's hand before closing her eyes again. "I'm sorry, Pin," Ronnie murmured. "I'm just worried. We are on the ugly edge. We can't be dancing on the precipice. We need each other, so I'll try not to go incendiary on you, and Newton will try to use some common sense, and we'll get through this."

"I'll try," Newton said with a humorously doubtful tone.

With her eyes closed and a dreamy look on her face, Pin smiled and said, "No more dancing with dragons."

He sat there with his mind tumbling through their circumstance. They were so short handed that he needed to tell them about Omni, so he could have a new crew member to put to work. But robustus people had some sort of primal hatred of the Kai. Bourne out by some very ugly setbacks, the robustus members of Fleet couldn't get past the fact that they were insects. What if knowing about Omni, having to work with Omni, was to hurt Pin? He was bothered by how hard some angry words hit Pin. She went ashen in an instant, skin cool to the touch, complete loss of muscle tone.

At least the color was back in Pin's cheeks, thought Newton, pink, from blood. Their blood was still contaminated, so much so that neither Pin nor he could work in certain areas. Maybe he could have Omni do the radiation tasks while they started their treatment for fragmentation disease. But if six years in the beam was dangerous to them, then what about Omni? What about Mot? Ronnie said treatment involved injections. How does the doctor treat Mot in the bio-cell?

Mot actually had good reason to be mad at Newton for the crash. Pin stirred in Newton's lap. "Thinking too hard, Newton, tell," said Pin.

"Not sure that's a good idea," he dodged, "an argument can make you sick."

Pin opened her eyes and looked up at him. "If I ask you, it hurts more if you don't tell." She lifted her eyebrows with expectation.

Newton hesitated before saying, "Standard procedure is to slow down once we're out of the beam. I didn't. I wanted to use the momentum to save us any travel time. Mot knew, cautioned me against that decision. That's why he was so angry." Newton paused and shook his head. "It wasn't the secret mission that caused the crash. If I had slowed us down, we would've probably been able to avoid the collision," confessed Newton.

Ronnie picked up her head from Newton's shoulder and looked at him. Pin also looked at him. After a moment, Ronnie said, "You messed up."

Pin held his gaze and said, "You did, but you found a living world. Hopefully, we won't be destroyed by the Sentinels." Pin closed her eyes and snuggled back into his lap.

They sat together on the floor for a while longer, but then Ronnie had them get up and took Pin back to sickbay for fluid and electrolyte replacement. Newton stayed in the galley and cleaned up after dinner. His next stop was the equipment room to get a light visor for those dark areas throughout the ship. Newton wanted to go back up to the crown to finish his cigarette.

On the way, he decided to check out the warehouse. "Hey, Omni! Are you in here?"

"Not alwayz," came a voice from a dark side of the warehouse. "I heard zomeone coming, recognize vootztepz," said Omni as she walked out of the darkness. "Here, vor you. Call me iv you need." Omni handed him a small disk about the size of a coin. "Vrequenzy can't be heard by Zoftin radioz." Newton accepted and pocketed the small transmitter. "You go zmoke," said Omni with the smell of cinnamon perfuming humor into the statement.

"You've been spying on me," said Newton.

"A vhaze, zmoking the crazy weed," Omni said. The insect looked at him with the smell of humor wafting gently in the air. "No judge," said Omni. "Omni think more Zoftinz zhould zmoke. Zoftinz dangerouz, crazy voolz without weed."

Newton realized that there was no reason to be embarrassed with Omni. He actually felt liberated that there was someone he could be completely honest with, someone he wasn't trying to impress. "Come on, then, let me show you the crown." The both went up the access tube. As Newton was opening into the crown, Newton said, "We just breached security. No one unauthorized should be in the crown, let alone a stowaway from an adversarial world."

"I not a zpy, Newtin," said Omni. "Don't care about politicz."

Omni and Newton sat in the crown, talking, smoking. Omni even smoked with him, putting the pipe to a breathing port on the side of her abdomen, having to open the spacesuit on the bottom and showing more of her wild coloring on the area where a person has a hip. Omni was somewhat bashful at first, not letting him see, but after a few hits, her demeanor relaxed. When he lit the rag cigarette, she wanted to try it and he held it out to her.

Omni muttered a curse and unsealed spacesuit at her wrist and took off the glove covering her hand. Newton privately marveled at the insect pincer gingerly accepting the cigarette. Her hand was a graceful, jointed claw on top where he had an index finger, a shorter jointed claw for the thumb, and a thin, tapered claw that flattened the hand or folded under to meet the thumb claw. Newton purposely did not roll Omni her own cigarette so he could catch glimpses of her hand in action as they passed the cigarette back and forth. Orange, black and green patterns of lines and dots on the top and outside, a pattern of color that got smaller toward the ends of the claws, with the undersides and inside a pearlescent white, he realized that Omni's entire body was vividly colored.

He also thought about how the term mantis didn't quite fit. It was correct for the overall shape, but the way the arms and legs bended was human-like, especially with hands on the arms and striding feet on the legs. There were two extra, smaller arms, but those, also, bent the right way and had little claw hands.

They talked about where they were in space. Newton confessed the crash was his fault, and told Omni about the crew, Mot in the bio-cell, Pin and Ronnie. Omni had actually heard about Ronnie's work on the Kai planet. Omni talked about what it was like to stowaway, how the life capsule was put on board during the outfitting of the ship. Omni also let it slip that her mission was somewhat rogue. Her orders were to keep track of Newton but to return to Kai if Newton was going to be deployed outside of the five planets of the known galaxy. She complained that her culture wasn't very adventurous, and she wanted to see what was out there. Omni stared at the yellow star for a very long time. The news that there was an uncharted, living world orbiting that star elicited a completely unfamiliar scent from the insect, the smell of acetone and honey.

"You could go there, if your pod is space-worthy. That planet is about twenty-three and a third marks away."

"Maybe," said Omni, her voice relaxed and low. "But maybe I wait, and Newtin goes to ezplore with me."

"Maybe, but we gotta fix this ship… we might get our asses kicked by the Sentinels. Mot could get out of the bio-cell and end all of our fun… Just saying, an escape plan to a living world, not the worst idea there is."

Omni handed him back their third cigarette. Newton took the cigarette with one hand and then surprised Omni by catching her claw hand and holding it, looking at it. "Awesome color," he commented. "Your whole body has color like this?" Omni stared at him but remained silent. "I noticed that when you opened your spacesuit. Woohoo!"

She laughed, saturating the crown with the smell of cinnamon. He let go of her hand. She pulled back her hand slowly and said, "Lust."

He blinked before saying, "You just said lust, with an S. I thought your kind couldn't pronounce S."

"I am very zstoned, Newtin, more relaxed." She laughed again.

"What do you mean lust?" he asked with a grin.

"It all about color and pattern, with my kind," said Omni. "I have rare color, considered so beautiful no one cares about anything else. So, I go to zchool, work hard, so I am taken seriously." She chuckled. "But here, varther than anybody ever go, and even a Softin lust for me," she said with an amazing amount of tone for a Kai, a humorous tone.

"You're just saying that because I noticed your color when you opened your spacesuit to smoke. I didn't mean any disrespect," he added with a grin.

She laughed with little clicking noises. She stood and closed the bottom of her spacesuit. "I know you respect me," said Omni. "I know by the way you talk to me. You respect my kind, too. That's why we stop the war." She paused and looked at him. A different, flowery smell rose up in the small room. "You made a very good impression." She continued to stand, with a subtle posture of indecision.

"Should we go down?" he asked.

"Yes, your crew needs you. I need to stay secret vor now. And you have a lot ov work to do, so get rest, avter you show me the reactor room."

Newton took a puff before dowsing the cigarette. "You're a language expert; what are you going to do?"

"I," she said as she pulled him to his feet, "am Kai, better at machines than any Softin, ever. I was making robots when you were ztill learning how to walk."

"Really?" he said.

"Really," she replied. Instead of putting the black spacesuit glove back over her hand, Omni flattened the glove, opened a compartment on the front of the spacesuit, and put it in a glove shaped recess. She also took off the other main glove and put in into a recess. Omni closed the front of the spacesuit in a way to suggest she was punctuating her point about technological superiority.

Newton went another way. Wearing a silly smile, he said, "So, even though you're strong enough to subdue a dragon, under that spacesuit, you're kind of skinny."

Omni smiled at him with the smell of cinnamon wafting around. "Does this make me look vat?" she asked. They laughed together as they got into the access tube. Newton turned on the light visor and they continued laughing as each floated down.

Newton stopped before the expected level. Omni was supple enough to bend past him after her foot grazed his shoulder, but when they entangled at the arms, she stopped facing him eye to eye, compound eyes to pupils. The individual hexagons were so tiny that Newton could barely distinguish them in the polarized, rainbow colored bands across the compound eyes. He reached behind Omni to open the hatch, momentarily bringing his face even closer to hers. She looked at him before going out the hatch first, leaving a new scent, tangy sweet, such as the blossom of a fruit tree. He wondered what the emotion was that went with this new scent. As he went out the tube and closed the hatch, he made a wild guess. "Did I embarrass you by getting so close?" he asked.

Omni's laugh sounded a little nervous. "Maybe," she said. "Maybe surprised, Kai supposed to be so disgusting to Softinz, but you touch my hand, look into my eyes. You just very weird, Newtin," Omni concluded.

He started them walking on the deck to the mechanical rooms. "You're weird, too," said Newton. "Whoever heard of a fat Kai?" Omni responded by stiffening her walk and making wide, teetering steps. They broke into laughter again.

After some relaxed walking, Newton asked, "Where'd you get that, 'does this make me look fat' line?"

"Serial comedies," replied Omni. "I ztudy Softins vor long time."

"I keep asking questions," he noted. "I'm not meaning to be rude; I'm curious, I guess."

"Questions are vine vrom vriends." Omni measured her wording. "Questions necessary vrom leaderz. You are both," she concluded.

Using his light visor, Newton kept the power off; for a good visual metaphor of someone up to no good, he searched around in the dark of the reactor room until he found a small canister of non-corrosive oil and some soft tissue paper. Newton used a spot of oil and tiny patch of paper to obscure every camera in the reactor section. Omni observed quietly. She followed him out to the reactor section's power panel and watched as Newton punched the sections he intended to power up into the grid. The ship's far-off gyroscopic engine responded by whirring in a slightly higher pitch.

They gazed at the panel for a few seconds, him watching, her set stone-still. Two of three light bars lit up; Newton threw a small lever. As lights came on in the reactor room, the full bar fell and the empty bar filled by small, corresponding amounts. "What am I looking at?" Newton asked Omni.

She put a claw point near each bar and said, "Power available, power used, and power out back to the ship, this power conditioner, not just zupply."

He nodded and said, "That's right." He then beckoned her follow him into the reactor room and quizzed her extensively on components and processes. After they discussed various possible strategies for the quickest way to have emergency power, Newton committed treason as casually as removing his insignia pin from his uniform and holding it out to Omni. "There's the telemetry key." He put it in Omni's upturned claw. "If there's a password request, like in the deeper operational schematics, two, seven, seven, two, a number bounce, two nines, eighteen, which compresses to nine, so nine is the derivative key."

"Nine," said Omni as she transferred the electronic badge to the smaller hand of one of her middle arms. The top arms did something at the neck and sides to crack open the breastplate of the black spacesuit. She pulled a necklace chain to the outside and resealed the breastplate. The necklace had a pendant that was a small cage containing a loose gemstone, a Winsor, a dark blue gem that gave off its own light in miniature, swirling, sparkling patterns. Omni opened the pendant and switched out the gem with the electronic pin. She then let the necklace drape on the outside of her spacesuit and held out the gem to Newton. She beckoned him to take the gem with a snappy nod of her head.

He hesitated. "I can't hold onto that for you," said Newton. "It's worth more than I make in a hundred revolves."

"So don't lose," Omni said. "Out here, no banks, no money, it just a pretty rock." She could see Newton's sincere reluctance and added, "Prove trust, keep vor me."

Truly humbled, Newton accepted the pea sized marvel. It looked like the living planet he found in the uncharted system, blue, with white clouds moving through the atmosphere and golden light glowing from the inside. It brightened and the swirls of white and rays of gold moved as it sat on his palm. "Accepted, I'll hold onto it for you."

Omni nodded and then turned to the computers to begin learning their system. He left her with the smell of rain in the reactor room.

Chapter V: Contests of Will

Newton kept the secret of their stowaway for a week. Although he would've denied it, he maintained the dynamic because every morning he woke up sleeping next to Pin was a blissful peace. He tried sleeping in the extra bedroom but she wouldn't have it. It wasn't sexual so much as sensual. They found sleeping positions where she fit in the spaces as he slept on his side, and he woke up with a warm, quietly breathing, petite perfection wrapped in his arms, her head with her shimmering blue hair and delicious smell tucked under his chin. Sleep had never been more restful. Once they were touching hands, their breathing would synchronize and gentle slumber would follow. Pin was also pulling more of a communication sync from the contact, so much so that often he only needed to start to say something and she could finish.

This greater connection was also problematic. Pin seemed to sense it when Newton spent any significant time talking to Omni. Pin didn't say anything but she would tense up to his touch, such a difference to the feeling of flowing together she usually had. It was enough for him to limit the times he spent with Omni, but that meant less work was getting done.

They were working on Engine No. 2, which was going far more slowly with Pin giving instructions instead of crawling around in the dismantled engine. Ronnie and Newton were slithering over the outer casing and tightening cover bolts while watching the torque indicators on their wrenches. "Did we miss any?" asked Ronnie.

"No," replied Pin. "I'd check those in the corners if we were going to run fluid, but this is just a test to see if it'll generate." Pin then began a check list as Ronnie and Newton got down from the engine. They took off their coveralls.

While walking toward the bridge for the engine test, Pin reached for Newton's hand, as she always did, but then she said, "Hold the doctor's hand, too." Newton caught Ronnie's hand in its languid swing.

Ronnie blushed and asked, "Why are we doing this?"

"You seem lonely," said Pin. "I know you like to be alone, to think hard, but you don't get to be lonely."

"It's weird, but I might be. Our routine has changed so my schedule of alone time versus working together is disrupted. It's ironic because I actually have been seeing more of you two lately," said Ronnie.

"Maybe..." said Newton. He turned to catch a glimpse of Pin's eyes.

She nodded casually and said, "Sure."

"No fair," said Ronnie, "I'm way behind you two on the touch communication."

"Well, seeing as your schedule is already disrupted, you could sleep in our quarters, take the extra room if you want," said Newton. They walked three abreast and hands in hands. Newton was beginning to feel somewhat spoiled and unworthy for having a woman on each side.

As they reached the end of the corridor and both women let go of his hand, Ronnie bubbled into laughter. The door slid open. Ronnie went through first, then Pin and finally Newton. Ronnie laughed again and said, "I know touch communication is supposed to be amazing and all." She made a point to catch Newton's eye. "Yet, seriously? A touchy subject like sleeping arrangements, you two worked that whole thing out not using words! How in five hells does that work?"

Pin also focused on Newton, interested in how he would explain it.

He thought for a moment and said, "People don't necessarily think in words. It's more images and feelings and ideas that stay formless but lead from one concept to another.

So, if Pin and I are sharing an idea or image or feeling, it has a different weight, greater volume; you can almost feel its weight inside your head. The way you communicate without words? Let's call them intention tones. The exchange you just saw. First, there's that feeling of warmth of waking up in bed, me with an image of Pin, Pin with an image of the bed linens, the intention tone of peaceful bliss." Newton made a sound such as a satisfied hum. "Then there are images of you, Doc, from Pin's perspective and from mine. Then there's another intention tone, worried." Newton made the sound. "Then," he continued, "I held out the image of the spare room until I felt Pin grab it. Then the final intention tone, going up in pitch like a question." He made the third sound. "That's how," he concluded.

"Incredible," said Ronnie.

A surge of uncontainable joy first twinkled in Pin's eyes, then pulled the outside corners into a smile, and when that wasn't enough, she jumped up and gave him a tight hug. She eagerly, blissfully, pressed her face onto his. "I love how smart you are," said Pin in a voice husky with enthusiasm. "That was great." She gave him a squeeze and the intention tone of great affection before getting down, still smiling at Newton.

"In case you didn't catch it, that was the squeezy love intention tone," Ronnie quipped. This started another round of laughter from all three of them.

Little waves of delighted laughter carried them into the bridge and each to a station for the engine test. The start-up went well, considering the internal parts of the gyroscopic motor moved extremely fast and the clearances were miniscule. Newton was thinking how the engineering approached the realms of magic.

The next stage was to properly mix the internal medium of oil and mercury, which meant running the engine for a couple of hours. Ronnie left the bridge to go and get some food and refreshments. Newton spent the time looking through programming schematics and Pin watched the indicators of the engine test. The temperature arc was going up a little faster than normal, but that could be attributed to the cold start. The sound from the bearings was within specifications.

Pin had built and replaced every piece. She watched the sonar screen. The swirling, colored patterns of density appeared normal, but if something went wrong, it would go bad quickly and the engine could destroy weeks of work. Pin also used some spare parts she couldn't replace. If they cracked a frame, for example, there was no way to make another one with the resources on board the ship. The ability to wind a fine wire ten-thousand times and then press the winding into a frame, this capability was in the ship foundry on Geddis, eighteen-some light-years away, according to Newton.

Ronnie noticed the silence of Pin and Newton concentrating on their screens when she rolled the food cart on through to the command table sitting at the top tier of the bridge. She touched a button to get an assist from a gyro motor, to get the cart over the stairs, three sets of two stairs.

The whine of gyros didn't break their concentration on the screens. Ronnie found the silence, amplified three times by gravity motor, troubling. She wanted to talk, but a core tenet of military discipline said not to interrupt the train of thought of a superior officer, not to take a crew member's mind from her work.

Yet still, Ronnie wanted to talk, even if it was because of the loneliness. Pin saw it. A touch of her hand through Newton verified Ronnie's loneliness, and their response, communicated by what Newton called intention tones, was so generous, caring, inclusive, just what she needed.

Setting the table, still with no acknowledgement, Ronnie dismissed the lame conversation starters that presented themselves to mind. She continued setting the table while being niggled by their offer. Did she want to share their sleeping quarters? She did. Not only would her presence keep the relationship between Pin and Newton from evolving into a sexual one, but it would give her a sense of family. Pin had talked about how Newton had old-fashioned books and would read to Pin before going to bed. Ronnie was baffled at the kindness in Newton. He reminded Ronnie of her father, so much patient wisdom, so unlike the sort of men who join the Fleet to become warriors.

But Newton was not Ronnie's potential problem. It was Pin. Ronnie hid her attraction to Pin behind a practiced veneer of professionalism, but all it would take is a single touch while Ronnie had sexual desire on her mind and Pin would know. Spending time with Pin in an intimate setting would increase those desires, put more images in her thoughts. Ronnie was already haunted by glimpses of Pin's body from putting her in the med-suit a week earlier; the perfect smoothness of her skin and awe-inspiring shape to every imaginable place on her body, it was maddening. Deciding not to accept their invitation, Ronnie let go a deep sigh.

"Be with you in a blink, Doc," said Newton.

"I want to start without command," Ronnie said.

"Go ahead," replied Newton.

Ronnie served herself from serving dishes of sautéed fruit, spicy meat over grains, cream soup and dumplings, steamed vegetables, and from pitchers of leaf brew blended with fruit and another pitcher of water. Newton was reabsorbed back into sifting programming codes, but Pin perked up to the aromas of a feast. Pin set up parameters for an emergency shutdown and took the glass off of a screen so she could keep watch on the gyro mix of conductive metal with insul-oil.

Pin pulled up a chair next to Ronnie, conspicuously close at the large command table. With a friendly swagger, Pin bumped shoulders with Ronnie as Pin sat down. Ronnie startled in a flash of panic before realizing Pin couldn't read anything from her shoulder through layers of clothing. Ronnie covered with a smile. Pin smiled back, ladled her beginning course, and asked, "Does he know there's food here?" Pin was concentrating so hard that she had been deaf to the exchange about beginning supper without Newton.

"Yes, and said to start without him," said Ronnie.

Pin gave Ronnie an ornery scrunch to her little nose and then an enthusiastic bob to her head. Ronnie laughed as Pin began eating and then Ronnie promptly began tasting her food. Both women were humming with appreciation for the banquet by the time Newton made it to the table and served himself.

The crew feasted for a quarter span when it was Pin who broke the silence. "How different are robustus from graces?" asked Pin.

"Ninety-nine point one percent the same genetic code, so point nine percent difference," answered Ronnie.

"Is that close enough to have a child?" Pin stared at the center of the table.

"Yes," said Ronnie.

"A healthy child?" asked Pin.

Ronnie paused and said, "Probably."

Even with this sensitive subject, Pin laughed in amused skepticism. "No way. You people are all long and delicate, more like how an artist would make a person. We busters, we're all bulky and bulgy. No way that different makes a kid. What would he look like, long and bubbles?"

"Same genes that make muscles in busters also make muscles in graces. Busters just have super-built versions of the same genes."

"Why? I don't understand. Some yes, some graces built but some not, some even fat, but every buster I have ever seen is two, three times the mass of a grace, all of us, every one." Pin wasn't letting it go and turned to meet her eyes with Ronnie's.

"Captive breeding," said Ronnie. "Busters were slaves for ten-thousand revolves. During that time, who reproduces? The strong, because they were bred like livestock, so for all that time, busters weren't marrying for love, so every buster alive today is descended from unnatural selection. All the other traits are the same concentrations, and both breeds dedicate the same fifty percent of genetic code to where the neurons are in our brains, so how we think and feel is generally the same, but busters come from a genetic niche of extreme musculature. As far as a hybrid, the child might have fused fingers and toes. That's mostly the difference, genetically." Ronnie went quiet, not sure how Pin was taking the information.

"Talk about someone looking like she was made by an artist," said Newton. "Five worlds, Blue!" He positioned his arm to look at his wrist flat to his view. "Look at you like this," he said. Pin did. "Where the wrist is edge on, straight, on me it's knobby, you, straight but round, then arm flairs with more straight roundness, like you're made of something smoother than flesh." Newton faltered. "Round with small, straight joints, you would be difficult for artists to capture."

Pin gazed at Newton, but asked Ronnie, "Is he exaggerating?"

"No," said Ronnie.

Pin laughed.

Newton's expression changed and he said, "Excuse me," and pushed back from the table. Newton got up and walked away, pulling from pocket what looked like a large coin, he fanned it out and the device became a screen and keyboard, and a message in Treomet: "*Incoming, folowing inside elipse, X 24, Y 08, Z 31.*"

Newton entered a response: "Cloak?"

"Turn on console, turn on cloak, thirty blinks and it will activate." The completely silent vibration triggered again and Omni amended her message. "Cloak or shields, not enough for both."

"Understood," wrote Newton. Pin and Ronnie were still switching from looking at each other or at him. He ignored them and went to the helm. Newton gained control of the large screens and focused in on the coordinates from Omni. He also went to the cloaking station and turned on the console. The computer math found and highlighted the moving object. Highly magnified yet closing fast from ninety-thousand strides away, it was a sphere with instrumentation and cuts in a folding pattern. Their ship was positioned just high of the elliptic and Newton watched the track of the sphere. In a few moments, the sphere's flying curve would put the horizon of asteroids in between it and the ship. That would be the time to disappear. Pin and Ronnie were now at their stations.

Newton waited as the sweep of the trajectory hid them and then he turned on the cloak. Thirty seconds later, the acuity of the screens sharpened until they looked like windows, a benefit of being under full cloak.

"What time is it in Mot's world?" asked Ronnie.

"Midbright late," replied Newton, "bright still in the sky, and these are magnified views, but all he'll have to do is notice the clarity of his window walls and he'll know we're stealth."

"Do I power up some weapons?" Pin's voice was more playful than serious.

"No," said Newton.

"Unless Captain Mot breaks into the what's what," chided Ronnie.

"Don't conjure it," said Newton jokingly.

Everyone on the bridge froze as they watched the incoming sphere slide to a complete stop, ten-thousand meters out, on the right side of center, the center occupied by the star that pulled the elliptic. The sphere unfolded and began measuring the asteroids around it with a quick, green laser. "What's it doing?" wondered Pin.

"Finding where we broke through, with motion anomaly. Maybe finding us by the wake," Ronnie concluded.

"We're invisible, remember? And Pin put us in the right flow for the rock belt." He added some humor. "Uh, right Pin?"

Pin responded, "We're invisible, remember?"

They all laughed. A quiet moment passed, but Ronnie had to spoil it, as she always did, with truth. "Regulations do call for this probe to become itty bitty bits."

"Regulations are wrong, and we're not going to arbitrarily destroy someone's snazzy little ball, that turns into a rectangle, thing." Newton thought of how he wanted to say it. "It's impolite to blow stuff up just because we can."

"Unless Mot," said Pin.

"Unless Mot," Newton conceded.

The probe moved slowly yet still in line with its orbit, then stopped again. It took more measurements with whips of green laser. "That's it. That's the hole we left with our collision," said Ronnie.

"Still not blowing it to bits," he said. "This far, we might miss, anyway, but that would sure ruin us being invisible."

After a tense pause, Ronnie said, "I can see your point."

They watched it hover. "This thing does need to be on its way, though, before any calls from the captain," said Newton. They watched even more intently, but then it slowly resumed its vector while folding back into a sphere. It gradually sped up while pulling away on the elliptic. The two graces sighed relief. Pin turned to concentrate her eyes on Newton's.

Ronnie, too, turned a discerning gaze at Newton. "Care to explain how you got this warning? It was too small and too fast for our computers to even catch at much distance. And then," Ronnie continued, "we have emergency nuclear for stealth, when we've worked twelve-span shifts on the engine?"

"I wonder why Captain Mot hasn't called," kidded Newton.

Neither Pin nor Ronnie would be sidetracked. "Tell her," ordered Pin.

Newton suddenly wondered how much Pin already knew. "We have a secret, unauthorized member of our crew, who's been helping with the nuclear power."

"Who?" asked Ronnie with a breathy voice.

Newton stuttered, so Pin answered, "She's a bug! From that place!"

"How'd you know that?" he asked Pin.

She narrowed her eyes at him and said, "You talked about how we share images. I see her when you see her. Tell Doc the rest of it."

"What rest of it?" he asked.

"How she has the hots for you, and you flirt with her," said Pin.

"What?" said Newton, sounding bewildered.

"Don't play stupid, Newton; you're no good at it," Pin said.

Ronnie chuckled before asking, "Who is it you're flirting with, exactly?"

Pin let out a mildly aggravated huff and walked off toward the command table to check on the gyro mix. Newton disregarded Pin's melodrama and answered Ronnie's question. "Omni, of the House of Reizha, I think."

Mild aggravation also sharpened some of Ronnie's tone. "Nice touch with the second thought. Your lack of conspiratorial knowledge is duly noted, but Omni, chancellor of the admiralty, first paragon, and daughter of Queen Tal Kai, that Omni, you would know. Is that who we're talking about?"

"Yes."

Shaking her head with disbelief, Ronnie said, "This just keeps getting better."

Newton crossed to the command table to talk to Pin. "It's Omni we have to thank for getting us emergency power, without you getting radiated. She gave us high-load power in thirty blinks. I don't even know how to do that, so we owe her some gratitude."

Pin looked up from her screen. "Maybe we do, but you need to show me you would choose me over her, always."

"I can't believe I'm having to defend myself here. You do realize she's not human, right?" Newton sarcastically asked. Ronnie began to gravitate toward the command table.

"I don't feel a whole lot of that mattering, not to her, and not to you," said Pin. "So show me who you choose for always."

Newton's voice betrayed some true annoyance. "How do I do that?"

"Give me that little planet she gave you," said Pin. "Not forever, I'll give it to you if she wants it back, but I hold onto it." The seriousness on Pin's face said she wasn't kidding.

Reluctantly, Newton found the gem in his pocket, took it out and looked at it, not sure he wanted it out of his possession, but then put it on the command table and started it toward Pin. She let it roll into her awaiting fingertips. "Graces don't always do this," said Pin shyly, "but with us, with me, you have to choose. To have me, you choose right, you choose me, only, always." Pin lifted her eyebrows and examined the Winsor, orienting the swirls between her fingers. "A fancy royal from the god planet," Pin sympathized, "you made a tough choice, but the right choice for me." Pin was gracious but Newton was dumbfounded. Pin put the gem into her breast pocket and buttoned it closed.

Taken aback by the exchange she just witnessed, Ronnie frowned as she waited for the way forward to present itself. She was already familiar with what Newton was just learning: Among the gracile, marriage had become a rarity, but with robustus, monogamy was imperative. Ronnie waited a little longer so Newton might catch up.

There was no need for more time, as fate would interrupt. "Report," demanded Mot over the radio.

"A probe flew by, noticed the gap we made with our collision but we were stealth," reported Newton.

"Was it destroyed?"

"No," answered Newton.

"Why not?"

"It was too small and fast for reliable targeting. I chose to stay in stealth in case we missed," said Newton.

"What's the other reason?" asked Mot.

Newton tipped his head before activating the radio. "Because it's impolite to obliterate someone's exploration device?"

"Thought it was something like that," said Mot. "I hope you're keeping track of all the procedural breakdowns because I lost count a long time ago."

"Accounting must be accurate and current," quoted Newton.

"Just tell me how you got the power. We have our Number Two engine?"

"No, working on a mixer test on Two, but that power was from emergency nuclear."

"Industrious," allowed Mot. "Pin, how long can we use nuclear and keep stealth?"

Pin made an exasperated face at Newton and replied over the radio, "I don't know."

"So who did the patch?" asked Mot.

"Newton set it up," answered Pin.

Mot made a sputtering noise before saying, "Pin, go to nuclear and make sure we are not going to explode. If it doesn't make us explode, then I would like a few brights, at least, with stealth, but not exploding. Understood?"

"Yes, Captain," said Pin.

"Rest of you," said Mot, "good work, carry on." The transmission light went dark.

Pin clicked her tongue and said, "He acts like we don't care if we explode." She turned to Newton and with teasing tone said, "You care if we explode. Come on, admit it, you don't want us to explode."

"I'm fine with not exploding," he confirmed.

"Me too," Ronnie agreed, "rather not explode."

"Right," said Pin, "let's not explode." Pin then shut down the gyro test and stood up from her seat at the command table.

"Now?" stalled Newton.

"We all agree that exploding wouldn't be good, and captain's orders." Pin started off the bridge. "And yes, I'll need to talk to your princess, and Doc wants to meet her."

Ronnie's hands pulled together in eagerness as she started to follow Pin off the bridge. "I really do," she confessed.

Newton stood for a second, realizing that they would continue even if he didn't follow them, and it would be better if he was there for introductions. He dashed off the bridge and didn't catch up with them until the women were entering the reactor room, and through the windows, saw Omni standing to face Pin and Ronnie. He whisked his way into the room and made hasty introduction. "Pin Pin, over with the blue hair, and Ronnie Chamberlain, Pin, Doc, this is her highness, Omni of Tal Kai." In a different outfit, this leather suit in black and green with straps that unified the bottom part with a vest, with the arms bare, Omni bowed.

No one knew what to say for a blink, then Omni said, "Pin, may I zhow you the power link?"

"Yes, please," said Pin approaching a counter with some engineering drafts. Newton's badge was also on the counter. "Begin with how you got a thirty-blink reach to full power."

"I preheat the water. I zhow, here." Omni turned to the counter and pointed a naked claw at a place in the drawings.

Soon Pin and Omni were bewitched by the engineering and went through several diagnostic programs, discussed the possible advantages and disadvantages of nuclear power supplement, and they realized they had their love of engineering in common, although Pin's body language indicated a controlled revulsion to Omni.

After half a span, Newton asked, "So, not going to explode and we get stealth for how long?"

Pin saw that Omni wasn't going to say anything, so Pin said, "For as long as we want, but we're making nuclear waste and will eventually run out of nuclear fuel. And, for radiation, we would prefer less before more."

"Tell Captain Mot he gets his few brights of stealth, then shut it down to conserve our emergency power," said Newton.

"Yes, Commander," said Pin.

Newton remembered that Ronnie wanted an introduction. He beckoned both Omni and Ronnie to him. They both approached. "Omni, I present Ronnie, our medical officer, and Ronnie spent time on Kai, finding medicines."

"It's an honor to meet you, your highness," said Ronnie, and then she held out her hand.

There was the smell of gratitude, a rush of thunderstorms on the horizon, then Omni shook Ronnie's hand. "It nize to meet you, Ronnie."

Ronnie held onto Omni's hand. "Thank you for helping us," she said before letting go of Omni's claw. Ronnie blushed.

"You're welcome," said Omni.

"Alright!" announced Newton, "I'm making a command decision. Omni gets her own quarters in the ambassador wing. Ronnie can show her to find a room."

"Nope, I'll show her highness to a room," interjected Pin. "And the ambassador wing is off limits to command." Pin crossed toward the door. "Your highness…" she said, waiting at the door.

Omni crossed quietly out. Pin shot Newton a smug look before escorting Omni away.

"Doc, been meaning to ask you," Newton drawled, "is it going to be bad for Pin to know about Omni? You know, that mind-body connection."

Ronnie smiled. "As long as you don't flirt with Omni, I think Pin'll be fine." Ronnie laughed as the conversation echoed in her mind. "I mean, nothing confusing about how Pin laid it on the line for you. That was stellar!" she exclaimed.

"She knew I was keeping a secret for a quarter-phase." Newton shook his head.

Ronnie gave Newton a pitying look. "Don't confuse nice with shallow. Pin's multidimensional as any of us. She's just so nice, you don't see it, till she deploys her thoughts, then watch out." Ronnie bubbled into laughter again. Ronnie's eyes got uncharacteristically mischievous and she added, "And don't worry, I'll flirt with Omni for you. She'll be fine." Ronnie walked out of the reactor room, turning up the hall toward the bridge.

Newton stood in the reactor room, stood dumb, pondering what Ronnie could have meant by what she said. Newton walked casually for someone going to demand an answer, as he was fairly certain that Ronnie would go back to the dinner table, perhaps to dine some more before clearing the dinner service.

And as it was so, he found her sitting at the table and wearing an amused smile. Newton approached with a double step up the three tiers. By her fleeting annoyance at her thoughts interrupted, Newton knew that Ronnie's smile was from something internal. He sat and finished some of the dinner that he saved for last. Then Newton asked, "What did you mean by what you said back in the reactor room?"

"Are you asking for my report? Because that's all I'm required to give," snipped Ronnie.

He relaxed and leaned in on his elbows. "Report," he simply said.

"Pin's right." Ronnie put down her dinner fork. "The top tier of the royal Kai, there's no limit to power. She can decide that she wants to build a university system that specializes in alien cultures, then it happens; the bureaucracy falls in line for the biggest, grandest scheme imaginable. Your girl did that at fifteen, had that kind of power her entire life. Omni wrote Treomet three years later, and had hundreds of universities to guide the process of an armistice, legions of scholars already in place." Ronnie gave Newton a look of impatience. "My point is Omni is also smart, and smart also increases the chances of someone getting what she wants. So she gets what she wants, so what's she doing here?"

"Pin says because she has the hots for me."

"Admit she's right or I end my report," said Ronnie sharply.

Newton sat up straight. "You're really testy about this; that's twice you've nipped, so yes, Pin's right. Omni even said a queen gets what she wants, in a conversation about her being here."

"So does a princess." Ronnie's expression softened. "Sorry, but we have a monumental leap, and we aren't going to make it if I have to explain things."

"I'm listening."

"We know the reason Omni's here. And it's a romantic tale, and perfectly reasonable. I even understand her choice." Ronnie smiled. "Your girl calendar is full, so don't read into that."

He nodded and said, "Noted."

"But, what might it look like to the five worlds, with at least a nine revolve delay in us communicating back to the worlds?"

Newton thought a moment and guessed, "Like we abducted the princess of Kai?" He sat there with a blank face as the thought fully landed, then he could do nothing but submit to tragic laughter. Ronnie laughed, also.

She sighed and then some of the admiration she had for Newton snuck back into Ronnie's eyes. "I am glad you're able to laugh. There are four of us in the entire five worlds who know the joke, and two of us don't think it's funny. So, to put the edge on our sword of truth, military assessment, how many of us, the Kai's adversary in a conflict, would they be willing to kill, if we held or harmed the princess of Kai?"

Newton shrugged while shaking his head. "Thousands, tens, hundreds of thousands," he said.

"Yes, perhaps millions. And she's just a girl run off because she's got a crush on this boy no one back home would approve of, so maybe she didn't tell her family much about this, so this could actually become an interstellar incident." Ronnie giggled. "Another interstellar incident." Ronnie's admiration for Newton blossomed into genuine delight. "You're getting good at those."

He rubbed his forehead while saying, "You're supposed to avoid those."

"I'll admit this, in another world, I think you and Omni would be a good couple, but now all you can do is decide whose heart you're gonna break," Ronnie leaned in on her elbows and added, "and Pin thinks you already made that choice, so factor that in." Ronnie's visage became loving. "End report, with a note of gratitude, you handled command with grace, again."

"Report accepted," said Newton. And that was the end of communiqué, of verbal communication, for the most part, for the finishing supper, clearing the dishes and scullery work. Ronnie and Newton worked happily together without conversation. They didn't miss a beat when Pin radioed in to Mot with her report, which Mot amended, a week of stealth before the conservation shut-down.

Chapter VI: Timing of Superiority

The nuclear power actually only had to run for three days of that quarter phase because once Pin had Omni's help, No. 2 engine took over power generation, and the gravity motor worked, after some dismantling and adjustments. Not just worked, sang, ranged through whirs and crackles; that's what a gravity drive is supposed to sound like, commented Pin, and they were mobile. A pyramid the size of a thirty-story building was able to move with staggering speed. Not that they were going anywhere, Mot said stay put, stay stealthy. Thus, Pin and Omni started repairs on Engine No. 1.

Then, a week to the hour, the entire crew, the evolved crew including Omni, Mot excluded, the actual crew was on the bridge, Pin at the helm, Ronnie at communications, Omni at instruments, Newton at the command station. The maneuver was to take down stealth and see what happened.

"Longest range to our sensors, scan for foreshortened movement." Newton specified, "All points."

"How do I look for foreshortened movement, exactly?" asked Ronnie while staring at the console.

"Omni, help Doc," said Pin. Omni reached over and tapped a dial for type of scan, putting her claw point on a setting with a symbol of an internal block with vibration lines around it. Ronnie set the dial. Without waiting, Omni also set the scan direction by touching a filled in circle in the signal bank. Ronnie and Omni exchanged a silent thanks and you're welcome with two quick nods.

An alarm sounded as a warning highlight appeared on one of the screens. "Magnify blip," said Newton. The screen looking low and behind the center of the system snapped to a view of something big, moving toward them incredibly fast. "Can we scan that at this distance?" asked Newton.

Pin and Ronnie were dumbstruck. Omni responded, "Iv we uze long range zcanz, it know we looking and will triangulate where we are."

"It seems to know already; it's coming straight at us. Scan it," commanded Newton.

"Yez, Commander." Omni's four hands worked switches on the console. The image of the incoming object flickered in different colors. "Zignal delay, give me vifty blinkz."

The object began to move faster, turning violet on the screen, the first color of a collision warning. "That just ruled out natural object. It did speed up, right?"

"Yez. It zpacecraft, large, ninety ztridez in vorward zillohuette, length unknown. It very denze." Omni adjusted the scan. "Drive unknown, traveling two perzent zublight. It made moztly of titanium alloy, but zo heavy, we have no drive that could move something that heavy that vazt." Omni looked up from the console.

"That's it? What about tech, weapons, instrumentation, origin?" asked Newton.

"All unknown. It made of very thick, very ztrong metal. That all we get by long range zcan, which we zhould ztop," Omni said.

"Stop scan," ordered Newton. "Ronnie, obviously, we are not taking down stealth, so keep it working, no matter what. Pin, in a way that doesn't give them a fix, evasive maneuvers, now," he barked.

Pin pulled the manual controls. The monitor that showed outside their ship leapt into a dizzying sequence of loops and diminishing objects. It was what Pin called the "death flower" and consisted of making loops away from a central point, but the trick was to mask the actual vector and be unpredictable because the loops were never the same shape. Pin also oriented the bottom of the pyramid away from the approaching ship. Pin called out, "Three quarters sub-light speed, that's about as fast as we got."

A huge asteroid whipped by their screens. "That's plenty dorking fast! Watch out! Shit!" exclaimed Newton.

Pin giggled and slipped between another two massive objects. All eyes went to the screen with the approaching ship. It transformed into a foreshortened streak and disappeared. "It went to light zpeed," Omni said.

"Find it!" said Newton.

Omni's four arms flurried at the console. "Line indicate, approach uz, zector vour, I think," said Omni.

"Park near one of the big asteroids! Bottom toward rock, now, before it comes out of light-speed," commanded Newton.

Pin maneuvered to an asteroid without slowing down. She stopped so suddenly that the gravity in the floor barely compensated. She hovered a hundred meters off the surface and quickly matched their drift with the asteroid. "Here?" asked Pin.

"I kind of wanted the asteroid behind us to the incoming, but don't move now. Let's see where it pops up." They all watched the screens.

A multicolored streak solidified into a ship. The side view was from about fifty-thousand meters out, shaped like a massive, metal V, which quickly changed course from the straight trajectory to a graceful summersault as it began searching between and behind the surrounding asteroids.

"What was the idea of parking by a big rock?" Ronnie asked nervously.

"With the amount of detail from an object instead of empty space, our stealth works better. We're more invisible."

The three humans on the bridge watched the ship stop. They all three drew the same worried breath as the point of the V hovered and oriented straight toward them.

"Weapons?" asked Pin.

"Can we hurt it, Omni?"

"Energy weaponz, no good," said Omni. "Mizzilez too zlow. I made vuzion slugz for machine gun, but only have a hundred and not loaded."

Newton scratched his chin. "No weapons, pulse laser would just make them mad."

"Can they see us or not?" asked Ronnie.

"Omni?" asked Newton.

"They veel uz. Not zee, but zenze we here. Motion zhow dizturbed zpace," said Omni.

"Are you sure we aren't leaking energy, showing ourselves somehow?" asked Newton.

"Nothing to be done iv we are," Omni replied, "nothing on, no com, no weaponz, no zhieldz, no zcanz."

A light blue flash glinted over every surface on the bridge. "What in five hells was that?" asked Newton.

Omni studied her console before responding, "I think that waz zcan, very ztrange energy wave, go through everything, neutrino maybe."

"Pin, get us out of here," Newton commanded.

Pin hit a fast sequence of switches and grabbed manual control. The pyramid jumped into motion, another death flower away from the V-ship. "Maximum speed, still sub-light, we can't outrun them," said Pin. The screen showing the V-ship whirled in away in a pattern of elongated loops, but then the image stabilized as the V followed them more and more precisely. "They're following and closing," Pin said in a controlled panic.

Something beeped on Ronnie's console. "We're being hailed."

"What?" asked Newton.

"Communication, in our formats, visual and audio, no translation program necessary," reported Ronnie.

"Receive with our end black, no reverb."

"I don't know how to do that," said Ronnie.

Omni reached over and adjusted the communications center. A center screen lit up with a multicolored image of small geometric shapes forming a human-looking face. The face said, "Stop and communicate or be considered hostile."

Newton commanded, "Full stop, def con three, battle posture!" Their pyramid froze in space and slowly tilted so the top of the ship oriented at the V-ship.

"Do we really want weapons hot?" asked Pin.

"Belay weapons," said Newton. "If we communicate back, they'll have a fix on us, so we're just supposed to just sit here with our pants down?" The V continued closing on the pyramid. "Ready standard guns and missiles, then give me audio com link." Newton watched for a nod from both Pin and Ronnie. He touched the com button and said, "Approaching ship, stop or be considered hostile."

The V-ship stopped, thirty-thousand meters away, a heavily armored battleship. Newton rubbed his chin and said, "They know we're out here, scan it."

"They could get a better fix," said Pin.

"They got that from our communication beam and from our shields. Scan it."

Omni went through a sequence of switches then reported, "Our energy weaponz would barely zcratch it. Gunz out of range. Zhip has hard weaponz, gunz, torpedoez. Nothing known on dezign or propulzion."

"Pyramid shaped ship, identify mission," said the pixilated face.

Newton tipped his head and said, "Open visual to com link." Ronnie touched the dial and nodded. He touched the dynamic com switch, letting the other ship get a look at them before saying, "Officer Keen, of Five Worlds Fleet, we are an explorer."

The pixilated face, of a young man, nodded. "I am Sal, of the guardians. What are you doing here?"

"We hit an object and are effecting repairs."

The pixilated face squinted thoughtfully. "You have weapons," said the voice. "Why does an explorer need weapons?"

"For protection," replied Newton. "If we were hostile, we would've blown up your probe." Newton knew this was presumptuous.

Again, the pixilated face nodded. "That restraint is why you're not already destroyed." The pixilated face turned and signaled something. A sustained muzzle-flash erupted from one side of the V and an asteroid in the foreground disintegrated into dust, in three seconds.

Newton shrugged. "I hope you're going to stabilize that gravity hole."

The pixilated face smiled slightly. "We will, and the hole you left. This is protected space. You are trespassing." Something happened to distract the face, which turned to the side, then back to the screen. "Officer Keen, may I address one of your crew?"

Startled, Newton said, "Sure, who?"

"You have a Kai on your bridge. I would speak with they who are Kai." Omni stood up and faced the screen. "You have a name," said the voice, avoiding a question with a statement.

"Omni Tal Kai."

The face transformed to that of a Kai mantis. "Your grace, your family thinks you have been abducted."

"No," said Omni, "I zecreted my way on thiz explorer. Tell my family I am well. Thiz commander waz welcoming to me."

"Your grace, please come with us. We can return you home faster than conventional signal. War will follow your family's declaration of blood vengeance."

Omni thought a second and said, "Zend word I am well."

The guardian face shook its head. "An emissary will not be sufficient. Only your presence, healthy and whole, will console them. Declaration has been made; time grows short."

Omni responded, "I will zend my jewel with your envoy. It have light az long az I live."

"Please reconsider, your grace," said the guardian. "This is protected space. It is dangerous for you to be here."

Tipping her head thoughtfully, Omni said, "Twize you zay thiz protected zpaze. You protect thiz zpaze vrom knowledge ov it?"

After a pause, the guardian said, "Yes."

"Zo, you destroy zhipz with knowledge of this zpaze."

"Yes," said the guardian.

A tart, metallic smell rose from Omni, the smell of fear. Her voice, however, sounded angry as she said, "I am Tal Kai. You will not lie to me. Iv I not on thiz zhip, you would deztroy it vor knowing thiz zpaze?"

The guardian looked at Omni for almost a full minute, then answered, simply, "Yes."

A different scent came from Omni, ammonia and burned meat, the smell of anger. "I will not leave my vriendz. Iv you harm anyone on thiz zhip or damage anything, you will know my vengeanze."

The mantis face tipped backward then turned around. There subtle motions back and forth as if engaged in an argument with unseen beings. The guardian turned back around and said, "Permission to ask a question, your grace."

"Granted," said Omni.

"How would you protect this space?"

"I would protect the zecret, but not with deztruczion, with intelligenze. I not tell of thiz zpaze, becauze a world muzt develop in itz own time, without the genozide of interplanetary conquezt. But I also know who to truzt, thoze who underztand all live iz zacred, like thiz crew." Omni worked hard to pronounce the F, "I keep zecret to protect life."

After a pause, the guardian said, "We accept and hold faith in your word."

"I granted you a queztion, zo I have queztion vor you."

"We are bound to truth, your grace," said the guardian.

"What give guardianz the right to deztroy livez to protect zpaze? We agree all live iz zacred," said Omni, "zo, what givez you the right to protect this zpaze?"

The guardian hesitated and said, "Technical superiority."

"That iz ability," said Omni, "not right." There was a strong resurgence of the ammonia smell; Omni was furious. "I am ovvended that you think zo little of killing my vriendz. I azk by what authority do you protect thiz zpaze?"

"The creator has dominion by divine right. What the creator creates, the creator can also destroy. We protect this space at the behest of the creator," said the guardian.

"Doez the creator create something juzt to deztroy?"

"In the balance of life," said the guardian, "there are prey and predator, life created to serve a purpose in its destruction."

Omni shook her head. "Nize try, but that iz a world without abztraction. We evolved into abstraction; killing to protect zecret iz killing vor idea, killing vor something that haz not happened. And, there are alwayz thoze who zay they act vor the creator, but the tezt iz, create or deztroy. Iv they uze creator az ezcuze to deztroy, they are lying. They work only vor themselves; they work vor greed. They deztroy because they are jealouz ov creation, zo they kill vor vun. I am beginning to think guardianz are thoze."

Ronnie and Newton turned and looked at Omni, both worried and impressed. Reprimanding beings with the ability to destroy them, it was a declaration of dangerous truth, but if they were going to die, better to die on the side of a truth boldly declared. Omni stayed statue still, staring at the screen.

"I apologize for having offended you, your grace. An offense to the Kai is an offense to the creator, as well. Please accept my apology," said the guardian.

"On condition," said Omni, "you will deliver my jewel to the known worldz, with my wizhez for peaze."

"It will be done, your grace," said the guardian.

The diplomat in Newton knew this was a good place to leave the negotiation. He cut in, saying, "We will send a probe with the jewel, and keep your space secret, Fleet Explorer Clarion, out." Newton touched the com button and the screen switched from the face to an image of the ship.

Omni reached into a wide, flat pocket on the front of her abdomen and got out a folio of metallic sheets of stationary. Seemingly oblivious to everyone watching her, Omni flipped through a few sheets—some with writing, some with drawings—selected a lavender colored sheet, pulled up a stool next to the science console, and began to write with a pen that set down a tiny bead of gold loops and lines.

"What happens now?" asked Ronnie.

"Omni?" said Newton.

She continued writing in an ornate, flowing script. "I write note, zay not to make war. Zay I ztowaway on zecret mizzion to zecret plaze, and crew good to me." Omni held up a perfectly composed page, heading, body, salutation—all rendered in precise, decorative handwriting. She then began to fold the sheet until she had a tiny box with a closable lid. Omni stood and crossed to the helm. She held the little, open box out for Pin and said, "Jewel, pleaze."

Pin looked surprised. As she reached into a hip pocket on her uniform, she asked, "Did Newton tell you I have it?"

"No, it vibratez with my live energy. I veel it no matter where it iz."

Pin put the Winsor into the little box. Omni closed it and then gave it to Pin.

"What did you mean by it having light as long as you live?" asked Newton.

"Iv you find one on Kai, iv it haz light, then light will come from zomeone. It hard to match light with being, but iv you vind the match, it ztrong connection. Only ninety match have been vound in all hiztory of Kai."

"So the guardians take this back to the worlds and it still gives off light if you're living, even though you are thirty light-revolves from it. It would still know, instantly, faster than light, times a hundred or thousand, or whatever?" Newton was intrigued.

"Yez, divverent side ov galazy, no matter, electroweak nuclear forze, diztanze make no differenze."

Pin flipped a few switches and announced, "We are hovering, and I am leaving the helm." She stood and crossed to the tube station at the back of the bridge. Pin looked at the tiny box for a second before putting it in a small pneumatic tube. She punched in a destination, hesitated, then sent the tube. She turned on a monitor and remotely controlled the tube being put into a delivery probe. Pin came back to the helm and set the targeting for the probe. Before sending it, Pin surprised everyone by turning to Omni and saying, "Your highness, that is a beautiful thing; come to find out, it knows you like no other, last chance."

Omni gazed at Pin with an uncharacteristic tremble. "Zend it, Pin," said Omni. Pin's finger paused above the trigger. "Pleaze," said Omni. Pin shook her head. With a weak voice, Omni pleaded, "Pleaze." Pin took a deep breath and touched the button. Everyone's head turned to the screens and watched the probe launch toward the guardian ship.

They all watched a magnified view as the probe closed on the ship and the rocket engine cut out, leaving it to coast toward the ship. A small, bubble shaped shuttle deployed to intercept the probe. It approached the probe, reversed motion to match flight, deployed mechanical tentacles which gently caught the probe. The shuttle pulled the probe inside and streaked back to the ship. Once the shuttle was on board, the V-ship pulled back. It turned in space and deployed another object where the obliterated asteroid had been. They watched as the debris began to coalesce around the object. The guardian ship then pulled away on a trajectory perpendicular to the elliptic of solar system. It streaked into light speed and disappeared.

All the humans on the bridge sighed relief. A different scent, pungent and sweet, perfumed the bridge. "Permizzion to retire to my quarterz," said Omni.

Newton, startled from his thoughts, said, "Permission granted."

Unable to control the trilling sound of emotional breathing, Omni left the bridge.

Newton, Ronnie and Pin sat at their stations, staring at the screens, speechless. Pin broke the silence, "Newton, go, tell her I forced you to give me the jewel."

He shrugged and said, "I'm not sure that's going to help."

Pin looked angry. "She's hurting. It'll help." Pin's voice became shrill as she said, "She just saved all of our lives! Go and comfort her."

Newton looked at Ronnie, who nodded. "Just the effort will help. Tell her we're grateful. Then hurry back, we'll wait," said Ronnie.

After a quick sigh, Newton said, "Ronnie, you have the bridge. I'll be right back."

Newton walked to the ambassador wing and found Omni in the hallway. She was weeping with little clicks and trilling sounds. She was standing in front of a canvas too large to put in her room. He remembered when she asked for art supplies. Newton approached and saw that the painting was a portrait of him. He didn't say anything but simply walked up and pulled her into an embrace. Omni weakly resisted but then returned his embrace. Newton was surprised at the texture of her shell, silky smooth, softly pliable and slightly cool to the touch. She wept in his arms for a couple minutes, filling the hallway with the scent of grief, sharp and sweet.

"I'm sorry, Omni," Newton whispered. "Pin pulled an image of the jewel from my mind, and images of you that whole time you were a secret. I needed to let Pin hold onto the jewel to prevent a total meltdown. She was jealous and I didn't know what else to do. I had no idea how important that was to you."

"I know," said Omni, "I juzt veel alone and ztupid."

Newton pulled away enough to put his forehead against Omni's. Her small, segmented antennas nestled on both sides of his nose. "You're not alone," he said. "You just have all of us to deal with. And you're not stupid. You saved us from the guardians, and we're all very grateful. I am very grateful."

There was a change in the scent, drifting back to the cinnamon-sweet of grief turning to humor. "You hugging a bug, you know," she said.

"I am hugging someone who bravely faced a deadly foe; I'm hugging a princess, someone I think is beautiful."

The smell changed again, back to grief. "You have Pin."

"Yes, and the rules say I can't love either of you, but I do love you, and Pin, so we're just going to get through this one bright at a time, and see what happens."

Omni pulled back and looked at him. "I love you, too." She caressed his face with the side of her claw before stepping back. "I don't want to make trouble vor you. Zo, one bright at a time," said Omni. The angry ammonia smell welled up and she said, "And I think the guardianz are the

Zentinelz. Guardianz, Zentinelz, they are zame thing, juzt divverent wordz."

Newton considered it with a nod and said, "That makes sense. And they were willing to blow us into bits for being here, until they saw we had a Kai on board." He smiled. "Thanks for being a stowaway," he added with a grin.

"Iv I waz hiding in the warehouze instead ov on the bridge, they *would have* blown uz to bitz. Thank you vor inviting me to be a part ov your crew," said Omni. "I not the only one who zaved uz."

"Well, crewmember, I'm going to give you some rest, but I want you back on duty before the dinner bell."

"I can go to the crown and zmoke?" asked Omni.

"Absolutely," said Newton, "you're welcome to the entire stash, hesh, rag, enjoy, and I wish I could join you, but they're waiting for me on the bridge." Without turning to look at the painting, Newton tossed a thumb in the direction of the large canvas. "So, what's this?"

Omni laughed with clicking sounds before pulling his shoulder and softly turning him away. "Never mind, Newtin." She gently pushed him down the hall, perfumed by the smell of cinnamon. "Not ready, and no command in the ambazzador wing," said Omni.

Newton continued walking and said over his shoulder, "Yes, Princess." He stopped at the end of the hall and looked back at Omni, a tall, slender mantis. She waved him off and he disappeared around the corner on the way to the bridge.

Smoking with Omni in the crown, that was one of his true pleasures, and he only got a week when that was an option, before he learned that Pin would see the images in his mind. Defiance welled up with the idea that he was the commander and he could just tell Pin to deal with it. Maybe he could go to the crown instead of the bridge. They told him to comfort Omni. Whether he was hugging her in a hallway or smoking with her in the crown, it was the same thing, he rationalized.

As he walked onto the bridge, he was glad he came directly back because neither Ronnie nor Pin had moved, so they were waiting for him, sitting there frozen in the moment. Newton took his seat at the command station. He stared at the screens. One of them played a loop of the guardian ship firing on the asteroid. The firepower was impressive, if not somewhat horrifying. A chunk of space rock twice the size of their ship was pulverized to dust in a few seconds. Their meanest, six barreled gun, throwing huge slugs at six-hundred per second, that gun would've taken perhaps an hour to have the same effect.

"She going to be alright?" asked Pin.

"Yeah, she's going to take a little time for herself and be back on duty before dinner," he said. Newton smiled at Pin. "She's emotional but strong, just like the rest of my crew."

Pin smiled back at him and said, "Poor Newton, has to deal with all these women who have all these feelings." Newton laughed, to be joined by Ronnie, then Pin.

They all appreciated the break in tension, but Ronnie had to ruin it with a question. "What are we going to tell the captain? We just had an engagement with a hostile force; engagements are suppose to be his, only his, call him to the bridge, his, but if we had done that, we'd be like that cloud of dust out there."

"His, but he's supposed to defer to me," said Newton, "the certified diplomat, so it's like he deferred to me, just after the fact."

Ronnie sputtered with aghast. "What imaginary world are you living in?" she asked.

"What imaginary? It already happened. Captain Mot doesn't know it, is all," said Newton. He lifted his eyebrows as if the gesture settled the matter.

The matter was far from settled. "A simple report," challenged Ronnie. "Do you mention our stowaway? She's the only reason we're alive. Regulations would have her executed. The light in the jewel goes dark and it starts a war back home, and the guardians come back and destroy us. That's the world we live in," Ronnie concluded.

"Is it?" replied Newton. He pointed to the screen with the loop showing the asteroid's destruction. "There's the power in this world. They said an offense to the Kai is an offense to the creator. The creator and the Kai are somehow connected. These guardians know what happens on the other side of the Black." Newton turned and switched his gaze back and forth from Ronnie to Pin. "How? Light-speed puts all communication out of range, for revolves, and yet they know. They said they could get Omni back, faster than light-speed. We can only do that one-way, and only with objects, not a signal. Say what you want about Mot, but he understands power. He knows we need to be smart, or be destroyed. And, we have the blessing of the creator, in this world, and back in the five worlds."

Ronnie stayed silent.

"You think the Kai really are connected to God?" asked Pin.

"I don't know," answered Newton. "What I do know is the Kai have a compassion that is godlike. They have a love and wisdom and humor that I have only seen in the aspirations of reaching for God. Yes, they are insects, and God seems to like paradox, so why not take the lowliest creatures to hide the true essence of the divine." Newton paused to smile at Pin. "It was the test of our faith, and we failed because we thought they were just bugs. The Kai lived in peace for a thousand revolves. Every religion I know of talks about peace but no other civilization has ever done that, not even close. And when we invaded, they responded with awesome power, like the very wrath of God."

"I thought you didn't believe in God," said Ronnie.

Newton chewed on the inside of his cheek before responding, "I don't believe in the god that religions use. That god seems like a rather transparent brainwash to exploit the masses. But, there is something in life that seems divine. There are forces of creation that I don't understand and I wouldn't say there isn't a God. I think there might be. Waking up with Pin in my arms, that warmth and peace, or sharing images and feelings from her mind, it feels like something from the divine." He looked from Pin to Ronnie. "Talking with you, Ronnie, when you impress me with your intelligence and humor, that also feels as if God gave me that moment. So, I'm not a believer, but I keep seeing these glimpses that make me wonder." He laughed. "And, here, through a series of impossible events, we are still alive at this moment. What happens after this doesn't take from the thousands of minor miracles it took to get here." Newton walked closer to the screens.

"As the one true atheist on this crew, I'd like to say that if God got us to this point just to quit on us, then I'm glad I didn't waste any time believing in a creator," said Ronnie.

"So what are we going to do about Mot?" asked Pin.

"Nothing," replied Newton. "I'm not going risk putting Omni in jeopardy. When it gets closer to the time to letting him out, I'll consider reporting this engagement. But," he hesitated, "if it came down to a choice of who lives or dies, I would kill Mot before I let him hurt Omni, so there's no real question in my mind. When it comes time to decide whether to tell Mot that Omni is on board, to give him credit for realizing the full details of this engagement, then I will let you both know. I want us all ready to protect Omni. If anybody's not willing to do that, tell me now." Newton left the question hanging, intentionally not looking at them to see if they were truly listening, if they had dedication.

"I have no problem killing Mot to protect Omni," said Ronnie.

"Me neither," said Pin.

He turned around to face them. "That makes us mutineers," he said.

"Don't care," said Ronnie. "You can give him a chance, tell him, give a full report that includes the fact that they didn't kill us because of her, but if he snaps and goes after, no way he hurts her. If he can't understand that the old rules don't apply, then he's just going to get us all killed."

Pin nodded. "Like that probe, Mot would've destroyed it without a second thought, and the guardians wouldn't even have talked to us. They would've just zapped us like that asteroid and been done with it," said Pin.

Newton looked at the clock. "Pin, put us back where we were. The sun goes down in seven spans, so when Mot has window walls, I want the view the same."

Pin pulled away from asteroid and said, "We were on manual helm, so I don't know if I can find it."

"I'll help with the calculations," said Ronnie, "although those maneuvers might make it a bit tough." She got up from the communications station and went to the navigation computer. After a minute, with three screens being dedicated to maps, Ronnie complained, "The navigation pulse didn't make a big enough spot map. This is going to take a while."

"We have seven spans, which sounds like a lot of time, but hurry," said Newton.

"Aye, Commander," said Ronnie, "and Pin, get us above the asteroid belt, please."

Pin pulled the manual helm and zipped past several asteroids. Once clear, Pin asked, "Here?"

"Much higher, I need to see the turn of the ellipse."

"Got it," said Pin. She maneuvered straight up until they were in empty space. The view of the small solar system was beautiful, a section of asteroids on a curve, a cloud of interstellar dust, a large, pale blue planet pointing the way toward a tiny yellow star.

Chapter VII: Pains of Awareness

Preparations were made for a moment that didn't arrive. A week before Mot was scheduled to be freed from the bio-cell, Newton sent a report about their engagement with the Guardians, a report that included the fact that there was a Kai stowaway on board. Sending the report was not a popular decision and Newton didn't want to do it either. Their living situation, before the report, had transformed them into a family. Ronnie moved in with Newton and Pin, and Omni would visit in the downtimes. They all organically fell into routines of fellowship and recreation. Pin and Omni would play at the ball court. They would get together after meals and Omni would play a stringed instrument for Ronnie and Pin to make up funny songs. Newton would read to all of them from the book he was reading to Pin.

And then, the report, they all went back to solitary living quarters and returned to the military divisions of crew and duty. Newton expected Pin to be upset and he was haunted by the images of her emotional departure. And if Newton was to accidentally encounter Pin going about her duties, she might start weeping again while attempting casual conversation. He was also surprised by Ronnie, who delivered a tearful speech as she gathered her things from the spare room. Her tirade suggested that exchanging the harmony they had found for the madness of Mot's command was a deadly mistake, and they all would pay the price, for a command structure that abandoned them to die. Omni, she didn't say anything but the smell of interchanging anger and sorrow would betray her if she talked to Newton for any length of time.

Yet, Mot didn't read the report and batter his way out of the bio-cell, as they all expected he would. Newton sat in the crown but stared a monitor and alarm he set up outside the bio-cell. He patched the motion sensor in the hallway to everyone, so they would have some warning, but there was silence, three days with no reaction. Newton began to wish there were cameras inside the bio-cell, but Mot said no when they were building the ship. Mot cited the observation principle, that observation changes behavior, and the animals in the bio-cell were already at a disadvantage because of just how small their jungle was. Newton remembered being impressed by Mot's reasoning. Now that decision was a problem because no one knew what Mot was doing in the bio-cell.

Mot was on the staircase up to the canopy room. About three-quarters up the staircase, according Mot's memory of the ship's construction, there was a place where the wall of the bio-cell met with a mechanical room. He knocked on the wall while listening carefully. With his long knife, Mot found a seam with the point. Three sparking cuts and a stiff punch to deform the panel, he was through the wall and walking in the mechanical room on his way to find that bug.

Omni was getting ready for a shift in the engine room when the hall alarm sounded a warning tone. The sensor she set was for endothermic beings, which means any crew member could trip it, but the tone was also size sensitive, so she knew by the longer tone that it was Mot.

Mot walked the hallways with slow, intentional inhales through his nose. There was a smell, like apple blossoms and musk; he had killed enough of the things to recognize the baseline odor of the insects. All he had was his combat knife, but he didn't want to be discovered going to and from a weapons hold.

When her door chime rang, Omni indulged in an appreciative look around the reception room of her ambassador suite, luxury sofa and chairs that didn't work for her body, low level, elegant lighting, a large window display showing that they were floating on the outer edge of a widely spaced asteroid field. The door chime sounded again. Standing by the beverage counter, Omni touched a button on the wall.

The door slid open. Mot streaked into the room but was thrown back with considerable force by the invisible web Omni had stretched across the entryway. Mot hit his back against the wall, bounced forward into a roll and stopped on his feet, crouched, wide stance, lead hand empty, hand with the knife low and away. Mot's motion blur resolved to see Omni pointing a gun at him.

And not just any gun; it was a rip gun. It looked like an ancient handgun, with cartridges in clips, slide and barrel, but instead of firing a metal bullet, a Kai rip gun fired an insanely fast moving hole in the fabric of space and time. It was difficult to miss one's target, not having to adjust for elevation or leading a moving object except for extreme distance or speed, and the wounds made by these guns were horrendous. Even being grazed by a rip round could pull an appendage inside out or liquefy bone, and Mot was staring straight into the barrel of one.

"Look, it's a big, filthy bug," said Mot.

"Look, it'z a zoft, ztupid grub," replied Omni.

As a test, Mot snapped into a sidestepping motion. The hit-point of the gun followed his movement perfectly. "Think you're quick," snarled Mot.

"Think nothing," said Omni. "Zee fazter, move fazter, zimple vact, and no one vaster than thiz gun."

Mot stared at the barrel and cringed with frustration. "I can't believe you'd bring one of those on my ship." He frowned with the hint of fear in his eyes. "Stop pointing that at me," he demanded.

"Put knive in zheath; I put down gun," said Omni.

Mot stared at her as he slowly sheathed the combat knife. After Mot's hand moved away from his knife, Omni set the gun on the drink counter. The tension in Mot's posture relaxed slightly. "Thanks," he grumbled, "hard to think with one of those in your face."

"What do you want, Captain Mot?"

Mot glared at Omni. "If we were in the Five Worlds, I would have to drop you at the closest port, but out here, I can dump you in space, dead or alive."

"Iv we were in known zpaze, I could get vivty million clips vor your head on Kai, ten million billetz vor your head on Geddiz." A smell of cinnamon scented the air. "I wonder iv they give money vor halv a head." The scent changed again, to the smell of ammonia and burned meat. "The mighty Mot, you make enemiez like mozt make vriendz."

"I don't need friends," said Mot.

Omni tipped her head in surprise. "You wrong about that, Captain. Vivty yearz vrom home, vriendz are only thing that matterz."

"So that's the reasoning? We're so far from home that the rules don't matter?" asked Mot. He crossed his arms and looked for places Omni may have used to string the web of invisible cord.

"Rulez change, thiz var away, yez," Omni said. "I azk again, what you want?"

"I want you off my ship."

"I have zhift working on Engine One; you zure you want me ovv zhip?"

Mot had to think about it. Newton credited Omni for the thirty-second nuclear power in his report, but prejudice didn't care. "I am sure. Everyone may think you're some kind of savior, but you're really just a spy, and a criminal, and a freak of nature," said Mot.

"How about trial by combat?" proposed Omni. "You win, I leave. I win, ztay a part ov crew." A resurgence of a cinnamon smell revealed her confidence, because she was amused when she said, "You get to try to kill me. You win vight, I die or leave."

Mot stared at the giant, stinking bug, realizing that if he lost the fight and survived, that he was making an agreement to accept the thing as a crew member. Disgusting as they were, the Kai definitely had skills, and the rest of the crew already accepted it as useful. An upwelling of revulsion quickly canceled all thoughts with the opportunity to kill it. "Combat how, when, where?" asked Mot.

"Bladez, now, bio-zell, zo we not interrupted," said Omni.

"Fine," said Mot.

Omni picked up the handgun. She went around behind the counter and opened a cabinet door and pulled out a belt with a short, curved sword. Putting the belt on with her smaller, middle arms, Omni said, "Captain leadz." She pointed the gun at Mot's chest and touched a button in the pocket of her leather vest. A flurry of moving lights consumed the invisible web. "Remember, I want to zhoot you. Try anything, I will."

Mot walked in front of Omni, feeling the menace of the rip gun behind him, remembering the magnetically charged splatter of comrades being hit by rip guns in battle, smelling the aftermath of a warrior's body being ripped apart and collapsing into itself at the same instant. Damn he hated those things.

When they got near the hallway with the entrance to the bio-cell, Omni said, "Go the way you came out. Thiz not the way."

Mot turned toward the engineering floor. He walked wondering how Omni knew he didn't come out the front door. Perhaps it was the same reason he didn't use the door, because the door would have an alarm on it, but that would mean that the crew was conspiring with the bug. But the bug knew, because it put up the web, so where was his crew?

Once Omni saw that Mot was going to an engineering room, she commanded, "You walk ten ztepz pazt door. I go in virzt. Count to thirty, then vollow."

Mot walked past the door, stopped then turned around and asked, "Why should I walk into a trap?"

Omni moved the hit-point of the gun from Mot's chest to his face. "Iv I waz going to zhoot you, I do it now. I not vollow you in convined zpaze. Iv you don't zee I try to be vair, I zhould juzt kill you vor being ztupid." With that, she backed up to the door, which opened, meaning she had an electronic badge, and then she disappeared into the engineering room. The smell of living things guided Omni to the hole in the wall. She quickly went in and descended the staircase to find her battleground in the bio-cell. Finding her place at the top of a gentle hill, loving the smells of the jungle and the sounds of flowing water, Omni unzipped a pocket and a vent, got out a cigarette mix of hesh and rag, and lit what could be her last smoke. She watched clouds move across the sky from the window-walls, recorded from an actual sky on one of the five worlds.

Mot came through the hole on the stairs and smelled the cigarette mix. She smoked while casually following him down the stairs with the sights of the rip gun. "Not smart, smoking hesh before a battle, it might slow you down," said Mot.

Omni laughed. "What do you care? You want to win don't you? Bezidez, I could be ztoned, and drunk, and old, and zick, and ztill beat you." She took such a big inhale that smoke escaped her breathing ports and her mouth.

Mot sauntered from the base of the stairs to a hidden cabinet in the rocks. "That so?" He said. He stopped and pointed at a place in the rocks. "I'm going to get my pipe, so don't shoot."

Omni straightened her arm and leveled the gun and nodded. Mot pulled out the Kai pipe that Newton had given him. He took a puff of hesh, held the hit, and blew out a big cloud. "That pipe waz a part of givt of Kai to Newtin," said Omni.

Mot smiled. "Yeah, well, he gave it to me for my birthbright."

They smoked in silence for a while, staring at one another. "Vunny, you call me vilthy, zoftinz make vive timez waste as Kai. You vilthy, leaking, dripping, shedding, oozing, excreting all the time, all this gunk," said Omni.

"At least I don't give off a hundred kinds of stink," grumbled Mot.

Pin was on patrol duty, wearing an armored vest and carrying a pulse pistol. There were regular patrols ever since Newton sent the report, but the others checked only the front and cargo doors into the bio-cell. Pin, however, had the architecture of the entire ship memorized, so after she confirmed the weld was intact on all of the doors, she rearmed the alarms and started toward the engineering room that shared a wall with the bio-cell stairway.

In the bio-cell, Mot closed the pipe. "You finished stalling?" asked Mot.

"Put down you zhit and zhow me what you got," said Omni.

Mot put the pipe into the hidden cupboard. Omni casually tossed the rip gun away and pulled her sword. Mot unsheathed his combat knife and charged. At the final ten meters, Mot leapt, spinning toward Omni and leading with the knife. Omni waited and made a graceful bend with her body, hooked Mot's knife arm with her sword's blunt edge and punched his shoulder to send him tumbling on the ground. He rolled then jumped to his feet. "One vree attack," said Omni, "next will cozt you in blood."

He ran at her, spun at the last second, but again, she was way too fast and easily ducked the vicious slash of Mot's blade. As his other hand came at her, she stabbed his palm,

126

pulled the point, pushed the sword into the dirt for leverage, and then kicked him off the small hill with both legs. Again, Mot tumbled away from the fight. She casually wiped the dirt off her sword with two swipes against her leg.

His roll changed from sideways to head first with a quick tuck. Three years of war without much hand-to-hand combat, Mot considered the fact that the legendary speed and strength of the insects may actually be true. Strange as it was for him, Mot would have to think to win this fight. "I'm doing all the work, here," said Mot. "You got moves enough to attack?"

"Vine," said Omni, "devend yourzelv." With a dancing sidestep, moving in a closing arc, Omni suddenly reverse into a backward spin. Mot had only enough time to stop her sword with his blade. She jumped over the top of him, pulling the edge of her blade into the flesh of his forearm. His other hand reached behind to catch her, getting just a finger hold of her vest, delaying her spin away enough to hit her leg with the point of his knife. Her two smaller arms seized his knife, so when he tried to pull the knife from her leg, he pulled her, sword ready, right to him. Close enough to embrace, Omni pulled her sword straight up, leaving a deep cut from Mot's waist to chest to shoulder. He punched her away and Omni tumbled backward but landed on her feet.

Mot wondered why a cut instead of a lethal stab. Was that thing going easy on him? Fury made him lunge at it, even though its stance was ready. Again, Omni shifted at the last instant, hooked his knife arm with her sword and punched his opposite shoulder to send him rolling away, but this time, she used the edge, cutting tendons on his inside forearm. He made it to his feet but looked down to see his knife on the ground. He couldn't close his right hand.

"Zay I am your crew and we ztop," said Omni.

"Don't trust him!" Pin shouted from the hole on the staircase. "Keep your distance, no matter what he says! I'm coming down!" Pin came through the wall, pointed the pulse pistol at Mot and tapped the radio button on the bottom of the handgun. "Code nine! Engagement! Bio-cell!"

With blinding speed, Mot lunged forward into a shoulder roll, grabbed the knife with his left hand and unfolded into a cartwheel attack on Omni. Pin fired the pulse pistol at Mot, pkCHOOM! Omni leapt up and deflected the pulse round with her sword, but she came down into a rounded slash from Mot's knife in her torso. It was more punch than stab, making a hollow bending sound, but there was enough energy to send Omni twenty meters through the air above jungle floor. Pin waited until Omni was clear of her shot, almost fired at Mot's head, but then dropped her aim and fired two more pulse rounds, pkCHOOM, pkCHOOM! hitting both of Mot's knees. He stumbled to the ground.

Pin walked slowly down the staircase, watching Mot the entire time. She approached Mot and when she saw that he still held the knife, with a casual indifference, Pin shot the hand holding the knife, pkCHOOM! Standing over Mot, Pin pointed the pistol at his face. Mot's eyes betrayed dismay. "Your highness!" Pin called out, her voice pinched with emotion. "You alive?"

Omni's voice sounded strangely relaxed. "Zort ov. How Mot?"

Pin grimaced with torment as her eyes filled with tears. "He's alive," Pin called back.

"Good," said Omni. "Don't be mad, Pin. We made a deal. No more vighting, no more hurt."

Omni's compassion hit Pin hard. She crouched down and pressed the pistol angrily into Mot's nose. "Hear that?" Pin hissed. "That's what a leader sounds like. I think you should die. I hope you do." Pin stood up and stepped back, tears running down her face.

Charges popped at the main door. The door slid open and Newton rushed in leveling a battle rifle. Once he saw Pin standing and Mot on the ground, Newton called, "Sitch stable!" He continued into the bio-cell. "Stand down, need medic!" He walked up to Mot as Ronnie looked around the edge of the doorway. Ronnie grabbed a medical pack and came into the bio-cell carrying a battle rifle. Mot turned and watched Ronnie approach, noticing that she, too, came armed, in direct violation to the regulations that governed engagements.

"Where's Omni?" asked Newton. Emotion choked off Pin's ability to respond verbally, so she just pointed. Newton started off in the given direction.

Ronnie walked up to Mot assessing his injuries, pulse gun wounds, which were essentially extremely bad burns, burns bad enough to cauterize smooth muscle and crumble bone, pulse gun wounds to both knees and the left hand, with simple but deep lacerations on the torso and right forearm. She knelt down and watched his eyes for a moment before touching Mot's neck. His heartbeat was slow, regular and strong. Amazing, she thought. Someone with his injuries should be going into shock.

Newton walked into a shallow valley and then up over a gentle rise before he spotted Omni lying on the ground. Dropping the battle rifle, he rushed to her and knelt down. She turned her head to him as a tinny, sharp smell reached Newton's nose. All he could think to say was ask, "How bad?"

"Don't know," she said, "avraid to look. Chezt hurt, really hurt."

"I'm going to look," said Newton. He began undoing the ornate hooks on her vest. Omni put her claws over her eyes. With an attempt at a lighthearted tone, Newton asked, "What are you doing?"

"Bazhful, Newtin, you undrezzing me." Newton opened the vest. There was a gray-green slash across the pearlescent white of Omni's front torso. The laceration was mostly just color that lightened as the blade went across both of the ornamental hooks of the vest, but at one end of the mark, there was an actual puncture wound seeping clear fluid. "What color?" asked Omni, still covering her eyes.

"Gray bruise in a line, mostly."

"Any break in my zhell?" she asked.

"Yes, you have a small puncture. What do I do?"

"Cut patch from inside one of my pocketz, zame vor ztab wound on my leg. Hurry." Newton got his knife and cut a hole in the knee of his uniform pants, thinking that the skin of his leg would conform over the puncture wound while he worked with both hands. He pressed the side of his calf to the wound and got to work on the patches. "Zoft vlezh, I vorgot, zmart," Omni said weakly.

Thinking to keep her talking as he worked, Newton asked, "This was not the plan, Nee," using his nickname for her. "What were you thinking?" He folded some of the pocket lining into the puncture wound on her leg.

"We need Mot to aczept me az crew, and he respect ztrength. Zo beat him in vight, then do what he zays. Zhow loyalty, zomeone who ztronger do what you zay." Newton placed the patch and strapped it down using his own belt. He was slightly amazed at what a graceful creature Omni was, her torso no bigger around than one of his thighs. He cut the extra length off his belt and closed up her vest. She uncovered her eyes and said, "Ztill might work, maybe."

Newton took and held her claw. "Why maybe? You definitely kicked his ass."

"Might not live," said Omni. "Bruizez and breakz in zhell can be very bad."

Newton shook his head in defiance. "Nope, you don't get to die. You don't even get to talk like that. You will be fine. Tell me what you need to recover."

Omni thought a moment. "Thiz plaze. Our hozpitalz are filled with plantz and living thingz. Let me ztay in here, pleaze." The sun broke through a line of clouds and warmed the bio-cell.

"Alright, we'll set you up in here." Newton looked around, unable to see over the gentle hill. "You hang on; I'll be back in a minute." As he walked over the rolling ground toward Mot, Newton realized the tinny smell must have been Omni's pain. Memory of the smell amplified Newton's anger until he could practically taste his rage as he topped the hill and saw Mot lying in the grass. "You dorking idiot!" Newton's strangely hoarse tone and charging strides triggered Pin and Ronnie to intercept. Pin folded her arms above her head and stopped in his path as Ronnie grabbed one of his arms and set her shoulder to check his advance.

Mot was surprised both at Newton's anger and surprised to see the female crew members defending him, surprised and a little grateful since he didn't have even one limb that wasn't severely injured.

"I am done defending you!" Newton yelled, feeling his anger drain into sadness through his hand touching Pin's arm. "I can't believe you'd risk all of our lives by hurting Omni! Right there on the feed I sent in my report, she is the only reason they don't kill us! They dorking said it!" He stepped back from the Pin and Ronnie barricade, looking into the jungle. "You care about a cursed dragon, but not the one who saved it! Omni saved it for you, which means maybe I should kill it!" Newton shook his head in disgust. "Ronnie, get him the hell out of here. The bio-cell is now Omni's for medical sanctuary."

"You giving orders over me?" asked Mot. Ronnie and Pin looked at Newton.

"Article seven point two, I am in command until you are able bodied. And I might consider slapping a sanity review on that, because risking your entire ship seems pretty damned crazy. Again, get him the dork out of here!"

"Yes, Commander," said Ronnie. She turned and started out of the bio-cell.

"Belay that," grumbled Mot.

Ronnie kept walking. "No, Captain, seven-two applies, and you are going to pass out in a sweep or two, anyway. But even if you don't, you are not able-bodied." She touched the switch on the outside and closed the door to the bio-cell.

Pin looked at Newton. "Orders, commander?"

"This is mutiny," mumbled Mot.

Newton ignored Mot. "Secure this battle site. Restore all of Omni's weapons to her. Be careful with the rip gun I saw over there, all battle rifles go back in the third-floor hold, keep your sidearm and issue a sidearm to Doc, and move all of Captain Mot's stuff out of the canopy room and to his quarters."

"Aye, Commander," said Pin. She set down her pistol a good distance from Mot, then crouched and rushed in toward Mot, throwing his knife into the pond, darting in and grabbing the belt of his shorts to pull and roll him face down. Mot grunted in pain from his many injuries as Pin patted down the pockets of his shorts. With the knife she had strapped to her foreleg, she then cut his belt and re-sheathed the knife. Pin purposely rolled Mot over his pulse burned left hand to get him on his back. She pulled out the belt and threw it away and felt his front pockets as his right hand moved toward the knife on her foreleg. She stepped back casually, remembering that his right hand was too injured to hold a knife. "He's clean for medical evac," reported Pin. She then went and holstered her pistol before gathering the two battle rifles.

When Pin brought Newton Omni's rip gun and sword, Newton asked, "You're afraid to talk to her?"

Pin nodded with a worried frown. "He really got her. She saved him from a pulse to the head, and he tried to kill her." Pin closed her eyes and shook her head with disbelief. She turned toward Mot and raised her voice. "She was fast enough to stop me from shooting him in the head, but that's how he got her." Her voice dropped to a sad whisper. "I feel responsible. She would've easily won if she didn't have to defend him. I'm afraid to see her."

Newton ran a soothing hand across her shoulders before carefully accepting the rip gun and the sword. "Carry on," said Newton. Pin nodded, picked up and slung both battle rifles over a shoulder, walked to the door and left the bio-cell. He looked at Mot, who was already looking at him. "Stay there until the gurney gets here, or I'll shoot you with this thing," Newton said, holding up the rip gun. Newton then turned to go back to Omni.

He found Omni laying face down on the jungle floor with her four hands and two feet dug into the dirt, her torso naked, the strap of Newton's belt interrupting the vivid patterns of color on her back. Using her rolled up vest as a pillow, she had her head turned to one side and there was less of the tinny smell. He walked up and sat on the side she could see him. Newton carefully put down the rip gun, pointing it away, and the sword. He stroked her arm and said, "That scent is diluted, does that mean you're hurting less?"

"You zo zmart," Omni replied. "Yez, pain goes into ground. Veel better. There iz healing energy in all theze plantz and animalz. Can you veel it?"

He let go a sigh, and admitted, "No, I can't feel it."

Omni surprise Newton with a change of subject. "Mot has the pipe we gave you. I wonder why we zmoke with ztupid toy inztead of Kai pipe."

"How on earth did you know that?"

"Bevore vight, I zmoke zigarette and he zmoke pipe." Omni made a soft clicking sound as a weak aroma of cinnamon touched Newton's nose. "I make thinking ov you. Iv I knew Mot get it, I not make it zo pretty."

With a low, confidential voice, Newton said, "I didn't know you made it. I gave it to Mot because he was going to be confined, and I thought if he could smoke some hesh in here, it might mellow him out. I guess I was wrong."

"No you weren't," said Omni. "He struggled with dezizion, talked, waited, made deal." She raised her voice. "He lozt vight, zo I am crew, right Captain?!"

Mot called back, "If you live, if you fix Engine One, we'll talk about your conscription rank, which won't have quarters in the Ambassador's wing, you stinking bug!"

A milder, more flowery cinnamon smell perfumed the air. Omni was pleased with herself. Newton was quietly amazed. Maybe Omni was smarter than all of them. "Make sure he getz hiz pipe," said Omni, "hidden cupboard in rockz by the pond."

The door to the bio-cell opened and Newton heard the sound of the gurney. "I will," said Newton. "I love you, Nee. After we get the captain situated in the infirmary, you are going to have a conversation with Doc about what else you need to get better."

"Yez, zleep now," said Omni.

Newton went to help load Mot onto the gurney, nagged by the recollection that the Kai didn't require but a fraction of the sleep that people did. Ronnie stood looking at the gurney and Mot, puzzling whether to use the straps to load Mot. She looked up at Newton with this question on her face. He shook it his head and said, "Let's just load him." Ronnie shrugged her shoulders and put on some medical gloves. She got a small canister of bandage foam out of the medical kit. While she was applying a line of foam on Mot's cuts,

Newton was wondering what Mot might steal from his mind by touch. He decided that he didn't care. He didn't have sex with Pin, and his more recent memories were the solitude imposed by military division of quarters and duties, which is why Newton ruined their family harmony for Mot. "I'll get the top," said Newton.

Ronnie reacted with surprise. "Want some gloves?" she asked.

"No," answered Newton, "and we're in a hurry, right?"

"Yes, actually, these are serious wounds. We need to get him in amniotic chamber before he goes septic, and I need to reconnect the tendons in his arm before he goes in the chamber," said Ronnie.

"So let's go, on three." Newton hooked his hands under Mot's arms and Ronnie grabbed his ankles. Newton counted down and they plunked him on the gurney. Mot got a few fragments of imagery from Newton's touch—Pin weeping on the bridge, Omni working in an engine room, Ronnie in sickbay with Pin on a hospital bed.

As they were going down the hallway with Mot on the gurney, the captain began mumbling in delirium, "Saw a fragment of light cord when I untied that dragon, knew something. I also heard you after that dart, trying to talk her out of experimenting on me." Ronnie looked nervously at Newton as Mot passed out.

They got into sickbay and Ronnie put a gas respirator on Mot. As she started intravenous fluids and hooked up a vitals monitor, Newton realized she was preparing for surgery. He started for the door but Ronnie stopped him, "I need you to stay and assist, and when we're done, I'll need your help getting him into the amniotic chamber."

Newton nodded and touched his radio. "Pin Pin, we need to boost power output. Pull clear of all gravitation matrix, then work the engines against each other to hold position."

"Yes, Commander," said Pin. "That means I take the helm without supervision."

"Yes," said Newton, "you might have to get my badge from Omni. Sorry."

Ronnie opened a surgical pack and said, "Newton, I need traction on these fingers. Put on those surgical gloves after you position that overhead light." He did as instructed. "Now, put on a mask and put a chuck under his arm."

"A what?"

"A chuck, that absorbent square, unfold it and put it under his forearm," said Ronnie. She took the scalpel from the surgical kit before saying, "Hold his wrist down so he doesn't move during the incision." She cut lengthways down the arm. "When tendons are cut, they shorten and fatten, so we need to stretch them back to reconnect." Ronnie was making small talk as she felt around the gore inside Mot's forearm. Once she found the tendon, she gripped it with a pair of forceps. "His middle finger, straighten it, and hold these forceps with your other hand." She found the other end of the tendon, set some forceps, and pulled them together. She got a stapler. "Sugar staples," she said, continuing her small talk. "They'll dissolve in a phase." With Newton's help, Ronnie positioned the two ends together and stapled them together. "Index and middle finger conjoined, so are the ring finger and the small, but they have the same number of tendons, so with some swivel in the joints, there's extra strength in the hand." She continued the small talk as they repeated the procedure on three more severed tendons. "I noticed you've been wearing your dress badge. If Omni has your regular badge, why did you apologize to Pin?"

"She's afraid to look at Omni. She'll have to talk to her to get the telemetry badge. Pin feels responsible for Omni's injuries."

"How bad is Omni hurt?"

Newton hesitated and then said, "Don't suppose you're certified in Kai medicine, too. She's got two breaks in her shell, one on the thorax, one on the leg." Newton hesitated. "Part of me thinks we're wasting time on the wrong injured."

Ronnie did some more surgery to prepare for closing and sounded distant when she said, "Everything we've done would probably be upheld in review, even darting and shooting the captain, as long as we don't kill him for convenience, as long as we give him medical attention. We can't cross that line, like you said, for our own sake. When he said he heard us talking about doing the procedure, I suddenly was glad that we're on the right side of the line, even if we are never before an inquiry by the Fleet. I like being blameless." Her words kept rhythm with the sutures closing Mot's arm. "You're right. We will do what we can for him, and the second he is stable in the chamber, I will go see what I can do for Omni, which, sorry to say, isn't much." Ronnie switched from the inside to the outside layer of sutures, impressing Newton with her quick movements as she used the small hemostats on the tiny, curved needle to nip the edges of skin and then tie the stitch with tiny whips and loops.

"They call us soft flesh, and look at you go," said Newton. "You didn't pick up any Kai medicine when you were there?"

"Open those two suture kits," said Ronnie. Newton complied and Ronnie began scrubbing the long cut on Mot's torso, finding the deeper areas of the laceration. Once involved in the sutures, she picked up on the thread of conversation, as well. "Kai medicine? I know that if a Kai eats too much, she doesn't get fat; she goes dark sooner and doesn't live as long, so instead of a hundred-thirty revolves, she'll get eighty or ninety. I know that more of their medicine is based on absorption rather than oral intake. They use the energy of living things to help heal, so their clinics

137

look more like greenhouses. They sometimes bury the severely injured up to their head and hydrate by watering the ground as much as by mouth." Ronnie looked up from her work. "I thought you already knew this, giving the bio-cell to Omni for medical sanctuary."

"Omni said something about needing to be in there, when I asked what we could do for her. The dirt eases pain, she said, with a scary new smell, sharp, strong enough to stray into other senses, like a taste, or the ringing sound of pain."

Moments passed as Ronnie put in dozens of sutures. Newton almost forgot where they were in their conversation when Ronnie said, "I hope there's enough bio-mass in there to actually help her. As far as medicines, they use poultices and aromatics, oral medications and surgery are a last resort. I'll see if can find my notes from Haza, 'cause I did ask about Kai healing practices, which sound more like poetry than science."

"Poetry?" said Newton.

"Maladies are like weather events and the remedies had corresponding elements. I'll ask Omni, too." Ronnie stopped suturing and made a point of getting Newton's eye contact. She said, "The straight physics go like this: She has internal struts; if a strut is broken inside a limb, she could lose and regrow that limb; if a strut is broken in her torso…" Ronnie slowly shook her head with a pained expression. "There are always tradeoffs in physics. To have energy in one place, you borrow it from another. Newton, they are strong beings, but it's as if that toughness means they weren't made to heal from severe or complicated injuries."

Newton burned with immediate panic. "You stow that shit right now! Because if Omni dies, I'm not playing, any more. I'll pull the plug on Mot and everybody is on their own!"

"What is that supposed to mean?" asked Ronnie.

"It means I'm abandoning ship, because when the light in that jewel goes out and the guardians come back and destroy this ship, I am going to be on our lander at full speed toward that planet. You and Pin are welcome to come along, but the chances of survival are practically nothing."

Ronnie shook her head in skepticism. "The guardians?"

"Yeah, use this ship as a decoy, but they may be too smart for that and destroy both the ship and the lander. Even if we made it, the planet could quickly kill us, ionic charge in the water, pathogens, kill us quick and gruesome, kill us ten-thousand ways."

"That's why that is a terrible plan."

"Well, we can't outrun them in this, not without all three engines, maybe not even still," said Newton.

"You are presupposing the guardians are going to come back and destroy this ship. We don't know that's what they are going to do."

"We have reason to think that is a possibility, and if they do, then we are stuck and defenseless. So, without Omni, I don't care. Fleet can kiss my rod!" Newton fumed.

Ronnie worked in silence for a moment. "You had Pin and me in your life before Omni came along," said Ronnie. "Why does all hope, the will to go on, why does it now pivot on Omni?" asked Ronnie.

Newton had to think about his answer. "The way she talked to the guardians, I saw that genius and courage during every negotiation we had with the Kai. And she came aboard because of me, so I feel like the universe gave me this responsibility, to take care of this extraordinary being, and if I fail," he trailed off, "it's kind of ... unforgivable." Embarrassment glinted across his face.

"I'm trying to listen through the religious connotation, but failing. Transpose 'universe' with God, and you giving up because Omni is a sacred mission, but that still doesn't do shit for me or Pin."

Newton smiled. "What's the better plan, the rational, nonreligious plan, then?"

"Let's start with that same premise. If Omni dies, you go crazy and avenge her by killing Mot. That makes you an outlaw, but me and Pin, we're fine with you avenging Omni, which makes us outlaws, too. So, outlaw, you take the two women you have left, one of whom thinks you are God's gift to her, and the other who thinks you're pretty alright for a man, and we run. If we live, we live however we want. We make the guardians or the Fleet find us, take a few of them with us if there's a fight. If we die, we die trying," Ronnie concluded.

With a grin, Newton said, "That sounds good."

Ronnie returned a more demure smile. "Never resign your fate, Newton."

Pin's voice came in over the radio. "We are point-eight sub-light, still with the solar wind off our star-side. At this speed, we still might be a phase from empty space."

"Copy that," said Newton, "change of orders, generate power by keeping us on the move."

"What direction?" asked Pin.

"Exercise full stop under stealth. Look perpendicular to the plane of solar system. Look for the emptiest space, with all sensors, then set course straight into the darkest of the black," said Newton. "Please summarize," ordered Newton.

"We stop under stealth, look for nowhere, then go there," said Pin.

"Good, now when we have enough power for amnio-chamber and stealth, about thirty-six gigs, then go on stealth, but failsafe priority to the chamber."

Pin sadly said, "I still haven't moved Mot's stuff."

"Don't worry about it," answered Newton, "I'll get it."

Newton watched the transmission light on his radio go dark. Ronnie got up from her work on Mot, pulled off the gloves and went to the far corner of sickbay. She activated a panel that lit up a room that contained the amnio-chamber.

"How long till we have power for the chamber?" asked Ronnie.

Newton touched his radio button and said, "And we need power for the amnio-chamber just as soon as we can get it."

"I'll create some drag with the rudder engine," said Pin, "and you'll have power enough in about three sweeps."

"Well, good, but why isn't point-eight sub-light enough?"

There was silence before Pin responded, "Omni's rebuild, it's without the regular parameters of friction, so there isn't the same amount of heat generated."

Chapter VIII: Uncertainty of Place

It took Ronnie and Newton almost half an hour to get Mot in the amniotic chamber. Once inside and even under sedation, Mot thrashed so violently it seemed he might crack the glass when the chamber filled with fluid. The fluid needed to have complete contact with the body, including sinus recesses and inside the lungs. Mot eventually reached biometric stasis and Newton asked, "If these things can revert someone to strict genetic expression, then wouldn't we lose everything we've learned?"

"No," answered Ronnie, watching several computer screens as the chamber began to learn every cell of Captain Mot's body. "The chamber takes a snapshot and maintains the brain exactly as it is. Why do you ask?"

"Because Mot has been smoking hesh. I gave him a pipe for being in the bio-cell in hopes it would mellow him out. Omni thinks it did. If he did calm down, I'd like to have him stay that way rather than turn into a more aggressive form of himself."

Ronnie turned from the computer screens to gaze at Newton's face. "I wondered practically every bright what was keeping him in there. And when he'd be so reasonable, you were drugging him!"

"Was not. He was drugging himself. I just gave him a really nice Kai pipe, worth enough to buy my own spacecraft, by the way, and I hoped he'd use it," said Newton.

She shrugged and turned back to the screens. "It's not forcing an electro-acupuncture procedure on him, I guess." She smiled to herself. "To answer your question, the change to neurotransmission of smoking hesh will last around three phases after cessation, so ninety brights to go back to his regular self, but hesh doesn't change the brain that much. It slows some uptake, with the net effect of making a person more patient and less anxious."

Newton looked at Mot in the chamber, a thickly muscled hunk floating in a blue fluid swarming with sonic vibration waves and tiny sparks of electricity. "How long is he going to be in there?" asked Newton.

"A quarter short of a phase, those pulse wounds are serious. Perfect center to the knee so every vital structure is involved, same way for the hand, hitting where everything comes together at the wrist, Pin is good shot. All that tissue will have to be rebuilt. It may take a phase. We'll see. Did you ever isolate the medical from the main computer?" asked Ronnie.

"Yes, and I cleaned up all the drives."

Ronnie paused out of habit but remembered Newton was very good at picking up past conversations. "Were there any suspicious connections between our mysterious mission and the main computer?"

"Possibly," said Newton, "as there were clusters of ride-along code. The code wasn't embedded, sort of added on as an afterthought. It also didn't change anything but it did send a report to the main computer. And then the main computer might've responded with changes." Newton suddenly had an urge to go to the bio-cell to replenish his supply of rag and hesh, as Mot was no longer preventing it.

Ronnie's voice sounded worried when she asked, "Any chance we'll figure out what the destination was?"

"Encrypted, but if I figure out the key, I'll get it. The weird thing is how much data I can account for; it's mostly all regular stuff. The file of our secret mission is not that big or it's being held in a separate source."

"I've been meaning to ask you something," said Ronnie. "It may sound a little accusatory but it's really not. And not because what's done is done; it's because I am just curious."

Newton smiled and said, "Now that I'm properly prepared, what's your question?"

"Why were we traveling for phases without you knowing we were off course?" She laughed and added, "Phrasing notwithstanding."

"The faster you are moving, the smaller the spot where you can see, and when you're in the beam you're blind, so the phase we were coasting the navigation spot was microscopically small and empty."

"That navigation spot, is it directly ahead?" asked Ronnie.

"Yes, absolutely true destination, and everything else is distortion."

She asked, "Even behind, the absolute place you're traveling from?"

Newton nodded his head before saying, "That spot is even smaller. There's a gravitational lens effect both front and back, but it's worse looking reverse because mechanical flight isn't stable when you're ripping through space and time, which you are when you get close to the speed of light."

"So you didn't actually cause the collision because you couldn't really see where we were going," said Ronnie.

"I caused the collision by not decelerating immediately out of the beam. The mission said to slow down and then let the computer take us somewhere for almost two revolves. That seemed like a waste of time, but at the speed we were traveling, with our longest sensor reach, there wasn't enough time. If I hadn't been right there, we'd be dead. If I hadn't broke procedure by turning the shields on and the stabilizers off, we'd be dead again because the shock went to the engines instead of tearing through the hull."

Ronnie turned and looked at him again. "So that's why you were practically living on the bridge once we were out of the beam?"

"Yes, and no 'practically' about it. I was living on the bridge. I'd turn off the alarms if I was close to the helm, but if more than a stride away, alarms on."

Ronnie further tested Newton's memory. "But you violated a direct order from the Captain with that collision."

He quirked half his face for a few seconds and said, "Save it or make sure we die?"

"Right, you crippled us in the Big Black."

"I thought saving the crew was the most important thing. Next time I'll save the ship or make sure we die."

She let her eyes start a smile that finished on her lips. "I'll go with Pin's take on this: You found a living world." The smile faded. "What's going to happen for the three-quarters of a phase that Mot's in this chamber?"

Newton shook his head and also gave a short shrug of one shoulder. "I don't think I could go through another separation, so we are sticking with military division of duties and personnel." He shook his head. "The grief you all put me through, you with your reasoning body slams, Pin with her tears during casual conversation, Omni with the smell of sadness and rage when she's being polite, that shit was heart breaking. I'm not going through that again a phase from now," grumbled Newton.

Ronnie let go a nervous gasp. "We really worked you over. Sorry about that. We were just so happy." She dropped her gaze to an empty space below the screens. "Really didn't know that every bright could be filled with nothing but joy, bright after bright, quarter-phase after quarter-phase. But, you were right. When I touched Mot's neck for a pulse, when you just grabbed him to transfer to the gurney, we couldn't have done that without some time as a buffer, and I don't blame you for not wanting to put everybody through that again, because…" Ronnie's voice carried a hint of anger. "We sure don't want to corrupt our lives with being happy."

Newton laughed. "Nowhere near as important as getting in a dig despite all practical considerations," said Newton. He started out of sickbay while adding, "The blink that Mot is stable, please check on your other patient."

"We should talk about that," said Ronnie in a voice that would carry the distance.

He stopped with an exasperated huff. "What?"

"Later," said Ronnie. "For the meantime, you need to talk to me before you visit Omni."

Newton turned to look back at Ronnie. "What the dork is that supposed to mean?"

She stared back. "Not now, but later, if she goes into a healing phase, you need to talk to me before you go in there."

"You're seriously annoying me right now," Newton said.

"Tough," replied Ronnie, "just talk to me when both of us have more patience."

Newton left sickbay, made his way to the crown, and smoked until the tension in his neck went away.

As the stars drifted on the projection layer of the windows, his thoughts drifted to Pin and a song she spontaneously created while Omni was playing a lute. They were all in the galley; Omni was plucking notes, perfect fourths with a slow, underlying meter. Pin began singing on a melody that shadowed the notes and found a direction of its own. "The stars, they follow and keep with me. The rocks and bramble stride away. Yet no matter, which star I choose, it stops and starts with my every step, and puts obstacles in front of me." And the bridge she came up with was haunting in its somber simplicity. "Why keep such distant mystery, so far in blue on black, flickering as you run from me, but next morning my star is back, there again, inconstant but steady." Pin sang the beginning verse two more times with small changes in melody and meter and then she closed with the bridge modified to resolve on a lower note. After they applauded Pin, Ronnie asked if Pin just made the song up, and she said she did. Ronnie was really upset by the idea that something so beautiful would be lost. Omni offered to write it down for Pin and gave her the sheet music a day later, written in the standard form of music notation and regular calligraphy. Pin was grateful enough to actually hug Omni's shoulder.

The drift of stars on the projection layer stopped. Pin was obviously on the bridge and exercising his orders: stopping under stealth and looking for their emptiness to go to. Newton sat in the crown and smoked the occasional cigarette for nearly an hour. He knew the serenity in the crown belied how busy Pin must have been on the bridge.

After a few cigarettes, Newton realized that Pin might be having a problem. He opened the question on his radio, "Pin Pin, you having trouble?"

Her voice was relaxed, carrying hints of affection that reminded Newton of his decision to stick with military division of duty and personnel. "We are in a cloud of wheeze, and it is dorking with my readings beyond."

"You sure it isn't methanol or cyanide?" he asked.

"I've run the scan three times. There isn't anything out there but pure ethanol and pure water."

He loved her voice and was second guessing his decision. He could have three weeks of that beautiful little chunk sleeping next to him. The thought put playful intonation into his voice when he said, "No ethyl formate for raspberry flavor?"

Pin had a little giggle in her voice when she said, "Nope, this stuff will get you drunk without even tasting it."

"Well, let's try some. Open the scoops and push to the evaporation tanks. As far as direction, get a color-spectrum image of the cloud. If it's big enough, put the cloud in between us and our former position. If the cloud is less than a phase of travel, then get out and scan for emptiness."

"Got it," said Pin. Her transmission stayed on. "How long is Mot going to be in the chamber?"

"Three-quarters of a phase, but we're keeping with military division."

"Not completely," said Pin with sweetness in her voice. "You, me and Doc are going to have meals together, again. We'll stop when it gets close to time. And I won't force you to sleep next to me. But I miss you and we are all sharing meals again. Right Doc?"

Ronnie's voice came in by radio. "Right," she said.

"Alright, but last time we went back to the rules was brutal, so keep that in mind," he said. "If I think dinners are going to create a problem, I'll shut it down," he added.

Pin's voice became harder, more resonant in the long tones, sharper at the starts and stops. "It was the princess who made us go easy on you. She said we had to respect command or we would be making you choose between love and command, and you would have to choose command. She was right, is right, about everything. But as bad as it was, it could've been worse." Pin's transmission light went out. Newton didn't know what to say. There was silence for the next several hours.

Ronnie was in sickbay, so engrossed with her work that she had no idea what time it was. Putting someone into an amniotic chamber was a complex process because the machine actually dismantled a person's body at the atomic level. It rebuilt the tissues according to the genetic code, so all the damaged cells were replaced by genetic blueprint with the elements in the fluid. The computer could actually make a person a healthier version of themselves. If a person had surgical hardware, for example, those pieces would end up at the bottom of the chamber and the bones the hardware stabilized would be in perfect condition. Mot had six skeletal repairs, five fillings in his teeth, and the signature for an autoimmune disease that would show up in a few years. Ronnie designed the computer response for each skeletal and tooth repair. The genetic repair to solve the autoimmune disease would take a week or two to implement.

Newton found his way to the engineering room that housed all the computer servers and controls. For the sake of finding the encoded secret mission, he spent hours defragmenting hard drives. The process was tedious but Newton had outfitted the room with a good stereo system and exercise equipment, so he would start a defragmenting program, exercise with background music, and then he would start the process on another drive.

Pin was the daughter of colonists, which meant she had a most unusual upbringing. The home world, Tarn, was an ecological wasteland. All agriculture was done indoors, with the uncivilized niches populated with a few dozen, disease resistant, surviving creatures—all of them ugly and dangerous.

But Pin, she was a girl who spent her childhood running barefoot in cool grass, climbing trees, tasting wild fruit and encountering wild animals. Most of the land masses on Meeri were massive deserts or frozen continents at the poles, but the islands amid Meeri's vast oceans, these places were green and full of life, tropical and isolated.

Many of the plants and animals in the bio-cell were from Meeri. After checking on and finding Omni asleep, Pin stripped down to her underwear and went hunting and gathering, a barefoot beauty with a simple, recurve bow. She spent even more time in the galley.

Pin surprised Newton and Ronnie with an invitation to dinner. They walked into the galley to a banquet of aromas, root mash with greens and bits of chicken, fermented greens and nuts, fruit salad, long grain and beans. Their molecular dehydration process allowed them to store foods indefinitely and reconstituted with really good texture and flavor, but this feast was as fresh and succulent as food could get, harvested just an hour earlier, with an infrared age generator to add a month to the fermented greens.

Halfway through the meal, all three of them realized at the same moment that they had eaten in silence, on the very brink of being overwhelmed by a flavorful bliss. They laughed together and went right back to eating.

And that was how things went for a couple of weeks. They ate meals together and occasionally spent an evening together just talking and listening to music. Pin snuggled up to Newton whenever they were together but otherwise respected their boundaries. It made him miss her more, which she knew by a touch. Her response, without words, said to be patient and happy, because he had her love in all the ways that truly mattered.

Omni did go into a state of dormancy. Her shell turned into a dull outer casing and Omni became immobile and silent. Ronnie assured Newton that this was actually a good sign. She also reminded him to check with her before going into the bio-cell. So, one day, when Newton thought to replenish his stash of hesh and rag, he stopped into sickbay. Ronnie was looking at computer screens to check on the progress of Mot's reassembly.

Newton called as he walked in, "Hey, Doc, I'm here to get the speech of what I need to know to go into the bio-cell, something about Omni, even though it's apparently fine for you and Pin to go in there, and I hear Omni's like a statue right now." He stood right next to Ronnie.

She didn't move her eyes from the screens. "Be very careful not to touch anything and take one step back," she said.

He complied. "What the hell?"

"The entire program is taking instructions, so it's all activated. One accidental button could erase all the work and probably kill the captain."

"Five hells, Doc!"

"Give me a blink, and don't move," said Ronnie. She went through a sequence of two-key commands and sighed relief. She turned to Newton. "Alright, what?"

Newton wanted to make a point. "Seriously? It would've been that easy to kill the captain?" he asked.

She widened her eyes. "Oh yeah, every cell in his body is sixty-one percent physical and thirty-nine percent energy, and they were all highlighted and waiting for instruction. Any buttons but the ones I pushed, in the proper sequence, and he's thirty blocks of organic mush. Next time I do a sequencing download, I'm locking the door to sickbay."

Newton smiled. "You are not a killer."

Ronnie's face went blank as she realized he was making reference to a conversation they had three and a half months earlier. An almost overwhelming gratitude moved the edges of her mouth and the outside of her eyes. "Shut up," she said.

"Nope, you tortured yourself and your every instinct is a healer. You could've gotten rid of Mot with a random touch of the keyboard, and you were in a panic until he was out of danger," said Newton.

Ronnie stood and with a pained look on her face said, "I want that hug now."

Newton chuckled and pulled her into a warm embrace. "I know, don't read into this," he said.

She laughed, holding his embrace. "Exactly. But, you know me better than any friend I've ever had, which is weird, because you're a man." She gave him an extra squeeze before letting go and stepping back. "Seriously," she asked, "how come you're so good at dealing with women? Are you a homosexual?"

He smiled and said, "You're the only homosexual we got on board."

"Am not," Ronnie said with a worried expression on her face. Homosexuality was condemned by the Fleet, with sanctions including demotion and discharge from service.

"Are too," Newton said with a smile.

"Am not," she repeated.

"Are too," he said with a little more certainty in the lift of his brows, added to his smile.

Ronnie cinched her brows together. "How did you know?" she asked.

"Pin said if she was ever feeling down about herself, all she had to do was touch you, because you have swoon, as she put it," said Newton.

Ronnie blushed. "Pin said I have swoon?"

"Yes, and when your friend came to say goodbye before we launched, Tillie, the look on her face was that of a lover, worried and sad and a little angry that her life is getting on a ship and may never return." He paused. "And your face said the same thing, only why are you leaving the better part of your life behind on Geddis."

Ronnie looked sadly at the floor. "It's been half a revolve and I still wonder that," she said quietly.

"So, to answer your other question, why I get along with women, without sexual tension or whatever, I've had my one perfect love." Newton shrugged. "I lost her in a transport accident, but we had six years together, and we packed a lifetime of craziness into our short time together, but I have no doubt how good love can be. Part of me is still satisfied, may always be satisfied, so I am relaxed in matters of love."

"What did she do?"

Newton paused, smiled and said, "She was a captain of a recon destroyer."

"Of the Intrepid?" asked Ronnie.

"Yeah, and that's what I mean. Every other phase we were rescuing each other from certain death, more adventures than most couples ever see, always helping each other, always ending up next to each other in sickbay after some epic battle. When Fleet demanded I be reassigned, she pirated me from the flagship that took me for duty review. She committed court marshal offenses and destroyed Fleet property to bust me out of the brig. We went on nine more missions before they demanded a hearing and then she threatened to resign her commission. That put a quick end to all the trouble from Fleet. They could not lose her. She was the most decorated captain in the history of Fleet with a mission success rate that is mythic. They decided she could be romantically involved with her first officer. And when we were evacuating civilians from a fire on a space station, the transport driver behind her loses control and cracks the hull of her shuttle. She made sure all the kids had pressure suits but there weren't enough for the adults as the fire spread from section to section on the space station."

"Amantha Hale, she gave up her pressure suit for a teenager two trips earlier," said Ronnie.

"You know that story," said Newton, sounding a little surprised.

"Yes, your crew saved four-hundred-fifty people, including the eight kids on that shuttle. Captain Hale had a nine-year-old kid sit in the co-pilot's seat, in a suit, and he docked the shuttle because she showed him how to use the radio."

Tears formed in Newton's eyes. "She definitely thought about contingencies, and I talked him in, knowing she was dead, strapped in the seat next to him."

Ronnie rubbed his shoulder. "Sorry for your loss."

"Thank you."

"It's even more of a loss that the official version doesn't make mention of the epic love between you two."

"Well, she did send audio diaries to her sister on Tarn. We're famous back home, books and movies about us."

"Really?"

"Yep, we even watched a few of the movies together. We would laugh because the real adventure was often more outlandish than the supposedly fictional one."

Ronnie nodded thoughtfully. "Could that be the reason Fleet wants you gone?"

He quirked half of his face. "Maybe, the Fleet is kind of portrayed as a bunch of bureaucratic buffoons trying to hamstring an obviously good, space conquering duo." They both laughed at the idea. "But," Newton added, "the shit we pulled, I could've spent twenty years in a brig. They recognized my contribution to our success enough to demote me from command rank to low level officer. Admiral Vital told me, privately, that they wanted to see if my promotions were because of my relationship with Captain Hale, or if I could rise on my own, so they put me back where I was when I got put on her ship." He shrugged. "I'm now a first officer again, and it took me the same three years, so I must have done it on my own."

"You're not going to report me?" asked Ronnie.

"No, not going to mention it to anyone, ever, not even to Pin. It's no one's business but yours and whoever you love."

She gave him a grateful smile. "I love you for knowing that."

"See?" he said with a grin.

Ronnie laughed. She walked toward her beverage maker while shaking her head. Raising her voice to carry across the room she asked, "So what did you want to know? I really wasn't listening, something about Pin and me and the bio-cell?"

"Yeah," he said, "I'd like to go in there and you said to talk to you first."

Ronnie said, "Come, get a cup and sit." Newton did as instructed. "When Omni comes out of her chrysalis, hormones will make her sexually aggressive. You may get sexually assaulted," said Ronnie.

"What the dork are you talking about?"

"When she comes out of that casing, survival hormones are going to be soaking her brain in supernatural concentrations. She's attracted to you, and she's three times faster and nine times stronger. Kai sexual behavior is a bit rougher in general. So, I'm thinking we may want to consider locking her in the bio-cell."

Newton gave Ronnie an incredulous stare. "So Omni doesn't sexually assault me," he said with tones of utter disbelief.

She took a deep breath and said, "I did not want to tell you this! And it's a damned tragedy, but that sweet, brilliant, gentle Omni that we knew is gone, gone for long time. Maybe we will never see her again."

Newton frowned. "You have my attention."

"We have a dilemma, because if we're going to get the sweet Omni back, we need to bring her in and socialize her back to us, but for the safety of this crew, and you, we should keep her in the bio-cell. Her memory is going to be intact, but her emotional makeup will be considerably more severe. Say, for example, Mot barks an order at her and adds an insult; she might not have the restraint she has previously demonstrated. And consideration for Pin's feelings with regard to you, that could be gone, too."

"You said she may sexually assault me. How would she rape me?"

Ronnie rolled her eyes. "You know where a wasp has its stinger?"

"Yeah, on the end of its abdomen."

"Right," said Ronnie, "that's where her sexual parts are, so instead of a stinger coming out, the exoskeleton opens, and with soft tissue, she has a space that goes in. Your phallus will respond to practically any stimulation, so she grabs you, bends her abdomen to you and bumps and brushes until you have an outy for her inny, and you're being raped by a girl. Now I'm not saying she's going to, but it would be irresponsible of me not to mention the possibility. She was so sweet that we never even had to realize that she is nine times stronger than a human. If you think you could fight her off if she wanted to have her way with you, you're wrong. We were safe only because of her kindness, and she might be a bit less kind for a while."

He took a drink of his brew. "I just wanted to go get some damned rag."

"And if she's still dormant, then that's no big deal. Have at it. But, if she's out and walking around, or flying, then you may want to let Pin harvest your rag."

"Flying?"

"Yep, Omni is going to re-emerge with a beautiful new set of wings, and her color may be slightly darker." Ronnie looked whimsical.

Continuing to make reference to earlier conversation, Newton asked, "Did you learn all this from your notes?"

"Sort of, my notes kept making reference to a book, Essential Kai, and we actually have it in our library. Not only does it have an outline of history and science compendium, but it has extensive chapters on Kai anatomy, physiology and medicine." Ronnie smiled and shook her head in amazement. "So, I heard that they may go dormant and emerge more aggressive, but after reading for three spans every dark for a half phase, I learned that the aggression has a strangely romantic character."

Newton made a puzzled frown. "Romance? Have I even seen a male Kai?"

"Sure you have. Every species has a different ratio of female to male. Mantis, it's like three girls for every boy. For spiders, ten females to every one male, wasps twenty to one, but beetles, the ratio is two to one. The Essential Kai, by the way, is a great read. There's a philosophical paragraph at the beginning of every section, some of them written by none other than our princess, and there are allegories plugged in difficult passages to make things easier to understand. Anyway, to explain the mantis ratio, Omni wrote that male mantis were fewer so they could get more attention. They couldn't create new life so their job was to help nurture the life that others created, to serve, and therefore be lavished with affection for their service. She added, with a bit of humor, that this service didn't exactly come naturally, so it needed to be encouraged."

She took a drink from her cup. "As for the practicals, a male mantis is slightly smaller, less brightly colored, and more rebellious and artistic in nature. There are some that are well educated and high in the social ranks, but they are more likely to prefer physical work, and in a couple, the male stays home and raises the children. As far as when you have seen them, pick any battle with the Kai. The males of all Kai species make up the bulk of the warriors. Not only are they more inclined to see themselves as expendable, but they like to fight. If the males were in charge, we'd still be fighting that war, because that was the most fun the planet has had in more than a thousand revolves."

"So the females were the higher ranks, the strategists, and the foot-soldiers were the males?" asked Newton.

"Yes, generally, but there's a difference between species; spiders, for example, females are also stupid."

"Which is the smartest kind of insect on Kai?" asked Newton.

"Mantis, with wasps, including ants, a close second, but mantis are the smartest. Mantis were first to evolve, first to build, first to have a written language, first to develop sophisticated technologies. They are about a hundred revolves ahead of us in all significant technologies, with a faster curve from fire to gravity propulsion. The energy beam that got us out here as well as the amnio chamber are based on Kai mathematics. The amnio chamber is experimental. We shouldn't even have one but I called in every favor my service could generate, including giving up a chunk of my pension to have the chamber. The Kai formulas unified matter and energy and quantum mechanics. We had been searching for a unified field theory for centuries. The Kai have had one for centuries. "

Newton nodded thoughtfully. "No wonder they won the war."

Ronnie scoffed, "We're lucky we stopped before we actually made them angry. They had plans and the ability to destroy Space Harbor Chastain. That would've been half of Fleet."

"If they got past our defenses," he said.

Ronnie rolled her eyes. "We didn't know they knew where it was, so imagine a few thousand Kai warships with impenetrable shields all appearing at strategic places at the same instant, all with crews that stay awake for seventy spans, with fuel and food to keep going for several revolutions, meaning they just keep going until we were exterminated. Haza told me that was the plan, but you and Omni kept trying to force a peace." Ronnie's face went blank and drained of color. "It's so strange to have you here, the one who saved countless lives, maybe our entire civilization, but those in power want to steal credit for the peace, so you're treated like an embarrassment, made to disappear. And Omni is here, too, the other one. And I'll bet they somehow made it easier for her to stowaway. Now they can rewrite the history. It's maddening," Ronnie concluded.

Newton smiled. "You once told me it hurts less if you don't stop. In this case, I disagree."

Ronnie smiled with a little pink coming back in her face. "Follow the story. You're alive, away from the deceivers. Omni's here with us; she's the reason the Guardians didn't destroy us, so the joke's on the manipulative assholes."

Newton had a question from an earlier part of their discussion. "So, are they smarter than us or just technologically ahead of us?"

"The Essential Kai answered that, too," answered Ronnie. "We used to think they were smarter, but it's just that their sensory input updates three times faster, so they see and hear and move faster, but if you solve for that, they fall on the smart side of normal, just like us, same distribution curve, regular is still smart, smarter is amazingly smart, same number of brain cells and connection matrix."

He gave her a thoughtful frown and asked, "Any appreciable differences?"

She smiled before saying, "That was a smart question, Newton. Only one, our brains are wired through the limbic system in such a way that we have an emotional state, near constantly, that they rarely if ever feel." Ronnie paused for a lift of her eyebrows. "Can you guess what it is?" she asked.

He thought for a second and with certainty in his voice, said, "Fear."

"Right," said Ronnie, "key to our evolution and survival, the most dangerous mind-state for a culture, the key to mind control, fear, and they rarely feel it. I remember the way Omni talked to the Guardians, such a clear thinker facing death. That's a very important difference, a fundamental difference."

"Yeah, like she could risk our lives with hers."

"Or," said Ronnie, "she doesn't like us because she fears loneliness. She's not nice because she's worried we won't like her. She doesn't cooperate from conditioning to authority or negative consequences. She genuinely cares, wants us to be happy. She does good for all the right reasons." Ronnie glanced across sickbay to notice one of the screens showing a line trailing off one half of a growing banner. "By the gods!" she exclaimed. The line jiggled to indicate a sound wave, then the line went flat again.

The line also responded to Newton saying, "What?" Without answering, Ronnie crossed to the computer console and threw a sequence of switches. Newton crossed to her and asked again, "What?"

She put her hand to her forehead. "Download triggered input," she whispered.

"What input?"

"Us input. Mot heard us talking. He's going to remember us talking."

"Can he hear us now?"

Ronnie shook her head but kept her voice low. "No, but I turned off ambient microphones. I keep them on because background sounds reduce disorientation, but there's no way to predict when the computer will allow an input, or for how long."

"So what did it catch?"

"No way to tell, it says three-hundred parcel bits, so about twenty parcel bits per sweep, so around fifteen sweeps before I caught it. That isn't all of our conversation, but it's most of it." Ronnie's face got a look of terror. "We talked about my secret," she whispered.

"Doc, that was like thirty sweeps ago, before we moved over there to have a cup of brew, when you were in front of the screen, which you would've noticed. And our conversations are epic, so that was more like forty sweeps ago." He smiled. "Mot could learn a lot from listening to us, learn what life would be like if he only had a little more patience." Newton laughed alone at first but Ronnie eventually did, also.

After a pause, she quietly said, "Busters kill homosexuals."

Also quietly, Newton said, "A hundred revolves ago that was true, but only the men. Females have a protected status; behaviorally, sexually, they get a lot of latitude that even includes that."

Skepticism wrinkled Ronnie's forehead. "Are you sure about that?"

"Positive, look it up."

"Look at you, educating me," said Ronnie.

"Yeah well, you might've been the smartest person in the room through every doorway you've gone, but you can't know everything," said Newton.

A sheepish smile formed on her face. "I've been too paranoid to do much research about that subject, not electronically, and it's hard to find a library with actual, paper books."

Chapter IX: Escape of Desire

Newton was reading in bed when the bell rang and he heard his front door slide open. He looked up from his book and saw Pin walking in wearing a sleep dress and a smile. He tossed his book to the floor next to the bed and said, "Explain."

She continued in and sat on his bed, still wearing a demure smile. "Doc says Mot gets out in a quarter, so we get tonight."

"He's been in for a phase, which is a quarter longer than she said already," Newton said with a smirk.

"Doc says he's gonna get crackles in a few revolves, so she's fixing it."

"She can fix a complex, autoimmune disease?" he asked.

"Yeah, just takes more time."

Newton got a sly look and asked, "Are we sure we don't want Mot to suffer a crippling and painful disease?"

Pin giggled. "She didn't even consider it."

He turned off his reading light. "Come here, Beautiful Blue." He pulled up the bed sheet and Pin snuggled into him. They simultaneously closed their eyes and breathed the same peaceful sigh. They relaxed for a while before Newton asked, "So, what's the idea, here? We spend the dark together and then go back to isolation for a quarter phase?"

"Sort of," said Pin. "I'm not the only one who is lonely." Newton was processing the statement when Pin brought her hand up and placed it gently on his face. He got an image of Ronnie waiting in the hallway and, with the shimmer of an imaginary image, the picture of all three of them in the bed.

He hesitated with indecision and then said, "Fine," with mild misgivings in his voice. Newton scooted over in the bed to make more room.

Pin followed him and lay on top of him, and with straightened arms, held her face just above his, gazing directly into his eyes in the darkened room. "Thank you, Newton. I love you." She lowered her lips to his. The moist softness of their first kiss was instantly arousing. She ran the tip of her tongue between the press of their lips before inviting his tongue into her mouth. They each swooned into the kiss until they had to stop. She lay on top of him, quietly panting and letting things settle. They spontaneously chuckled together. "You got it going on," she whispered.

"It's you, Little Blue, and I love you, too."

"I know you do, and you've been very patient." They heard the door slide open. While Pin moved to the middle of the bed, she whispered, "So have I."

Ronnie came into the room wearing matching pajama shorts and shirt. She hesitated at a place in the room where she could either go toward the bed or slink off into the spare room. "We have one shot at the loneliness therapy," said Pin, "and it's right here, next to me." Ronnie made her choice by going closer to the bed but she hesitated yet again. "We promise to be polite, and I will stay in the middle, but you need the warmth of sleeping next to someone," said Pin. She lifted the bed linens. Ronnie smiled shyly and got into the bed.

After they found their sleeping positions, Pin thought of something and said, "Newton, I forgot to tell you; there's a trajectory detection on the scan."

"It is a ship?" he asked.

"Yep, point zero nine sub-light, straight as a laser," said Pin.

"What trajectory?"

Pin hesitated and then said, "I looked at your calculations on the light boards; it was our trajectory before the collision."

"What?"

"Our trajectory, we cleared the path, so it went straight through."

Newton asked, "Any signal?"

"No," answered Pin, "traveling in stealth, small."

"How did you see if it was under stealth?" asked Ronnie.

"Because of our position," said Pin. "We're a third-thousandth parsec directly above the star, the center of the system. And," hesitated Pin, "the stealth was the same energy waves we use." She repositioned herself to lay on her stomach.

"Strange," said Newton.

"Is there any way they saw us?" asked Ronnie, sounding worried.

"No," answered Pin. "We are stealth and absolutely still, in deep dark, with nothing behind us. Moving that fast makes them more visible and it closes off where they can see." Pin stirred in the bed and settled on her side with a hand gently caressing Ronnie's forehead. "Even if they stopped and scanned, I doubt they'd see us. We are seriously in the middle of nowhere out here, power equilibrium, stealth at near perfection. Probably the only thing that could find us is one of those neutrino scans that the Guardians use."

"What could that mean, though, following our trajectory, using our style of stealth?" asked Ronnie. Neither Pin nor Newton answered, both hoping the question would just fade away. Ronnie's tone spiked with more urgency when she asked, "What's a bolt?"

"Damn it," whispered Newton. His voice carried both anger and worry. "Doc got that from you, didn't she, Blue?"

"Sorry," whispered Pin.

Newton huffed and said, "Well, Doc, you're fascinated by touch communication, what did you see?"

"Pin was stroking my hair, and when her fingers touched my forehead, I saw her look at you and say a word, which I didn't hear but felt my mouth and throat say 'bolt'."

Newton tried a diversion. "Is touch communication supposed to work that well?"

"Everyone in Fleet is profiled and rated for potential clairvoyance," answered Ronnie. "Much of it in the annual psychological test, and command thinks it's bunk, incidentally. Most of us are a one or two; Pin's the top potential, a solid five, so, in her case, touch communication is going to work exceptionally well, if there's anything to it." Ronnie's tone became serious. "So, now that I've answered your question, what in the five hells is a bolt?" Pin pulled back her hand as if Ronnie's head was hot to the touch.

Newton answered, "It's a theoretical ship, from the clandestine services of Fleet, that gets sent to kill defectors, or destroy ships that go rogue. They are nothing more than myth, according to command."

They all laid there in isolated silence. After a few minutes, Ronnie broke the silence. "Myths don't show up as detector traces."

"It doesn't make sense to put us on a ship if they just wanted to kill us," said Newton.

"It does if they're keeping up appearances. They start skimping, a review would catch it and trigger an investigation. But they get us on the other side of the Black, nine revolves between transmission and reply by radio contact, the mission could get us, and they send a bolt to make sure," concluded Ronnie.

Newton lay in bed with his eyes closed. "That's paranoid," he muttered.

Ronnie chuckled. "Which doesn't mean they aren't after us."

Newton also chuckled. He yawned and drifted off to sleep. Ronnie fell asleep soon after Newton. Pin, however, lay awake for quite a while, with her large eyes open and shining in the dark.

At some point in the night, Newton turned onto his side and found Pin's hand. She smiled and held his hand. Their breathing synchronized as they fell back asleep.

Coming out of the night's sleep, Newton felt refreshed but something pulled him back to a dream-state. At least it felt like he was dreaming, but the imagery was from his present moment, lying next to Pin, with Ronnie next to her. He felt Pin's hand as the imagery gently transformed into the same hand, his hand holding Pin's hand, flowing down Pin's arm and to her small breast, which immediately responded to his touch. He relished both the sensual imagery and the subjective feel of her body. For several minutes, image and sensation interchanged until a new image faded into view, both the silky slide and image of Pin pulling up her sleep dress. The imagination took Newton's hand to flow over Pin's body, seeing her by touch and feel. For a long time his fingers caressed and explored the small and intimate contours, and when the moist warmth enveloped his finger, the sensation was so convincing that Newton had to open his eyes to check if it was actually happening.

He was lying next to Pin, just holding her hand, and Ronnie was holding Pin's other hand. Pin pulled her hand from his and softly covered his eyes before taking his hand again. With his eyes closed, they went back to the intimate touch. A shimmering image of how to stimulate her by a tapping touch with his thumb as her body tightly held a finger of the same hand. Newton could sense her strength as her back began to arch and her waist flex involuntarily. Waves of imaginary pressure moved up and down his spine. Pin's writhing stopped. Her breathing clicked in erratic starts and stops.

Newton narrowly opened his eyes and saw both Pin's and Ronnie's faces fluttering between intense pleasure and pain, their bodies stuttering in a suspended ecstasy. He closed his eyes again. He lay next to the women, listening as their breathing slowly returned to normal, silently marveling how imagination could trigger an actual orgasm.

They drifted back to sleep for another hour. They roused to have breakfast and return to their respective duties, and no one mentioned what happened during their one night all three of them spent together. The only hint of what happened was the sly crinkle Pin's eyes would get sometimes when talking to Newton. Ronnie's demeanor changed toward both Pin and Newton. The stiffness was gone, the brittleness in her voice, gone. Ronnie felt comfortable enough to touch both of them in casual interactions.

Once they were back into their military division of duties and rank, they saw each other less and less. Ronnie put the finishing touches on Mot's recovery. Pin worked on Engine No. 1, casting and machining parts. Pin wished she had Omni's help.

Newton got used to going into the bio-cell and seeing Omni encased in a dull brown shell, so when he went in, he didn't even check. What struck him was going from the light of the hallway to the darkness of night. With stealth, the clarity of the window walls showed the star-scape and ring of starlit asteroids above the jungle. Pin parked the spaceship upside down to the star, Newton realized. "Bio-cell, working point lights," called Newton. He checked his watch to see it was the last minutes of the thirtieth hour. Small lamps brightened spots on the staircase and in certain places in the rocks and jungle. Newton went in and climbed the hill to the ravine with the hesh grove.

Three terror birds near an escarpment perked their heads as Newton came into the ravine. The largest, a male, stood up and moved between the other birds and Newton. The weak light from a point on the escarpment showed red and green feathers on the terror bird's collar at the base of its long, thick, short feathered neck. Newton pulled the stun gun and placed the red target dot on the bird's chest.

Surprisingly, the bird looked at the dot and responded by sitting down. "Good decision," said Newton, holstering the stun gun.

He harvested some hesh by pulling buds off the bottom branches of certain plants, occasionally casting a wary eye toward the terror bird. Pocket filled with the last of the mature buds, Newton walked from the ravine and followed the small lights down the path.

A rapid chopping noise and a gust of air moved in front of him. Newton froze in the path, searching the dark silhouettes of scrub and tall trees. He started down the path again, his hand on the stun gun. The scent of apple blossoms and musk stopped him, stopped him in a strategically bad spot under a large tree. He looked up along the tree trunk and in the darkness, he could barely make out a familiar face. Omni. She was holding onto the trunk upside down, looking at him. A pungent, unfamiliar, tangy sweetness hit Newton's sinuses so strongly that he almost felt light headed. The physical sense was overtaken by an emotional upwelling. He had no idea how worried about her he was, how much he missed her.

Stone still, upside down, the mantis gazed at him. Newton showed open, empty hands and walked slowly closer to the tree. In the dimness of night, he saw Omni's head follow his steps. "Good dezishion," said Omni. Her voice was different, colder, even more mechanical.

"Omni, come down here, please."

The human sized insect clicked backward as if she felt the sound wave of Newton's voice. Omni didn't say anything but her wing covers snapped slightly open, and the scent became even stronger.

Surprised at the sound of his own voice, Newton begged, "Please, Omni, please come down and talk to me, please."

A motion blur condensed into Omni standing straight and statue still on the path in front of him. She was smaller, thinner, darker, her calico pattern of green, orange and black stronger, the pearlescent white of her front now more gray. "What?" said Omni.

Newton swallowed back a wave of fear. "Omni," he said, "I want to touch you."

She tipped her head as her wings fanned open. "Why?" asked Omni.

"Because I was so worried about you. I miss you. You're my friend."

"Zovtin, I can't zmell what you veel," said Omni. "How I know you vriend?"

"I love you. I've told you that before. I've held you before. Trust me now," said Newton.

Omni's wings folded back under and the shell closed. "Yez," she said.

Newton slowly stepped forward, gently, carefully wrapped his arms around her. He thought about how she was the one who, with his help, stopped a war. The worlds had her to thank for millions of lives, and they almost lost her. Tears of gratitude reached his eyes. Even Ronnie's warning about Omni possibly being a danger didn't dampened his gratitude.

Omni felt the slight tremble in his body, smelled the chemical trace of tears. She pulled back from the embrace enough to look at his face. "What'z thiz? Zovtin cry?"

"Stop calling me that," whispered Newton.

The smell of an approaching rainstorm, gratitude, flooded the air around them. "Newtin," said Omni.

He gazed at her. "Yes, you saved millions of lives. The universe isn't right without you in it. And I thought we lost you."

"Did, almozt lozt," said Omni. She stepped back from his embrace. "Zome lozt," she added, looking away.

Shaking his head in denial, Newton grabbed her claw, knowing his movement would need to be quick and insistent, and she did start to pull away before she sensed his determination. "Nothing is lost," he stated emphatically. "You are here. I will help you. Doc will help you. Pin will help you. Give it some time. You just need to remember."

Omni looked at his hand holding hers. "Maybe," she said.

"What do you need?" he asked.

"I need to think. I need to rezt. I need my toolz, big box in room." She paused. "I need you to let go hand."

Newton let go but asked, "Why, don't you like me anymore?"

She gazed at him for an awkward moment. Finally, she said, "You warm, like vood."

He was oddly amused by the idea of Omni being reduced to such a primitive state. Really, a sophisticated being who helped her end a war, just food? "Well, you get to stay in here, and evolve, but if you eat me, you will be undoing a lot of good, because this tasty morsel was the guy who helped you stop that war." He laughed. "Seriously, there are a lot of critters in here, and I'm sure that none of them helped you elevate the character of civilization."

A waft of the cinnamon smell, humor, lilted past his nose but quickly faded. "You underztand. I will ztay in here. You bring my toolbox."

"Anything else?" asked Newton.

"Don't let Mot in here. I kill." Omni stepped back, snapped open her wing covers and launched into the air. The chopping sound faded as Omni disappeared above the dark canopy. "Thank you!" Omni called from a distance.

"Thank you for being alive!" Newton called back. He shook his head, walked down the path and out of the bio-cell. Outside in the hallway, he changed the door setting, turning off the automatic opener, requiring a pass-code to exit and enter, one number, 9. If Omni thought hard enough, evolved to her true self enough, she should be able to think of that. He got a marker from his uniform pocket and started to write a nine on the wall but stopped himself. No, Ronnie or Pin would have to talk to him before getting into the bio-cell.

Newton set off toward Omni's suite in the ambassador wing. If the goal was to help Omni evolve back to the beautiful soul he remembered, then giving her the toolbox could help. She said that she was building robots before he was even walking. He knew that the difference in their ages made that impossible, she being the equivalent of twenty-four revolves old and him fifteen revolutions older, but the point was the Kai were exposed to engineering in early childhood. So, her therapy would include some engagement with whatever she wanted to do with her tools.

Once in Omni's suite, in the kitchen, Newton was looking at a toolbox that was more the size of a travel trunk, and next to the tool trunk was a stack of sheet metal, coils of different gauges of metal, a bench mounted roll press, and what looked like a small smelter and metal foundry. Newton went and got a warehouse truck, loaded it with all the engineering stuff, and he also went into the bedroom and found a suitcase full of Omni's clothes. There were more of her clothes in the dresser drawers, but the packed suitcase had her crown jewels, finery and favorite outfits. Apparently, if she were to leave in a hurry, these were the things Omni would always want with her.

He put her suitcase with the engineering stuff and took it all to the bio-cell loading dock. Again, he set the bay door to require a pass-code before pushing the truck onto the landing of the ground floor. As the bay door opened, Omni came flying out of the darkness of the jungle. She picked up the tool trunk as if it weighed nothing and walked off to an alcove in the rocks. Newton remembered what a struggle it was to get it on the warehouse truck, being able to only lift one side at a time, and this spindly creature just picked it up and walked away, leaving footprints pushed deeply into the jungle floor. He put the portable foundry, the sheets and coils of metal, and the roll press on the ground, and Omni would come back and carry them to her place in the rocks. She came back and Newton held out the suitcase. Omni accepted it with the smell of gratitude in the air. "You more than food," she said quietly, and then she walked to her spot in the rocks. Newton smiled, turned, pulled the warehouse truck out of the botanical cell and secured the bay door.

Omni opened her suitcase and turned on a built-in light. She pushed aside her clothing and found the small computer tablet at the bottom. Touching a sequence of icons, she was soon looking at photographs that she took with her jewelry camera. There were pictures of Ronnie, Pin, and Newton. Omni wanted this suitcase, she realized, more than her tools, but she wasn't thinking clearly enough to ask for it. Newton just knew to bring it somehow. She turned off the tablet computer, closed the suitcase, collapsed to the ground and fell asleep.

Ronnie was on the first rotation, hours one through ten, so there really wasn't anyone else to call to announce the momentous event. She hit the switch that drained the amniotic chamber. She touched the radio on her uniform. "Um, if anybody's awake, I thought you should know, Captain Mot is being born, and will be walking and talking in a span or two," Ronnie announced.

"Omni was just reborn, too," announced Newton's voice.

Ronnie blinked with surprised. "You saw her?"

"Yeah, I brought her some of her tools and secured the doors to the bio-cell."

"You alright?" asked Ronnie.

"Yes," replied Newton, "she just emerged, and she's in a primitive state of consciousness, said my warmth reminded her of food, so we're going to let get her bearings." He paused and added, "And we need to keep Mot out of there. She said she'd kill him. I believe her, so let's be careful as we coax her back to us."

Pin's voice came in on the radio. "What's the code to get in?" she asked.

There was a pause. Newton said, "Not sure I want to tell you."

"That's crap," said Pin. "I miss her. I need her help. I am going to help coax her back, just as good as you can."

That wasn't exactly true, thought Newton. He replied, "Not over the radio, you and Doc, face to face, I'll tell you the pass-code."

"We do need to be careful," said Ronnie. "This phase of her healing, she's going to be different than we remember her. She is going to need time while her brain chemistry recovers, and in the core of her mind, we are the warm blooded prey of her primordial self. And she's faster and stronger than even the captain. If she wanted to kill him, she would've, easily. Her mind will clear, but it will take a couple of phases."

"Phases?" asked Pin.

"Yes. She could be functional sooner, but that gentle Omni we knew, it could be a long time before she's back."

With an emotional constriction in her voice, Pin sobbed, "I miss her."

"I know, Pin," soothed Ronnie, "I miss her, too. And we're really lucky we didn't lose her. If she didn't have the bio-cell, immediately, she probably would've died, so this is good, but it's going to take some time."

Pin sounded sad but accepted the situation with a single word, "Alright."

Newton went back to the original topic. "Well, since everybody's up, put in a management meeting at the tenth span, to brief the captain from all departments. Doc, you figure out a way to tell Mot that the bio-cell is off limits."

"Thanks," said Ronnie.

"What's it going to do for Omni's recovery if she kills and eats the Captain?" Newton asked with a humorous ring in his voice.

"Good point," Ronnie conceded.

Mot awoke feeling refreshed. The cover of the amnio-chamber was open and he had a towel covering his naked body. Across sickbay, he saw the doctor working on something with her back to him. There was a chair with his undergarments, uniform, sox and boots, and the equipment belt that he always wore. The belt wasn't part of the uniform; it was just something he always wore. She must have gotten it from the canopy of the bio-cell. It even included his knife, the one Pin threw into the pond. He must still be in command, he thought.

Mot sat up on the slab. There were no scars on his arms or body. Mot looked at a large glass jar next to the chair. He recognized the plate and screws that held his femur together, another set of orthopedic hardware from his back. Mot took a deep breath and stretched, with no pain. He couldn't remember a time when he didn't have some pain.

"Please let me help you stand," called Ronnie.

"Hurry up, then," said Mot.

"Impatience, that's a good sign." She typed a few more things on a keyboard. Mot interpreted the finishing touches on what Ronnie was doing as a reason to ignore her request. He stood, but his vision went gray and he fell back to the amnio-chamber slab. Ronnie rushed over to him, putting on gloves as she crossed sickbay. "You're so dorking willful," she exclaimed. She just reached him in time to grab his arm to keep Mot from rolling off the slab.

"Why can't I stand?" demanded Mot.

"You need to turn your hydrostatic switch back on," said Ronnie. She caught both hands and pulled with all her body weight, leaning back at a severe angle, to get him sitting up on the slab. "Look at me." She checked his eyes. "To turn that switch back on, take a deep breath, hold it, tighten your stomach until you feel pressure in your head, then exhale." She placed both of his hands on the slab. "Do it," she ordered.

Mot gave her a look, followed her instructions until his head turned red and veins bulged in his neck and temples. He exhaled a huge puff of air and felt a few stronger beats of his heart.

"Now, take a normal breath, hold it, pinch your nose closed, push the air, not too hard, and release it quickly by opening your mouth as wide as it'll go." Mot, again, gave her a look to suggest he wondered if she was messing with him. "Please, it'll help," she said. He followed her instructions and heard a creaking sound in his head. "One more and we're done," said Ronnie. "With your shoulders straight, shake your head wide and slowly, for ten blinks." Mot began and Ronnie counted, "One, two, three, four, five, six, seven, eight, nine, ten." Mot stopped. "Good, now, how do you feel?" Mot nodded. "Then let's try standing again, but if you feel dizzy, just sit back down."

Mot stood, dropping the towel to his feet. Even though he was standing nude in front of her, Ronnie was watching for signs of unsteadiness, marveling at the physical presence of the man, more than twice her width at the shoulder, three times her weight in skeletal and muscle mass. Mot stood and moved his broad, muscled shoulders, sampling and appreciating the limberness in his back.

"Good," said Ronnie. "Go ahead and get dressed." She walked back to her computers and stood, occasionally pushing a sequence of commands, watching one of the screens.

Getting dressed, continuing to appreciate the ease of movement, Mot spoke so his voice would carry across sickbay. "When do I address the crew?"

"There's a management meeting at the tenth span, all departments are giving you their reports."

"What total time is it?" asked Mot.

Ronnie hesitated while looking at the clock and said, "Mission time, fifth phase and second quarter phase, third bright, seventh span, forty-fifth sweep."

Surprise stopped Mot mid-motion. "Why was I in for so long?"

"I needed to rebuild both knees and a hand. You also had tags for crackles, so I needed to fix a place in the strand, in every cell of your entire body," said Ronnie.

"Crackles?"

"The pain in your elbows, hands, back, ankles, all that was going to get progressively worse," said Ronnie. "Did you have a grandparent with crackles?"

Mot nodded and said, "Yes," remembering his grandfather, starting life strong and formidable but stooped and crippled his later years.

"It usually skips a generation."

Mot strapped on his equipment belt. "It's impossible to fix a genetic disease."

"Not impossible," she replied casually. "If you have an amniotic chamber and spend about nine-hundred spans doing computer modifications to the strands. I haven't gotten much sleep for the last phase."

Mot was listening but was also noticing the painless range of motion in his wrists. "Gracile," he commanded, "look at me." Ronnie turned at the shoulder and looked at Mot with the same forced patience she always had dealing with him.

"Why not just fix the wounds?"

Ronnie gazed at him a moment and shrugged her shoulders. "It was a challenge. Changing every strand was theoretically possible when the Kai gave us the different components of the amnio-chamber, but it's never been done before. If we were back in the worlds, I'd be famous, probably get an Enterprise Commission."

He held her gaze. "Never done? Was it dangerous?"

"Yes, I saved your life probably ten times a bright, but I gave you twenty more revolves of life," she said. "And, since the pain was causing you to grind your teeth while you slept, I rebuilt those, too."

For the first time ever, Mot looked at Ronnie with eyes showing respect. "Any chance this goes wrong and I sprout another head or something?"

"Nope, I was very careful. That's why it took so long."

Mot's face actually softened to a brief but unmistakable expression of appreciation. "Thank you, Doctor Chamberlain," he said quietly.

"You're welcome," she answered. Ronnie turned back to face the computer screens and hide her astonishment.

Mot walked over and stood next to her, looking at the graceful woman who saved his life ten times a day, saved him from decades of degeneration and pain. It was confusing, this grace, skinny like a child, tall like an adult. She looked so fragile, so tall and thin he wondered how it could stay upright, more like a stalk of wheat than a person, pretty face, though, sky-blue eyes, golden hair. Speaking gently, Mot said, "You don't like me. You're not getting famous out here. Why save my life ten times a bright?"

Ronnie let go a deep sigh. "It's what I do. I'm a doctor. I heal people."

Mot waited, a smile forming on his face. "So, that was the good stuff," he said, "so tell what you don't want to tell me."

She gave him a sidelong glance. "The bio-cell is off limits. We have immunity. You don't."

"Immunity from what?"

"Omni went through a healing process. Because we were around while she pupated, we can go in there. You weren't, so it's dangerous for you."

Mot sensed something and said, "You're lying." He then grabbed Ronnie's delicate wrist with his bare fingertips. He caught some fragmented images of Omni in a brown shell, of Pin in a medical suit, and then he saw a stronger image of Ronnie's hands placing the Kai pipe in the box and putting the box on desk in his room, on the desk next to two jars, one full of hesh, one full of rag. The image distracted Mot enough to allow Ronnie to pull free of Mot's fingers.

Ronnie stepped back with an angry flush on her face. "If you don't believe me, go in there and die and waste all the dorking time I spent saving your life."

After seeing the forced patience come back on the doctor's face, Mot nodded and walked out of sickbay. He loved the bounce in his steps and the freedom of walking through the ship. When Mot got to his quarters, a living space he hadn't seen in months, he found the box, with the pipe, right there on his desk with the jars of hesh and rag. Mot loaded the pipe and smoked hesh, then rag, and spent an hour showering and grooming, tending to months away from a mirror. His hair cut in the bio-cell was to take the electric razor to his face and head. This left fine bristles sprouting around his nostrils and the tragus of his ears. His month in the amnio-chamber gave him a half inch of dark green hair on his head, which he kept.

Mot arrived three minutes after the appointed time. Pin, Ronnie and Newton stood at attention as the captain walked up to the command table at the top tier of the bridge. Although it hadn't been worked out before that moment, Pin and Newton wore their administrative level uniforms, with insignia and regulation footwear. Even Mot had forsaken the equipment belt for the belt with the strap that went over one shoulder. He nodded and everyone took a seat at the big table.

"Engineering report," said Mot.

Pin sat up and said, "Engine One is completely dismantled. Omni was about to make a handheld X-ray spectrometer, which would make the process go much faster. She also found cracks in nine places computer modeling missed. I really need her help. Without it, estimated time of completion is ten phases."

"This ship and mission is designed for you to work alone," said Mot. He turned to Ronnie. "Medical officer's report, include details concerning the conscript in the bio-cell."

"Our engineer, first officer and I have all been on oral supplement to reverse the slight genetic damage caused by fragmentation disease. Your fragmentation disease was reversed while you were in the amnio-chamber."

"What fragmentation disease?" interrupted Mot.

Ronnie picked up one eyebrow. "From being in the beam for six revolves," she said.

Mot's face didn't reveal whether this was a surprise. "Continue report."

"Sickbay is down six percent on irreplaceable compounds, not even a half revolve into the mission, but both Pin and you required some extraordinary measures. As for the conscript, the bio-cell is essential to her healing process, which has completed a critical term. The one thing to note is she will be volatile for a few phases," reported Ronnie.

"Define volatile," said Mot.

"Her personality is changed by the healing process. She will be duty-ready in a quarter phase, probably, but she will be angry and impatient. The reason to note this is because if she became combative, we would not be able to subdue her, so I would recommend we not assign work for three quarter phases, and nurture a transition back to duty."

Mot looked annoyed. "Recommendation noted," said Mot. He turned to Newton. "First officer's report."

Newton chewed on his bottom lip for a second. "We are parked fifty marks above the axis of the star. The uncharted system is stable, four billion revolves in age, three billion left on the star, one live planet. We engaged with a hostile force known as the Guardians, technologically far superior but they demonstrated an interest in keeping the conscript alive, and we should assume we are being monitored. There was also a ship's signature following our trajectory with our form of stealth. We were undetected," said Newton. After a brief pause, he added, "Other than Engine One, the ship is in good shape, Engine Two running better than specifications on all outputs; ship stores above projections; biomass in the bio-cell is back to pre-collision health; computer systems are back to optimum."

"What's the rotation?" asked Mot.

"Doc is on first rotation. I'm on the second. Pin's on third."

Mot nodded slowly. "Who's on galley?"

"Doc has been on galley for phases, but we rotate the duty on an informal basis."

"How much of that informality has been going on?" asked Mot.

"Some," said Newton without hesitation. "We have shared meals together, but we've been extremely busy so we drifted back to military division for about a half phase."

Mot looked at Pin but asked Newton a shocking question. "Who was Pin's caring hand after she got mercury poisoning?"

Again, Newton did not hesitate. "I was," said Newton.

Mot frowned through a thoughtful pause. "Did the doctor explain the need for that?"

"Yes."

"Did you cross the line to abomination?" asked Mot with an angry glare at Newton.

"No."

"Why not?" asked Mot.

Newton shrugged and replied, "We have a good dynamic, love each other like family, including Omni, and I will not risk that."

All three of them fixed their eyes on Mot. This unity was somehow quite convincing. "Crew dismissed, except Pin," said Mot.

Newton and Ronnie apprehensively stood and left the bridge. Mot waited and said, "I claim you as my breeder."

Pin's eyes stayed on the table. "We have two engines, and with Omni's rebuild, Engine Two gives us more than three-quarters sub-light." She met her eyes with Mot's. "We are not marooned."

"We are if I say we are," said Mot. "I won't declare it officially, yet, going to observe first, but don't be surprised if I make that our status."

Pin stood up with anger giving her cheeks and forehead a pink glow. "Most men, real men, they get a woman willing by proving themselves. To just command someone to be your girlfriend, that's sick." Pin walked away and left the bridge without permission.

Chapter X: Reversal of Ultimatum

With Ronnie's objections and Mot's insistence, Newton was assigned the task of socializing Omni back to being a productive member of the crew, and there were advances and setbacks. Ronnie had given him an instruction program that included warnings, so when Newton walked into the bio-cell just in time to see a small jungle cat fighting for its life, he knew to postpone the day's lesson.

It was also disturbing to watch. Omni tormented the little spotted cat until it froze, and then she snatched it out of its defensive posture and tore out its innards before it could even make a sound. The warning was that what she ate affected Omni's mood, and meat would trigger primal aggression. Newton shouted for her to not eat all the predators. With blood dripping from her mandibles, Omni shouted back that she knew the balance better than he did and that predators tasted special.

Newton sealed the door and walked away from the bio-cell. Feeling a little isolated and hopeless, he went to the engineering level and went into the large bay of Engine One. Not only was there no sign of recent activity, but the task log's last entry was from three weeks earlier. A chill went down Newton's spine. It wasn't unusual for crew on rotations not to see one another, but three-quarters of a phase earlier, that was about the time Mot emerged from the amnio-chamber and reassumed command.

Worry put speed in his steps on the way to sickbay. If something happened to Pin, then Ronnie would know. Even if Ronnie wasn't there, Pin might be, or records. Newton almost bounced off the door to sickbay because it didn't slide open on his approach. He pushed the button for manual opening. "Member identify," said the computer lock. Newton put his thumb on the scanner. The door slid open.

Sickbay was mostly dark so Newton said, "Sickbay, lights, forty percent."

"Override, twelve percent," said Ronnie's voice from the darkened shadows of the corner. "Seal the door." When the lights came up, she gestured for Newton to follow her into the glass enclosure of an isolation room. She patted the bed. Newton cinched his eyebrows together. In a quiet voice, Ronnie said, "You don't feel well, in case he comes in here and sees us."

Newton got on the hospital bed. "What the dork is going on, and where is Pin?"

"You didn't go to her quarters did you?" Ronnie asked in a panic.

"No, I stopped by Engine One."

Ronnie attached some leads and turned on the monitor. "As best as I can tell, Pin disappeared moments after our management meeting with Mot. I noticed that she hasn't been taking meals or her quarter phase medications. Four brights ago, Captain asked me for the files to install biometric locks. He didn't say anything, but I think it's so if she goes through certain doors, he can find her," whispered Ronnie.

"What about her transponder?" Newton asked quietly.

Ronnie shook her head. "She doesn't have one. I took it out for treatment of the mercury poisoning, and she didn't want me to put it back. I didn't want to force the issue."

"Does Mot know that?"

"No, I lied, said her body rejected it."

Newton smiled. "Lying to a robustus, that's risky."

"It's not that hard. All you need is an image, strongly reinforced, to cover the lie. If he touches you, that's all he gets," said Ronnie.

"Are you shitting me? And has that ever worked?" asked Newton.

Ronnie rolled her eyes. "Yes, on Captain Mot, even. I juiced him with an image of the transponder impacted in pus on Pin's back. He pulled back his hand like it was on fire. And I knew he might check because he's done it before."

Newton shook his head with a grin forming on his face. "You're brave."

"Only with tyrants," said Ronnie. "I'm not brave enough to tell Pin she can't violate Article One, and that both of us could get busted back." She shook her head. "Focus, this is serious. Pin has disappeared and the captain is acting weird, like he knows why."

Color drained out of Newton's face as he thought about the situation. "If she was injured, we wouldn't even know," he whispered.

"Exactly, injury and isolation could kill her, and I wouldn't know. And the captain restricted me not to say anything to you, so something is seriously dorked up and I can't go looking for her, and you can't." Tears formed in Ronnie's eyes. "If they had some kind of fight, she could be dead in some dark corner of this ship. We may never know what happened," Ronnie whispered.

Newton's expression brightened to a hopeful widening of his brow. "But this is Pin, who thinks in that third dimension, as we've seen, so maybe she was prepared, an exit strategy, then all Pin needed to do was get out of the room."

Ronnie slowly accepted the idea. "Yeah," she sounded relieved. Gratitude made Ronnie's posture wilt for a moment. "Yes, thank you. I needed an idea to hold on to. That's exactly right. Pin knew Mot would be stomping around the ship again at some point, and she would prepare for that set of contingencies." She melted into another fleeting swoon. "Yes. Thank you, Newton."

"You're welcome, and now your turn," Newton replied. "What do we do now?"

She blinked a few times and said, "Don't appear to do anything. The trigger is Mot, so we don't act like we know, until circumstance would naturally lead us to require Pin, when we're talking to the captain. Then we ask, and even let him divert the issue a few times before we press it, if that's how he wants to play this," added Ronnie.

"And when he orders the search party?" asked Newton.

"Then we search for her, for her, not Mot." Ronnie looked nervously at the door. "Now, get out of here."

Newton nodded thoughtfully and left sickbay.

They knew yet pretended not to know for week after tortuous week. It was especially difficult for Ronnie, who prepared survival packs and would secret them to the dark recesses of the ship, but when they would go untouched, Ronnie would become more depressed with worry. She would move the survival packs further into seclusion, thinking Mot may find them, or she would make them easier to find as worried desperation weighed heavier on her mind. All this took a toll, and Ronnie began taking a sedative to stop obsessing about Pin. Ronnie was disciplined, taking only enough to slow the intrusive ideation, not enough to feel a narcotic effect, well below the addiction threshold.

Newton didn't have as much time to worry. Although Mot didn't say why, Mot pressed relentlessly for Newton to get Omni ready to work. Yet, when he went into the bio-cell, Newton never knew what he would find. Sometimes he would find a creature patient enough for a conversation or a card game. Sometimes he would find a savage, dressed in animal skins and adorned with bone jewelry and armed with stabbing and throwing weapons. One attempt to get Omni working in an engine room resulted in her merely harvesting some mechanical components from a lift robot and circuit boards from the power supply. She left the engine room with the smell of cinnamon trailing behind her. Omni thought it was funny. She knew he was powerless to stop her. Newton followed her back and watched her dial nine and go into the bio-cell, still with the smell of cinnamon hanging in the air.

Another attempt to get Omni to work resulted in her cannibalizing more components from the engine room, so Newton realized he was going to have to tell Mot that the effort wasn't going so well. Newton never got the chance. Mot called a meeting in the administration office, a room with a window wall, a mandatory meeting for Ronnie, Newton, and, worrisome to Newton, Omni was also required to attend.

Newton shouted into the bio-cell to Omni that he was going to walk her to the meeting at the top of the hour. He closed the door and wondered if Omni was going to at least put on some actual clothes. She was bashful before the change.

When he went to pick her up, Omni walked out of the jungle wearing a leather cover over the sharpened tip of her abdomen and straps that crossed at the top, as well as a vest of braided metal strands and matching necklace. She looked primitive and technologically sophisticated at the same time. Newton was mostly just thankful for Omni's cooperation. Her posture was relaxed and her movements fluid.

They walked through the door to find Ronnie and Mot already in the administration room. Ronnie stood and waited for Omni to take a seat, which she did by turning the chair back to one side. Newton sat next to her, across the table from Mot.

"You are a conscript, and will be addressed as such," said Mot.

"I am alzo of the Royal Houze, zo I will keep rezidenze in the bio-zell and the ambazador wing," said Omni.

Mot looked irritated but said, "For now, but I have concerns about the ecosystem of the bio-cell, so if I think it needs a rest, then I will declare it off limits to everybody."

"Kai keep jungle better than Zoftinz."

"I realize your species is good at maintaining natural systems; that's why you're still in there. But I have the final say. Acknowledge," ordered Mot.

"Yez, Captain." There was a brief scent of burnt meat and ammonia.

Mot leaned back and crossed his arms. "I reviewed the recordings of our encounter with the Guardians, the conscript was at the science station and assisted with com function. What can't you do on the bridge?"

"Nothing," said Omni.

"And you got us emergency nuclear power in thirty blinks, and did a superior rebuild of Engine Two," said Mot. "The doctor says you may or may not be ready to interact with the crew. Are you ready to work?"

Omni sat stone-still and waited. After a moment, she replied, "Yez."

"I want you on third rotation, taking Pin's roster of duties, starting tomorrow," said Mot.

Newton thought it was finally time. "Where's Pin?" he asked.

Mot shifted in his seat and replied, "Unknown, derelict in her duties." He rubbed his chin. "The conscript was a stowaway for phases. Would it help me find Pin?"

"No," answered Omni. "Iv I hunt zoftin, I might loze control and eat."

Mot sat there, blinking his eyes with confusion. Eventually, he looked at Ronnie and asked, "Is that thing kidding?"

Ronnie replied in a distracted monotone, "I don't think so."

Mot bristled. "Answer like you're addressing the captain. Explain why you don't think so," growled Mot.

Ronnie straightened up and looked at Mot. "The ability to lie is at six on the sentience scale. Omni's a nine, and ten is reserved for a super-being, if one is ever discovered. So, she has the capacity to deceive. The reason I don't think so is her recent condition. Hormones are giving her intrusive thoughts and violent impulses. Her executive thinking is barely in control, and the stimulation of a hunt could overwhelm that control." Ronnie hesitated. "And referring to her as 'it' or a 'thing' is dangerous."

Mot's face turned red. He kept his eyes on Omni but addressed Newton. "First officer, the conscript worked under your command," he prefaced. "So, is there a danger to my crew or not?" asked Mot.

"Before, there was no danger, but things have changed. As for present danger and as your diplomat, some acknowledgement and good manners will get us through this adjustment period, because that's really all this is, an adjustment period."

"Acknowledge what?" asked Mot.

"Acknowledge who she is. Omni is royal Kai, and the president of the Five Worlds would call her if there was a problem. Acknowledge that she's showing restraint because she could physically overpower any of us, so her cooperation is proof that she wants to help. We should also acknowledge the remarkable breadth of skills and knowledge that she brings to our crew. Fleet couldn't even recruit so much talent in a single officer, let alone an unpaid conscript."

Mot nodded thoughtfully. "Good manners, then?" said Mot with a quizzical tone.

"Again, royalty, a lifetime of being addressed respectfully, so a little respect, some patience, a bit of tact will make it easier for her, and it doesn't take anything from us but a second thought." Newton shrugged.

With a frown of acceptance slowly fading on Mot's face, he nodded. "Fine," Mot said. He stood, to be followed by Newton, Ronnie and Omni. Actually saying her name, Mot commanded, "Omni starts third rotation at hour twenty, tomorrow. And all, carry on."

"Yes, aye aye, yez zir," Ronnie, Newton and Omni said at the same time.

Mot nodded and walked out of the administration room.

Ronnie's mouth trembled in a slight frown as she looked at Omni. "It's good to see you, your highness."

Omni nodded, with the subtle smell of an approaching rain. "You understand, Ronnie. You zay how I veel. Newton zay it get better. Iz that true?"

"Yes. Yes it will. So soon after emerging, you undoubtedly feel miserable and it doesn't seem like it's getting better from one bright to the next, but eventually, you'll gradually feel better, you'll notice moments of clarity. I promise it will get better. Everything will be back to normal in about three phases," said Ronnie.

"Three vhases! I veel zick all the time. I don't know iv I lazt that long. Can I do zomething now?" asked Omni.

"Yes, smoking hesh will help. Rag will make it worse. And eating fruit is good, but meat will make the mood swings more dramatic. Also, if you keep your temperature down, it'll help, so get wet periodically," advised Ronnie.

Omni nodded as she listened. "I cool down yezterbright, thought it waz my imagination, veel better a zweep or two."

"Your mind will play tricks with you. Ask yourself, does this hurt or help?"

"Hurt or help," Omni repeated. "That good. I can do that." Omni looked from Ronnie to Newton and back to Ronnie. "What I vorget?" asked Omni.

"We are very worried about Pin," said Newton. "Thank you for not hunting her."

Ronnie nodded with tears forming in her eyes.

"I not hurt Pin," said Omni.

Newton escorted Omni to the bio-cell.

Weeks passed. Mot spent a lot of time stalking the lower levels of the ship. He suspected that his emotional involvement was making his searches less than systematic, but the idea of designing a circuit and flushing plan gave Mot a headache. He rationalized that random searches would keep Pin from recognizing a pattern. And since he had a crew member that needed access but wasn't in the database, wasn't even human, Mot eventually decommissioned all lock and tracking protocols.

Ronnie was still haunted by the idea that Pin was languishing or dead somewhere on the ship. She stopped putting out survival packs when Omni came into sickbay, dropped off two survival packs, shook her head, and left without a word. Ronnie realized if Omni could find them, then so could Mot.

Omni worked her shift, and even though she needed less sleep than humans, she did no more than duty required. She spent hours in the textiles warehouse and the equipment bays. Omni also spent a lot of time either soaking in the bio-cell pond or in her bathtub in her suite.

Newton, oddly, didn't have much to do, or, more accurately, didn't feel like doing much of anything. He was supposed to be assisting Omni, and watching Omni under that guise, but she became ill at ease with him in the room almost immediately. When machine components began to break and tools began to bend from Omni handling them, Newton decided that monitoring Omni wasn't worth the wear and tear on the ship. He had yet to tell Mot that Omni was working independently.

It was the fifteenth hour of the fifteenth day, midday, midmonth, seventh mission month, midyear, when the defense alarm sounded. Flashing lights accompanied the wails of the alarm in every room and hallway on the ship. The alarm sounded for a full minute before Mot's voice came over the loudspeakers, "All hands on the bridge, all hands on the bridge, all hands on the bridge." The flashing lights and alarm resumed.

Newton was in the access tube on his way to the crown. Flicks of the rungs upward plunged him down in zero gravity. He rode the tube whisking his knuckles against the walls for drag, slowing enough to stop at the first floor, the floor of the bridge. Of the two hatchways, Newton chose the longer approach to the bridge, the causeway to the hall entrance.

In the hall, Omni was leaning against the wall, as though certain of his arrival, and ready to enter the bridge together, so she snapped to the hallway to match his walk. When he got to the door, Newton let Omni go through the door first. "Conscript, helm, Newton, com," said Mot. They took their stations. Newton's hand drifted toward the alarm controls. "Not till everybody's on the bridge," said Mot. Ronnie appeared in the doorway then entered. "Doctor at the science station." Newton silenced the alarm.

Mot gestured toward Omni and said, "Do we have emergency nuclear?"

"I give it to you with three zweepz in engineering," said Omni.

"Go," said Mot, "I'll take helm if necessary." Omni walked quickly off. "Doctor, thirteen zip, one eighty ziks, tell me what that is."

Ronnie tuned the instruments to see but not be seen. "This is a ship shadow, our stealth at higher cycle rate, coming from solar system center, going to the place where we hit the fringe."

"Pull it up, on screen, another screen where we see the center. Also give me a macro-view with ship and destination highlighted." Mot wandered over to the weapons station next to the helm and flipped a couple switches. "And since we have a destination, let's calculate an intercept line."

"Apparent destination," said Ronnie. "It's a simple line so far."

"Duly noted," said Mot.

"What kind of intercept?" Ronnie asked.

"Blind and behind." Mot muttered. Ronnie prompted the computer for complex calculations. Three lines, red, blue, yellow, appeared on the wide view. Mot looked at the lines. "Show me high and lying in wait." Again, Ronnie started the computation and three more lines appeared on the screen.

"These are at top speed and the optimum line will disappear in five sweeps," said Ronnie. She did more computation. "Other line opportunities close soon after."

"Or, we could stay put, lay low," said Newton.

"You know what that is?" asked Mot.

Omni walked onto the bridge and took her place at the helm with Mot going to the command chair. "Emergenzie nuclear iv you need, three zweepz, thirty blinkz vrom ready zwitch."

Mot turned to Omni. "Prepare to follow high trajectory line yellow." Omni nodded. Mot shot a glare at Newton. "Again, do you know what that is?"

"It's paranoid myth," said Newton.

Mot shook his head, his face showing some pity for Newton. "Wrong," said Mot. "The instant that myth sees us, it will unload on us with actual weapons. We will try to destroy it before it successfully destroys us." He paused. "Conscript, hit it."

The stars on two screens lurched into motion at different speeds, depending on the magnification of the view, but the wide overview showed a moving blip. Omni flew up to full speed, modifying the line to ride lower into the blind spot.

"You're dragging," said Mot.

"Ztaying in blind zpot, while we have maneuver time."

Mot frowned but then nodded. "Fine, approach blind, adjust for intersect."

"Captain, defensive condition change," said Ronnie.

"What?"

"A Guardian ship, was paralleling ship on the other side of the elliptic, now inbound to the intercept point."

"The place we crashed through the fringe?" asked Mot.

"Negative," Ronnie replied, "our intercept, presumably calculated from our course, also approaching in the blind spot, at light speed, so their intercept will just follow ours."

"What are they doing?" asked Mot with a rhetorical tone.

The electronic growl from Engine Two suddenly went silent and there was an alarm tone from the helm. Omni pulled at the control stick, flipped a few switches, and tried the helm again. "Report," commanded Mot.

"We lozt Engine Two," said Omni. "Zenzorz zay not cataztrovhic vailure, but not gravity zpot. Input go dark on all power zircuitz."

"Bring up a camera on screen seven," said Mot.

Omni's four arms and clawed hands blurred over the console. "The bridge haz been bypazzed, to unknown control board. Jumping zourze mean we can't vind the camera veed or engine control." Omni slapped a few more switches and rolled a dial. An image of the pyramid shaped ship appeared on a screen with a field of color coming off the one, small rudder engine. "Thiz iz zeriouz. There zhould be zome gravity az gyroz zlow down. Nothing."

"Show me temperature," ordered Mot. Omni clicked a switch. The ship graphic showed the rudder engine glowing, the nuclear reactor warming up and the mechanics of Engine Two cooling down. "What do we do now? We're in the middle of an attack maneuver!" shouted Mot. "How long until electrical power from Engine Two is gone?"

"Three zweepz," answered Omni.

Mot surged from the command area to the console with the emergency nuclear power. No sooner than the instant he initiated the system, another alarm sounded. "Now what?" demanded Mot.

Newton replied, "That's a bay door alarm."

"Stop it and give me a visual," said Mot.

"Can't," said Omni, "also on hopping zourze."

Mot held his hand to his forehead and stared at the screens with disbelief. "We still in the blind spot?"

"Yez, but we zpeeding, iv launch, we deztroy it by zpeed and angle," said Omni.

Mot gave Omni an annoyed smirk, and said, "Rotate bay door to the safest angle to the line of motion. She might damage us with a foolish attempt."

"Aye Captain," said Omni. She hit a flurry of small adjustments, and the view turned at different increments, but all of them sluggish motion, since the rudder engine was weak to the exponential forces.

Once the facet with the bay door was exactly on the trailing shadow, the ship's landing craft, about the size and general dimension of a transport bus, leapt into the wake and disappeared quickly with the velocity of the ship. The landing craft first followed the ship to catch up to relative speed.

Mot said, "The instant she goes out of our spot, while visible, she makes us visible." He dialed into the emergency nuclear. "Provided we also stay invisible ourselves, meaning we have emergency nuclear power." The captain hit a switch and a graphic appeared on the bottom left corner of all the screens. It depicted a nuclear symbol and a graph of power levels, available, used, returned to the ship. "And we won't pop into view," grumbled Mot. "Acknowledge Conscript," Mot announced. "How much we got for capability?"

"Enough vor ztealth, zhieldz mostly, not enough for tractor beam too," Omni replied.

Mot nodded. "We still need to make an attack with nothing but a rudder engine. That means we should decide if we're still attacking at all." He tipped his head toward Omni and asked, "What else do you got? Because this, we're screwed."

Omni squared her large, compound her eyes to Mot's. "We have three hundred rip rounds vor machine gun, Captain," Omni answered.

"That gun eats three-hundred rounds in half a blink."

"Theze are good one at a time." There was a hint of cinnamon in the air.

Mot pondered what she was saying. He chuckled and said, "Rip rounds, in our gun. Yeah, we'll shoot those one at a time." After rocking in place to comfort himself, a nervous tick, not a confidence builder to see the leader rocking his head back and forth such like a simpleton child. "Good. Give me trajectories that don't need acceleration but that attack by behind from blind, and another, intercept with target going after Pin, 'cause she strays across line while visible, it might pursue."

As if the deserter on board the landing craft heard him, the lander zipped off in a new direction toward the center of the solar system. The two trajectory lines appeared on the macro view, with the ship's blip already moving further toward the protect-intercept line. Mot agreed with the new line. "Good course correction, keep on this line as long as we're stealth."

Moments passed, Pin's ship accelerated toward the star, still well under the ship's capability in speed, still visible. Even Mot began to wonder if Pin was intentionally setting herself up as bait so the Clarion could destroy the bolt, which had yet to alter course. Ronnie drew a surprised breath as the bolt slowed to a stop. Energy signals changed as the bolt reoriented, perhaps redirecting toward the landing craft. "If the target goes full speed to Pin, can we still intercept?" asked Mot.

"Maybe, we muzt change courze, vront attack iv they zpeed up," said Omni.

"Understood," said Mot. "I take weapons to the command chair." He shifted away from the console back to the command chair. He took a seat.

The bolt accelerated to intercept with Pin's course and Omni adjusted their trajectory to catch the uncloaked landing craft. "Guardian battleship also adjusting course," said Ronnie. "To an intercept after us," she added. Ronnie was distracted enough for her voice to fade in energy when she said, "Target is trained on lander, and just powered up weapons and shields."

"We match weapons and shields," commanded Mot.

Omni and Mot touched switches. Another two graphics popped up on the bottom of the main screen, weapons and shields on the bottom right. Ronnie broke in, "Drain on shields, target is taking a better look in our direction."

"Straight axis, backward spin, precise line to sync with stealth, we will disappear, now!" barked Mot. Omni was ready and the helm spun them backwards. The bolt blasted energy waves their direction for a couple of searches, but couldn't see the pyramid, so it again focused on Pin's ship. "Slow backward spin for targeting sync, so pull axis to the target ship," Mot said.

"Aye captain," said Omni. She made the adjustments to the helm.

"Prepare to block all communications, especially powerful, long range and directed communiqué," ordered Mot.

"Yes, sir," said Newton.

The confrontation closed in. At the last second, the bolt lunged at Pin's ship, which also lurched forward and disappeared. The bolt answered with blaster fire ripping into a calculated line of the invisible ship. There were no contact explosions. Pin must have veered off the instant she was invisible.

"We zpin too vast to take zhot?" asked Omni.

"No, we'll lose speed; just keep to its line!" said Mot. He set up the stick on the arm of the command chair for a manual shot.

There is no way he makes that shot manually, thought Newton. They approached the bolt oriented upside down and spinning backwards. A transmission light, Newton patched it through. "Cannot locate primary target, negative primary, evidence of location," reported the bolt. Still at great distance, Mot took a shot, KchZOOM!. "Landing craft, contact coordinates…" A jamming whistle accompanied the transmission.

"Don't lead, zhoot direct!" shouted Omni.

Mot waited for the spin to bring the target to sights. He fired two shouts, ChkZOOM, ckZOOM!" All watched as the impact explosion ripped the nose off the invisible ship, making it instantly visible, but then the second rip round disintegrated stern. Momentum sent the damaged bolt tumbling through space. A low, cruel laugh started in Mot's throat and flourished into a truculent guffaw. "Two rounds kill a ship with full energy shields, rip rounds," said Mot. He watched their line and commanded, "Steer clear, they may have auto destruct."

"Aye," said Omni, pulling the lazy helm.

"What the dork was that?" asked a voice.

"Ship-to-ship com from the bolt," said Newton.

"Reply with visual," ordered Mot. The screen with the bolt jumped to an image of the bridge of the bolt, with smoke and warning lights, with two crew members, the commander and crewman. "That was a couple of rip rounds, courtesy of our Kai conscript," said Mot. "How did you like them?" he asked with a grin.

"Rip rounds, you're an asshole," said the commander.

"So says the spook sent here to kill his own dorking comrades!" bellowed Mot.

The commander's face withered to an expression of genuine fear. "Sorry. If you're so good, don't leave us out here. Just put us on that live planet. Please. If not us, my tech, she isn't even clandestine services. At least save her." Mot looked at the brown haired gracile. Mot began to form sympathy until her face betrayed worry.

"Nope, can't trust either of you," said Mot. "And you kill from cover. No mercy for cowards."

"Our autodestruct is out," said the commander.

"We'll help." Mot signaled to cut communications then turned to Omni and said, "Pull us to contrary line, make sure the Guardian ship isn't in the background."

"Aye," said Omni. She adjusted the helm and waited for the weak response. Once their line was more to the side rather than straight down, Omni changed the spin.

"Good, angle, don't slow down," said Mot. He caught Newton's eye and nodded. Newton reopened communications. "What are your names?" asked Mot.

"I'm Kale," said the commander.

"My name's Bree," said the tech.

Mot nodded. "Goodbye Kale and Bree. I'll give you a sweep." The commander and the tech looked at one another. Their bridge image disappeared. Mot put his hand on the gun-stick and waited until the spin would give him an opportunity. One pass, two passes, third pass, long before a minute, Mot fired one round. The bolt imploded then exploded into a flash of fire, leaving a dark blossom of tiny fragments.

"Harsh," said Newton.

"Real," Mot replied. "Full stop!" he commanded. Omni adjusted the helm.

Newton gasped with amazement. "Sir, all we got for navigation is our forward momentum and a rudder. If we stop, we're paddling a small boat in a rough ocean."

"Understood," said Mot, "but it is customary to stop when communicating with other ships, and the Guardians are going to be here. Right?"

"Correct," said Ronnie.

"My hope is the rudder engine will even stop us in time for this not to look clumsy," Mot added with a strangely relaxed demeanor. "Well, Conscript? Can we stop anytime soon?"

"Yez, but we are wazting a lot of move power," complained Omni.

"Can't be helped. We're not discussing it more," said Mot. "Helm, face wherever they take the diplomatic stage."

"Aye," said Omni. They spent the next agonizing five minutes coasting to a stop, but the Guardian popped into view a minute after they ground to an actual fixed position. The v-shaped battleship oriented to face them and also came to a full stop, thirty thousand meters apart, with the yellow star behind and below the Guardians.

"Com from Guardians," said Newton.

"Patch it, all modes, dynamic," said Mot.

"Aye," Newton said.

A shape-pixilated face appeared and said, "Greetings, Captain Mot. I am Sal."

"How do you know my name, Sal?" asked Mot.

"Her grace, Omni, said that Mot commanded the Clarion."

"True," murmured the captain. Mot returned to his command voice. "What can I do for you, Sal?"

The pixilated face of a young man paused before saying, "You could tell us why the craft you launched, for a decoy, is now speeding toward the system center."

"We are having a personnel issue, a misunderstanding, which we will resolve. And we expect some consideration to deal with it, protections of understanding from the

Guardians," said Mot, speaking as if this sort of rational thought was second nature.

"What is our understanding?" asked Sal.

Mot picked his chin with mild aggravation. "We will never reveal this space to the worlds. Pin, the pilot of that ship, she also agreed to protect this space, so you will let us work this out, not interfere, for as long as it takes."

"That's a lot to ask on one man's word," said Sal.

Mot nodded, and said, "My word and two lives of my countrymen, whom I killed to protect this space, or did you not notice that?"

The pixilated face looked from Mot, to Newton, to Ronnie, and then to Omni. "We noticed that," said Sal. "We have an understanding, purchased with two lives." Sal focused on Mot. "Anything else?"

Mot turned to Newton. "Anything else?" asked Mot.

"A question for the Guardians," said Newton.

"Please ask, Officer Keen," said Sal.

"Any news on the diplomatic package sent by Her Highness?" asked Newton.

"It was well received by her family, a phase ago, when the light of the jewel was strong again," said the Guardian, almost sounding as though they were waiting to deliver it until Omni recovered enough to emerge from the brown shell. "War has been averted," said Sal.

"How did you get through a nine revolve time barrier?" asked Newton with a smile.

"It's a secret," responded Sal with different smile. "You have a last, serious question?"

"How much do the worlds know about us, here, now?" asked Newton.

Sal flashed a grin of delight before the pixilated face became stoic. "The worlds know that the princess joined the crew of a Fleet explorer, commanded by Mot and Newton, with Ronnie and Pin, to a lost destination, on a secret mission. And we delivered the parcel from the other side of the Five Worlds," added Sal.

Newton tipped his head back to Mot, who turned to the screen. "Thank you for your part in keeping peace," said Mot. "Good future to you."

"Good future," said Sal. The communication view blinked off the screen. The Guardian ship tipped over and backwards before swooping away in an arc. The ship vanished into a streak toward interstellar space.

"Damn!" exclaimed Newton. "You been studying diplomatic packets?" Newton asked Mot with a surprised tone.

Mot smiled. "You make this shit harder than it really is." Newton laughed, then Mot laughed. Ronnie laughed with disbelief that Mot could be amused enough to laugh at anything conversational. Still with a smile in his eyes, Mot turned to Omni. "Conscript, please go to the engine room and tell me what happened to Engine Two."

"Aye, Captain. Helmzman leaving bridge." Omni left the bridge with the subtle scent of cinnamon and apple blossom.

Chapter XI: Place of Mind

What happened to Engine Two was sabotage, precise, critical, irreversible sabotage. Pin used hydraulics to pull the braid, a bundle of room temperature, super conducting wire to transfer the gravity from the engine to conductive plates on the hull. The gravity motor wouldn't work without that braid, and nothing on the ship could be used in place of that braid, a two meter weave of wire with connectors on both ends.

The autopilot was directed toward the place they were, the fifty-mark axis point to the entire solar system, but top speed of just the rudder engine would take weeks, so they pointed, powered up and began the slow crawl.

Searching for the braid became the all consuming task. Mot's obsession with finding it was goaded by the idea that Pin didn't have that much time to hide it from the moment it was pulled, to the point the shuttle left the bay. Newton argued with Mot, explaining that she planned well before the sprint through the ship to the launch bay. Pin had already hidden the spare braids to Engine One, even though it didn't fit and the engine was dismantled, and the spare braid from Engine Two. Newton understood why Mot was so determined. What if she took the braids with her? They would have to live out their lives stranded in interstellar space.

The members of the crew, besides Mot, put halfhearted effort into the search and waited for Mot to realize that he needed a secondary plan, one that involved getting Pin back. Finally, Mot called a meeting.

Ronnie and Newton were the first to arrive, then Mot, with Omni the last to arrive. She was still dressed as a primitive, the only acknowledgement of her place on the crew was Newton's all access telemetry pin on her handmade vest. Omni gave Mot a quick salute and sat at the boardroom table.

Mot looked at Omni and asked, "Conscript, is there any way to built some sort of detector to help us find the braids?"

"No," said Omni. "Metal detectorz uze electromagnetic wavez, but braidz are zuperconductorz, zo all wavez, all ambient energy will be not be returned. I make detector to try and zee absorbed energy, but it not work. Iv I could tune it, it might, but I need a braid, and we only have one, and it working on rudder engine. Taking our lazt engine ovv line iz too risky, even vor a little while."

Mot nodded. "If we took the rudder offline, and let you work with the braid, what are the chances your detector could be tuned to work?"

"Not good," Omni answered. "The energy hole iz theoretical. Modelz zay it won't work. I built it becauze vizual zearch iz wazte of time."

"Not if we find them," said Mot.

"We azzume they can be vound," said Omni. "They could be in zomething, or Pin took them. We need to think ov divverent ztrategiez."

Newton made a conscious effort to keep his face blank. Omni's courage when speaking truth to power was privately appreciated by Ronnie, too.

Mot turned to Newton. "We're dorking stuck. What's a different strategy?"

Newton shrugged and said, "Pin knows where the braids are. How about we find her, appeal to her, reassure her that she can come back to us? You know, rescue her. Give her immunity from any trouble so she'll stop running away."

There was an uncomfortable silence that lasted for several minutes. Eventually, Mot cleared his throat a few times and asked, "With the engines of the landing craft, how long will it take for her to get to Freeland?" Mot used the name Newton gave to the live planet.

"She could be there in a phase, maybe, if she took the safer course above the elliptic, so, she could be orbiting Freeland in a quarter plus a few brights," said Newton.

"What do we have? Can a shuttle make it there and back?"

"A shuttle is slower, has less sensor range to avoid collision, so traveling safely to Freeland would take three phases."

"I have zhip," said Omni. Three surprised looking faces turned to Omni. She looked back and forth to all three of them and settled her gaze on Mot. "It in piezez, take me zeveral brightz to put together, but it much fazter. It be at Vreeland in a quarter phaze."

Mot let go an aggravated huff, which gave way to another long silence. This time, Mot turned to Ronnie. "What would a contact mission on Freeland even look like?"

Ronnie shrugged and said, "All scans indicate that Freeland has a preeminent life form about five thousand revolves into a civilization arc. That puts the populations at crop cultivation, animal husbandry, city-state political structure, contract armies with hand weapons." She fell silent, stifling a thought.

Somehow, Mot picked up on the very thought Ronnie dismissed. "A preeminent life form, what do they look like?"

After chewing on her lip, Ronnie answered, "Probably a lot like us."

Mot scoffed and pointed at Omni. "There's a preeminent life form than doesn't look anything like us. How do we know Freelanders aren't giant bugs, too?"

"Ninety-nine percent of preeminent species follow the same evolutionary pattern, starting with tiny primates, insectivores for the extra protein to build brain power, eyes facing forward for stereoscopic vision, arboreal for development of hands and feet and inner ear balance. The primates that develop the striding foot, or go through an aquatic phase, will become evolved enough to develop weapons, and hunted protein will create more brain development. That's the pattern and that's why every one of the five worlds has or had preeminent beings that are just like us. Part of the evolutionary process is temperate zones, areas of cooler climate." Ronnie paused, looked at Omni, then continued. "What Kai doesn't have is temperate zones. The entire planet is a tropical climate. The species that would have evolved to something like us, on Kai, those are still primitive form primates. The Kai are the exception to prove the rule. Freeland, however, has temperate zones, cold areas, deserts, and tropical areas, and saltwater oceans on two-thirds of the planet, similar to every living world with primate-based preeminence."

"I alwayz wonder about that," said Omni, "why zovtinz vrom divverent planetz look the zame, why zovt vlezh animalz on Kai not zmart."

Mot ignored Omni's comment and asked, "So we have reason to believe there is a chance that Pin may be able to assimilate with Freelanders?"

Ronnie looked uncomfortable. "There's a scenario that could put her at risk. If the Freelanders look similar enough for Pin to think she could fit in, but maybe she would stand out. Specifically, if the people on Freeland looked like graciles, as do nearly all primate based preeminent species, then she may not realize they don't have a robustus line, which is unique to the evolution of Tarn. Pin's hands, feet and blue hair would mark her as an alien, in a world of superstition and magical thinking."

"So she is comfortable to interact with graces, not realizing they would immediately know she doesn't belong," said Mot.

"Right," said Ronnie, "probably in a world where everyone still believes in supernatural powers and monsters, and other stupid crap."

"But we don't know what they look like," said Mot.

"And if they look very different, she'll know to stay hidden, but if they look like graces, she may not," said Ronnie. "Technological sophistication always precedes intellectual, so at such a low level of development, we can safely say they are unsophisticated and hostile to things they don't understand."

Mot sat frowning a moment. He then made his decision. "Searches for the braids will continue. The conscript will assemble her ship. When ready, the away team will consist of the conscript and first officer; the mission will be to contact, and if necessary, rescue Pin." Mot stood up. The crew followed him to their feet.

"Captain," said Ronnie, sounding alarmed, "We just discussed how the preeminent species probably look like me and Newton, so Omni would be in extreme danger on planet and is not able to act as safety second to Newton. A conscript isn't authorized to go on away missions, anyway. Please reconsider the away team."

Mot shook his head. "No. The conscript can pilot her ship. We may not be able to, and we need that ship because we have a daunting time barrier to Freeland. And, more importantly, I want you here, because if I let you and Newton go to that planet, I doubt you would return. You two would find Pin and all three live happily in dereliction of your duties. You'd abandon me out here, probably hoping that the conscript and I kill each other." Mot started toward the door. "No, one of you will be my hostage, always, because I am the only thing standing in the way of you all becoming pirates with the resources of the Fleet." Mot left the administration room.

Omni looked at Ronnie, the ammonia scent of anger being replaced by the smell of cinnamon. "Mot zmarter than he look," said Omni. She left the room. Ronnie and Newton exchanged grim looks and left the room without a word.

It took six days for Omni to assemble the Kai ship from components hidden in food silos and tools in spare parts. She worked around the clock, but not always in the transport bay. She also spent countless hours in the materials warehouse.

One morning when Ronnie was supposed to be sleeping and Newton was supposed to be searching, they ran into each other in the hall outside the transport bay. Newton could see that Ronnie was worried. "We will come back," said Newton.

"Even if you find her, what's changed? She obviously left to get away from Mot," said Ronnie. The door slid open and they went into the transport warehouse, talking as they walked.

"How is that obvious?"

Ronnie clicked her tongue. "Think about it. Things were fine until Mot got out of the amnio-chamber. He comes out like he's brand new, no scars, no physical pain, feeling as beautiful as he is ever going to be. He thinks he finally has a chance with Pin and makes a move. She disappears. That's pretty obvious."

They stepped passed some heavy machinery into the open bay with Omni's ship, and Omni standing next to a cart laden with tools. Without turning to look at them, Omni said, "You two zpeak too vreely. Mot here ten zweepz ago."

Continuing in with Ronnie, Newton said, "Point taken. We are too reckless about that." He touched Ronnie's shoulder and caught her eye to make certain she registered the idea.

Ronnie and Newton stopped next to Omni, taking in the sight of Omni's ship. It was shaped like an ancient terra-craft roadster, long hood with fenders for the front wheels, grille at the front and ornament at the nose. Mid-ship, it had windows forward and to the side, some space behind the bridge with hatch doors, and the stern tapered to a lifted boat-tail and a massive armature that held the single, rear wheel. Although its shape suggested a small roadster, the size was far more massive, six strides tall, nine strides wide, fifteen strides from tip to tail. It was also unmistakably Kai, a masterpiece of aesthetic and engineering, beautiful, sleek, gleaming black with hardware decoration in gold metal.

Newton bubbled into incredulous laughter. Eventually, he asked, "Where the hell did you hide this dorking thing?"

"Beanz," replied Omni.

Both Ronnie and Newton turned to Omni. "Beans?" asked Newton.

"Thirty monolithz of beanz, rize, corn, emergenzy reserve for planting or eating," said Omni. "I hide partz in thoze tankz. If you need, ten tankz only halv vull."

Ronnie changed the subject. "It's so beautiful. Does it have a name?"

"Brina, my mom's name, zhe dezign zhipz that you put together," said Omni. "Thiz one iz zpecial. Zhe gave it to me vor givt."

All three of them spent a moment admiring the ship. "What do we need to go?" asked Newton. "And when are we leaving?"

Omni looked down to the floor. There was a tangy-sweet, tree blossom smell. Newton tried to remember the emotion that went with the scent. He then remembered a context, their first accidental embrace in the zero gravity access tube. This scent was embarrassment. "I make clothez and thingz vor Newton. I need another day to vinizh. Zhip almozt ready."

"That's right. If, when, he has to interact. He'll need period appropriate clothes," said Ronnie. "Damned worlds! What else?"

"Middle evolution clothez, weaponz, money, ztuvv with hidden tech toolz, and stuvv for dizguize iv they look divverent. Moztly clothez, ztring closure, zome buttonz, cotton, linen, leather, vur." As Omni talked, Ronnie got the feeling that these ideas were too familiar with softin civilization. "It can be divverent in ztyle, like Newtin come from other culture, but must be carevul about ztuvv too zmall, too advanzed."

"How do you know all that?" asked Ronnie, "unless you saw Pin prepare."

The smell of anger rose up around Omni.

"Don't say anything, Omni," interjected Newton. He turned to Ronnie. "Don't ask. If the Kai enter into hidden alliance, they never betray them. They keep confidences to their death. To even ask is an insult." Newton recognized some of the hydraulics that had been rigged to pull the braid as the very same machinery that Omni pirated from Engine Room One. He already suspected and was comforted by the thought that Omni helped Pin escape, provided Pin refuge in the bio-cell, the one place on the entire ship that Mot couldn't go, a place without surveillance.

The scent of anger faded and Omni changed the subject. "Told Mot we launch tomorrow, at twenty-vith zpan," said Omni.

"How can I help?" asked Newton.

"Meet me in textilez warehouse, in three zpanz, zee what I made, iv it vitz." Omni looked at Ronnie. "Ronnie come, too, make zure it right." Omni went back to work, abruptly fading from the conversation. Newton spent some time looking at the ship. Ronnie wandered the ship just thinking, daring to hope that Pin did have some help.

When Ronnie got to the textile warehouse and workshop, Newton was already there and looking at his clothes. She approached them as Omni laid out the jacket, caramel brown leather, bloused for room in the upper arm, thickened leather guard at the elbow and forearm, with a long opening for the cuff, brocade over the chest and shoulder, roll collar, double closure with crossover loops over brass buttons. There was white linen shirt with smocking and embroidery, short, matching leather pants, long stockings, and tall boots. Ronnie smiled and said, "The quality is a bit much. I doubt even the highest echelon has finery this nice."

"We're looking for anachronism," said Newton.

Ronnie pointed at the leather vest with a front closure made of nine small brass rings on each side, a leather ribbon to interlace it together and tie at the top and buckle together at the waist. "That's way too sophisticated in fashion and execution."

"Too late now," said Omni. "There will have to be a plaze on Vreeland where they make ztuvv like thiz."

Ronnie wasn't quite sure what Omni was saying. How could it be too late? A sudden flash of impulse told her that Pin had a similar vest, and that matching outfits may help Newton find her. Ronnie changed the subject. "The boots don't fit either, with internal stitching to the sole and a heel. That's a risk, very late middle period in a civilization arc."

Newton smiled and said, "I don't care. Those are snazzy."

Omni crossed to a cabinet and brought back a leather bag with a shoulder strap. She presented some of the contents a small leather sack with gold coins, a folio with paper and quills, a small ink well. She also retrieved weapons, a straight sword with an intricate guard around the handle, with a matching long knife and a smaller one.

He chuckled as he picked up the long knife and pulled it from the sheath. "The legendary strength and craft of Kai steel, we'll have to ignore the fact that there is no equal anywhere in the known galaxy."

"Not a thing to lose on planet," said Ronnie. "If it survived to technical proficiency, it would be a mystery long enough to make a legend of itself, until it becomes confirmed as an extraterrestrial artifact."

"That's what Kai does," Newton said with a sound of sincere reverence, "sets off wonder of a grander existence."

Omni wavered a little bit as she faced Newton. The scent of gratitude growing, she went about unpacking and presenting more useful things. Ronnie looked at the items, each far too fine in quality, and Ronnie knew that love was the material that fashioned everything. "I don't mean to be tedious," said Ronnie. "These things are so beautiful, and your contributions are very appreciated and truly lovely." Ronnie gave Omni a quick bow of her head and then departed the warehouse.

Omni watched after her, waiting until the sound of the door indicated Ronnie's absence. "Ronnie haz to be on bridge when we launch?" asked Omni.

"Thinking we should take her with us?"

Omni nodded, with a smoky, musky sweetness, the smell of grief.

"Mot will make certain she is standing right next to him when we launch," said Newton. "Regulations also kick up, if there are only two members of a crew, so he doesn't have to let her out of his sight. Mot knows, so Ronnie is trapped."

Anger filled their space with a sharp, ammonia smell.

Newton turned to Omni. "Patience, my beautiful princess, there are many more chapters in the better outcome." Without even asking, Newton pulled Omni in for a hug at the shoulder. She turned and reached to him in an embrace with all her arms. She held him an instant before pulling away. Omni left the textile workshop.

A day later, Ronnie was standing beside Mot at the consolidated console on the bridge. Mot had all navigation and weapons, Ronnie with communication and sensors. They were looking at the monitor with the view of the Kai vessel Brina.

"Reconnaissance Vessel Brina, please sync data, signature and com," said Ronnie.

"Copy, zync now," Omni said. There were some lights that blinked, and eventually a screen displayed a view of Omni and Newton on the bridge. He was taking the helmet of a spacesuit off, while Omni looked at him dressed in her version of a middle period, dark ages outfit, linen blouse under leather jacket. "Iv zomething bad happenz vor thiz zhip to loze atmozvhere, we dead anyway," said Omni.

Newton turned to the screen and said, "Apparently, pressure suits are an unnecessary precaution in Kai ships."

"Get on with it," grumbled Mot. "Stabilize proximate atmosphere and gravity and open the bay door."

"Aye," said Ronnie. She made some adjustments on the console.

"We have a total sync, with mission clocks and computer protocols?" asked Mot.

"Yes."

Mot faced the screen. "How long of a delay are we going to have with our transmissions from Freeland?"

"Zeven zpanz," answered Omni.

With a sour look and a nod, Mot commanded, "Kai Recon Brina, you are clear to launch. Upload progress reports daily, until you reach Freeland, then switch to every span, and watch for a flag requiring two-way communication. Both acknowledge."

"Yes, Captain, daily to Freeland, then by span, watch for flag," said Newton.

"Yez," said Omni.

Mot cleared his throat, getting strangely emotional. "Good future," said Mot.

"Good future, my captain," said Newton.

Omni driving, the Kai ship rolled to a place in front of the opening bay door. Once in position, Omni said, "Beltz." Even though they were standing up, they buckled themselves to the padded back portion of what could be a seat. She checked on him, adjusted some controls, took the stick and said, "We vorget something?"

"Yes," said Newton.

Omni pulled out of the bay and accelerated away from the pyramid shaped ship. Newton looked out the side window at a rear view mirror. The Clarion shrunk to invisible in two seconds. There was the sound of the wheels folding inside the ship slightly before the low pitched song of Kai gyros reached a plateau of effortless, impossible speed. The stars in the periphery blurred as the forward view formed a circle of stars in fine focus. Judging from the size of the circle, they were three-quarters the speed of light and steadily accelerating.

Omni spent the next hour talking Newton through the workings of the Kai helm, showing him how the seat would form under and behind the pilot, or one could adjust the gravity setting to lay down flat with the window and the controls still within reach. She unbuckled and then beckoned him to follow her through the ship. The living quarters of the ship kept with the luxurious style of Kai; there were four sleeping berths, a kitchen with a dining nook, a bathroom with a toilet, sink and shower, and two reclining chairs in the back, with all of these spaces having actual windows to the outside. Newton opened a tall, narrow closet next to one of the sleeping berths and saw his clothes for Freeland. He realized this was his side of the living quarters and took off his pressure suit. Once in his linen shirt and some shorts, he joined Omni at the table in the small nook.

She waited until he was seated and then handed him a pipe. It was a different color of metal, a brighter gold, not as much decoration, but otherwise quite similar to the pipe Newton had given to Mot. Newton smiled before touching the tip and taking a long inhale. It was nicely cured and delicious tasting hesh. He handed the pipe to Omni, who also took a generous puff, waited, and then blew a light cloud into the air.

They passed the pipe back and forth another time before Newton noticed that Omni was smoking the regular way. "You no longer smoke by breathing port?" asked Newton.

Omni tipped her head and replied, "Healing ztage, it makes better connection from lungz to mouth. I breath both wayz now. Iv Kai hurt bad, sometimes bury bottom halv to open passage to lungz. It zuppozed to make me talk better, breath by mouth, but that not zeem to happen yet." Omni held the pipe to him.

Newton waived the offer. "No thank you. I'm good. And you're doing fine. I can understand you."

Omni nodded. "I wanted to go see Vreeland with you. Now we go."

Newton chuckled with delight. "I know, it's so nice to just have a while to be with you." He caressed her shoulder. "You finally feeling better?" asked Newton.

She nodded and smiled slightly, her mandible blades separating up and down and side to side. "Better, Ronnie right, cool down, hesh. Zlow progrezz, but now I can think sometimes."

Newton sat back and gave her a mischievous smile. "So, what's the temperature Kai run on board their ships?"

Omni clicked a short laugh. Newton realized it was the first time he had heard Omni's laugh in more than three months. "Zixty sparks," she answered.

"So what's it in here now?"

"Vivty zparks."

"That's still kinda warm," said Newton.

Omni nodded with a smile. "Yes, Newtin, we can turn down heat." She turned to him and said, "Tell Brina."

Newton raised his eyebrows with surprise. "Brina, would you please adjust the temperature down to forty-five sparks?"

A pleasant sounding, female computer voice responded, "I can, and I am instructed to follow all orders from Newton, but, her highness is sensitive to temperature. Her joints begin to stiffen at forty-five sparks. How about forty-seven?"

"Absolutely, forty-seven sparks, please." Again, Newton ran his hand over Omni's shoulders. "And Brina, can you solve visual distortion and show us the planets as we go into the system?"

"Yes," answered the computer. "The first significant object is a dwarf planet with it's own satellite, an unusual moon because it's practically a third as large as the dwarf planet." What Newton thought was a wooden table with an intricate rectangle of inlay, displayed a screen with an image of the dwarf planet with a large moon in orbit.

"Thank you," said Newton.

"Gravh pleaze," said Omni. A top view of the solar system appeared in the top corner of the image. The outer belt of small points had a dot highlighted, one with a tiny dot in its orbit. There was also a blip for the position of their ship.

For the next few days, Omni and Newton relaxed into a routine of checking the helm, occasionally discussing the workings of the ship, eating, smoking, and dozing in their sleeping berths or in the recliners. They were quite compatible, both able to enjoy one another's company without much talking. In fact, some of the days passed without a single word but plenty of communication with looks and casual touch.

Whoever noticed the image of the next planet to appear would beckon the other's attention to the screen and they would gaze at it together. They saw blue gas giants on outer orbits, one with an oblong orbit and one tipped on its side. There was spectacular view of a planet with a ring system. Unlike the blue ones, the ringed planet was in an obit that was underneath and relatively close to their trajectory toward the center of the system. The next planet in was on the opposite end of the elliptic but was so large that they could get really good images, anyway, swirling bands of red, yellow, pink, white, with an immense red storm in the southern hemisphere, more than sixty small moons.

On the sixth day, Brina called their attention to ship navigation. "Excuse me," said the computer, "your highness wanted to know if we were approaching a challenging course in. We are above an asteroid belt but will have to adjust to stay safely high to the orbital plane."

"Adjust and accelerate to keep our arrival time," said Omni.

"As you wish," said the computer. Both Omni and Newton casually went to the bridge and settled in, the separated back and seat support allowing Omni's abdomen through the seat. They watched a distant wedge of asteroids drop in the forward circle of focus.

"Can we fly through for the fun of it?" asked Newton.

"Better iv we don't," said Omni. "We might pull something out of stable orbit. Living world is two planets in."

Newton nodded. "It's all fun until we drop an asteroid on your world."

"Right," said Omni.

They watched the approach and Newton pulled up an image on one of the screens available on the helm. He was able to do this because Omni had outfitted his side of the helm with buttons and sliders. Controls for Kai were holes and grooves to accommodate the tips of their claws. Newton learned that the last thing Omni did before outfitting the ship was make the buttons for his hands. He remembered Ronnie once saying that he and Omni made a good couple, and Newton could see that all these signs of her consideration for him indicated that hers was genuine love. Could he seriously be intimate with such a different creature? He glanced sideways at her. He wasn't disgusted. It was interesting how his affection for her seemed to soften the startling contrast, how his love put pleasure into her alien face and body.

Yet, they were on a mission to find Pin. That was a reason to dampen the entire notion, but if it was just her and him, their obvious differences didn't actually didn't matter to them. Was it a reason for Newton to grab the controls and disappear with Omni? Almost, but he loved Pin, also, and he was desperately worried about her. Stay the course, he thought.

Without discussion, they both stayed at the helm for the final approach to Freeland. Fourteen hours, they flew over an asteroid belt and the orbit path of red planet on the far side of the star. And then, there it was.

"It looks like your jewel," said Newton. The planet had vast oceans so was mostly blue, but weather systems of white clouds and green and brown land masses added definition to the color. There were also white masses at the poles and showing the mountain ranges.

"It really doez," Omni said quietly. She took the control stick and hit some switches to take the ship off autopilot to start a deceleration. She flew a loop outside the orbit Freeland's moon, careful not to fly between the planet and the star. "Going in, approach on dark zide, invisible moon, stealth up," said Omni. Newton remembered and engaged the cloaking feature. He also turned on all sensors. Going slow enough to see all directions without distortion, they floated over the top of the moon and leveled out; they approached the north hemisphere on the night side of the planet.

"There are no radio signals and negligible artificial lighting," said Newton.

"Where?" asked Omni. "Zovtins have better eyes."

"Top far right quadrant," answered Newton. "Brina, crescent shaped cumulative light source middle land mass, other light sources on an island above and mid-peninsula below, magnify and display on helm screens." Overhead views of three nebulous masses of orange lights appeared. "Magnify center view," said Newton.

The view zoomed in until they could see streets lit with various points of flickering orange, with buildings made of timber, stucco and stone. There was a river going through the middle of a city, a dark ages city with an island in the river, an island in the heart of the city. There was a concentration of lights on the island, firelight arranged around what might have been some sort of construction site. "Any more magnification?" Newton asked.

"Magnification at maximum," the computer replied.

"Let's follow the dark to this other land mass, see if we can find a less populated area so we can get closer, maybe catch a glimpse at what they look like," suggested Newton.

"Yez," agreed Omni. She steered left over an ocean, following night to a more pristine land with less permanent structures. Newton was busy with scientific instruments. Oxygen, nitrogen, carbon dioxide, water with the right ionic charge, carbon based life, the world was completely wholesome. "Well, this planet toxic?" she asked.

"If I'm reading this right, we could breathe the air, drink the water, eat the food, forever. There is nothing that we would classify as pollutants. It appears that Freeland is a virgin world," he murmured.

"No zhit?" said Omni, sounding surprised. She leaned over and peered at the sensor readings. After a moment she exclaimed, "I can't believe it, a virgin world!"

They flew from a coastline in to an uninterrupted forest that covered the eastern third of the continent. The forest gave way to huge lakes and river basins. The signs of the preeminent life forms disappeared past the lakes. On the plains, just before they reached a mountain range that divided the continent, Omni doubled back to set down on the bend of a river at the base of a mountain that ran the wrong way. Newton was watching the sensors and knew the closest preeminent was half a continent away. There was, however, life outside the spacecraft. They flew over a herd of large, wooly, short-horned animals that numbered in the thousands.

He knew the protocol was to go out one at a time, so Newton was first into the airlock, to perish outside if the sensors were wrong, but once his feet touched the grassy riverbank, he forgot protocol and was eager to share the experience. The sweetness of the air almost brought tears to his eyes. After a few minutes, he remembered that he was supposed to wet a finger and touch the soil then taste it. The hatch opened behind him. Omni stepped out and handed him the wrist radio he was supposed to be wearing.

"All vun till you locked outside your zpazeship," she commented. They wandered around the riverbank for a while, tasting the water, examining plants, gazing at the stars.

Sitting on a grass covered bluff, gazing at an immense mountain shaped like an ocean wave that reached both ends of the horizon, Omni asked, "Should we even vind Pin? This iz a beautivul planet to live on."

"Well, we still need to know what they look like. If she's out somewhere like this, she'd be fine, but if she tries to mix and it goes badly, we can't abandon her here. These preeminent beings might be really horrible," said Newton.

"How we vind her?"

"Her ship has a transponder. It signals if something goes wrong, so we would've got a signal on the way in if she didn't land. You can't disable it. Once stationary and powered down, it gives a different signal. We search for that signal, which is a pulse every span. We are going to have to design a search pattern for the entire planet, listening for that pulse." Newton pulled a long stalk of grass and nibbled on the green end. "So let's go back the way we came and try and catch a look these preeminents."

"Yez," said Omni.

They reluctantly got back into the ship and steered east. Once in the big lake country, they continued until they followed a river that cut its way through dense forest in an effort to drain to the distant ocean. They saw a village of longhouses and moved closer while fully cloaked. Hovering at the line of trees, they waited. The eastern horizon brightened as a breeze whispered through the treetops. A light flickered and grew in one of the longhouses. A man wearing leather leggings brought a burning stick outside to a fire circle. Closer to the ship, a figure came out of the woods to the riverbank. It was a woman in a tanned hide dress decorated with shells around the top opening and medallions of quillwork in a line down the front. Her long dark hair was gathered in three thick braids, reminding Newton of Pin. The woman slipped out of her beaded slippers, pulled up her skirt and waded waist deep into the water. She glanced up at the sky and fixed her gaze on the ship. "Can she see us?" whispered Newton.

"Zovtinz have very good eyez," Omni whispered back. "Zhe see outline az contour curve around edge." The woman stared directly at the hovering ship. "Thiz cloze, zhe might hear us, too. Zhe came vrom outside village."

"What do we do?" asked Newton.

"Wait for the blink zhe lookz away, then jump." The woman sidled in the direction of the bank while watching their portion of sky. She turned her head; Omni yanked the stick and they pulled away and behind the line of trees, pulling higher and accelerating toward the coast.

"The preeminent species are graces," said Newton, "with hunter-gatherers on one continent and middle period city dwellers separated by an ocean."

Chapter XII: Signs of Loss

They searched for Pin for nearly a month, taking a
couple of breaks in the tropical areas of the planet so Omni
could enjoy the environment. Each time they went back to
the ship Newton felt it was cruel to take Omni out of the
jungle because she was so happy flying from tree to tree,
tasting fruits, and swimming in wide, warm rivers.

But then they received the muted ping of Pin's ship,
coming from the island with one of the three cities they saw
on their initial approach to the planet. After methodical
passes, they narrowed it down to a lake in the northern half
of the island. Pin submerged the landing craft to hide it. The
water and the iron ore in the surrounding geography
dampened the signal. Pin was smart enough to know this was
very good place to leave the ship.

What worried Newton was a good place for the ship
didn't necessarily make it a good place for Pin to assimilate.
The villages and the land in the area were agrarian or
pastoral, so there were few wild places for Pin to hunt and
stay in seclusion. Another troublesome idea came from
Ronnie. In all their sightings of the people on Freeland, they
were all graces. They didn't appear to have a robustus line.

After making certain that Pin wasn't in the lander, Omni
and Newton argued about the next step for an entire day.
Finally, he pulled rank and told her how it was going to go:
She would drop him off in a forest clearing well outside a
village, and then she would park under water next to the
landing craft. She would give him a week, six planet days,
and then rendezvous at the clearing. He had an emergency
call button disguised as a medallion on a silver chain. No
radio contact between him and the ship, just the frequency to
his subdural transponder, upload the plan to the Clarion and
then go silent. Newton stepped out of the ship and found

himself standing in a meadow as the barely visible, shimmering outline of the Brina floated up and away into the night sky.

He walked till he found the path to the village. Once on the road, he loaded a pipe that Omni had carved from wood. She told him not to use the lighter she made in front of the indigenous, but he was alone, walking in a starlit night. He smoked rag and walked in full costume, sword and long dagger on a bandolier, his belongings bag hanging at the other hip.

A little after sunrise, Newton reached a large stucco building with a thatch roof. A wooden sign with picture of a mug hung outside the door. He heard activity inside so he pulled a string to unlatch the door and entered. There were five men inside, two at one table, two at their own tables, and a stocky man with a red beard standing in a doorway to the kitchen. Their clothing was considerably more crude, but at least the idea was right. A vest over a cotton shirt, with stockings over short breeches and leather shoes, and three of the men had knives under or on leather belts. All of the men stopped their conversations at the sight of Newton. The man with the red beard approached and said something. Newton said he didn't understand him. The man then lifted his palms as if to ask what Newton wanted. The innkeeper then gestured as if he were bringing food to his mouth. Newton nodded, hoping it meant yes. The man then beckoned Newton with a gesture to a table in a private niche with an open, wooden hatch window. Newton thought about all the men eyeing his sword as he took his seat.

Luxurious as a Kai reconnaissance ship was, it didn't have the storage for complex foodstuffs, so Newton had spent a week eating little more than concentrated nutrition wafers. Even primeval food would be an improvement. The innkeeper put three coins on the table, a small copper coin, a small silver coin, and larger silver coin. He looked at Newton, then the coins, and back to Newton.

Newton pulled the small money bag from his accoutrement and opened it under the table where the innkeeper couldn't see it. He selected a small silver coin that had the impression of a bird's head. He handed it to the innkeeper. The man looked at the coin for a while and nodded with satisfaction. He then slid the sample coins off the table. Newton then pulled out his pipe and held his palm up. The innkeeper smiled, nodded and walked away. Soon the man returned with a lit candle and a long taper of wood. He used the candle to light the wood and smoked his pipe. People came and went; some would pause for a double take at the sight of Newton, but he figured it was the quality of clothes that caught their attention.

The innkeeper brought Newton's food in three trips, serving porridge and flat bread, strawberry tarts and two roasted doves. Newton smiled and waited for the innkeeper to walk away before he got out the tester stick. He stirred the porridge and poked the bread, tarts and doves. None of them triggered a color change on the stick. There were no poisons. The innkeeper then brought Newton a mug of ale.

He then tested the ale, which also passed. Newton spent the next hour relishing every mouthful. The porridge tasted a bit murky, most of peas and barley, but it was still an improvement to nutrition wafers. The tarts were good, the doves were even better. Newton finished the food and took sips of the ale until it was gone.

After he cleared the table, the innkeeper again gestured the question of what Newton wanted, this time offering a room with pantomime of sleep. Newton nodded an affirmative. The innkeeper rubbed the tips of his thumb and forefinger together. Newton again hid the money bag and pulled out a coin. This coin was slightly bigger, with a man's face on one side and a lute on the other. He smiled when he handed it to the innkeeper, hoping the man didn't notice the face on the coin looked a lot like Newton.

The innkeeper led Newton out of a side door and up a cobblestone path. They stepped over a creek to three small huts. The huts had loosely fitting doors and a window, thatched roofs and were arranged in line with the creek. Paving stones formed an area to the get to the water in front of each hut. After waiting at the entrance of the closest hut, the innkeeper registered Newton's confusion and opened the door. He went in, came out with a pitcher, filled the pitcher with water from the creek and took it back into the hut. Newton followed the innkeeper in; the man smiled, showing some missing teeth, and departed.

Newton's room had a sleeping pallet and small table with a pitcher and basin. He pulled the bag from his shoulder and set in on the dowel and leather caddy. Newton was about to take off the bandolier with his sword when he realized that he couldn't simply sleep. Thinking in the third dimension required a vulnerability test. He was in an alien world, and even though the discussion with Omni of what they should do deprived him of sleep, his presence was going to generate attention. Different clothes, money, weapons, strangers were considered a threat more often than not. He needed to be sure.

He let go a heavy sigh before putting the strap to his bag back over his shoulder. Newton opened the small wooden door to look out the window. The view allowed a look at the back of the inn and a vantage into a street of the nearby village, with a few people milling about in simple clothes. In the foreground, a red haired girl with a short broom herded a group of geese to a wide, stone-lined part of the creek. Newton watched her for quite a while; she had skin so white that it seemed to glow with the sunlight. The girl watched the geese closely and would sweep any droppings away from the creek. The geese drank and played in the water. Newton wondered why the birds didn't just fly away.

At the back of his room was another hatch window. Newton made certain there was no one to see him, put his accoutrement and bandolier out the window, crawled out himself, picked up his things, and headed into the woods behind the hut, keeping the hut behind him to block the view from the inn. Newton moved stealthily into the forest, pausing every now and then, making sure he wasn't seen by anyone, moving to high ground. He found a place in some rocks. Bushes covered the shadowed niche, a place to retreat if necessary, and a view to the cluster of buildings of the inn. Six-hundred strides down the hill, he watched the hut where he was thought to be sleeping.

Morning passed; afternoon clouds thickened from the northwest and in the mellowing light of early evening, Newton was beginning to think the vulnerability test was pointless. But then the innkeeper rushed from the inn toward the hut as a man at arms on a horse appeared on one side of the inn and then two more from the other side. The innkeeper turned to face them. It was way too far away to hear anything, but the body language told the story. The innkeeper was protecting the front door of the hut, while the three men dismounted and crowded closer to the door. Another man rode up to the group, dismounted, approached them, and knocked the innkeeper out of the doorway. The forth man then kicked the door in, let the door snap back as he stood aside, pulled it off its leather hinges and tossed it away. He motioned for two of the men to go in, which they did, and soon came out to report the hut was empty.

The leader glanced inside before walking around to the back of the hut. He examined the ground outside the window as a light rain began to fall. With an angry hunch in his shoulders, the man stared in the direction of the trees. Two of the men got on their horses and started slowly toward the forest, watching the ground. Newton had already surveyed the land behind the rocks so he knew he had barely enough time to get down a ravine and across a meadow to a denser wood. Moving made one more visible, but if the men on horseback were familiar with the area, then they would know of his hiding place. He watched their methodical advance to the trees. With rain and darkness falling, Newton squeezed through the crevasse behind the escarpment, checked for a clear course and started down the ravine.

Newton walked for three days, mostly by night, toward the highlands. Flying over the area with Omni had taught him that the villages clustered around larger estates and more orderly tracts of land. This was also the direction from which the riders came, and if his purpose was to find Pin, then it made sense. Word of a man dressed in similar fashion to Pin had brought the men from where she was being kept. He realized the plausibility was scant, but it was all he really had. Newton also realized that getting closer to the source of armed men was reckless, but he needed information.

He was walking at dusk in an unusually dense wood. Thickets seemed to repel casual travel, filling in spaces to reflect paths away from the heart of the forest. He defeated the bramble barricades numerous times, sometimes with mild injury, always with a compromise of time. The atmosphere changed in the darker heart of the wood. With the absence of breeze, the air was more humid and sweet. Then Newton noticed the gardens. Rocks would form a pool from a spring or creek and hand cut irrigation trench and the pool would feed the garden. Some were herbs, some cherry or berry bushes, some hand woven arbors with strawberries or peas. There were also clearings with patches of grains, barley, oats and wheat.

Something in the periphery made Newton look left. In the mellow light, coming from a shadowy depth of forest, a shaggy animal was closing on him. Narrow, waist high, a long face and piercing gold eyes, the way it fixed its gaze but moved in silently suggested this wasn't a wild creature. Newton knew that primitives had companion animals, but he had never seen one. He had mere seconds to decide his response; was he going to fight or run? Think in the third dimension, he told himself. Be nice. Don't be a threat. Newton dropped to one knee. With sing-song tones, Newton said, "Hello, ugly beast. Are you a nice monster?" The large animal was so surprised that it skidded to a stop and looked at him with its head tipped.

Seeing the confusion, he continued. "My name's Newton. I'm new to your world. I saw in a book somewhere that primitives had pets. Are you a pet?" The animal gave its tail a slow sway back and forth. "Come here, let me see you," he coaxed. The beast approached and started sniffing the air in his direction. Moving slowly, Newton put his hand a little closer. With tentative steps, the beast closed in enough to smell Newton's hand. It seemed to like his smell and licked his hand. Instinct told him to pat the animal's head. It moved even closer and leaned into him, enjoying a rub behind its ears. He was privately amazed, kneeling eye-to-eye with this strange creature.

"Loop," said a voice. Newton looked up to see an old woman standing in the evening shadows. There was enough light to make out the woman's facial expression. She looked somewhat surprised and even more angry. The woman called the animal again and this time it pranced to her. Newton stood, not sure what to do.

After studying him for a moment, the woman asked him a question. Newton shrugged his shoulders and told her that he wished he could understand her language but that he was impressed by the landscaping he noticed in the area.

The old woman approached Newton, saying something that sounded like a complaint, keeping the animal at her side. She stood at slightly more than a conversational distance, still grousing that there was a trespasser at the edge of her barley plot. The woman fell silent and spent a long time just looking at him, his face, clothes, hands, boots, accoutrement, weapons. He also looked at her, hair pulled into braids so long that the gray streaks reached halfway down to her waist, ending with brown at her knees. Her dress was made from a light blue, shimmering linen with an under blouse of white. Laces gathered the bodice and the skirt was gathered with pleats around the waist.

The woman seemed amused by something about him. She seemed to make a decision and turned, beckoning him to follow with a gesture and a word. They walked for a while, stopping as she would start a fire in a basket. One fire was difficult to start with the flint and iron. When the old lady wandered away searching the ground for kindling, Newton used the Kai lighter to start the fire. She came back to a crackling fire and she actually smiled. Newton smiled, too.

She led him to a cottage in clearing. There were other structures behind the cottage but the cottage was lit from within, visible through small, actual glass windows with open shutters. Smoke rose from the chimney. The woman called to someone inside the cottage. Someone called back. With a raised voice, the woman said something that took numerous words to say. Newton also worried about the urgency in her voice. If Newton hadn't placed the voice inside as a child, he would've busted in through the door before they could complete their preparations.

Another compromise Newton allowed was the jacket. She made a gesture to suggest it was hot in the cottage and gave his jacket a quick tug at the sleeve. Newton said how he didn't believe her for a blink but was going to play along to get inside to see what was really happening in the cottage. He took off the sling for the bag, the bandolier and the jacket. With these items draped over his arm, he waited for the trap.

Making sure the animal stayed outside, the woman opened the door and went in, stepping aside and holding the door. She closed the door behind him as Newton first noticed a table holding a candelabrum with a dozen lit candles, saw a young woman across the room to his left and a boy in the closest corner to his right. Both had loaded crossbows pointed at him. In tones of both reassurance and warning, the woman took the items folded over his arm and put them in the corner to his left. Newton turned his head and watched woman become interested in the weapons. She unsheathed sword and spent a moment with the blade, feeling the edge, looking closely at the steel, bouncing it in the air to sense the weight. She said something aloud, held the point off the wooden floor and dropped the sword. The sword bit into the wood and stood straight up from the floor. Keeping her distance, she ducked under the girl's line of fire and stood in front of Newton.

With a motion for the girl, skinny, early twenties, with a huge tangle of dark hair, to move to the weapons corner behind Newton, the woman waited and then moved closer. The woman untied a string at the cuff of his shirt and the leather strip on his vest. After saying something to the girl, the woman looked at his wrist and his forearm, and she then felt under his armpits. She made expressions to show her his teeth and open his mouth, which Newton did. She felt the glands under his jaw. She seemed fascinated by his hair, pulling the tight curls straight at his temple and again behind his ear. The girl behind him asked a question that provoked a scoff from the old woman. The woman said something back, a statement that involved turning Newton's hand, touching the lines of his palm and pressing the ends of his fingertips and watching the blood flow back. She said something else and felt for the pulse in his neck, which caused her to nod when she found it.

Newton's patience was wearing thin when the woman stepped away and came back with a length of cord. She tied his wrists together at the front. When she pointed to a stool for Newton to sit on at the end of the table, it set off some tense discussion between the girl and the woman. The woman's tone was firm but patient, pointing to Newton's boots, vest and head. She again indicated for Newton to sit at the end of the table, which he did.

Part of Newton's training was to plan a response in complete sequence to any defensive scenario, and once the raffish haired girl moved back to the distant left corner of the room, the scenario changed to where Newton could subdue them without hurting anyone. He let the girl get set with the crossbow and the woman to take a seat to Newton's right.

Still, he waited for the tension to put focus somewhere other than on him. The woman began to say something, not to him, but aloud, sounding rhetorical, but fatefully, pulling attention off of Newton for a second.

He took hold of the seat to the stool and lurched into motion, rolling backward, holding the stool as a shield, THUNK, a crossbow bolt from the boy. Once on his feet, still crouched, he spun and cut the cord between his wrists with the sword stuck in the floor. Newton then went into a shoulder roll toward the girl, unfolding and springing up, snatching a platter off the table with one hand and pushing the girl's crossbow up with his other hand, the bolt being launched into the ceiling, SWIP. The woman screech as the boy fired another bolt at the corner. Newton used the platter to stop the bolt from hitting the girl, SWACK. He tossed the bolt pierced platter at the boy to delay a reload, tossed the girl's crossbow to the corner with his sword and he jumped, tucked into a roll over the table and unfolded in front of the boy. Newton pulled the crossbow from the boy's grasp and tossed it to the corner. The entire fracas took five seconds, leaving the girl, the woman and the boy dumbstruck.

"Basic training for Fleet takes two revolves, and only nine out of a hundred actually graduate," said Newton with a casual tone. He guided the boy by the shoulders to a seat at the table next to the woman. He pointed at the stool, on which the boy sat. "To stay in Fleet, we have a trial by combat once a revolve. Even admirals have to fight to stay on active duty." He rounded the table to the girl, who was protecting her right hand with her left. Newton gently took her hand and found a cut on her middle finger. He got a handkerchief from his pocket, bit the edge to start the rip and tore a strip. The girl watched him with confusion as he bandaged her finger with the strip of cloth. He then pointed to a place at the table. She went to take a seat. "So, the idea that I could be apprehended by an old woman, a mop-headed girl and a scrawny whelp, it's a little insulting," he concluded.

Newton went to the corner and got his belongings bag, moving it to his former place at the end of the table. Three dimensional thinking caused him to stop, look back, pull the sword from the floor and poke it into the threshold, holding the door closed.

Picking up the stool and working the bolt free, he tossed the bolt to the corner and took his seat. All three of them gazed at him with more curiosity than fear. He patted his open hand on his chest and said, "Newton." The girl and the woman repeated his name.

He gestured to the woman. "Mary," she said.

A look and a nod at the boy, "John," he said.

He then gestured to the young woman. She gave him a shy smile and said, "Sarah."

With a satisfied nod, Newton said, "Well, Mary, John, Sarah, I'd like to begin with a note of appreciation. You people smell a lot better than the other Freelanders I've met, and you seem healthier. Like you, Mary, you have all your teeth. I saw an innkeeper, half your age, half the teeth he should have. So, whatever's going on here, keep it up." They didn't understand him, of course, but his tone seemed to put them at ease. Mary even seemed amused.

"Now, the reason I am here, I need to find my girlfriend. Her name is Pin, and I have a picture of her, drawn by my other girlfriend." Newton paused and smiled. "Please don't tell Pin I called Omni my other girlfriend." Newton opened the bag and brought out the folio. He flipped into it and brought out the pencil drawing of Pin, of her entire figure dressed in her middle period outfit, of her standing with her re-curve bow and wearing a demure smile. Newton couldn't help but be pulled into the drawing for a second; it just looked so much like her, proportion, shading, perfect, with blue colored pencil for her hair. He handed the drawing to Mary.

Mary was confused at first, spending some time feeling the paper, looking at the reverse side of the page and touching the edge of the drawing, smudging the pencil mark. Eventually, Mary showed the drawing to John, who nodded first but then shrugged.

When Sarah saw the drawing, however, she said something excitedly to Mary. Mary and Sarah talked back and forth for quite a while, with Sarah pointing to the drawing's blue hair and Pin's hands. Sarah held the drawing for a quiet moment as Mary sat with her arms crossed, looking at Newton with concern.

Newton saw that Omni included three colored pencils in the folio, black, red and blue, so he got a blank page and drew two boxes, one with a stick figure with blue hair standing at the shoreline of a lake, with the distinctive shape of the rocks above the lake. He slid the page to Sarah and pointed at the empty box; he also held his hand palm up with a questioning look on his face before holding out the black and blue pencil.

Sarah said something to Mary that seemed to be asking whether she should tell Newton what she knew. Mary thought through a pause, let go a worried sigh, and conceded with a nervous nod. Sarah took the pencils and drew four stick figures that were horses, a smaller stick figure lying on the ground with antlers. She hesitated, looking at Newton. Newton held his hands in a worried question and begged, "Please tell me what happened to Pin." Sarah took a deep breath and drew two human stick figures on horseback and two standing on the ground holding something. She glanced nervously to Newton before drawing in the central stick figure, the one being held, and finishing the central figure with a curved line of blue hair.

Newton stared at the sketch for a moment. He drew a third square and an arrow to the blank square. On the line of the arrow, he drew five stick figures, with two holding the one in the middle, the middle one with blue hair.

Again, Sarah seemed to ask if she should answer the question, and again, Mary relented. Sarah drew the towers, wall and fortified door of a castle.

Newton stood and began gathering the two drawings and pencils. He put the folio away and got his coin-purse, pulling out three gold coins and putting them on the table in front of Mary. This set off a passionate discussion between Sarah and Mary. Newton didn't care. He just found out that Pin was in trouble. He needed to get back to his ship, and then these primitives would have a serious problem. He went to the corner and started getting ready to leave.

Sarah approached and touched his arm. He looked at her, oval face, large, wide-set eyes, narrow nose, full lips and wide mouth. She was a truly beautiful girl, except for the dark red birthmark on her cheek, a red stain shaped as a partially broken human skull. He made a point of looking in her eyes as she spoke to him with plaintive tones.

With gentle but assertive tones, Newton said, "I am all that Pin has. I have got to go and help her. I'm going to go and help her." He held her shoulders. "I appreciate you telling me, but don't try and stop me."

Newton tried to turn back to his preparations but Sarah reached up and touched his face. She spoke more urgently, pinching the skin on the back of her hand and pointing to his hands, touching his face and then her own, her hands then moving in a frustrated effort to explain something to him. He shook his head and put on his jacket, shouldered his bandolier and bag. He pulled his sword out of the threshold. "Newton," called Sarah. He looked at her. With both hands seeming to press with a downward motion, Sarah asked him to wait. Sarah then spoke to Mary. The old woman considered something then nodded. Sarah climbed a ladder to the floor above the room. They stood around listening to movement above their heads, with Newton wondering what he was waiting for, wishing he could just leave. He had three days of walking to get to the rendezvous point. Sarah dropped a bag and climbed down the ladder; she was wearing a cloak and leather slippers. Newton realized that she intended to go with him. He shook his head emphatically. Mary said something to Newton, pointing from Sarah to him and lifting her eyebrows as if to say he needed her. Sarah shouldered her travel bag, walked up to him and stood. The expression on Sarah's face told Newton there was no point in denying her. Mary said something to the boy, who dashed off into a small room off to the side. The boy came back with a leather sack, which Mary looked into and then handed to Newton.

Sarah then kissed Mary on the forehead and ruffled John's hair. Newton waved to them and opened the door. Sarah shooed the animal inside then closed the door to the cottage. She then smiled, letting Newton lead the way.

They walked by night and rested by day. Sarah seemed to appreciate Newton's style of stealthy travel. The talked quietly, although neither could understand what the other was saying. He enjoyed her company and was slightly taken aback when she stripped nude and bathed in a pond. Her limbs had such a subtle definition, looking straight and seemingly the same width of her elbows and knees, but the volume of muscle was so smooth and graceful. She was also chesty, with round, highly set breasts. When she came out of the pond, shivering, he opened his arms to warm her up and rub her down with his spare shirt. She came to him without hesitation, and waited in his arms until she was warm. In the sack that Mary had sent was a ham, berries, and some flat bread.

They did have a few close calls. There were riders who patrolled the roads, and with a waxing moon, they prompted a search that forced them to hide for half a day. They moved from cover between patrols and escaped into a hedgerow.

When they stood at the edge of the meadow, Newton wondered how he was going to get on the spacecraft with Sarah standing next to him. Maybe she would be frightened away. He didn't intend to take her with him and thought that would solve the problem. This was the assumption as the shimmering outline of the Kai ship lowered to the center of the clearing. Newton walked out to meet it, and when the door opened — a hole in the world — Newton turned to say goodbye. Sarah's jaw dropped with surprise. Newton stepped up into the airlock and waved goodbye, but Sarah shook her head and jumped up and held him in a tight hug. He started to pull free but her arms tightened even more.

Omni's voice came by intercom. "What doing? Cloze door. Vreelanderz coming fazt, on big animalz, vour hundred stridez."

"Shit," said Newton. He closed the outside door and opened the inside hatch. He pushed into the living area and pointed to the table with the seats. Confusedly, Sarah let go and took a seat. He pointed to tell her to stay put and called over his shoulder, "Omni, go!" The ship pulled up and tilted so fast that internal gravity almost didn't compensate. Newton wavered while the gravity stabilized and then sat down next to Sarah. "Brina, put the navigation view on the table screen," said Newton. The screen lit up with trees flowing under the ship. Omni stopped, hovered, and pointed the ship at the road behind four riders on horseback. They rode away, toward the meadow.

Omni then turned and flew back toward the lake. Sarah watched the screen but also took glances out the window next to the dining area. When the ship tilted nose down to go into the lake, Sarah grabbed the table in a panic. Newton soothed her with a reassuring hug at the shoulders. Omni put down right next to the landing craft. A school of fish swam up to the light of windows. Sarah touched the window and turned to Newton with wonderment on her pale face. You haven't seen anything yet, thought Newton. He got up from the table to meet Omni.

Omni's voice led her approach from the bridge to the living space. "You good? Next time, I go on mizzion and you ztay here and worry." Omni stood close to Newton, opening his jacket, looking him up and down.

"I'm fine," he said with a grin. He grabbed and held Omni's claw. "I should introduce our guest."

She tipped her head while looking at him. "Why do we have guezt?"

"She insisted on coming with me. I thought the ship would scare her away but she grabbed me in the airlock and wouldn't let go." Both Newton and Omni looked at Sarah, who appeared as if she might be going into shock.

"Courze zhe wouldn't let go," said Omni with the smell of cinnamon getting stronger. "How many girlz do you need?" asked Omni.

"Quit," said Newton, "I don't know what to do."

"Why not juzt let her go? You vriendz with zcary monster bug. Zhe probably go away now," said Omni.

"Why not? She knows about where Pin is," said Newton.

"How you communicate?" asked Omni.

Newton took the bandolier and the bag strap off his shoulders. Putting the folio on the table and dropping the bandolier and bag on the floor, Newton introduced Sarah to the Kai. "Sarah, this is Omni," he said, holding Omni's shoulders. "Omni," he repeated. He dropped his hands. "Omni, this is Sarah," he said with a gesture to Sarah.

"Zarah," said Omni.

Sarah pursed her lips but then said, "Omni."

Newton opened the folio and showed Omni the drawings. Omni surprised them both by getting a blank page and quickly drawing three different castles. Watching Omni draw was amazing in itself; she didn't outline and fill in but rather went across the page at various angles with lines and dots, and she was quick. Each drawing took a minute but had depth and a spare but undeniable photorealism. Sarah pointed to one of the castles.

"Thiz iz helpvul," said Omni. "I do recon, know where this iz." Omni went to the closet next to her sleeping berth and got out the pipe. She handed it to Newton, who took a puff of hesh. He and Omni passed it back and forth. Sarah got a blank sheet of paper and held it up, apparently asking if she could use it. Omni went to the table, flipped through several sheets, pointed at Sarah and nodded. She also touched the pencils, nodded and pointed at Sarah. Sarah got a page and pencil and started doodling.

Omni and Newton smoked for a little while, relaxing in one another's company. "There'z something I not tell you," said Omni.

"What?"

"Zal wantz to talk to you."

"Of the Guardians?"

"Yez, he waiting vor you to get back."

Newton smiled. "You were going to tell me, eventually?"

"I mizz you. Hell with Zal. You can talk to me virst," said Omni.

Newton laughed and hugged Omni's shoulder. "Well, let's go talk to Sal." He turned and called, "Sarah?" She looked up. He pointed to himself, the bridge, to her, and then gestured with an open hand to ask her to stay. She nodded.

Once Omni and Newton were on the bridge, Omni opened the communication station. "Kai Recon Brina to Zal," said Omni.

"This is Sal," said a voice. The view-screen formed a face.

"You wanted to talk to me?" asked Newton.

"More than that, I need you to get the landing craft off planet, as quickly as possible."

"Why?"

"Because every blink it is there it presents an enormous danger of cultural contamination. It could destroy the arc of scientific discovery, and the faith of everyone on the planet. We have shown great patience, but it is very stressful for us to have it there. Please, please, get that off the planet. We could destroy it, but out of respect for you, we would prefer you just pilot it away, back to the Clarion," said Sal.

"We haven't found Pin yet," said Newton.

"And we will help you find Pin, but the culture of this world must be protected."

"Not just find Pin," said Newton. "Rescue Pin. She has been abducted."

"How do you know that?" asked Sal.

Newton hesitated and answered, "A Freelander, a girl from this world, drew some pictures. Pin was seized by soldiers on horseback and taken to a fortress. This girl, by the way, refused to let me go, which means she's on board. I mention that because if you're worried about cultural contamination, what do we do about Sarah? She's already met Omni."

Sal nodded and said, "Patch me through to Sarah." Omni looked at Newton. He nodded. Omni put the communication through to the screen on the table. Sarah saw the light come up from under her drawing. Sal greeted her and introduced himself in her language. Newton got up from the chair on the bridge and looked back to the living quarters. Sal and Sarah talked for a quarter-hour and she had more questions than he. Eventually, Sal said something and Sarah pointed at Newton.

"Take back com," said Newton. Omni changed the source as Newton took his seat at the bridge. "What do we do with Sarah?" asked Newton.

"Every sentient being has autonomy. You could expropriate her, but she wants to stay. She says she can help," said Sal.

Newton squinted thoughtfully. "You can speak her language?"

"Yes, we represent the creator, who knows every language."

Newton dismissed the topical diversion. "Alright, here's my decision. Give me three spans; I'll get that lander off this planet and back to the Clarion. It's going to take a phase to get it back to the ship. Omni will take this ship back and be there in a quarter phase, and Sarah is going with her, to teach us her language and help us when we come back." Newton's voice became angry. "If something happens to Pin between now and then, I'm going to blame you, Sal, because I think we should blast our way in and get Pin right now. You're worried about cultural contamination but I'm worried about Pin!"

Sal nodded. "Understood, and we will be prepared for your return."

Still angry, Newton said, "Give me something else, because I hate this deal. How about a dorking dictionary with this planet's language and ours?"

"I'll send it, two copies, one for the lander and one for the Brina," said Sal.

"That would be great," growled Newton.

"Thank you, sincerely," said Sal. "How else can I help?"

Newton forced himself to think about the question. "Please explain to Sarah that she will be on board this ship for a quarter phase with Omni, without me. Tell her I won't see her again for a phase, and then ask her if she still wants to go with us to a ship deep in the night sky."

"Considerate phrasing and summary," Sal said, then nodded to Omni. She switched the com station back to the table. Newton leaned over and looked back to watch Sarah and Sal talk again. He could see Sarah's reactions. She nodded, and listened, and shook her head. She looked up at Newton, who signaled for Omni to take back the com. Sal's face popped up on the screen at the helm. "Sarah wants to go. She understands that you will go in a separate ship and that your journey will take longer. And she still wants to go."

"How do you explain a primitive having such courage?" asked Newton, "such understanding?"

"Intelligence and information are not the same things. And courage, Sarah says she found a little green mantis in the garden once, and said it looked at her while she was looking at it," said Sal as if this explained everything.

"These are remarkable beings," muttered Newton.

"Yes, which is why we need to protect them," said Sal. "Good future to you."

"Good future. Brina out," said Newton. Omni cut the com.

They outfitted Newton with his pressure suit and waterproof case with his belongings bag and a supply of rag and hesh, among other things. Newton hugged Omni and Sarah before he put on the helmet went out the airlock. Sarah and Omni watched Newton swim to the landing craft and go inside. The pilots of both ships spent an hour getting ready. The last thing Omni did was take button adaptations off Newton's side of the helm and have Sarah sit in the other seat. Omni buckled Sarah in and had the bottom part of the seat pull under her.

"Kai Recon Brina, this is Clarion lander, come in." Newton's face appeared on the screen. "Guess what I found in the lander," said Newton.

"The braid for Engine Two?" asked Omni.

"Good guess." Newton smiled. "Sensors indicate we're six-hundred strides clear, stealth up, top axis out, three-quarters atmosphere speed, then give her all she's got, ladies first."

Sarah watched with amazement as the Kai ship pulled up out of the lake, up off the green of the island, off the planet and out to space.

Chapter XIII: Death of Illusion

As they pulled away from Freeland, they saw the Guardian ship in a high, geosynchronous orbit above Sarah's green island. Omni flew around the planet for Sarah to see her world. Once both ships were outside the orbit of the moon, the lander and the Brina hovered for a moment to dial in their courses. The Brina then zipped away and accelerated to her impressive speed. Newton followed and noticed that Sal didn't send the dictionary file until the landing craft was past the orbit of the red planet.

Newton smiled to himself and started studying the Freeland language. This was how he would spend a month, studying, smoking a little hesh and a lot of rag and checking his ship status and navigation.

On board the Brina, Omni and Sarah had a lot more fun. Omni was indeed a language expert, and with the dictionary file and a native speaker, and with some techniques she designed for learning a completely foreign language, Omni was nearly conversant in a couple of days. They could communicate well enough to enjoy the journey.

Omni's facility with language also helped her realize that despite Sarah's primitive upbringing, the girl was smart. Sarah was illiterate, but once seeing a page of paper and a pencil for the first time, she was fascinated by the ease of drawing. Sarah's alacrity for learning would appear in other ways, too.

When Omni opened the scoops to pull in some hydrogen for the fuel cells, it provoked a discussion about basic matter. Omni tested Sarah to see if she truly understood the concept of atomic particles. She asked Sarah for an example to prove that something which was invisible was still made of small pieces. The girl thought for a moment and then blew a puff of air into her hand, closed her hand and then opened her hand, tossing the air toward Omni. Omni laughed with delight and told Sarah she was right and that she would answer any question, would teach her as much as she wanted to learn.

Sarah took advantage of the offer, although the discussion of electricity seemed to be more frustrating than satisfying. She got that lightning was made of one form of electricity, but Sarah didn't understand why the instruments didn't blow up from the vast energy. Again, the inspired question was: If electrons were moving through wire and circuits, why didn't we eventually run out of them?

With drawings and description, Omni illustrated that for the electricity in the instruments, the electrons bumped into the electrons next to them, and it was the moving wave of being bumped that made the instruments work. Sarah asked if that was enough. Omni assured her it was because certain metals, as the metals used in wires and circuits, had so many electrons that being bumped made for strong waves. Sarah looked at Omni with one eyebrow lifted. She then patted Omni on the knee and said the Freeland equivalent of "if you say so." Omni laughed with delight.

Another example of Sarah's humor was when Omni pulled up an image of the giant planet with a large red storm in the turbulent atmosphere. Sarah said that was her planet. When Omni asked why, Sarah pointed to the red spot on her cheek.

Omni also started Sarah on the alphabet, which she enjoyed so much she ran through every blank sheet of paper they had on board the ship. Omni adapted a tablet computer and a stylus to serve as a practice tool. Sarah was writing words on their pass of the last planet in the solar system, and Sarah was so engrossed that she asked Omni if she could take a picture so she could look at it later, and Sarah went right back to work.

After Omni called Sarah to the bridge for the approach to the Clarion, the girl came up and buckled herself to the back support. Omni never actually taught Sarah to do that, she just put it together after seeing that Omni was strapped in. Omni used her smaller, middle arms to pull the belt ends to prompt Sarah to tighten down her harness, which she did.

The Clarion was still oozing its way toward the fifty-mark axis point, still months away, completely visible, a pyramid drifting toward empty space. Omni touched the com station buttons and hailed the ship, "Kai Recon Brina, on docking approach." There was silence. Omni slowed her approach. "Vleet Ekzplorer Clarion, come in," said Omni. Still, there was no answer. Omni adjusted her course and flew under the pyramid, keeping the nose toward the ship. In Sarah's language, Omni said, "*Zarah, you have better eyez, look vor damage, holez, lightning, dark zpotz.*" Omni slowly flew around the ship, looking at every side.

"*I've never seen a sky ship before, but it looks good to me,*" said Sarah.

"Vleet Ekzplorer Clarion, this iz the Brina, come in," said Omni. She piloted to the side with the bay door and matched her position to the lazy drift. Omni worked some adjustments to the instruments, pulling in sensors and a trying to communicate to the computer. "Fleet Ekzplorer Clarion, open bay door."

"Unable to comply," said a computer voice.

"Check your zync, thiz iz Kai Zhip Recon Brina," Omni growled.

"Checking," said the computer.

"*Who are you talking to?*" asked Sarah.

"*That zhip'z computer, thinking mazhine,*" answered Omni.

"Sync found, mission found, no authority for docking filed," said the computer.

"Dorking Mot," muttered Omni. "You zo ztupid. Vorget we coming back?" Omni spent a moment hacking into the Clarion's intercom system, specifically for sickbay. She punched in a sequence that made a shrill whistle for a call tone. She pushed for the tone again, waited, pushed it again. With a crackling noise, Ronnie's voice said, "Is there a reason my intercom is making strange sounds?"

"Ronnie, thiz iz Omni, we outzide, bay door won't open."

"Shit! I'm sorry. I'll be right there. Hang on," said Ronnie.

Two minutes later, Ronnie's face appeared on the bridge console. "Hello, Ronnie," said Omni.

"Hello, your highness," said Ronnie, with an odd, disheveled aspect to her. "Welcome back to the Clarion." The ship rotated the bay door to the trailing side, with Omni matching the languid turn.

Aboard the Brina, they watched the yellow lights at the corners start flashing and the bay door slowly slide open. Omni put out the landing gear and hovered gently in and touched down on the floor of the bay. Omni told Sarah to wait while the bay closed and the indicator lights for gravity and atmosphere said things were stable. They remained buckled and watched the lights on the wall. Gravity was stable as they hovered in, but it took a few minutes for the atmosphere lights to go green on all four walls. Omni still did a thorough sensor check before letting Sarah unbuckle.

Omni instructed Sarah in airlock protocol while they disembarked the Brina. Sarah stretched and looked around the bay. They heard the door open. Ronnie approached eyeing Sarah with confusion. Ronnie stopped, bowed her head, and said, "Good to see you, your highness. It's been far too long." Ronnie seemed a bit shaken, but Omni not being able to smell Ronnie's emotional state, missed the cues.

Ronnie then looked at Sarah. With a worried tone, she asked, "Who is this?"

With a surprised glance from Ronnie to Sarah and back to Ronnie, Omni said, "Thiz iz Zarah, our contact with Vreeland." Ronnie gave the girl a little wave. Using the Freeland language, Omni introduced Sarah to Ronnie. "*Thiz iz Ronnie. Zhe iz a healer, and zhe the nizezt perzon on the zhip.*"

Sarah smiled and said, "Ronnie."

"Sarah," said Ronnie with an uncertain tone. Sarah nodded and reached for Ronnie's hand. "Sarah," Ronnie said with more confidence. The two held hands for a minute. Ronnie let go, glanced nervously at the ship and asked, "Where's Newton?"

Omni tipped her head back with surprise. "Mot not tell you?"

"Tell me what? You're scaring me!"

"Newton vine," said Omni. "He bringing the lander, be here later. Why didn't Mot tell you the mizzion?"

"Mot's losing his dorking mind, that's why," grumbled Ronnie. Tears formed in Ronnie's eyes as she nervously checked the direction of the door.

These signals were not too subtle for Omni to understand. She touched Ronnie's hand. "You good? He not hurt you, did he?" asked Omni.

Tearfully, gratefully, Ronnie shook her head. "No, he hasn't hurt me, but he's getting weird, standing too close, smelling my hair. I think it'll go back to normal now that he's not alone with me. And he's also hard to find. I have no idea where he is most of the time." Ronnie let go a sigh. Gazing at Omni, Ronnie exclaimed, "By the gods! It's good to see you." She grabbed Omni for a long hug. After she let go, Ronnie asked, "Is Pin coming back in the lander with Newton?"

"No. Guardianz want uz to get it ovv planet. We rezcue Pin later."

"Rescue?" asked Ronnie with a pained look.

"Yez. Zarah help uz vind her. Guardianz will help, too."

Ronnie shook her head. "Well, I think you should have Sarah in your suite, to protect her and continue learning her language. And, while we get her settled, how about you brief me on everything that's happened?"

Omni nodded and turned to Sarah. *"You remember how to open doors?"* The girl nodded. *"Go get your things and we will show you your room,"* said Omni. Sarah bounced her chin, went off to the spacecraft, went in, and after a moment, she came out with her traveling outfit and travel bag.

As if she suddenly realized something while looking at a pretty girl with a huge tangle of dark hair, dressed in a dark green hooded cloak, a bag hanging at her hip, pale, skinny legs sticking out from under a brown skirt and finished by leather slippers, Ronnie said, "A girl just barely civilized made friends with a Kai, got into a spaceship and taught you her language? What the hell?"

Omni nodded and said, "Newtin vound a good one. Pin vound the ztupid, ignorant, zuperztizhouz onez. But he vound her. Zhe invatuated with him."

Ronnie laughed. "Of course she is." Ronnie beckoned Sarah to follow.

The three of them walked to the ambassador suite, where Sarah stashed her things in one of the bedrooms. Sarah flopped on the bed and then played with light switches. Then they went on a tour of the ship as Omni filled Ronnie in on all the details of their mission.

Sarah would ask the occasional question or make the occasional comment, one of which was how she really liked Ronnie's clothes. When Omni translated, Ronnie offered an outfit and they stopped by Ronnie's quarters. Doctors in the Fleet were allowed to wear civilian clothes with insignia or badge. Ronnie outfitted Sarah with underwear, socks, boots, pants and matching jacket, shaped undershirt and belt—all with the strong, light, soft fabric, the ornament and detail of contemporary high fashion. The clothes fit Sarah well; she loved the details, zippers and pockets, snaps and seams.

When Ronnie pointed to the full-length mirror, after a second of confusion at seeing a mirror, Sarah laughed and struck different poses in the mirror. But then she noticed the red birthmark on her face. She got close to the mirror and touched it. She asked some questions and Omni translated, also translating Ronnie's answer. Sarah asked if something could be done about it. Ronnie said they would talk about it when they could talk to one another directly.

"Does that mean she can?" asked Sarah.

"Yes," answered Ronnie, intuitively guessing the question.

"Yes, but she needz to hear it vrom you," said Omni.

Sarah glanced to Ronnie and then focused on Omni. *"To be fair?"* asked Sarah.

"Yez, Doctor Ronnie haz great medizinez and toolz but zhe also carez," said Omni.

The three then continued the tour of the ship while Omni continued to brief Ronnie. She was especially interested to learn about the dictionary the Guardians gave them. Ronnie asked for a copy; Omni clicked her version of a chuckle and handed Ronnie a small flash drive. Another point that gave Ronnie pause was to learn that the braid for Engine Two was on the landing craft with Newton.

They were in the hall that led to the bio-cell. Ronnie stopped them in front of the door. She attempted to code-in the door. It denied entry. Omni punched in another code and the door slid open. Humidity and jungle smells flowed into the hallway. They walked a little way in, where the window-walls showed it was the morning side of midday. The door closed behind them as Omni was telling Sarah that although the bio-cell was beautiful, there were some dangerous plants and animals, so she shouldn't go in alone. Sarah gave a distracted nod as she stared into the verdant landscape. Ronnie motioned for them to go outside into the hallway. Once the door was closed, Ronnie said they needed to inform Mot.

She waited to call him from the hallway in case the bio-cell was a needed refuge. Ronnie touched the radio on her forearm. "Ronnie to Mot, Omni is back, with Sarah. When do you want a briefing?"

"Who the dork is Sarah?" asked Mot.

"Our Freeland contact." The transmission light went out and there was a pause.

"Admin, top next bright," said Mot.

Ronnie nodded and said, "At least he gave you a bright to rest. Tell Sarah I'll bring by some bathing, skin, and hair products. I also have other clothes that'll fit her." Ronnie lowered her voice. "And for now, let's not let her wander the ship alone."

Omni agreed with snappy nod and she and Sarah went to the suite. Ronnie went to sickbay and downloaded the dictionary, studying for several hours. Mot figured he better catch up on Ronnie's hourly reports that he had been ignoring.

Ronnie stopped by the suite the next morning and discovered that Sarah had been in the bath for more than an hour. Sarah invited Ronnie in and they spent hours going through the beauty products Ronnie brought, shampoo and conditioner for Sarah's hair, soap, lotion, deodorant, cotton swabs, disposable razor. Ronnie combed out Sarah's hair, manicured her hands, tweezed her eyebrows, showed her how to brush and floss her teeth. Sarah started taking double takes in the mirrors, appreciating the transition from wild child to beautiful woman. Ronnie also brought a clingy undershirt with a built-in bra.

Once dressed, Sarah looked so sophisticated that Omni took one look at her and decided to change her attire. They smiled as Omni came out of her bedroom wearing the black and green leather suit.

At hour fifteen, Ronnie, Sarah and Omni were sitting in the administration room. They all stood as Mot entered the room. He signaled for them to sit with an annoyed flit of his hand and took his seat at the head of the table. There was an odd moment with Mot glaring at Sarah, and she, rather than withering, her nostrils flared and she glared back, matching if not exceeding his contempt. Ronnie was quietly amazed at the exchange. It was a safe assumption that Sarah had never seen a robustus man before, two heads taller and more than three times her weight, and Sarah wasn't intimidated. Rather, she reacted to a contempt she could not possibly have earned. Ronnie's respect for Sarah bloomed.

Mot turned to Omni. "Why are the Guardians dictating where we park our lander?"

"It a legitimate conzern," said Omni. "Iv they vound that zhip, it could take the reazon to learn, the reazon to try, the reazon to ekzplore vrom the whole world. Bezidez, Newton command the mizzion, and he dezide. Don't you want the braid back?" The light scent of ammonia and charred meat came and went.

"I would rather that you had brought back the braid so this ship isn't floating helpless in the middle of nowhere. Instead, you bring me a scrawny little savage," said Mot, pointing at Sarah.

Sarah immediately began talking to Omni in assertive tones. Omni started to say something but Sarah touched Omni's arm and continued talking while looking directly at Mot. When she finished, Sarah nodded.

"What did she say?" asked Mot.

"Zhe zaid that her name is Zarah, and that we don't know her world. Zending Newton was a miztake. The way he was drezzed was a miztake. Zhe can help uz get Pin. And no one elze is ovvering to help uz," said Omni.

Mot thought a moment and asked, "Why was sending Newton a mistake?"

Omni translated the question. Sarah gave the question a long reply. Omni nodded and said, "The lazt black men, men with dark skin, were in her country with the 'Romanz,' zo long ago that mozt people have vorgotten. Newton will be notized and not welcome."

"What does she mean by 'Romans' and why wouldn't he be welcome?"

Again, Omni translated and listened. She translated the answer. "The Romanz had black men az zlavez."

Mot sat back and crossed his arms. "Graces as slaves? Would you take smack at explaining that, Doctor?"

Ronnie shrugged her shoulders. "It's as I feared. There are no robustus on Freeland, only gracile. So, apparently, the climate niche in which graces evolve will create different features, and when these varied and isolated populations meet up, the distinctions become a part of the power structure. We never focused on the differences between characteristics because the differences between robustus and graces were more pronounced."

Mot nodded and said, "Interesting." Mot stood, followed by Omni, Sarah and Ronnie. Mot looked at Ronnie. "Learn her language; figure out what else she means by our mistakes, and make sure she doesn't dork anything up on this ship, and make sure she isn't carrying diseases or parasites," said Mot. He left the room.

Sarah stared after Mot's departure, her expression one of mild disgust. "*Ugly monster*," she said.

"*Carevul*," said Omni. "*He really iz, and monzterz are dangerouz.*"

Ronnie gave Sarah a warm smile. Talking to Omni, she said, "Ask Sarah to stop into sickbay for a checkup, no hurry." Ronnie left the room.

The next couple of weeks were good for Sarah. She helped Omni and Ronnie learn her language, and they made a lot of progress. With Omni's language learning technique, with the dictionary from the guardians, with a computer algorithm Ronnie wrote, and with some brain mapping done as Sarah talked while in the dry amnio-chamber, Ronnie set up the chamber to add polarizing patterns to her own brain, polarizing the neurons to aid learning the Freeland language. Ronnie was soon fluent. Although the polarizing would not work for Omni, her talent for learning language kept her on par with Ronnie.

Sarah eventually asked Ronnie how she would get rid of the birthmark. Ronnie explained that the amnio-chamber would change her cells to energy and then make adjustments. Sarah asked if it was dangerous, and Ronnie said there were risks, and the procedure was a little scary because she may feel as if she was drowning, but it would only take a couple of hours. Ronnie tested Sarah to see if she was vain, asking if there was anything else Sarah wanted to change. She shook off the idea, saying she just wanted normal skin on her face, just like everyone else she had ever seen. Ronnie assured her that the red spot was something that happened to other people, and agreed to do the procedure.

When making the request for emergency nuclear power to run the amnio-chamber, Ronnie lied to Mot, saying it was necessary to get a genetic read and make certain there wasn't a threat. Mot agreed and assigned Omni to power up and shut it down as soon as the procedure was complete.

Once Sarah was in, the astonishing thing for Ronnie was the genetic blueprint. Freelanders were not just similar to graces, they had exactly the same sets of genes and chromosomes. Every preeminent species of the Five Worlds had a similar but a slightly different arrangement of chromosomes, the DNA pattern using different elements, compounds or proteins, but these aliens were made by an identical genetic processes. It was impossible, but there on the screens, every marker, unique to the individual but common to the organism.

Ronnie told Sarah it would take a couple of hours because she expected to have to solve for the differences. The actual procedure took her half an hour, and that was finding and fixing more of the red spot that was under Sarah's hair on the back of her head. Once the chamber was drained and Sarah came out of the shower, she got dressed and gave Ronnie a tearful hug of speechless gratitude. Sarah could only whisper thanks and leave sickbay.

Later that day, Mot told Omni to bring Sarah to the bridge. Once there, they realized that, much to Mot's aggravation, Sal wanted to talk to Sarah. They conversed at length, some about specifics of Sarah's province, some of the conversation was Sal merely checking to see that Sarah was being treated well. Sarah being able to report Omni's kindness and instruction, and Ronnie's eagerness to learn her language and removing the red spot, these details gave Sal the reassurance that he needed. When asked what Sarah thought of Mot, she said she never really saw him and figured that leaders were typically strong and aloof. Sal nodded and said they were working on a diplomatic solution to Pin's situation and the Guardians were going to ask for her help. Sarah assured Sal she would help. Mot was further annoyed that the communiqué ended without an acknowledgement of Mot or the Clarion.

A day later, Sarah was walking down the hall in front of the bio-cell and thinking about how she couldn't wait to show Newton her face without the red spot. The door to the bio-cell interrupted these thoughts as she looked at the keypad. Most of the doors on the ship just opened for her because she had the little broach that Ronnie gave her. Mot appeared at the end of the hall, stopped, then walked up to her. Without a word, Mot punched in a code. The door slid open and Sarah went in but stopped, remembering how she wasn't supposed to explore the jungle alone. Mot looked up and down the hallway and went in after her. The door slid closed.

Omni called Ronnie when Sarah didn't show up to get ready for dinner. Ronnie said that they would see if she showed up for dinner. The instant Omni signed off, Ronnie pulled up the frequency of the telemetry badge that Ronnie had given Sarah. The day's accesses popped up and then one denial, the last known location, the botanical cell. Ronnie strapped on the pulse pistol that Pin had assigned her months earlier and started for the bio-cell.

Her access was denied. Ronnie closed her eyes and cleared her mind. She listened for the tones that Omni had used to override the lock. Eventually, she heard them, low high, low high. There was one more, even higher, the highest tone, nine. Ronnie dialed it in, two seven, two seven, nine. The door slid open. Ronnie drew her pistol and entered a jungle in early evening light and the sounds of an active rainforest.

Ronnie did a methodical search to higher and higher ground. Just as Ronnie was beginning to hope the search was an overreaction, she broke from thicket to a small clearing and her movement disturbed a cluster of animals, carrion toads. The largest one leapt in her direction and she fired, pkCHOOM! The dark blob exploded into a cloud of red mist and the others scattered into the underbrush. What they were eating, it was pale, smooth skin. Ronnie had learned the graceful shape of Sarah's back and shoulders. Ronnie fell to her knees. In a sudden eruption of grief and anger, Ronnie vomited. After a time on her hands and knees, anger pushed the grief into the background, and anger focused her mind.

She stood and moved to examine the body, headless, signs of sexual assault. Her heart beating madly in her chest, Ronnie searched for Sarah's head. She spotted a tangle of hair some distance toward a grove of fruit bushes. Her walk gave her time to think and time for grief to replace the anger. Tears of genuine sorrow fell on Sarah's face as Ronnie reached down and turned the head. The critical information was that the head was severed by tremendous strength, more of a crushing pressure than any sort of cutting.

Mot. Mot killed Sarah. This knowledge was the end of everything. Ronnie forced herself to think. If Omni knew, Mot would be dead soon after, the same with Newton. She must think in the third dimension. Ronnie gently laid the head back the cradle of grass. Ronnie walked out of the jungle and out of the bio-cell. Pin was still in need of rescue, and an outbreak of murder and vengeance could destroy Pin's chances.

Ronnie made her excuses to Omni for missing dinner, saying they weren't supposed to be eating together anyway, and she would spend the time seeing if she could find where Sarah had gone off to. Every hour there were forces working to destroy the evidence. Hopefully, before Omni discovered her, the jungle would reclaim most of the sin.

Luckily, Omni presumed that Sarah would cooperate and was unable to get into the bio-cell. Omni's worry, however, plagued her every moment, searching the ship frantically, calling Sarah's name. For three days, Omni searched without rest.

Interruption came by the hail of Newton from the landing craft. No sooner than he had signaled his final approach did Ronnie take the opportunity to check inside the bio-cell. Animals, insects and bacteria had reduced the body to bones. Ronnie found the skull and put it back with the rest of the bones. She hurriedly left the bio-cell and made her way to the bridge.

Mot and Omni were already at their stations when Ronnie rushed onto the bridge. Seeing Newton's cheerful face on the screen made her secret almost unbearable. "Clarion Landing Craft knockin' at the door," said Newton, wearing his pressure suit.

"Orient for docking. Stabilize proximate gravity, draw atmosphere and open the bay door," commanded Mot. Omni responded to the command for the helm. Ronnie was at the science station but she really didn't hear the command. Omni looked up from the console, and brought Ronnie to the task with a touch to Ronnie's shoulder.

Once the bay door was open and Newton docked next to the Brina, the sensors beeped. "Guardian ship coming in fast, top-forward X axis," said Ronnie.

"Close and return atmosphere. Draw up and full stop," said Mot. Omni made the adjustments. The helm slowed the ship to an ungainly stop. "Damn graceful," Mot grumbled sarcastically.

"The braid iz on the lander," said Omni.

"What's going on? You all look very distracted," said Newton, taking off the pressure suit helmet.

"Hurry up and report to the bridge," said Mot.

The Guardian ship took the diplomatic stage thirty-thousand meters out. For some reason, the ship just hovered out there without communicating. Everyone on the bridge stared at the screen, which is how Newton found them when he came onto the bridge. "Oh, company," said Newton.

As if the Guardians somehow knew that Newton was on the bridge, Sal's face appeared on the screen. "Hello, Captain Mot and crew of the Clarion. We have made progress."

"What progress?" asked Mot.

"We have contacted the house that is holding Pin. They were under the impression that she is without family or estate. Negotiations are proceeding, and presently, we have a neighboring house of significant estate who agreed to forward the matter. We have audience in a half phase," said Sal.

With emotion putting tension in his voice, Newton said, "How is Pin supposed to last that long? How has she lasted this long?"

"Our emissary has seen Pin, and told her you were working for her release. She was already aware that you were in the country. Apparently you caused a stir." Sal smiled. "Pin told our emissary that she is holding on for you."

Mot interrupted the moment. "What do we expect from this audience?"

Sal frowned and answered, "All attempts at paying ransom have been rejected. The remedy may come down to a show of force. They assert that Pin is guilty of poaching and the only thing that can redeem her is a trial by combat, so we contract a company of men-at-arms. The display should dissuade a trial."

"Why avoid a trial by combat?" asked Mot.

"To keep from getting Pin's champion killed," said Sal, "or killing one of them, if it can be avoided."

Mot scoffed and asked, "Why should we care about that?"

"Because they have kept Pin alive, by our petition, in spite of a crime that carries a death sentence. They are following a course of communication. We must follow diplomacy at least until we think it may fail," said Sal.

"We are aliens to these savages, so I doubt diplomacy will do much but play it out. We could liberate Pin with a precise, well timed attack."

Sal took a moment to summon some patience. "They know someone wants Pin liberated. At the first sign of attack, they could kill her. And you have the means for diplomacy. Sarah tells me that Ronnie is fluent, and with

Sarah's knowledge of the customs and region, your delegation is well prepared." Sal looked around the bridge. "May I speak with Sarah?"

Newton turned and looked from face to face with hopeful expectation. Ronnie's eyes filled with tears. Mot's face betrayed nothing. Omni said, "Zarah iz mizzing."

"What?" asked Newton.

Ronnie swallowed hard and said, "Not missing, dead. I found some remains in the bio-cell just as Newton's approach sounded on the intercom." Ronnie's composure disintegrated into uncontrollable sobbing.

"Doctor, leave the bridge," said Mot. Ronnie departed in tears.

Disbelief froze Newton's face in a look of horror as the scent of grief rose up from Omni.

"What is a bio-cell?" asked Sal.

"It is wild space within the ship, full of dangerous animals," said Mot.

Sal looked at Mot for a moment. "Captain Mot, you purchased our understanding with two lives. With the loss of Sarah, one of those lives is forfeited. So, now, our understanding rests on one life. Since the house may require a champion and their mark may also die, your life is the balance. You, Captain Mot, will be in the contingent, and if there is a trial by combat, you will be the champion."

"What of your faith in diplomacy?" asked Mot.

"Ronnie will go for diplomacy. You will go if diplomacy fails."

Newton said, "What about me? I've been there."

"No," said Sal. "You would be a distraction." Sal paused before saying, "We know you bring compassion and courage, and we will strive to that on your behalf." Sal moved his gaze to Mot. "Captain Mot, stage the away mission no closer than the red planet. We will contact you when you are there. You have twelve of your brights until the audience. It would be wise to give your team at least a day on planet to prepare." Sal's face disappeared and the Guardian ship fell gracefully away and streaked into the darkness.

Mot turned to Omni and commanded, "Conscript, go to the landing craft get the braid and install it on Engine Two."

"Aye," said Omni. She left the bridge.

Newton looked at Mot with consternation. Mot said, "Take a bright to rest from your mission. Dismissed." Newton left the bridge.

He was still in his pressure suit when he walked into the bio-cell. Newton wandered in until he saw Ronnie standing in a small clearing. Standing next to her, Newton waited a moment before he said, "She came so far, just to die."

"You should leave. She wouldn't want you to see her like this." Ronnie paused. "We shaved her legs, and underarms, tweezed her eyebrows, brushed out her hair, removed the stain on her cheek, dressed her up, all for you. She was so excited to see you, for you to see her." They both looked down at a tattered flesh skeleton lying on a bed of darkened ground.

Newton shook his head. "I had to use an override code to get in here. How did Sarah get in here?" asked Newton.

Ronnie intentionally kept her eyes down as she replied, "She saw Omni use the override code once. She learned to read and write in a quarter phase, and she was brave enough to go from candlelight to spacecraft. But this place, it's an unnatural concentration of horrors, even for a smart, brave girl."

"That's dorked up," grumbled Newton. "Something is going on around here, and I am going to figure it out." Newton left the bio-cell.

Ronnie was thankful he walked away. She could not have held up against another second of his questions. Ronnie searched the warehouse for a shovel, the textiles room for a roll of shining white cloth, and after arming herself with the pulse pistol, she dug a grave below the flowering bush where she found the head, wrapped the remains and laid them in the ground.

She heard the door to the bio-cell open in the distance. With a heavy sigh, Ronnie waited. Omni and Newton walked up and stood next to her. Ronnie said, "I didn't call you. How did you know?"

"Don't do that," said Newton. "We just knew. We all lost Sarah. We will miss her," Newton said in a distracted voice. "Although I didn't even know her family name."

"Dughall," said Ronnie. "She was living with the old woman, but her family sent her there to learn healing arts and cultivation. She told me that her family name means dark stranger. She laughed and said that's how she knew she had to go with Newton." Ronnie's head jittered a moment while looking at the shroud in the grave. "She laughed because she was not superstitious."

They all looked into the grave for several minutes. In hushed tones, Newton said, "I'll cover her."

Ronnie nodded, took a handful of dirt, sprinkled it in and walked away. Omni also tossed some dirt into the grave and departed. Newton filled in the grave.

Chapter XIV: Foray of Consequence

Mot was beside himself as Omni took a few days to repair the braid. Being pulled with hydraulic actuators, while transferring tremendous amounts of energy, damaged some of the connectors. Newton made the point that Omni could actually repair something they could not. Room temperature superconductors were made and repaired at the shipyard that built the Clarion, eighteen light-years away. Mot snarled and stomped off as if this undeniable fact was some kind of hard-sell. Newton's patience with his petulant captain was running dry.

He was also plagued by the loss of Sarah. Newton found Ronnie in the incinerator room, throwing clothes and boots into the furnace. He asked her why she was burning her clothes, and Ronnie said that Sarah had borrowed them and it was too painful to keep them. She seemed to dread the question as it formed in his mind. Why was she naked? Ronnie said she must have gone for a swim in one of the ponds. The image of Sarah bathing in the pond on Freeland came to his mind, but Newton was left wondering if Ronnie knew about that moment. Did it also make enough of an impression on Sarah for her to tell that story?

Newton also knew that Sarah's room and belongings were left untouched in Omni's suite as if they were some sort of shrine to the departed. Was that merely the difference between the way Ronnie and Omni handled their grief? He didn't dare even say Sarah's name around Omni because the ammonia smell of anger would be strong enough to make his eyes water. For Omni, grief had turned to a smoldering rage.

Finally, Omni announced that the braid was ready and she was running engine diagnostics. Mot called for a pre-flight meeting in the administration meeting room. Mot, Newton and Omni waited almost fifteen minutes for Ronnie to show up, and when she did, her expression was odd, her movements slow. She sat without a word.

"You're late," said Mot.

"I'm here," she replied.

"You drunk?" asked the captain.

"I'm ill. Maybe I'll puke so you believe me. Otherwise, I suggest you make this meeting quick," Ronnie murmured.

"You were supposed to make the calculations for the mission. Did you do those?" grumbled Mot. She nodded. "Well?" asked Mot.

"We better hurry; top speed says two spans to launch."

"Cursed hells!" exclaimed Mot. He turned to Omni. "Can we?"

"Maybe," said Omni.

"Conscript, go, I want Engine Two in one span." Omni surged from the chair and out of the room. Mot then said, "Newton, you're responsible for the doctor, and I don't care if she's got a puke bag pinned to her shirt, she will be on the bridge with her computations in the navigation computer in thirty sweeps." Mot stood and stormed out of the room.

Newton sat calmly across the table from Ronnie. He waited until he was certain that Mot was long away from the room and said, "I watched your eyes follow Omni out of the room. Instead of smooth motion, your eyes tracked with stops and starts. You're gacked on something. What?" he asked.

"Dremiline," she replied.

"Which is?"

"Just about the strongest anti-anxiety drug made."

He smiled and said, "And you don't share?"

She managed only half a smile. "This shit's a little dangerous."

Newton's mood switched to serious. "That's why I am not letting you out of my sight for the next thirty spans. And based on your behavior during that time, I'll decide whether

I am going to put an ankle bracelet tester on you. The captain gave me that authority before he left the room."

"You're a rod," Ronnie muttered.

Anger lit his eyes as his face tipped down and he glared at her from under his brow. "You're acting like a coward. You can fall apart AFTER we rescue Pin. Until then, you are going to impress me with your courage and resourcefulness," growled Newton. He commanded, "Start now."

Ronnie swallowed hard and said, "The navigation is already in the computer."

"Good, that does impress me," he admitted. "The next thing is you are coming to my room, where you are going to shower in the spare washroom. And while you are doing that, I am going to search your clothes."

Rolling her eyes first, she let go an exhausted sigh and said, "They're in my boot. Please don't embarrass me."

"Once we're in the spare room, you hand them over and I'll let you go in the bathroom with your underwear, but addiction is every bit as smart as we are, and in your case, that's too dorking smart for me, so modesty is only going to work this one time," said Newton.

They walked to Newton's room in silence. Ronnie pulled off her boot and handed him an adhesive pouch with three tiny tablets. With a mournful look, she stripped down to her bra and panties and stood. He visually checked but did not trace the fabric for hidden pills. Instead, he kissed her forehead. A single tear ran down her cheek as she whispered, "Thank you," and went into the bathroom. He noticed the similarity between Ronnie's and Sarah's bodies, tall, thin, delicate bones, straight shoulders, narrow waist, small butt, long limbs. The shower seemed to help Ronnie's mood. She at least stood a little straighter, moved a little smarter as she dressed.

Newton and Ronnie stopped by the galley for a snack and some hot brew. By the time Captain Mot walked onto the bridge, Ronnie was at the science station with courses and contingencies. Newton was feeling a little nervous at the com station. Mot went to the command chair and sat; they all just sat, staring forward, waiting for Omni to report.

After several minutes, the door slid open and Omni made her way to the helm. "We have Enginez Two and rudder. Power up and go," said Omni.

"Do it, then," commanded Mot, "fast as she'll go to the Red Planet." Omni punched in instructions; there was the distant sound of a gyroscopic motor whirring up to full power and the sound of a slow pressure build in the electrical turbines. The screens showed a shift in the stars before the distortion of extreme acceleration.

After a few minutes, Omni announced, "Thiz iz good az we got. Two perzent zlower than Engine had bevore, damaged braid."

Mot looked at Ronnie and asked, "Did you calculate for a slower engine?"

"Yes," she replied. "I calculated for a ten percent loss, so we're in good shape. At this speed, we're five brights out from a landing zone on the red planet."

"What do we need to do with that time?" asked Mot.

"You and Ronnie need expeditionary clothes, weapons, money and provisions," answered Newton.

"I'll make thingz vor Ronnie," said Omni.

"And me," said Mot.

"No," said Omni.

"Why?" asked Mot.

"I don't like you," said Omni. "Not ovvicial duty, zo I don't have to."

Ronnie and Newton were aghast. Mot was angry. "Your duties include anything I tell you to do."

"You can punizh me vor not vollowing orderz, and you have no helmzman or engineer while am in the brig. That would juzt be ztupid. We have mizzion and time puzh," Omni said with casual confidence.

There was a painful silence. Newton rescued them from the situation. "I'll make clothes, weapons, armor and provisions for Captain Mot. I've seen their stuff. Omni's accoutrement was way off, anyway," said Newton.

Mot nodded. "Fine, patch all alarms and alerts to my quarters and personal radio. And put the navigation graphics ship-wide." Mot started off the bridge. "Carry on," he said, and then he left the bridge.

With the spicy scent of humor getting stronger, Omni waited and asked, "Whatz wrong with the ztuvv I made?"

"Princess, the stuff you made was the nicest stuff on the entire dorking planet. And by all means, with Ronnie as our diplomat, she should have some finery, too. But the crap I make for Mot will fit right in with their pathetic arts." Newton started for the door. "You girls relax for a while, and I am going to bring us dinner at the command table."

"I love you," Omni said.

"I do, too," added Ronnie.

In front of the door, Newton turned back and smiled. "My lovely ladies, we're going to go get your sister, and we'll be a family again."

On a flyover of the red planet's northern hemisphere, they saw a formation that, in the shadows of evening, looked a little like Ronnie's face. They set down next to the formation, outfitted the Brina, and Newton watched as they all flew out of the thin atmosphere of the red planet. He was alone on the ship. Newton did a safety diagnostic for a complete shut-down. Taking a gyroscopic motor to total stall was always a risk. The magnetic fields worked a sort of magic that kept everything functioning. Once quiet, there was a small chance the motor would seize. Newton didn't care. He was depressed, alone, powerless. The planet's gravity was a little weak, but the ship was immense, so it's not as if the feeble currents of air were going to move the ship. He went up to the crown and watched the darkness descend, realizing the bright star in the green of dusk was Freeland.

Omni and Ronnie sat on the bridge of the Brina as Mot sat in one of the recliners, the recliners being a seat that could actually accommodate such a massive person. Sal sent the coordinates and a situational dossier of the mission. Ronnie read for a couple of hours as Omni piloted to the morning crossroad where they were supposed to meet their escort, keeping her eye on the heat sensors showing a company of forty men, most on horseback, but some riding a carriage, and some in a wagon. With the ship under stealth, Omni oriented the airlock away from the rider's approach on the road. Mot jumped out and Ronnie and Mot offloaded their things quickly. Ronnie sealed the inside door, leapt to one of the large travel chests, closed the outer hatch and stepped down to the ground as the Brina flew away. To the riders a mile away, it looked as if two travelers with luggage simply materialized at the crossroads.

Geddis being an industrialized world, it had been years since Ronnie had been on a fresh planet, the smell of the air, the depth of infinity in the blue of the sky, the complexity of the verdant life folding into the contours of the landscape. It was so beautiful that the virgin world brought tears to her eyes.

"Get your crap together," ordered Mot. "You'll make us look more ridiculous than we already do." He faced the direction the riders would approach. Mot was dressed in a long, chain-mail shirt, leather pants, leather boots with armored shin guards. He also had armor breastplate, shoulder guards, forearm guards, and helmet with eye slits and holes to hear. Mot held the helmet at his hip. His belt held a broadsword, a knife and three of his throwing darts.

Ronnie looked at him. Ridiculous? Speak for yourself, she thought. Ronnie loved her clothes. Omni took what she learned from Sarah's dress and made the under-dress of luminous white, with a top smock of dark blue linen, with the white sleeves using an elegant pattern of gathers and lace, with the matching leather bodice a variation of the rings with the leather ribbon that Pin had on her vest. Ronnie's generous blue linen skirt had layers of white under skirt, and under that, Ronnie's bloomers were blue leather, with stockings and sturdy, tall boots. For femininity, Omni completed the costume with a braid of gold to go around her head with a mesh of finer gold to work as a veil or to frame her face. She also had a close fitting necklace of Kai pearls, a gold ring, matching blue gloves, and two, thin, ornamental daggers that fit into the seam holding the rings of the bodice.

The riders rode up and encircled them. Rather than form ranks to subdue, they turned their horses toward the approaching carriage, dismounted and took defensive positions on the outside. One rider dismounted and handed off the reins of his horse. He then took the lead horses of the carriage and positioned the carriage. A man came off the driver's place of the carriage, opened the door and folded out an iron step. An elegantly dressed woman in a black embroidered dress and white headdress emerged from the carriage. "*Stand and recognize the lady Margaret Ainsley,*" announced the footman. Lady Margaret was brunette, petite, with an intrigued wideness to her dark blue eyes. She smiled, widened her skirt with one hand, held her other hand with the palm up toward Mot, and lowered into a curtsy.

When the lady stood, Ronnie said, "*Lady Ainsley, you honor us greatly to present yourself to this company from so far away. I am the lady Ronnie Chamberlain, of Tarn. This is the Lord Mot Hammer, from Clarion.*" Ronnie curtsied low but held both hands forward, palms up and crossed at the wrists. Mot gave her a stiff bow of his head.

She waited for them to straighten their stance before Lady Ainsley asked, "*I don't understand your gesture, Lady Chamberlain. Here, that hand position means that you are bound by service.*"

"*And we are here to entreat much from your house. It is impolite for us need so much before we are met, but we are strange to this country. A beloved daughter of our estate has found peril in a neighboring house. And without a friend, we fear she will be lost. Lord Mot will champion her if needs be, but without a banner to press her case, we cannot hope. That is why we are at your service and grateful for any charity,*" said Ronnie. Her eyes filled with tears.

Lady Ainsley was touched and cleared her throat before she said, "*You have my hospitality and the banner of my house.*" She stepped forward and pulled a lace handkerchief from her cuff and handed it to Ronnie. Ronnie dried her tears and handed it back. Lady Ainsley gestured for the footmen to load the wagon with their luggage. Lady Ainsley gestured to the coach and Ronnie turned to look at Mot.

Mot looked at the carriage and said, "I don't think I'd fit in that thing. I'll ride on the cart. Find out what you can. Brief me when we get settled in their big pile of rocks." Mot's movement spooked the nearby horses as he picked up the weapons chest. He was easily a head taller than every single one of the men at arms. They watched Mot with mixture of interest and dread. Not all of the men focused on Mot. The footmen and the men who were close enough to hear Ronnie speak, these men put their attention on the ladies. One came to the door, positioned his arms to create a sort of railing but turned his face to protect her modesty. Lady Ainsley got in first, but when Ronnie started in, the carriage shifted. Both footmen caught Ronnie under her arms. She didn't say anything and took her seat opposite Lady Ainsley.

The company got organized with the shouts of leaders giving orders and soon they were moving along the road. Inside the coach, Lady Ainsley was looking at Ronnie. She smiled and said, "We go to our big pile of rocks."

It took a second for Ronnie to realize that a Freelander just used the language of Tarn, that Lady Ainsley had understood Mot. "I wondered how Sal got a message from Pin. Are you a guardian?" asked Ronnie.

"No, highland girl, born and raised," said Margaret. "I learned this language because some runt of a man disturbed my dreams for more than a phase to teach me." She shrugged. "Then that same slight man showed up at my door, with a chest of gold and a favor to ask."

Ronnie searched her face for indications of magical thinking. "How do you explain such a thing? Normal men do not visit us in our dreams and then appear in the flesh."

"How does one explain anything? There isn't a goldsmith in the world who can make threads as fine as those in your veil. There have been stories of a dark skinned man bearing pure silver coin and a sword made of moonlight. Stories of two invisible dragons breaking from the deep of the lake and flying to the dark between stars," said Margaret. She got up and took a seat next to Ronnie, turned Ronnie's wrist and ran her fingertips over Ronnie's palm and fingertips. "We don't know until we do. Your words open a way forward. I don't put faith in God or give a thought to sorcery. I know people, and I feared for Pin until I heard your eloquence and saw your tears."

Ronnie scoffed. "I'm eloquent compared to Lord Mot, who called our host's home a big pile of rocks." The ladies laughed together. They relaxed in silence for a time. "Seriously," asked Ronnie, "how can you be so rational, and how does a lady lead a household in world of men?"

"That is why," said Margaret. "All the men of my noble house squander the blessings of creation to go and kill other men with a different notion of God. No god would want such devotion. Such madness proves that there is only what men do in the guise of God."

Ronnie gasped and whispered, "Lady Ainsley…"

"Maggie, please."

"Maggie. And I am Ronnie."

The ladies talked for hours, switching languages to make up for deficits in what they wanted to say. Ronnie was curious about the virgin world and Margaret was curious about everything else, Ronnie's knowledge of anatomy, physiology, chemistry, mathematics, physics, botany, astronomy. Margaret would occasionally remember they needed to focus on the audience, but having someone who could describe the workings of the universe, it was an inviting digression with temptations littered throughout every conversation.

On the day of the audience, they marched on Wainthrait castle with a company of a hundred chargers on horseback, sixty heavy men at arms with siege weapons, another sixty men at second with shields and pike to assist sixty archers. Mot, Ronnie and Margaret were with the laager in the middle of the formation. As they drew up to the keep, parts of their force brought defensive lines and poised themselves to defend or move to strategic steps around the defenses. They were in position, banners of black and red, the thistle in black, banners undulating in the bright, clear morning. The Wainthrait banner was a yellow hedgehog on blue.

A shrill horn sounded as the portcullis cracked and groaned as it pulled up with doors opened behind. A rider with a white cape rode out and made his way toward the laager. The rider approached and invited the ladies and champion into the keep. Ronnie diplomatically refused, saying the field of honor was in the sunlight where all could see. The rider went back in and drums began to throb. In rhythm, forces deployed on the walls of the castle and spilled out of the gate. Moving to the places not already occupied, the tension built. The forces were fewer, their vestments and equipment shoddier, but still, steel was poised against steel and men glared at their opposite number. Finally, three chariots emerged and took a place near the laager, and then came the wagon.

Pin was dressed in a white gown, with her hands tied in front and standing behind a wicker pedestal while men in armor drove the wagon to a place under the wall full of archers. One chariot had the nobleman, one a cleric, and one a large man in armor, the champion. *"Walter Wainthrait, I present the Lady Ronnie Chamberlain, of Tarn, and the Lord of Clarion, Sir Mot Hammer,"* said Margaret. *"Lord Hammer speaks only the language of Clarion, the language of your captive, but Lady Chamberlain speaks our tongue."* She turned to Ronnie. *"Lady Chamberlain, this is his lordship Walter Wainthrait, regent of the Iron Harrow."*

Ronnie bowed her head. *"It's my privilege to meet you, Lord Wainthrait. I bear thanks."*

He looked a bit puzzled. *"For what do you bear thanks?"*

"I thank you for this audience. I thank you for allowing Lady Ainsley to visit our Lady Pin Pin. I thank you for keeping well a cherished daughter of Tarn. To restore her to us, you would have the gratitude of a great house," said Ronnie.

"You say she is from a great house. I say she is a demon with cloven hands and feet, a creature fashioned by evil," said the cleric.

Ronnie made sure to look only at Walter. *"Where I am from, a man does not address a lady without an introduction. Surely, just as there are different customs and languages, there are different peoples."*

"Stay out of this Friar Titus," grumbled Walter. *"You said she came from the depths and therefore was without*

271

estate. The great host of petitioners you see before us says you are mistaken. You said she spoke only words for the devil's ear, and Lady Ainsley, besmirched nowhere, speaks with her." He looked over his shoulder to Pin for an awkward pause. Walter turned back to Ronnie. *"What is her condition?"*

Ronnie had to think about what he meant by the question. She guessed and said, *"She is betrothed, to a powerful baron, who sends me as an emissary, with the bounty of his gratitude, or he sends Lord Mot to answer the pains of justice,"* said Ronnie. *"Blood has not been spilled, and I thank you again, but blood is in the balance, because she is sworn to another."*

An odd poutiness took over his face. He struggled with a thought for a time and then shocked all within earshot with the question, *"If I defiled her, would the baron still want her?"*

Ronnie tried to control her anger. *"Yes!"* she hissed. She worked for more composure and said, *"If you tarnished her, his wrath would be for you, not her. He knows her heart; he wouldn't blame her for someone else's wickedness. His wrath could lay low this entire valley, but for her, he keeps only love."*

Walter thought for a moment and said, *"What a land of wise retribution she comes from."* He laughed, shrugged his shoulders and asked, *"So how do I keep her? Though she comes from a land of conscience, I want to keep her."*

"You are bewitched, my lord," said the cleric.

"Be it so," Walter said quietly. Giving Ronnie a solemn look, Walter asked, *"If my champion bested Lord Mot, would the baron accept that verdict and leave her to be a part of my house?"*

She thought about the question and said, *"If it was a fair fight, he would be honor bound to accept the verdict."*

Walter looked at his champion and asked in a rhetorical tone, *"How could it be a fair fight? Lord Mot is the grandest man this world has ever seen."* He took a deep breath and shouted, *"The Iron Mark and Lord Mot will engage in a trial by combat! The loser may yield, but the winner conveys the fate of the captive! Make a field and leave all to the honor of the champions!"*

As the rhythmic roll of drums set up the battle, the armored champion stepped off the chariot and sauntered out to the clearing. Standing on the wagon, Mot amazed the spectators by taking off the metal shin-guards and then the breastplate and shoulder guards. Mot jumped to the ground from the laager, without his helmet, without his sword, wearing just a chainmail shirt, leather pants and tall boots. Rather than take the field with a walk, Mot lunged forward, tucked into a shoulder roll, unfolded into a cartwheel and stopped instantly about thirty yards from the champion. The drums went silent.

Sunlight was dampened by a cloud. The armored champion pulled an iron cross from his belt and threw it at Mot, who stood, shifted to the right at the last second and caught the cross with his left hand. He tossed the iron cross gently up and over his shoulder, but at the same time his left hand went lazily up, Mot's right hand blurred forward. A throwing dart penetrated the champion's left eye. The man's arms dropped limp and the armored champion fell backward, lifeless. An audible gasp rolled through the ranks around the field.

"What witchcraft kills without object?!" shouted the cleric.

"Mot, show them a dart!" commanded Ronnie. Mot whipped around and froze with an extended hand. A thick metal dart bit deep and held in the shell of the cleric's chariot, inches from Friar Titus's hand. Ronnie closely watched Walter's face. The verdict was clear, but would

Walter accept it? "*Mercy*," said Ronnie. "*It ends well. It ends here.*"

"*I cannot*," said Walter.

Ronnie shouted to Mot. "Mot, they will betray us! Wait for it to start! Apprehend their leader!" Ronnie forced herself to wait. Mot's weapons chest, armor and helmet were on the laager next to hers. Margaret, too, forced herself to stand still.

Walter shouted orders. "*Take the captive back into the keep! No harm to her! Archers, kill any who approach the captive! All others, kill who challenges you!*"

There was a second of peace with nothing but the sound of banners in the breeze. All the men at arms set their footing, gripped their weapons and eyed their opposite man. The cart started to move, touching off a flurry of action at various places throughout the battlefield. First, Pin's wagon suddenly lost one of its knights as she crushed the helmet with a war hammer and pulled his sword as he fell. She engaged the other knight as some of Margaret's men lunged forward to help her. This prompted a volley of arrows from the wall, and archers from the ground answered. Their seconds drew up shields to protect them for reload. Other skirmishes started on the ground, but Margaret's men had the more defensible ground. Mot was running toward Walter's chariot, with two dozen men running to head him off. Ronnie leapt to the other wagon, snatched up Mot's helmet and threw it into his path. He rolled over it and came up running and buckling on his helmet.

Mot charged and hit the first of his attackers at a full run. For the first six men, Mot didn't even engage bringing weapons. He turned their own weapons on them and dispatched the men with tremendous speed and strength. More men ran toward the fight, and another figure closed on the fray. With the skirt of Pin's white gown cut and knotted to make shorts, she ran with a sword in one hand and a war hammer in the other. Mot was dealing with three attackers when she jumped over them to defend Mot's back. They coordinated their fight, switching hands, advancing or retreating in a box pattern, calling in threats, signaling intent with taps to the other. Mot would also call to Ronnie for assistance. He broke a sword and shouted for another. Pin lost the war hammer and Ronnie threw them a small shield.

Ronnie's place at the wagon was fairly safe, as the Ainsley ranks around the leaders held their ground and let other groups answer any attack. Occasionally a stray arrow came in, and Ronnie shielded Margaret a few times, and she even saved Walter once by throwing Mot's shoulder guard at a broken ax flying from the fight. But the leaders were off limits in this battle, and Margaret's men would respond to any threat with brutal focus.

The fights on the perimeter died down as all eventually realized the contest hinged on the battle closest to Walter. Ronnie shouted for Margaret's men to prevent any others from approaching the center field. And with Mot and Pin left standing back to back unchallenged, and with Walter unprotected, quiet settled over the field of honor. There were thirty-six dead and dying men littered around them. Margaret exclaimed, "*Sweet Jesus!*"

Ronnie shouted, "*Men at arms for House Ainsley! Victory for the brave!*" A great cheer roared from the battlefield and echoed from the walls of the stone fortress. Ronnie called to Pin with a worried pinch in her voice, "Pin, your condition?"

"A little banged up, some minor cuts, but I'm alright," she answered.

"Captain Mot?" asked Ronnie.

"I'm better than these assholes," said Mot.

Ronnie untied the leather lace in her bodice and coiled it into a quick knot. "Pin, are you well enough to arrest Lord

Wainthrait and drive his chariot for a span to cover our retreat?"

"Absolutely," snarled Pin. The cleric hurried off toward the castle.

Ronnie addressed the men, "*All men at arms! Lord Wainthrait will accompany us to House Ainsley. He will be granted boon to share with all his men! If any of his house follow, that man's share is lost and he puts his lord in disgrace! Blood was spilt to form this trust! Bind your wounds! Bury your dead!*" Ronnie let this statement ring for a sense of resolve. "*Men of House Ainsley! Bring us our fallen! If you cannot ride, or walk, these wagons, also, will bear you home. We will withdraw with lord and ladies within the column! Banners will be furled to be borne another day! For this day, there is honor for all!*" Everyone watched as all the flags were rolled up; this symbolic act changed the mood on the battlefield.

Men who were set to kill each other now helped one another. The three wagons of the laager were separated and turned into hospital trucks where the wounded and dead lay next to rolled up flags and weapons. Pin tied up Walter and had him sit in the chariot. Mot sat in the champion's chariot. The cleric's chariot was used to move men and supplies. Ronnie did triage with the wounded. An hour and a half after the final ring of clashing weapons, the column was leaving the battlefield.

Ronnie and Margaret were in the cleric's chariot. Margaret's face held a transfixed wonder looking at Ronnie. Eventually, Maggie asked, "Have a lot of experience as a war general, do you?"

"I'm a doctor in the military, but they keep us away from the fighting so we can treat the casualties. This was my first time commanding a battle," said Ronnie.

Maggie shook her head, bewildered. A little while later, she asked, "Do you have a husband, Lady Chamberlain?"

Ronnie looked at Maggie, deciding how honestly she wanted to answer. She decided and said, "No husband. I would want a wife."

Maggie chuckled and said, "My question was more to ask if you could be a wife."

"I could be a wife, to a wife," said Ronnie.

Ronnie then thought of the wagons filled with wounded men and the chariot far ahead carrying Mot. He downplayed his injuries. He had a dozen cuts and puncture wounds. And those were just the ones she found before he lost patience with her examination. She didn't even get under the chainmail shirt. There were nine dead and twenty-six wounded men in the wagons, and one probably wouldn't survive the ride to the castle.

She couldn't take it a second longer. Ronnie handed the reins to Maggie and pulled the transmitter that Omni gave Newton from an inner pocket of her bodice. She fanned out the coin sized device and began typing a message in Treomet. Omni was in orbit directly above the island, and Ronnie needed her to go to the red planet. Omni wrote back, asking if Pin was rescued. Once Omni learned that Pin was well, she immediately agreed to make an emergency trip to the Clarion. Margaret watched Ronnie use the device but said nothing.

When they got to the castle, Ronnie put a small chest of gold on Walter's chariot. Pin worried Ronnie as she seemed to be considering whether to kill Walter or let him go, then she said, "Goodbye, you little worm." Pin sent off the chariot without cutting loose Walter's wrists and lifted her arms to Ronnie for a hug. Ronnie held Pin for a very long time, two ladies standing on the road. Four knights escorted Wainthrait's chariot. Soldiers moved around them and set up an encampment around the fortress. Pin eventually let go, sensing that Ronnie wanted to get to work. Pin went into the keep and searched for Margaret to ask for better clothes.

Ronnie took off her gold veil and bodice and got to work. She organized the courtyard into an infirmary. Whatever request she made, there were men and women eager to fulfill it. She started a detail for boiling bandages and creating splints, a detail to find cots and make awnings over the wounded, a detail for collecting tools she might use for surgery, a detail for cleaning containers and filling them with sterile water, a detail to make soap, a detail for gathering certain plants and grains. She worked tirelessly, watching the progress of the different wounds and trying to time when to do what.

Maggie tracked her down. "The magic runt of a man casts a shadow in front of the hearth. He asks for a word."

"I'm very busy," huffed Ronnie.

"I told him. He promises to be quick." Maggie smiled. "And while you're there, I've had a small dinner set. You'll drop in your tracks if you don't get something soon."

"Thank you," sighed Ronnie.

"You need a wife, I think." Maggie looped a lock of Ronnie's hair back behind her ear. Maggie then summoned a girl to escort Ronnie to the hall.

The girl pulled a chair at the large table and Ronnie sat. Water, wine, flat bread with cherry jam and honey, boiled oats with chunks of mutton, she didn't realize how hungry she was until she started eating. Sal approached the table and poured her wine into a goblet. "You did well. Your leadership saved many lives. You preserved the dignity of all involved. And you rescued Pin."

"And yet…" said Ronnie.

Sal smiled. "And yet the Brina is making way to the Clarion without you, or Pin, or Captain Mot."

Ronnie ate some more, thinking about her answer. "We preserve dignity, even in battle, so people aren't emotionally wounded, and so they'll bring more love instead of hatred to the world. Helping heal their physical wounds does the same thing. For every life we save, we don't have a widow or orphan. We have a man who is grateful for his life and more likely to value life," she said. "When Omni delivers the medical supplies, I'll send Pin and Mot back to the Clarion, but there are a dozen men who will die without my help, and half as many again who will be debilitated. I need another bright and then I'll leave."

Sal's visage paused for something between love and resignation. "As you wish."

Ronnie returned to eating her meal as Sal walked toward the entrance to the hall. His footsteps went silent and the Guardian vanished. Ronnie was finishing the goblet of wine when she got a message from Omni. Margaret arranged for litter to be made to carry Mot, and she volunteered to help with getting the supplies, although she wasn't sure what that actually entailed. It was dark by the time they put Mot's stretcher on a wagon. Pin, Ronnie and Maggie then got on and started toward a higher course of a lesser road.

"Why can't I ask for a retinue of men to help load?" asked Maggie.

"Because you're the only one I can trust to see our bark," Ronnie answered. "This is a ship that sails between stars." The horses pulled the wagon until they entered a shadowed stretch of road between rock walls. "The ship will come from the sky, land and offload a box. The pilot is our friend, but she doesn't look like any person you've ever seen." They watched the outline of the Brina float down and land behind the wagon. The horses pulled against their traces when the cloak faded and the ship appeared. Margaret had to work to calm them.

Pin hopped down from the wagon and went to wait at the door. As it opened, Pin greeted Omni, "Hello, your highness."

"They zaved you!" declared Omni.

Ronnie was checking on Mot, who was unconscious and running a fever. "Omni, I need my travel bag."

"Yez," said Omni. She turned back into the craft. When Omni came back out and handed Ronnie the small medical kit, Maggie was so shocked she could hardly breathe.

Ronnie pulled a small instrument from the bag. "He's going septic. This can't be." Ronnie lifted the chainmail shirt and found a stab wound near his navel. She went into the bag and prepared a syringe. She gave him an injection near the stab wound. "Omni, you're going to need to give him another of these injections in six spans." Ronnie put a monitor on his wrist. "Omni and Pin, you're the only two strong enough to get him on the ship. Put him in the recliner and I'll set up an intravenous drip." The stretcher wouldn't make it through the door, so they moved him to the edge of the wagon, with Omni getting his top and Pin getting his legs. Ronnie followed them into the ship. Maggie moved so she could see inside. Omni and Pin laid him into a chair as Ronnie was hanging a bag and connecting tubes. Then she did something on Mot's arm and connected the thin tubes to the arm. Omni then brought out a box and loaded it on the wagon.

Omni looked at the ship in a thoughtful pause. Maggie asked, "Did I hear Pin call you highness?"

"Omni, Prinzezz of Kai," she offered Maggie her claw.

Maggie shook Omni's claw. "Where's Kai?"

Omni looked up at the night sky. She leaned one way, then another, searching the stars. "I vind it when I above your world." She searched and then pointed to the ridgeline. "There, where that pointed rock and tree have ztar between. That'z Kai ztar."

"My name's Maggie, and Ronnie says my star is the sun." Maggie looked at the ship. Her voice was worried as she asked, "Is Lord Mot going to make it? If you have a ship that goes to different stars, you should have some good medicine, yes?"

"Maybe, but the body healz, or not, dependz," said Omni. "Many have tried to kill Mot, too many to count. It would be strange vor him to die here, where none who want him dead will know. We zo var away." Omni turned to Maggie and said, "I go get zhip ready. It waz nize to meet you, Maggie." Omni went inside the ship.

Pin came out to give Maggie a hug before getting back aboard the Brina. Ronnie exited the ship, went to the box, opened it, and used a small light to search the contents. Maggie saw Omni appear in one of the windows. Ronnie signaled Omni. The side door closed, and not long after, Pin appeared in the window next to Omni. They made preparations for a time, waved, then with a whirring sound, the ship floated up, and it disappeared while streaking away.

Ronnie spent the next day dressing wounds and doing medical procedures. She made medicines from plant extracts and fermentation vats. She set bones and did surgery. Even some of Wainthrait's men had heard about her medical success and Ronnie treated them, too. Maggie joked that Ronnie was going to be stuck there forever if she didn't lose a few patients.

After nightfall, Ronnie and Maggie loaded the box onto a wagon, along with William, Maggie's five-year-old son, and ventured into the darkness to a place where rock walls hid the road. The Kai ship Brina floated down to take on some medical supplies, luggage, and three passengers, leaving an empty wagon and two unharnessed horses.

Ronnie and Maggie were having tea at the table when word from the Clarion came through on the table view-screen. Mot died of his wounds. Ronnie reminded Newton to punch in Mot's transponder frequency to register the death with the ship's computer. He could then access the secret mission. An hour later, Newton called back. The mission: illuminate darkness.

Chapter XV: Resurrection of Hope

The Clarion was still parked on the red planet, sitting next to a mountain that, at the right angle of sunlight, from orbit, looked like a face. Newton had purposefully set down far enough from the mountain that one could see the entire formation with a glance out a window. It even sort of looked like an immense face in profile from the ship's position far away on a distant plain of orange dirt and black rocks.

This was the view when he and Pin sipped cups of brew on the bridge and watched the Brina as she floated down, bringing in the away team. A mission wasn't complete until everyone was accounted for and the ship was returned. Once Newton realized that Ronnie had brought two more extraterrestrials on board the Clarion, he opened the entire ambassador wing for everyone to choose a suite, scheduled three days of liberty and finished those three days with a mandatory meeting for every soul aboard ship.

Somehow liberty did not keep people from doing useful things. Pin set up power, plumbing and environmental controls to favor the living areas and conserve energy elsewhere. She also deployed a fleet of carts and dollies so people could move to new quarters. Ronnie and Margaret set up the galley so anyone could have prepared food and beverages at any time. Newton put Mot's body in a cryogenic tube and figured that the funeral services would be a topic during their meeting. Omni spent a lot of time in the textile and machine shops, but everyone was so busy that this went largely unnoticed.

At the fifteenth hour, everyone, including five-year-old William, gathered at the administration meeting room. What struck Newton was that no one was in uniform. By some odd coincidence, they were all dressed in their Freeland costumes. Another thing that struck him, as they met around the table, was the way Pin greeted Omni with a playful series of hand slaps and ending with a hug. Newton realized that even though they had moved just across the hall from Omni, he hadn't actually seen Pin and Omni in the same room for months. He waited as everyone chose a place and Newton sat at the head of the table. He first turned to Ronnie and said, "Would you care to introduce our new ... crewmembers?"

Ronnie smiled. "This is Lady Margaret Ainsley, Maggie, and her son, William. Maggie, this is Newton Keen, captain and commander of the Clarion." Pin started a heartfelt applause, to be joined by Omni, and then Ronnie. Newton and Maggie gave one another a little wave. William added his applause before the moment subsided.

"Welcome," Newton said with smile. His smile faded as he rubbed his forehead. Newton sighed and said, "So, we're fifty revolves from home, if we repaired Engine One and it ran well enough to compensate for Engine Two, so we are actually somewhere between seventy-five to a hundred revolutions from home. Keep in mind that we were discarded, because every scan indicates the destination was the emptiest of empty space, and don't forget they sent a bolt to destroy us out here in the Big Black." He paused and then continued. "All this leads us to the first and most important question: Do we want to go back home?" He looked from face to face at the table.

After a thoughtful silence, Ronnie said, "I think we should."

"Why?" asked Pin. "We could live our lives, happy, free, at peace. Why go back?"

"Because they wanted to get rid of us," Ronnie said angrily. "They want to rewrite history, because the two beings who saved the Five Worlds are sitting right at this table."

There was a knock at the door behind Newton. He launched to his feet and started for the defense cabinet at the close corner of the room. Ronnie headed him off, held up a hand and called out, "Sal? Is that you?"

"Yes," answered the voice from outside the room.

"Apparently, the guardians can materialize and dematerialize. It happened on Freeland," said Ronnie. "Permission to let him in?" she asked.

"Granted," said Newton with an uncertain tone.

Ronnie went to the door, which opened with her proximity. Sal walked into the room with a bundle that contained Pin's bow, quiver of arrows, clothes and other items. The guardian was a slender young man, also dressed in the costume of the ancient world of Freelanders. He put the bundle on a small cabinet at corner of the room. "These are items which could cause cultural contamination issues," said Sal.

Newton gave Sal a half smile, gestured to a chair and said, "Thanks, and would you care to join us? We were discussing whether we wanted to go back to the Five Worlds. Pin thinks not. Ronnie thinks we should because there's a chance that Omni and I were sent out here to disappear, so they could rewrite history back home."

Sal, Newton and Ronnie took their seats. "That is why the Clarion was sent into oblivion," said Sal.

"How do you know?" said Newton.

"When we delivered the message from her highness, it was welcomed on Kai, but the news that the princess was with a Fleet vessel created a tremendous tumult at the Five Worlds Ministry of Information. Several official annals had to be recalled and revised, and the Royal Kai had to sue the World Court three times for a correct record on all worlds," said Sal. He paused before adding, "Geddis and Phaeton both suffered attacks from unknown terrorists, and all records of the Clarion and the beaming were destroyed within spans of your launch, and these attacks were not reported, still have not been reported. No record of this mission or any member of this crew can be found, even though Queen Tal Kai has sued for these records."

They sat at that table for several minutes in relative silence, although William entertained himself with a toy cart and made little noises from the far corner of the room.

Newton looked at Sal for a moment and said, "Thank you, incidentally, for your assistance in rescuing Pin, and, even though I may regret it, I now ask what the guardians think we should do."

Sal looked serious and said, "You can't stay here, not all of you. Newton and Ronnie, and Lady Ainsley and William, obviously, could choose to live on Freeland. Newton, your prosperity and happiness may require a different culture than the one you visited. Ronnie and Newton are genetically compatible with this world, so, settlement here is only a matter of being careful with artifacts. But, alien beings could disrupt the planet." He made a point of looking at Pin. "If you go back home, however, you would have to scuttle this ship. The Kai ship is suitable as a craft to return with, and we could have you back in the Worlds in a few phases. Yet, the political situation is worse than I indicated. You have to return in a way that does not reveal your identities and thereby threaten knowledge of this world."

"I have island," said Omni, "that could be revuge vor all ov uz."

Newton's eyes went from Omni to Sal. "What about that?" he asked.

Sal knit his brow and said, "Actually, Kai is a protected world. That would be ideal."

Omni looked at Newton and then Pin. "Problem iz, one ov the reazonz I leave, iv I go back, I muzt marry. I can chooze, but must marry." Omni turned to Pin and touched her hand. "Pin, can I marry Newtin?"

Pin chewed her lip and said, "Yes."

Newton's gaze jumped from Pin to Omni and back to Pin. "Did you just give me away? Why would you agree to that?"

Pin's gaze fixed on Newton's face as her eyes filled with tears. "I love you, but this whole thing with a lie in the history of worlds, it's about you and the princess. I don't care. I don't want to be a part of it. When I left for Freeland, I wanted a living planet with real air and real ground. I was starved and drugged and raped lots of times, and all I could think about was my phase on that virgin world, the sweetness of the water, the smell the air, the beauty of the sky." Pin wiped the tears off her face and straightened in her chair. "Omni saved my life, helped me escape, and this big lie does need the truth. It's about you and Omni. If the Guardians say I can't live on Freeland, fine, I'll live on Meeri. It's fresh, too, so far from everything, nothing anybody wants."

Ronnie trembled with worry and asked Pin, "Do you need medical attention?"

Pin shrugged. "Too late," she said quietly.

Newton dropped his jaw in shock, thinking of how happy Pin had seemed ever since she returned to the ship. He had no idea. Their touch communication was joyful, their time together loving. Apparently, Pin could carry a great emotional burden without letting it darken the moment. "Are you sure?" he asked.

Pin let go a deep sigh and nodded. "I wasn't until just this minute, but now I am. It's weird because I knew you would make sure I got away from that disgusting little man. You showed me how good love can be. I'll always be grateful. Someday I may be ready, but now I'm messed up and I want revolves by myself, in a green world." Pin turned to Sal. "Can I have that?"

Sal nodded. "Yes. We can talk about where, perhaps Meeri."

An interlude of thought eased all the tension from the room.

Omni looked at Newton and proposed, "Newtin, will you marry me?"

He blinked with confusion before saying, "Yes, I will marry you." Ronnie, Sal and Maggie smiled. Newton added, "Aren't royal weddings about making heirs? What do we do about that?"

A cinnamon smell perfumed the table. "My little zizter a tramp; zhe make all the heirz we need." Omni laughed, to be joined by Ronnie and Sal, and eventually Newton and Pin.

Sal waited until a sense of calm settled over the group. "So, just to be clear, there are no plans to settle on Freeland."

"Not too thrilled with scuttling this ship," said Newton. "The bio-cell has thousands of life forms, flora and fauna, some of them extremely rare. I don't suppose there's a way we can save all that life?"

Sal thought about it for a moment and then nodded. "Yes, we'll work something out. We'll transfer the contents of the bio-cell, along with other possessions, onto an unregistered Five Worlds transport outside this solar system. The Brina and the transport will be pulled in an energy bubble. We'll drop the Clarion into the next star. I need to talk to Pin and Omni about where we will be taking you. The secrecy surrounding the Guardians and this system are still paramount." Sal stood and said, "I'd like to have that conversation with Pin and Omni with the benefit of a computer to show me precisely where they imagine for relocation sites."

Ronnie stood. "Can I take Sal to the bridge to use the navigation computer?" she asked Newton.

Newton lifted his eyebrows. "Permission granted."

"Thank you, Commander," said Sal. Omni and Pin stood.

Ronnie's face eased into a loving recognition. "By your leave, Commander?"

Newton nodded and Ronnie, Sal, Pin and Omni quietly departed the room, leaving Newton and Margaret regarding one another with the same perplexed smile and little William playing in the far corner of the room.

"I don't suppose you speak our language," said Newton.

"Actually, I do." Maggie smiled.

Newton's head tipped back with surprise. "Is everyone on Freeland a genius? Seriously, how could you learn a language from a world nine stars away?"

Maggie laughed at Newton's exaggerated expression of surprise. His expression relaxed to a mild curiosity. "That whelp who was just here, he taught me your language as I slept. Then he darkened my doorstep and asked me to help secure Pin's freedom."

After a pause, Newton said, "So you're the one who helped us. There was a battle?"

"Pin's captor, Lord Wainthrait, lost his champion in a single heartbeat," said Maggie, "but Walter was bewitched by Pin's beauty and he refused to accept the verdict. As he ordered Pin to be taken back into the keep, the battle ignited."

Newton got up and took a seat next to Maggie. "Obviously, I haven't debriefed Ronnie, so anything you could tell me would be helpful. Where was it? Was it neutral ground? Who commanded the forces? How many combatants? How many casualties?"

Maggie repositioned herself in her chair and put a hand on Newton's shoulder. "I mustered more than three-hundred men at arms, chargers, archers and infantry with siege weapons. We marched on the Iron Harrow and Ronnie commanded the battle. She chose a field on advantageous ground outside the keep and positioned all forces before the parley began. She also saw that Lord Wainthrait was going to break the oath of outcome and prepared Lord Mot and Lady Pin. They bested forty men at arms; twenty-seven of them were commissioned knights. In all, five hundred took arms, a hundred-fifty wounded, seventy-two dead. Ronnie brought forty-nine men, friend and foe alike, back to a productive life with her healing arts."

Newton set his hands to both sides of his face in aghast. He stared at Maggie as the significance of souls moistened their eyes. She gave him an understanding nod and placed her hand on his shoulder. He sighed deeply and stared at the center of the table.

The walk to the bridge was made in silence. Ronnie stood by the door to keep it open while Sal, Pin and Omni entered. Ronnie followed them in and started up the navigation computer. As she pulled up graphics for the different planetary systems, Ronnie asked, "Are you pregnant, Pin?"

She sighed. "I think so. I'm three-quarters late," said Pin in a quiet voice. "Which could be a good thing," she added.

"How is that?" asked Ronnie.

"It gives me a certain status with my family. The women will take care of me. The tribe protects me and adopts my child. Being pregnant by assault used to happen a lot. We busters don't blame the woman. And I can stay unmarried as long as I want."

"Interesting," said Ronnie.

"Indeed," said Sal. He made certain to catch her eye contact. "Do you have family and a tribe on Meeri?"

"Yes," replied Pin. "We were put there as a prospecting colony, but we never found anything valuable. Now we just harvest salt from the ocean and let the jungle and coral feed us. There's about fifteen-hundred people, rogue births, mostly, on an island the size of the one on Freeland. The space harbor is on the other side of Meeri. My village isn't on any map. My dad paddled a canoe for fifteen brights to get me to a recruiting contest, because I wanted to join Fleet and travel the stars. I did, and now I want to go back home."

Epilogue

Newton was dressed in cream-colored silk and green leather finery as he walked through an atrium in the central palace on the island of Li. At the base of a tree, he saw concentric rings of rag growing in the rainbow-lit mist from a nearby waterfall. The rag was recovered from the botanical cell of the spacecraft he had watched vaporize above the surface of a star. This tree, that flower, that little salamander on a rock next to the pond—all these plants and creatures looked so perfect in their new habitat.

Quiet footsteps announced someone's approach on a wide path of red marble. He turned to see Ronnie, wearing a long gown of white silk and gold details, fine brocade and ribbons in shining golden thread. Her hair was braided into a crown with more gold thread and jewels. Around Ronnie's neck was a pendant with a single jewel, a pea-sized gem, blue, gold flecks and white wisps swirling with light radiating from within the stone.

"You look great," said Newton.

"You look late," said Ronnie with a mischievous smile.

"The wedding isn't for another span."

"But for Kai weddings," said Ronnie, "everyone in the wedding party is supposed to be on the stage while the guests come into the hall, so Omni, princess of this planet, is looking like you're going to stand her up on her wedding day, if you don't come with me, right now."

Newton smiled, held out an arm to escort Ronnie, started them walking and asked, "Is that jewel what I think it is?"

Ronnie subconsciously touched the jewel with her free hand as they walked. "Yes. It's also a Kai tradition that the bride's matron wear the symbol of the family bloodline for the ceremony. Queen Brina put this on me and told me not to worry about anything. She said Omni is so revered that we will always have a place of honor in her family, and in the history of the worlds."

"Damn," breathed Newton.

"Right," said Ronnie.

They walked from the atrium to an enormous dome built of marble, gold leaf and colorful stained glass. As they passed through a palisade of marble columns, giant wasps dressed as footmen opened huge doors and bowed reverently. The floor split into a circular staircase in both directions. Ronnie let go of Newton's escort arm and pointed the direction he should go. They climbed stairs in separate directions until they arrived at the center stage of a monumental sized amphitheatre. Five thousand seats all had a good view of the stage. Hundreds of meters overhead, graceful arches of metal held great sheets of colored silk, which shaded the amphitheatre but allowed the breeze.

Newton took his seat on the groom's side of the tiered seating, the last of thirty places, the other seats already full with trusted representatives of the Five Worlds, including Newton's brother, sister and mother, friends from school and male members of the Kai royal family.

Ronnie escorted Omni out to the bride's side of the stage. In a gown of white and gold, similar to Ronnie's but with a more elaborate crown, Omni gave Newton a little wave before she took her seat. Ronnie aesthetically arranged Omni's bridal gown and kissed her claw. Maggie sat on the second tier behind Ronnie's seat.

Once Ronnie had taken her seat next to Omni and the last of the wedding guests had been seated, Queen Brina Tal Kai made a small gesture for the ceremony to begin. A sumptuous harmony of strings, horns and drums swelled within the amphitheatre as five thousand souls stood to welcome a new era of peace, joy and love.

About the Author

Daniel Sandoval has had versions of this story haunting his fevered mind for decades, and the only way to placate a frustrated muse is to manifest something, to entangle her with at least the threads of what may lead to fulfillment. Whether these lines weave a snare or tapestry, ultimately, it matters not, for the story is told and he is freed to his next literary campaign.

While telling this tale, the author sought other pursuits, as when he married a woman his equal in will and spirit and intellect—an arrangement not entered into by the fainthearted. And Mr. Sandoval continued his tenure as an elected official of a city in the western United States.

This is his fourth published novel, and his first work of science fiction, should he be pressed to label its genre. As with all his books, they defy categorization. This is also a romance, a character study, and a theological essay.